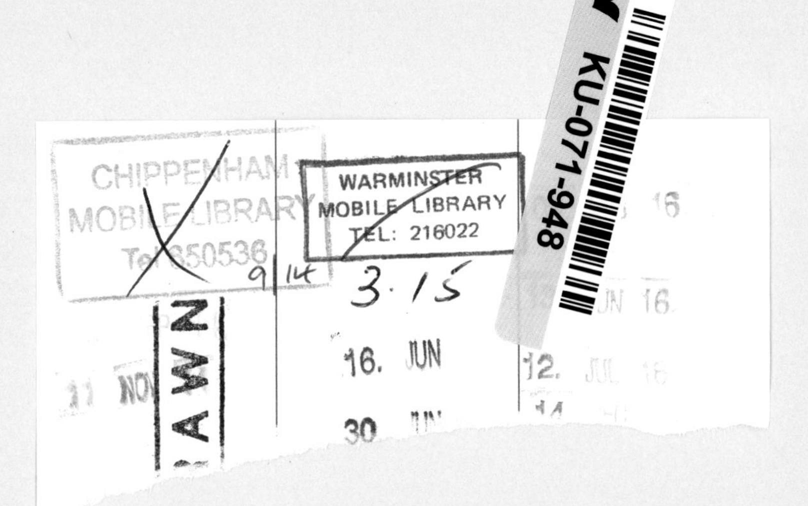
CHIPPENHAM
MOBILE LIBRARY
Tel 650536
WARMINSTER
MOBILE LIBRARY
TEL: 216022
KU-071-948
16. JUN
12. JUL

4 908554 000

SPECIAL MESSAGE TO READERS

This book is published under the auspices of

THE ULVERSCROFT FOUNDATION

(registered charity No. 264873 UK)

Established in 1972 to provide funds for research, diagnosis and treatment of eye diseases. Examples of contributions made are: —

A Children's Assessment Unit at Moorfield's Hospital, London.

•

Twin operating theatres at the Western Ophthalmic Hospital, London.

•

A Chair of Ophthalmology at the Royal Australian College of Ophthalmologists.

•

The Ulverscroft Children's Eye Unit at the Great Ormond Street Hospital For Sick Children, London.

You can help further the work of the Foundation by making a donation or leaving a legacy. Every contribution, no matter how small, is received with gratitude. Please write for details to:

THE ULVERSCROFT FOUNDATION,
The Green, Bradgate Road, Anstey,
Leicester LE7 7FU, England.
Telephone: (0116) 236 4325

In Australia write to:
THE ULVERSCROFT FOUNDATION,
c/o The Royal Australian and New Zealand
College of Ophthalmologists,
94-98 Chalmers Street, Surry Hills,
N.S.W. 2010, Australia

Born in Newport, Monmouthshire in 1931, Leslie Thomas won worldwide acclaim with his bestselling novel *The Virgin Soldiers*. In 2005 he received an OBE for services to literature. *Dover Beach* is his twenty-ninth novel.

DOVER BEACH

Summer 1940. The evacuation of Dunkirk proves that the British can rise to a challenge. But now the soldiers walk the streets of Dover and take weary turns on the town's skating rink. Life must go on, and people take comfort where they find it. Toby Hendry, a fighter pilot, meets Giselle, a young French woman. Can their love affair withstand the forces of war? Meanwhile, reserve naval commander Paul Instow has been called up to fight in a war for which he feels too old. Distracting him from his worries is Molly, a Dover prostitute. And then there are Harold, Spots and Boot: three boys desperate to fight the German invaders, armed with catapults and a stolen Bren gun . . .

Books by Leslie Thomas
Published by The House of Ulverscroft:

THIS TIME NEXT WEEK
SOME LOVELY ISLANDS
THE LOVES AND JOURNEYS OF REVOLVING JONES
ARRIVALS AND DEPARTURES
DANGEROUS BY MOONLIGHT
MY WORLD OF ISLANDS
DANGEROUS DAVIES AND THE LONELY HEART
OTHER TIMES
WAITING FOR THE DAY

LESLIE THOMAS

DOVER BEACH

Love, Life and Death in Wartime England

Complete and Unabridged

CHARNWOOD
Leicester

First published in Great Britain in 2005 by
William Heinemann
The Random House Group Limited
London

First Charnwood Edition
published 2006
by arrangement with
The Random House Group Limited
London

British Library CIP Data

Thomas, Leslie, *1931* –
Dover beach.—Large print ed.—
Charnwood library series
1. World War, *1939 – 1945*—England—Dover—
Fiction 2. Dover (England)—Social life and customs
—Fiction 3. Large type books
I. Title
823.9′14 [F]

ISBN 1–84617–429–5

Published by
F. A. Thorpe (Publishing)
Anstey, Leicestershire

Set by Words & Graphics Ltd.
Anstey, Leicestershire
Printed and bound in Great Britain by
T. J. International Ltd., Padstow, Cornwall

This book is printed on acid-free paper

For Matthew and Alexandra

Ah, love, let us be true
To one another! for the world, which seems
To lie before us like a land of dreams,
So various, so beautiful, so new,
Hath really neither joy, nor love, nor light . . .

Matthew Arnold
'Dover Beach'

'*We must fight for command of the Strait.*'

Winston Churchill

1

From below his cottage window the scene abruptly dropped away: an elderly wall with a stile, fields dotted with buttercups and sheep, then the town and harbour, silent at their distance, and cloud shadows skimming the sea. On clear days you could see across the Channel to occupied France. The Germans had mounted a big searchlight over there which, when the sun caught it, flashed like a taunt. His wife Nancy had left the window open and the commonplace summer sounds, birds and buzzing, came into the room. It was one afternoon in 1940.

Ships had always sailed close inshore on the Dover side of the Strait to steer clear of the Goodwin Sands and these days to hug the coast in case of attack. Cotton observed the convoy, solid shapes against a silvery sea, standing at the window, his head touching the flowered pelmet. As he did so a pattern of smoke puffs appeared below the clouds and above the twenty coasters plodding east. He opened the window fully. The airraid siren floated thinly from the town, and detonations began to roll up the hill. Quickly he took a pair of binoculars from their leather case on the hall stand, and focused on the ships. 'Christ,' he said quietly.

They were being attacked by Junkers dive-bombers, Stukas. He could clearly hear their trademark screams as they descended. He had never seen a dive-bomber except on the cinema newsreel but he knew what they were; swiftly falling almost vertically, dropping their bombs and ponderously climbing again. He opened the window wider. The bombs were causing spouts on the sea. Anti-aircraft fire from some naval escort ships made soft useless-looking puffs in the sky. His telephone sounded. Still watching the ships he stretched and took it from its cradle on the wall.

'Frank!' It was Nancy. 'Look from the window. They're bombing our ships!'

'I was watching,' he said. He kept his voice calm. 'Stuka dive-bombers.'

She was working at the hospital. 'The patients are all up at the windows,' she said, tumbling over her words. 'Somebody's going to fall out. Where are our planes, Frank?'

There was a roar across the roof above him, then two more. He peered up. 'Our fighter planes have just turned up,' he said flatly. 'Three Defiants. They might as well send three coppers on bikes.'

'I'll call you back when I can,' she said. 'I've got to get these patients in.'

He said: 'I'm going down the police station, Nance. I'm due on duty anyway.'

'Be careful,' she said. 'Please.'

'You as well,' he told her. 'I'll stick my tin hat on.'

He reached for his steel helmet and his canvas gas-mask case, and opened the front door to the dull warmth of the July day, the sound of the explosions and the high whine of aeroplanes. He picked up the binoculars. One of the RAF Defiants was already peeling away and beginning to roll and fall helplessly, black smoke trailing from it. He heard excited voices and looked along the lane to where three boys were shouting and jumping on the stile in the opposite wall.

'You kids!' he shouted. 'Take cover!'

They looked around with almost disdain. They wore lanky khaki shorts and carried bows and arrows. One had a dustbin lid held like a shield and a bread knife in his belt. 'Get under cover,' Cotton ordered striding towards them. 'Get under the roof of the shed there.'

The tallest of the boys, about twelve, who he thought he recognised from the juvenile court, said: 'Those Jerries are miles away.'

'Get under here,' Cotton ordered pushing them beneath the corrugated-iron roof of the shed where he kept his Austin Seven and the lawnmower.

They obeyed sullenly. 'Lot of good this is,' grumbled the taller boy noisily banging the wall. 'This won't take no direct hit.'

'*You'll* get a direct hit in a minute — from me,' Cotton said. 'There's a ruddy air raid on. Those Germans could be overhead in ten seconds.' He glanced at the bows, the arrows, the dustbin lid and the knife thrust in the snake-buckle belt. 'What do you think you're up to anyway?'

'Waiting for them, the enemy,' said the second boy grumpily. He had scrappy ginger hair and a face full of freckles. 'We've got our own defence patrol.'

'We're going to willy them,' said the smallest boy.

Cotton said: 'You'll what . . . ?'

'He means *harry* them, not willy,' sniffed the tallest glaring at the small one. 'Like it says on the wireless the resistance do, *harry* the Germans.'

'I'm getting the car out and taking you lot back into Dover,' Cotton told them. 'You're not going to harry anybody.'

'A bomb could drop on us, easy,' pointed out the ginger boy. He nodded at the small car. 'That's an easy target.'

'I've got to go to the police station,' said Cotton. 'And I'm not leaving you up here.'

'I knew you was a copper,' sniffed the leader.

'I've got 'Police' written on the front of this steel helmet, haven't I,' pointed out Cotton. 'Anyway, we've seen each other in the juvenile court. What's your name?'

'Harold Barker. And I got off.'

The explosions from the sea rumbled grimly. The boys watched the diving planes.

'Let's get you home,' grunted Cotton. 'Where is it you live?'

'Me and Spots, 'ere, lives in Seaview Crescent. And Boot . . . well . . . '

'Hostel,' said the short boy.

Harold added: ' 'Cos 'e's a refugee.'

Cotton had opened the door of the Austin and they piled in, thrilled at the novelty of being in a car. He glanced towards the sea. The battle went on. Smoke was mixing with the low clouds.

Spots began turning the window handle. The

glass slid down. 'Like my uncle's,' he boasted. ' . . . My mum's friend.'

Going to the front of the square bonnet Cotton powerfully swung the starting handle. The engine fired first time.

'Good starter, mush,' said Harold.

'So's my uncle's,' said Spots.

'Don't call me mush,' Cotton said. He climbed into the driving seat next to the smallest boy. 'Where are you a refugee from?'

'Poland,' he said. 'I been in Dover since last year. My mum's English, she teaches dancing and she's here but my old man ain't. We had to leave him behind. We don't know where he is.'

'That's why he's called Boot,' put in Harold. 'Polish, see. *Boot polish*. That's right, ain't it, mush.'

'That's right,' shrugged Boot. He glanced at Cotton. 'They think it's funny.'

Cotton drove the car from the shed. The wall in the lane obscured the view but they could hear the planes and the reverberations echoing off the sea.

'Why ain't you dressed like a copper, except for that tin hat?' asked Harold.

'I'm plain clothes.'

Boot put the window down a bit more and the battle noise increased. They were unafraid.

'If that's plain clothes, what's your best suit like?' enquired Spots. They all sniggered.

'Stop being lippy, mush,' said Cotton. 'And if you see a plane — duck.'

They were getting into the town. The sea came into view again. Eagerly they stretched to see the aircraft. 'Look at everybody!' suddenly guffawed Harold. 'All up on the chimley pots.'

Cotton could scarcely believe it. Every upper window was occupied by people looking out to sea. There were men and youths on the roofs, some holding on to the brick chimneys, others on top of the chimneys, sitting astride the round pots, shouting and pointing. A Dover Corporation bus had stopped and people were crowding the upper deck. The driver and conductor were on the bonnet and there was a man standing on the roof.

'They're mad!' Cotton bellowed. 'Bloody mad!'

'No swearing,' said Boot solemnly.

'Not in front of children,' added Spots.

'A Jerry!' shouted Harold almost deliriously, pointing directly ahead through the windscreen. The plane was coming low, straight up the street at them, the machine guns on its wings sparking.

'Down!' Cotton bawled. 'Get down flat!'

Before any of them could do so the aircraft, at less than two hundred feet, had roared above them and gone. Spots was struggling with his bow and arrow. 'Next time I'll get 'im.'

'See the crosses on the wings?' said Harold breathlessly.

They had no fear. Cotton had swung the car to one side. Now he righted it and charged it along the street. There were still people on the house tops with others scampering and sliding down tiles, ladders and drainpipes. He searched frantically for shelter. A side turning appeared and he flung the vehicle into it, braking violently in front of a wall.

'This is a petrol garage, mister,' pointed out Harold flatly. 'If that German comes back and hits the pump we'll all be blown to Folkestone.'

'Look!' Spots was pointing from the window. 'Bullet cases. All over the place.'

Cotton tried to stop them but the trio flung the door aside and tumbled from the car. Angrily he shouted but they were dodging about the street picking up brass bullet cases. Other children appeared and ran in excited circles. 'Still hot!' shouted Harold throwing a spent bullet case in the air, catching it and blowing on it.

Cotton got from the car and almost threw himself at them. 'Get under cover!' he bellowed. 'He'll be back in a minute!'

The plane was. It came, guns firing, from the opposite end of the town this time. Children scattered and resourcefully flung themselves flat against walls and railings. The boys piled into the car. 'It'll be this petrol pump next!' shouted Spots.

Cotton was the only one in a panic. The tyres screeched as he backed the car into the road and plunged his foot on to the accelerator. It went between the houses at forty miles an hour. Transfixed, he saw the German plane bank almost lazily above the town and come howling back, its guns hammering up the street. He threw the wheel over and the car went into a front garden.

Now the plane hung to one side as if the pilot

sought a better view, made another run and, flattening out, dropped a single bomb. All the earth around them seemed to rise. They felt the car heel. The blast was numbing. Cotton was trying to crouch under the steering wheel, the boys were piled together on the floor. The windscreen splintered.

There was silence. Harold was the first to raise his head and look out. 'They've bombed the Co-op,' he said almost with wonderment. 'Wiped it out.'

⋆ ⋆ ⋆

'Early closing,' shrugged Sergeant Wallace from behind the police counter polished by years of elbows and arms. A bulky man, his shrug was heavy, and his steel helmet too small. Cotton thought they might exchange because his was oversized. The steady all-clear siren began sounding.

'They bombed the lightship,' said Wallace. 'Two crew dead.'

Cotton said: 'I thought lightships and lighthouses were supposed to be neutral.'

'Well, the Jerries don't, by the look of it. It was sheer luck with the Co-op, empty, but the Huns weren't to know that. That Co-op could have been packed, housewives, mums. But even the manager was out on the cliff with everybody watching the fun.' He regarded Cotton gloomily. 'I don't know if we got any of them. I saw two of our boys go down, poor buggers.'

'Defiants,' said Cotton.

'With the little beehive gun turrets,' nodded Wallace sadly.

'Flying coffins,' said Cotton.

Wallace sighed. 'No serious casualties in the town though. Two of them half-brained kids fell off the roofs. One got saved by his mother's clothes line, the other demolished a coal shed, broken arm. Only the Co-op cat got killed. Spread all over the counter so they say. Better be careful what you get in your rations this week, Frank. Watch out for lumps of fur.'

'Thanks, I will. We ought to swap tin hats, Wally. They'd fit us better.'

Without replying Wallace took his helmet from his hot and balding head and Cotton handed his across the counter. Wallace put it on. 'That's better,' said the desk sergeant. 'More comfy.' He took out a big blue handkerchief and ran it around the interior of his own helmet before handing it over.

'I was due to go to the Co-op anyway,' said Cotton putting it on and adjusting it. It fitted. 'Some London wide boy has been sounding out the manager about black-market lard. Now there's no shop.'

The black telephone on the counter rang. As he picked it up Wallace said to Cotton: 'They've got 'undreds of branches, the Co-op. He'll have to try to flog it to one of them . . . Hello, police station Dover.'

He listened, then said: 'Detective Sergeant Cotton has just come in, sir. Yes, I'll tell him. Everybody else is out there anyway. Somewhere. Right, sir.'

'The super,' he nodded when he had replaced the telephone. 'They want every copper down on the pier. They're bringing the casualties in from those ships.'

* * *

Outside Dover dock gates, wedged along the side of the street, were people eager to see the casualties come ashore. People had stood there just over a month earlier when the angry soldiers from Dunkirk, throwing their rifles into piles, bloodied, beaten, had been brought from the evacuation boats. The spectators outside had clapped them with extra cheers for the badly wounded. But it had been no time for applause.

Now ambulances waited, their doors expectantly open; there were awkward groups of dockers and doctors. Gulls flew noisily around nervous nurses.

'Cricket will be off tonight then,' said one of the dockers.

'Clergy have cancelled,' said the man beside him. 'Play next week.' He nodded towards a group at the town end of the pier. 'There's some of 'em up there, getting ready to say their prayers.' He scanned the pale blue sky behind the town. 'Would 'ave been a good evening for it too. Here comes the lifeboat now.'

The shoal of rescue craft headed across the bland sea back towards the harbour mouth, led by the shoddy minesweeper HMS *Petrel*, her captain, Lieutenant Commander Paul Instow, grim on the bridge. She was a wooden-sided vessel safe from magnetic mines but said to have mice in her hull.

Instow was irked because that afternoon it had taken too long in his estimation to get up steam enough to leave harbour and reinforce the anti-aircraft defences of the convoy ships. The pom-pom gun on the bow and the Lewis gun on the stern had both loosed off at anything that looked like a German plane and had hit nothing but low clouds.

Everything about Instow's craft was shabby; he felt shabby too. Shabby and useless. He was a reserve officer and his crew were reservists. The steersman had not been near the sea for years and was as uncertain as the ship he nudged towards the harbour entrance. Instow prayed he would miss the wall.

Forward, around the base of the pom-pom with its multiple barrels, sprawled some of the convoy's survivors who had been lifted from the sea. Two of the ships had been set on fire and one of them had exploded. The minesweeper had arrived after the lifeboats from Dover and Folkestone and some fishermen. By now the sky was unoccupied, an innocent early evening, the Germans gone, the long white Dover cliffs gleaming, smiling blandly, and the green of the Kentish countryside rising above the strong, neat town.

There were six merchant seamen lying, smeared with oil, on the fore deck and another four at the stern, two of them crouching as if ready to run a race. Three canvas-covered bodies were laid on the tarpaulin of the lifeboat. The minesweeper's crew had handed out mugs of coffee and whisky and brought blankets. There was not much noise and not much movement. Anything said was only a whisper masked by the revolutions of the engines. It was oddly peaceful.

From the west two aircraft approached. The klaxon warning honked and Instow bellowed: 'Action stations.' The sailors attempted to drag the wet and oily injured men away from the guns, but Mancroft, the second officer, shouted from the deck below: 'They're ours, sir. RAF Spitfires.'

'Bleeding Spitfires!' suddenly screeched one of the men on the deck managing to get to his knees and shake his fist. 'Young bleeders!' Others, some of those who were able to, followed him, shouting and punching their fists at the planes which mistakenly dipped their wings in salute.

Instow recognised they were older men. You could tell that even though they were coated with oil. You could tell from their voices. He turned from them and watched the lifeboats trailing him into harbour and beyond them the low and labouring fishing vessels. Altogether they must have pulled thirty men from the sea he thought. How many were alive?

The helmsman, who he noticed for the first time had a nervous tic, correctly placed the bow between the red port light and the starboard green light at the entrance to Dover. As the view into the harbour widened people could be seen grouped on the quay and along the pier, and there were ambulances waiting against the grey buildings of the town. Instow was deeply conscious that they had already lost a battle. How many more would there be? 'Bloody hell,' he muttered.

'Yes, sir,' agreed Sub-Lieutenant Mancroft on the wing of the bridge. He was scarcely twenty, and he was trembling. He surveyed the men on the deck. Two of their crew were rubbing one of the merchant seamen with bare hands. One looked up at Instow and then Mancroft and called: 'Trying to keep 'im warm, sir.'

Mancroft glanced towards Instow, then shouted stoutly: 'Keep rubbing him, boys, we're nearly there.' It made him feel better.

HMS *Petrel* eased alongside. One of the sitting survivors by the gun coughed and called up. 'Skipper, sir, ain't the navy got anything better than this tub?'

Instow knew. 'I'll tell the admiralty,' he called back.

'You wouldn't have made any difference,' the seaman wheezed. 'Not with these popguns.' He turned his soaked and blackened back to Instow who knew he was right.

Now they were against the jetty, lines were thrown and tied. As the gangway rattled down there was a movement, at first hesitant, of medical men, service and civilian, to board the ship. A group of dockers trailed them timidly, almost with embarrassment. The land men stared at the burned sailors on the deck. The Dover and Folkestone lifeboats and the trawlers were coming to the jetty. The ambulances began to move almost timidly on to the pier.

Stretchers were hoisted aboard, tenderly loaded and carried carefully ashore. The clutch of clergymen hovered uncertainly. Prayers went unsaid. It took an hour before the final casualties were unloaded. The dockers stood afterwards, hapless, unspeaking, until the foreman grunted: 'That looks like the lot, boys. Go on home to your tea.'

One of the men said: 'All old men. They looked so bloody old, didn't they.'

'You'd look bloody old if you'd got all that muck over you,' said the foreman. He slung his canvas bag over his back. His lunch was still wrapped in its newspaper. 'Want a pickle sandwich?' he asked.

'No, thanks. I'll have my tea when I get home.' The docker's face sagged. 'I 'ope it ain't going on like this.'

* * *

A boy with a nosebleed and a woman with a sprained ankle had been hurriedly treated and ushered away. The casualty department was clear. Doctors in white coats, looking uncomfortable in a silent group, waited alongside starched uniformed nurses, some smoking, others drinking coffee, all looking towards the main door. Sister Nancy Cotton had posted herself outside and she saw the first ambulance. 'They're coming,' she said thrusting the double doors wide. They stubbed out their cigarettes, put down their cups and tried to keep calm.

The injured merchant seamen were almost

shoved through the entrance by stark-faced stretcher bearers who had never seen anything like it. Twenty were manoeuvred into the department through the entrance and directed to spaces marked with chalk on the cleared floor. Three of the men had already died.

Nancy clenched her teeth and her hands. Shadowing the senior surgeon she moved around the stretchers and finally to the side of one of the prone men. He had a beard, sticking out like a tar-brush, his eyes protruding savagely from a riven face. His mouth was like a hole. 'What you goin' to do wiv them scissors, nurse?' he croaked.

'Cut your clothes off,' replied Nancy primly. 'And I'm *sister*.'

'Wouldn't let my sister cut my togs off,' cackled the man. 'But I'm buggered down there somewhere, missus. I can feel all my guts hanging out.'

She began to scissor his wet, clogged clothes away. It was as if she was taking peel from his body. The blood and oil looked like heavy paint. Around them doctors and nurses bent working, the men groaning and crying or lying silent. A tubby priest came panting through the main door, blinked and made a swift sign of the cross. Muttering to himself, not to God, he cast his eyes about the room. An Anglican vicar, thin but unfit, came in and pulled up. Blood wriggled across the floor. The vicar almost hung on to the priest. 'We must do what we can,' said the Catholic trying not to vomit. 'You can't tell one from another.'

'Not much point in asking,' said the vicar.

A shadow approached the door. 'Dear Mother of God,' breathed the priest. 'A three-card trick. It's the rabbi.'

Tentatively the trio of holy men went among the wounded, the dying, and those tending them, stepping carefully. A man died with a stoical grunt and the vicar nudged the priest forward. The rabbi hung back, his hands across his mouth. Then an inner door was flung open like an explosion. Some of the casualties jumped. A man shouted: 'No!' Angrily Nancy turned to see a fat woman in a blue bonnet and a red dress splashed with huge white flowers. Her big folded face was convulsed.

'Bertram Bartrip is dead!' she bawled. 'Don't nobody care?'

The surgeon bending above the man whose clothes Nancy had cut away lifted his head. 'Bartrip was always an awkward man,' he said stoically. He glanced at Nancy. 'Get shot of her.'

Nancy turned from the casualty area and after a moment the young rabbi followed her. 'I think I'm a bit surplus here,' he said to no one in particular. 'It's no time to ask religious details.'

Nancy strode professionally up the corridor after the bouncing woman in the large red frock. The elastic in the short arms dug into the woman's flesh. 'I'm sorry, Mary,' said Nancy tightly as she caught up with her. 'But we've got an emergency.'

The woman snorted. 'Oh yes, I can see that! It's all the glamour, ain't it. Just like on the pictures. Never mind my father pegging out.'

Pushing ahead, thrusting doors open, Nancy said: 'Who said he's dead anyway?'

The rabbi followed timidly, catching the door as it sprang back.

' 'E's dead all right,' insisted Mary. 'I know 'im better than anybody.'

They reached an unrealistically bright ward, the late sun streaming in on the cheery quilts and flowers. Expectantly upright in their beds were ten men in striped pyjamas. Screens had been placed around the bed at the end. Someone turned off the wireless.

'We put them around, sister,' said one of the patients. 'The screens. Once we knew . . . '

The man in the next bed said: ' 'E'd started to gurgle.'

Nancy stayed them with a glare. Swiftly she went around the screen, Mary padding after her, now dumbstruck. The rabbi peeped around after them. There was no mistake. Bertram Bartrip was no more. She tested for a pulse and lifted a limp eyelid. 'The doctor will have to certify he is dead,' she said. 'As soon as he's not so busy.'

'Who,' demanded Mary swinging a plump arm towards the rabbi, 'is this bloke?'

'A man of God,' said Nancy firmly.

Mary rolled her eyes. 'Him,' she scoffed emphasising the aspirate. 'God! My father wanted nothing to do with God.'

'I'm a rabbi,' said the young man.

Mary's face colour deepened. 'A Jew!' she howled. 'A Jew boy!'

'Most rabbis are,' he responded evenly. 'I'm Joseph Bentick. If I can be of any help . . . '

Suddenly Mary deflated, the dress crumpling like a huge coloured balloon, tears gushing down the channels of her red and rough cheeks. 'I'm going 'ome,' she sobbed. 'To tell them.' Hugely inhaling she rallied. Nancy patted her.

Nancy said: 'Mary, as soon as the emergency is over we'll arrange things. You come back tomorrow. We could get Mr Palfrey, the undertaker . . . do you know him?'

'I know Mr Palfrey,' snivelled Mary. 'He arranged my mother. I'll come back tomorrow. I'm sorry about those poor blokes in there. 'Onest I am, poor sods.'

* * *

'Bertram Bartrip,' sighed Nancy as she slumped at the table. 'God knows how many deathbeds he'd had.'

'And he had to pick today,' grunted Cotton putting two boiled eggs in front of her. With bread and margarine. He poured her another cup of tea. The cottage was touched by a hushed wind from the distant sea. She put her face in her hands. 'If it's going to be like this . . .'

'It looks like it is,' he said. 'They bombed the lightship, you know. Killed two of the crew.'

'I heard,' she said. 'I thought that was out of bounds.'

'I'm not sure there are going to be any bounds.'

Nancy began to eat tiredly. It was almost midnight. 'Were you all right, Frank?' she said.

'Well, that bomb cracked the car windscreen.'

She sat up. 'Oh God, oh Frank. I should have asked you.'

'I didn't have a scratch. I had three kids in the car, three lads. They enjoyed it, terrific fun. I was trying to get them home when that Jerry came right up the street and demolished the Co-op.'

She leaned across the kitchen table and kissed his cheek. 'I should have asked you,' she repeated.

'Apart from that, and trying to get the gawpers away from the dock gates, Christ, those people . . . Otherwise, everything was all right,' he said. 'Oh, and the key to the emergency mortuary went missing. It just would, wouldn't it. In the end I kicked the door down.'

He stood and went to the wireless set on the sideboard. 'Might as well get the official story,' he said. The midnight news had just begun.

> '*In the English Channel today seven German planes were shot down by the RAF as they unsuccessfully attempted to attack a convoy of merchant ships. One of our aircraft is missing.*'

Cotton glanced at his wife. She seemed to have aged since that morning. 'Well, well, well,' he grunted. 'Fancy that. *Seven* Germans shot down. And we didn't notice.'

Nancy said: 'There'll be a lot more lies told before this war is over. It makes you wonder how many lies have been told up to now.' As she spoke the howl of the air-raid siren came on the placid air, floating up the ridge from Dover.

'No,' she said firmly looking up from the table and pushing her plate aside.

'Finish your egg,' he said gently. 'It's probably a false alarm. It's all dark out there.'

'I'm not going into that air-raid shelter,' she said. 'I've had enough of war for one day.'

Cotton went behind her and rubbed her shoulders. 'Thanks,' she sighed. 'I'm so tired. I want my own bed.'

'That's where we're going,' he said.

2

Dover had ever been in the front line. The first aerial bomb ever to drop on Britain fell on the town on Christmas Eve 1914, four months after the start of the First War with Germany, exploding in the garden of a house in Taswell Street and blowing a Mr Terson out of an apple tree which he was pruning. He was unhurt, though shaken. People came from miles to see the hole. It was only five years since the Frenchman Bleriot had been the first to fly the Channel, his cloth-and-wood machine coming to earth at Dover, only a few yards inland, a place that is today marked with the outline of his aeroplane.

Through history the town had been the cornerstone of England, its famous folding cliffs later afforded even greater fame by a sentimental wartime song composed in America by a man who had never seen them and called 'The White Cliffs of Dover'. In reality they stood like a wide and irritating grin, often visible to the enemy in conquered France.

Early tribes had colonised and fortified Dover against incomers until the Romans landed. They built Britain's first lighthouse, and the Normans built a castle, both still standing solidly above the town today.

Over centuries, fortification was piled on fortification and carved from the chalk of the cliffs, and in the rising country behind them were voluminous caves where guns had awaited the invasion of Napoleon Bonaparte. The British then muttered among themselves: 'Boney is coming,' just as in the first summer of the Second War they said: 'Hitler is coming.' Neither came.

That summer of 1940 began with forty thousand people in the town; behind it the county of Kent rising to the thick meadows, apple orchards and hop fields. They still call it the Garden of England today but they say the original name was the *Guardian* of England, because of the cliffs and ramparts that faced the straits.

It was an early destination for the spreading railways of Victorian times, passengers leaving the trains to board the ferries for France. By the beginning of the Second World War in 1939, there were steam trains five times a day from London taking two and a half hours to three and a half for the journey, depending on where they stopped on the way.

* * *

At eleven on that July morning in 1940 the train from London, trailing its emerald carriages, came into Dover Priory, the town station, two minutes late. A tall man with a clerk's slightly bent back and briefcase, trilby, umbrella and raincoat, despite the firm promise of a fine day, marched to the trembling engine. 'Late again!' he shouted above the steam. 'Every day now it's late. It was not like this once.'

'You tell the governors of the Southern Railway, sir,' responded the driver easing his greasy cap away from his forehead. His face shone, black streaks ran down his cheeks. The furnace roared at his back. 'Ain't no use you going on at me.'

The guard with his polished brasses and pressed uniform, his watch-chain glowing, approached along the platform, manoeuvring between the departing passengers. The driver said: 'Ask him. He knows more than me.'

The guard halted, stood straight and touched his cap. The toes of his black boots caught the sun. 'Two minutes late, I'll give you that,' he said. 'But you see, sir, since this twenty-mile exclusion zone's come about we have to make sure that nobody is on the train that shouldn't be on it. Mr Churchill don't want unnecessary people down here. Any minute Hitler might invade.'

As if contradicting him a group of six women, chattering in American voices, well dressed and excited, trotted towards the station exit. 'They've got passes,' said the guard defensively. 'From the American embassy in London.'

The tall man snorted, performed an irritated turn and strode towards the booking hall where the American women had been met by a confused Royal Engineers officer. 'This is an exclusion zone, you know,' the tall man warned waving his umbrella. 'Hitler may be on his way. At this very moment.'

The women's widening eyes followed him as

he left. Captain Robin Cartwright grinned and said: 'I'm afraid he's right. I was amazed when I heard you were coming.' Cartwright, in common with many soldiers then, did not look the part. The officer's uniform sat uncomfortably; he had a good-humoured but studious demeanour. It seemed he might have been more at home in a silent study.

They were a brightly hued group. A small, pouting woman and another, in large spectacles, wore trousers. Few women in Dover had ever worn trousers. It was not a place of fashion. All the Americans had hats, two with upstanding feathers, and in each lapel was a paper Union Jack.

The leader of the group, the most conservatively dressed, laughed uncertainly. 'I'm Sarah,' she said. 'Sarah Durrant.' Cartwright thought she was the youngest. She was neat, even dainty, with fair bobbed hair, calm eyes and an American smile. 'We all have our passes.' She shook hands with him, took the passes from her handbag and unnecessarily showed him. 'We're just hoping we can keep them for souvenirs.'

'To show our folks that we've been at the war front,' beamed a woman in a red satin coat.

'Only twenty-one miles from those Nazis,' said another expanding her bosom.

A porter who had begun to casually sweep the booking hall nodded. 'They're not far away, missus.' He studied their extravagant clothes and said: 'I should keep out of sight if I was you.'

Cartwright told them: 'Well, we'll get through as much of the programme as we can. It might be difficult. We had an air raid here yesterday . . . '

They were thrilled. Sarah Durrant said: 'Here? The radio news said there was action in the English Channel.'

One of the other women whispered: 'How exciting.'

'It was offshore, most of it. The Germans attacked a convoy of merchant ships,' he told them confidingly. 'One bomb was dropped on Dover and they shot up the place a bit, but fortunately they mostly missed. The casualties were on the ships.'

'Would you . . . would you prefer it if we returned to London?' asked Sarah. The faces clouded.

Cartwright was about to say that he would, but the women quickly chorused in disagreement. He said instead: 'At your own risk, I'm afraid. If the Germans come back we'll have to get you under cover like everybody else.' He tried an assured smile. 'But . . . for the moment . . . I've arranged coffee at the Marine Hotel.'

* * *

Furniture and boxes were piled in the hotel foyer. There were mounds of dusty rubble and a tangle of curtains on the floor, windows were without glass. A space had been cleared for the reception desk and a fair, slim girl, wearing a green summer dress, rose from behind it. 'Good morning. *Bonjour mesdames, monsieur*. I am Giselle.'

The American women surveyed their surroundings with curiosity and a little misgiving. The foyer lights began to flicker, went out, then came on again.

'The Marine Hotel is not usually like so,' said Giselle spreading her slim hands. 'We have been visited by the Boche.'

The jaunty feather in the hat of one of the women had become bent as though it was part of the damage. Catching sight of herself in a cracked mirror she left it as it was. She took out a notebook and wrote savagely. The others with some nervousness continued to look about them.

'Coffee is served in the lounge,' said the French girl trying to be bright. She smiled towards Cartwright. 'As reserved by *monsieur, le commander*. But please to go through the dining room today. The usual way is . . . poof! . . . ' She blew out her cheeks.

Still wishing they had not come, Cartwright ushered the busy party through the dining-room door. One of the long patterned-glass panels was missing from it, and the windows facing the street were boarded with plywood. The women wriggled with excitement, took out cameras and began busily to take photographs. 'Is this permitted?' asked Sarah cautiously.

Cartwright said wryly: 'I can't see why not. But it probably isn't.' He led them through the dining room and into the lounge with its drapes and red velvet chairs.

A woman in an apron was ineffectually flapping around with a feathered mop. 'Years of dust came up . . . ' She began to cough. 'Charlie will get the coffee. They're trying to put back the ceiling in the kitchen.'

She brushed each chair a little more emphatically before each guest sat down. The dust rose. They covered their noses.

'How far away was the bomb?' Sarah asked.

Eagerly the others leaned forward. 'Can we see the hole?' asked the smaller of the trousered women.

The cleaner said: 'It finished our Co-op.'

'About two hundred yards on the other side of the road,' said Cartwright. 'Fortunately it was the shop's early closing afternoon and the place was empty except for the cat.'

Every American eye was on him. 'Which hasn't been seen since,' he added. The feathered woman wrote briskly in her book. They grouped in a half-circle. The cleaner continued flapping.

'As I told you earlier,' Cartwright said earnestly, 'I honestly didn't expect you to turn up as arranged today. After yesterday's events I imagined someone in London would have . . . well, warned you.'

Sarah, sitting next to him, said quietly: 'We wanted to come.'

'Up to yesterday, it's been pretty quiet here,' he continued. 'As far as direct attacks have been concerned, well, there haven't been any. And it's been more or less like that over the whole country. Nothing much has happened this side of the Channel, anyway. In America they've been calling it the phoney war, haven't they?'

'The bore war,' added one of the women.

Cartwright continued: 'We had begun to

wonder if it would ever get started. Even while it was all happening in France, the evacuation of Dunkirk and the rest of it, here it has remained peaceful, apart, that is, from the Dunkirk troops being landed here. Yesterday the quiet was shattered. Two ships were sunk just outside Dover harbour and, as you can see around you, the town itself was attacked.'

They listened intently. He was conscious that his uniform was not well fitted; his face was too gentle for a soldier. The one with the notebook had stopped writing but still had a poised pencil. Another with a camera put it on the table. 'Frankly,' said Cartwright, 'I am responsible for your safety and even now I have a sneaking feeling that you should have reboarded the train and gone straight back to London.'

'That would have been a big disappointment,' said Sarah firmly. Her companions nodded and adjusted the Union flags in their lapels in turn.

'We were invited,' said one.

'Right,' said Cartwright attempting to sound pleased. 'But, with your permission, I will make this a short tour, have lunch and get you on the train. According to the rumours the Luftwaffe prefer to make their raids in the afternoon. They don't like early starts.'

Nobody smiled. 'So,' he said, 'I will start, as I usually do with these visits, by explaining that my name is Robin Cartwright, I have the rank of Captain, and I am a professional archaeologist who has been called up — appropriately into the Royal Engineers.' He tapped the regimental flash on his shoulder. 'In the British army the engineers are called sappers because they dig trenches and tunnels, and that's what I do in civilian life — dig. They sent me here because there are miles of caves and holes in the Dover chalk, some of which are still being excavated by the military, and I'm supposed to ensure that they don't dig up and throw away anything the British Museum would want preserved.'

'Have they done that yet?' asked one of the women. 'Found anything exciting?'

Cartwright smiled over his almost cold coffee. 'Nobody's been looking very hard,' he said. 'I volunteered for the armed services when the war started but, to be frank, once I was in the army they had no idea what to do with an archaeologist. Once I'd finished my basic training and my officer's course they sent me down here and mumbled something about me being useful.'

The Americans remained intent. Charlie came in and gathered the coffee pots and cups. He looked disappointed that little coffee had been drunk. 'A lot of the kitchen ceiling fell down,' he muttered.

'So,' continued Cartwright, 'we can see a few things on the tour. The Roman lighthouse, the place where Bleriot's plane came down after he became the first man to fly across the Channel, and perhaps Dover Castle, if they'll let us do any of these following the events of yesterday.'

'Then the store,' the lady with the crooked hat feather reminded him. 'The bombed store.'

'That will be the first stop,' he promised. 'Then we'll be back here for lunch, providing there are no warlike interruptions.'

'Because we were coming here,' said Sarah Durrant, 'we all read 'Dover Beach' by Matthew Arnold. It's the most moving poem. He must have been very famous in this town?'

'Not very, not at the time,' he smiled. 'It's said he only passed through on the way to France — on his honeymoon. Unfortunately just now that beach is covered with obstacles, barbed wire, and it's mined. We can see it but we can't step on it.'

'And the white cliffs?' asked Sarah close to him. She paused: 'Of Dover.'

'To see them properly we would have to go out to sea. That's not permitted either. I'm sorry. As everybody tells you — all the time — there's a war on.'

* * *

There was a silent and small crowd on the pavement opposite the mounds of rubble that had once been the Co-op, waiting as if they expected something else to happen. Some of the angled roof timbers jutted from the debris like the prow of a wrecked ship. Various groceries which had remained visible after the bombing had been taken away in Co-op vans to forestall rain or looters. 'Wonder where the cat went?' a girl asked her mother.

'Straight up in the air, I 'spect,' mumbled a man.

The six American women had grouped at the edge in respectful silence before Cartwright suggested they should go to see the Roman lighthouse. 'That's another ruin,' put in the man. 'Dover's full of 'em.'

A woman said: 'And there'll be a few more yet.' People laughed.

Doris Barker had collected the weekly rations for herself and her son Harold from Leeston's grocery shop in Snargate Street. They were not heavy in her basket. She had gone early because of a swift rumour that the dispossessed Co-op customers would, on the instructions of the local food office, be taking their ration books to Leeston's. She paused at the group viewing the bombed site and looked about to make sure Harold was not there when he should have been at school. He was not. The American women were moving away, following Cartwright.

'Look at them lot then,' said a woman called Kath Fox who she knew but did not like. Reluctantly she walked with her along the pavement.

'Nice slacks,' said Doris.

'Yanks,' persisted the sharp-faced woman. 'Showing theirselves off down 'ere, done up like dogs' dinners. My old man says they'll take their bloody time before they come in the war. Like last time.'

They neared the new Belisha beacon street crossing. 'Shame they can't have the orange lights on the top now,' said Doris attempting to change the subject. She calculated how long she would need to walk with the woman. 'Quite cheery I thought, like balloons.'

'That bloke Belisha's made plenty of money

out of them,' said Kath Fox sullenly. 'Another Jew.'

As they paused at the crossing a platoon of soldiers marched along the street, goaded by a stiff-backed sergeant, the peak of his cap only just above his nose, in his hand a short drill stick. 'Squad . . . squad . . . halt!' he bellowed. Taken by surprise the soldiers pulled up untidily. The two women watched but remained at the kerb.

'Ladies,' breathed the sergeant. 'I 'ave 'alted these fine fighting men to let you cross the road.'

The women with their shopping baskets hurried over. Doris waved a modest thanks. The sergeant bawled: 'Squad . . . squad . . . By the right . . . quick march!' He thrust his stick under his arm and the parade clip-clopped forward.

'Soldiers,' sniffed Kath. 'Call them soldiers. Poor little buggers. Some of 'em look like they've got rickets.'

'They are a bit on the scrawny side,' agreed Doris cautiously. 'Maybe the army will build them up, fill them out a bit.'

Kath put her head confidingly close. 'Now, them Storm Troopers, them Germans what you see on the pictures, on the news, they look like *real* soldiers. Jaws sticking out under their 'elmets and trained bodies. That's what I like, trained bodies.'

Doris was measuring the distance to the next corner where she knew she could turn off. 'Where's your old man?' asked the other woman.

'In the army,' said Doris. 'Africa.'

'Fighting the Wops, soon he'll be,' sniffed

Kath. 'All they're good for is selling hokey-pokey.' She confided: 'Mine's trying to keep out of it. Disabled, or 'e's going to make out 'e is. Says we can't win anyway now, so you don't want to be in bleedin' uniform 'cos you'll only get shot.'

Doris was thankful when they reached the corner. She walked down Seaview Crescent alone, wondering whether she ought to take Harold and get out of Dover. Some people had already gone. There were empty houses. Dover was in the front line and she had a sister in Northampton, in the safe middle of England.

Her house was one of a terrace with a rack of bay windows dipping down towards Dover Beach. She had never read the poem, and had never heard of Matthew Arnold, although the town was her birthplace.

She unlocked the door and as she opened it peered at her face distorted in the knocker, giving the brass a rub with her sleeve although it did not need it. Walking straight through to the kitchen she put the kettle on the gas and her rations into the food cupboard, small packets of tea, butter, margarine, and a pound of sugar. She wondered if she ought to bake a cake for her husband in prison. The last had been a month ago. It was all that was left between them. Her cakes and Harold.

She turned the knob of the wireless set. They usually lived in the tight kitchen. It was warm in the winter and it kept the front room tidy. The everyday *Music While You Work* programme was being broadcast and the band was playing 'I

Remember You'. The kettle joined in insistently and she put a single spoonful of tea, levelled off carefully with her finger, into a teapot on whose side there was a faded picture of Buckingham Palace and the words 'A Gift from London'. There was a knock at the front door.

Cotton almost filled the frame. 'Sorry to barge in,' he said. He showed his card. 'I'm a policeman. Detective Sergeant Cotton.'

'What's he done?'

Cotton grinned. 'Nothing very serious, don't worry. Is he your only one?'

'He's quite enough.' Doris allowed herself to return the smile. 'Come on in.'

She poured him a cup of tea. 'I've cut out sugar for the duration,' he said.

'Just as well, the amount we get allowed.' She handed the cup to him. 'What's my Harold been up to?'

'Over-patriotism,' he said. 'Him and some of his pals. They're out to defeat the Germans.'

'What does that mean? They're only kids.'

He nodded but said: 'Yesterday, when the air raid was going on, I found them on the ridge — you know, above the town — and I brought them down in my car to get them home. That bomb cracked the windscreen.'

Doris put her hands to her face. She said slowly: 'He didn't tell me that. He did say that some man had given them a lift home and dropped them at the end of the street. But he didn't say the police. He was all excited about the bomb, but I didn't realise . . . '

'Where's his father?'

'Maidstone jail,' she said looking straight at him. 'Three years for burglary. Harold thinks he's in the army in Africa.'

Cotton could see how hard it was for her. 'The point is,' he said carefully, 'Harold's got some idea of taking on the Germans on his own, or with his mates anyway, a ginger lad and a Polish refugee boy. And they could get hurt even if it's not by Jerry. These Local Defence Volunteers — Home Guards as they call them — don't know what they're up to. They're more dangerous than the Germans. All they want to do is to fire their weapons and if they see someone crawling in the grass they're as likely as not to take a pot-shot.'

Doris said: 'I'll tell him not to do it but he's so keen. The three of them spend half their time in our air-raid shelter. They say it's their headquarters. But they're only playing.' There was a sound from the front door. 'That's him,' she said. 'You tell him. He'll take more notice of you.'

Harold came down the passage disentangling himself from his school satchel and pretending to be a landed paratrooper escaping his harness. 'Any biscuits?' he said. He saw Cotton and his face altered. 'Oh, 'ello.'

Doris said: 'I think you ought to thank this policeman for looking after you in the air raid yesterday.'

The boy pulled a face. 'It was 'im nearly got us killed,' he said. 'We was all right where we was, up on the ridge, but he made us come down in 'is car.'

Cotton put his head in his hands and nodded.

'He's got a point,' he said, looking up and studying Harold. 'Sorry.'

' 'S all right,' said the boy pleased at the apology. 'You didn't know.'

Cotton, suppressing a grin, glanced at the mother. 'But I've come to tell you,' he said to Harold, 'that you and your mates had better stop thinking you're the resistance. Roaming around like you are.'

Harold picked two biscuits from the round tin decorated with a Highland scene which his mother put on the table. She reminded him: 'Harold,' and he handed the tin to Cotton who took one of the biscuits. 'That's nice,' he said biting it.

'She makes them,' said Harold.

'As long as I can get the stuff,' said Doris. 'How long that will be God knows. There's no onions in the shops now, you know, because they can't get them from France. We should grow our own onions. We've got gardens.'

Her son looked at the clock on the dresser. 'Football this afternoon,' he said. 'S'posed to be. But the ball's punctured and there's no master to take us.' He glanced cagily at Cotton. 'So we go over and make out we're playing, like pretending — except we haven't got a ball. The head can see us from the school but he don't realise there's no ball.'

'Anyhow, you've just got to pack it up,' said Cotton firmly. 'This fighting the Germans. They haven't turned up yet.'

'I wish they'd 'urry up,' said Harold.

'You'll get yourself shot,' said Cotton pointing

his finger like a gun.

Doris put her hand to her mouth and whispered: 'Dead.'

Cotton said reasonably: 'What do you think you could do with your bows and arrows and bread knife against a Panzer division?'

Harold said seriously: 'When I give the signal I can call out a hundred kids in Dover. We could ambush them and cut telephone wires and that.'

'Probably ours,' pointed out Cotton.

'We could do *things*,' Harold insisted. 'We've planned it all in the shelter out at the back. Honest. I can't let out our plans. A hundred kids. And the grammar school've got their own unit. If they get in with us they'll want to be the officers. They've got an Officers Training Corps, and they've got uniforms and they had some rifles but the LDV blokes came and took them away.'

Doris leaned forward, her lips tight. 'He's got a gun,' she whispered.

Cotton swallowed heavily. 'What sort of gun?'

'Like a machine gun.' Her face had gone white.

'Mum,' groaned Harold. 'For Christ's sake.'

Cotton said: 'I'd like to see it.'

Harold turned but his mother said: 'I'll get it. I know it's under your bed.'

'It's heavy,' said the boy. He looked defeated.

'I'll get it,' she repeated going out. 'I'm used to carrying things.'

Sullenly the boy regarded Cotton. 'We found it.'

Cotton felt his jaw sag when Doris returned

down the stairs. He stepped to help her but Harold got there first, taking the weapon from his mother and heaving it on to the table. 'Mark 2 Bren gun,' he announced.

Almost timidly Cotton touched the barrel. 'In working order?'

'A few bits missing,' said Harold. 'And no ammo.'

There came a knock on the front door and Harold seemed alarmed. 'I'll go,' he said.

'No, I'll go,' responded his mother going quickly into the passage.

Cotton studied the boy and then the Bren gun. 'What next?' he breathed.

As though in answer Doris ushered two boys through the passage, Spots and Boot, the Polish boy. They stared at the policeman and the gun.

'We've been betrayed,' Harold said to them.

Doris handed each of the boys a biscuit from the tin. Boot glanced about him as if considering making a run for it. Harold took another biscuit, then, on a thought, passed another to Cotton who took it. 'There's no ammo,' said Spots.

'Where,' asked Cotton, 'did you get it?'

'Found it,' put in Boot defiantly. 'Somebody lost it.'

'Careless,' sniffed Spots.

Harold said: 'I'll do the talking.'

'Right you are,' said Cotton turning to him. He sat him on a kitchen chair. 'Where did you get this weapon?'

Doris dabbed her wet eyes.

Harold said: 'Up the Folkestone road. Those Local Defence blokes, the LDV . . . '

'Look, Duck and Vanish,' smirked Spots.

Harold said: ' 'Ome Guards now. They was supposed to be practising fighting. We was hiding in the grass and watching. Talk about a laugh.'

'Like *Keystone Cops*,' put in Spots.

'Anyway,' went on Harold impatiently, 'they were up there with a couple of old rifles and some spear things that was in the museum and an axe and that, and their armbands saying 'LDV', and they were putting some tin dinner plates in the road . . . '

'Mines,' said Boot. 'Supposed to be.'

Harold grinned. 'It was funnier than the pictures.' The two other boys began to snigger.

'And this?' pressed Cotton nodding at the Bren gun.

'They left it behind,' shrugged Harold. 'Forgot it. It was up in the ferns at the side of the road so we took charge of it . . . and there it is.'

Doris regarded Cotton anxiously. 'Are they in a lot of trouble?'

The boys eyed each other. Boot looked as though he might start to cry. Cotton said: 'I've got to get my car. They're putting in the windscreen. Then I'll take this weapon to the police station.'

'What are you going to tell them?' asked Doris.

'I'll say I found it,' he said. 'The Home Guard must have missed it by now, but they may have tried to keep it quiet. But you three . . . ' He regarded them grimly. 'Keep out of trouble. You can't fight the Germans, even if they do turn up.

They'll kill you. You're . . . you're not old enough.'

* * *

When Italy had entered the war in June, Giuseppi Laurenti, manager of the Marine Hotel, had in a day become Joseph Laurence. He was as English as Dover and he now had his British passport displayed above the reception desk in a glass frame which, like much else in the hotel, had been cracked to a spider's web by the reverberations of the bomb. He had taken his Italian grandfather's name only in the cause of business and at a time when Italians had been old friends. When Italy, under the dictator Mussolini, entered the war after German forces had conquered Europe, angry civilians in Britain, eager for action, had taken local revenge by wrecking harmless Italian hotels, unprotected restaurants and ice-cream carts. Now Joseph had not only abandoned his former name but with it the professional operatic accent. He also shaved off his romantic moustache.

'Ladies,' he addressed the six American women who had entered the hotel dining room in a file. He revolved to face Cartwright. 'And sir. Good day. I would have liked to offer you a table at the window but, as you see, we have no window.'

The woman smiled and shook their heads. 'And,' he was beginning to spread his hands but then dropped them, 'if you find a piece of glass in your soup, then I will not be the least surprised.'

Everyone laughed bravely. Lunch was limited because of the kitchen ceiling. Mushroom soup, lamb and vegetables, and Kentish strawberries and ice cream. The only other guests in the dining room were two unsuitably suited businessmen immersed in papers, and a sadly thin old lady who lunched there every day.

The Americans' tour of the town had been disappointingly short; most places they had wanted to see, including the Roman lighthouse, had been guarded by soldiers with fixed bayonets and with little idea of what they were guarding. The lady with the notebook had earnestly asked one of the sentries when the Roman lighthouse had last been in use. 'No idea, missus,' he mattered. 'It weren't shinin' last night.'

The party had gone back for a second view of the bombed Co-op. Men were burrowing through the debris. 'Digging for the cat,' said the informative man who had been there earlier.

At the table the visitors drank Italian wine for which Joseph apologised. 'We are saving the French wine for the victory celebrations.' Once again he stopped himself spreading his hands.

Cartwright asked the woman with the notebook if she had found enough to write about. 'History,' she said happily. 'I'm recording history.' They voted their enjoyment of the Kentish lamb.

Giselle, serving the vegetables, said: 'Best lamb in England.'

Sarah sat next to Cartwright at the end of the

table. 'I'm sorry the tour has been so unsatisfactory,' he said. 'A week ago it would have been much better.'

'But then we would not have seen the bombed store,' she said. 'Tonight they'll be writing home like crazy, bragging that they have been in the front line.'

He thought there was some sadness about her. Something that had happened to her perhaps.

To his surprise she suddenly asked: 'Are you married?'

He replied slowly: 'I suppose I am.'

Sarah said: 'I'm a widow.'

'Oh, I'm sorry. You are very . . . '

'Young,' she finished. 'I know, I know. I didn't plan it like this, believe me. We had just come to the London embassy. Last November. He was run down by a taxi in the blackout and he died three days later in Guy's Hospital.' She smiled slightly. 'That sounds very American doesn't it, Guy's Hospital.'

'That's very sad,' he said. 'The blackout's killing more people than the war.'

'I believe that.' She was eating the ice cream and strawberries. She extracted a small triangle of ceiling plaster from the ice cream and said: 'Well, he did warn us.'

He took the spoon from her and handed it to Charlie who said: 'Looks just like vanilla, don't it.'

'How long they are going to let me remain at the US embassy I don't know. I was lucky to get a job in the archives department and that's saved me so far. Sooner or later, though, they're going to ship me home. They've sent some folks already.'

Cartwright regarded her. She had green eyes, almost grey. 'We came to London from Washington knowing it could be dangerous, that was okay, but we hadn't reckoned with an invisible taxi.' Charlie had brought another dish of strawberries and ice cream but, without fuss, she waved it away. 'You only *suppose* you are married?' she said.

He made a grimace. 'My wife is Irish, and she left for her home town in County Wicklow on the second day of the war — on Monday 4 September last year. She said she didn't agree with it. I haven't seen her since although we write now and then. I don't think she's coming back.'

'How long can Ireland stay neutral?' Sarah said. 'If the Nazis occupy this country then they'll be next.'

'Clare says she trusts them.'

'You don't look like a soldier,' she smiled.

Cartwright shook his head. 'I don't imagine I ever will.' He tugged at his battledress. 'None of this seems to fit. Uniforms are not meant for some people.'

'And some people are not meant for uniforms,' she replied.

Then there was an explosion, distant but enough to make the room tremble, followed belatedly by the warbling air-raid siren. All the talk stopped, all eyes turned towards Cartwright. Charlie, big eyebrows arched, hurried from the lobby followed by Giselle. 'I think we should withdraw to the cellar, ladies,' Cartwright said.

The old lady, who had lunched as if she were alone in the room, said loftily to Charlie: 'The Hun will not prevent me finishing my dessert.' The two businessmen hurriedly gathered their papers before leaving a shilling tip on the table and making for the door. As they reached it there was another explosion which made it tremble. A pane of glass slowly slid out.

'Yes,' said Cartwright rising, 'I think the cellar.' The woman with the notebook was scribbling furiously, not even halting as they were ushered out by Charlie and Giselle. Then Charlie put a steel helmet over his sparse hair. He returned at an amble. 'Can't see 'em,' he said.

The solitary old lady was unhurriedly gathering her belongings. 'I am prepared to leave,' she announced.

The hotel cellar was down a double flight of wooden steps. It was lit by only two bare bulbs which made stark shadows on the old brick walls. There were ancient barrels and dusty wine racks and three wooden garden benches which Charlie attempted to brush down with newspaper before the Americans sat on them. 'You are quite safe down here, ladies,' he said solemnly. 'Unless we get a direct hit.'

Cartwright said to him: 'Where's the old girl?'

'Don't worry, sir, she's gone off. She's got a car and a chauffeur so she's off home.'

Another explosion sounded and the cellar trembled. Brick dust trickled from the ceiling on to the women's hats and they took them off and shook them. The scribbling lady hardly looked up.

Charlie uncovered a bundle of candles in a dark corner and they set them up and lit them. 'I wonder how long the enemy — I mean the Germans — will keep it up?' said the American woman with the pout.

'Till they get bored, I 'spect, missus,' said Charlie.

Sarah quietly said to Cartwright: 'I would love to see Canterbury.'

He said: 'Perhaps I could show you around. I was born there.'

'Is it still possible to visit?'

'It was possible last week,' he said. 'Before all this serious stuff started.'

'You will show me around? The cathedral?'

'I'd like to.'

The group sat in the dimness. 'What luck,' enthused one of the Americans. 'We can say we've been bombed by the Nazis.'

There came a further explosion, though still distant. The group huddled closer. Cartwright was conscious of Sarah's slight form against his battledress. Then the lady with the notebook slammed it shut and began to sing badly but determinedly:

'There'll always be an England . . . '

The other Americans joined her.

'While there's a country lane,
Wherever there's a cottage small
Beside a field of grain.'

The big latch on the door of the cellar sounded. The singing stopped. The door swung open to frame the large uniformed legs and waist of a policeman. He bent his helmeted head and peered in. 'Bombing in the east of the town,' he said solidly. 'Hit some houses and there's some casualties. But they look like they've cleared off.'

Cartwright said to him: 'I'd like to get these people to the station.' The all-clear siren began to sound its steady groan.

'Train to London is in twenty-eight minutes,' reported the policeman, still bent almost double but managing to consult a large watch. 'I'll get a couple of taxis. That ought to do it. They been sitting in the bus shelter doing nothing but counting the bangs.'

3

Civilian travellers were still boarding the Dover ferries for France even during the first year of the war. Motorists, intent on holidays and with reservations, arrived expectantly at the ferry dock only shortly before the British army, fleeing Dunkirk, came in the opposite direction. In the months before that advertisements had appeared persuading well-off people that the Côte d'Azur was still a place of sunny peace; Paris — soon to be a subjugated city — was seen to be bright and unchanged. In the first winter of hostilities some snow resorts of the Alps retained their attractions and there were special excursions to ever-neutral Switzerland where, from cleverly constructed lookout platforms on the German border, tourists could view enemy soldiers goose-stepping on the other side of the Rhine.

Dover had been designated a 'safe area' by breezy estate agents hoping to induce the gullible to buy houses there, and 400 London children were evacuated *into* the town in the autumn of 1939 — although many became bored and missed their home streets, so their mothers took them home.

When the expected early mass destruction by dive-bombers did not happen people came out from the chalk caves, blinking, into the Dover sunshine. They sniffed the ozone, had tea in the promenade cafés, and bathed in the sea-water pool; some even skated in the outdoor roller rink.

Life and conversation became normal: the films at the cinemas, the new bill at the Hippodrome music hall, births, deaths and marriages.

Then the sweeping German victories in Europe brought the enemy to the doorstep of Britain, and Dover was that doorstep.

During the Dunkirk evacuation more than 100,000 defeated soldiers disembarked in the port. The wounded were taken off in trains and were angered to see from the windows white teams playing at cricket as if nothing had occurred. Hundreds of other men were left to wander about the town after dumping their rifles. They shuffled along the pavements among the Dover housewives occupied with their Saturday shopping. They were sunburned and dirty and some seemed to be sleepwalking. They drank the pubs dry and slept on park benches. Some gladly took off their boots and paddled in the sea.

The convoy bombing of mid-July was the start of the everyday war. Air raids on the town caused death, damage and consternation. In the harbour HMS *Sandhurst*, a supply ship loaded with high explosives, caught fire and three Dover firemen had earned themselves the George Medal before the flames were put out. The population was urged to evacuate because of the immediate threat of invasion and many did. The armed forces took over. Barrage balloons floated above the roofs.

Conversation in public houses was often tense.
'Fourteen thousand quid for a footballer — for *one* blinking man!' said the sailor to the soldier in the four-ale bar. 'That's bloody madness, mate.' There came a remote explosion and the glasses on the bar quivered musically.
'Folkestone,' said someone.
'Not too much for Bryn Jones,' argued the soldier.
'He'll be a lot of use to the bloody Arsenal now,' the sailor said. 'They won't be playing for years.'
Giselle, on the other side of the full, dim and smoky room, asked: 'Why is it the soldiers and the sailors argue so much?'
Toby Hendry, a young airman, realised she was asking him. They had not spoken before. 'They're getting ready to fight the Jerries,' he suggested. 'Getting their dander up.'
'I have not heard that, dander,' she smiled.
'Temper,' he said. 'Bad temper. Would you like a drink?'
'*Merci*, I would like a glass of wine. I came to meet a friend who is not here.'
He went to the bar. The bald barman rolled his false teeth in his mouth. There came another distant explosion. 'Folkestone,' he confirmed. He looked at the clock over the bar. 'Time the Jerries went home, anyway. Past their bedtime.'
Hendry returned to Giselle with the drinks. 'They had French,' he said. He held a pint of Kentish beer in a glass mug with a handle. They exchanged names.
She said without looking at him: 'I saw your

name in the Marine Hotel register, pilot officer. I work there.'

'That's me,' he tapped the bands on his sleeve. 'Defence of the Realm by Air.'

She studied him quietly. He looked boyish, and his uniform accentuated his boyishness.

'I booked the room because I was expecting to see a lady friend for dinner,' he said. 'We were engaged once but then it was off. Tonight was supposed to be making-up time. But she didn't turn up.'

The sailor and soldier were still arguing among the smoke on the far side of the bar. 'Listen, mate, *how* is Hitler going to get across the flamin' Channel? Swim?'

The soldier sniffed. 'They said 'e could never get through France. But 'e did.'

'This time he'll need boats,' pointed out the sailor. He patted a badge on his sleeve. 'We got a navy. And what about 'is 'orses. They've got thousands of 'orses. The Jerry army can't move without the ruddy things. 'Ow does he get them over 'ere?'

'So you fly in an aeroplane?' enquired Giselle. She made a movement with a small flattened hand.

'I didn't today because I bent the prop — the propeller — when I was landing yesterday. On a tree. But I'm up there again tomorrow. Give me a wave.'

'I will.'

'And you? How did you get here?'

'I came with the soldiers from Dunkirk. I hitched a lift, as you say. My mother also. But she has gone back to France.'

Hendry looked astonished. 'Back? Why did she do that? *How* did she do it?'

The girl stared into her wine. 'She came with me to England but she went back on the same boat, when it returned to get more soldiers. We had left my father on the farm. Somebody had to look after the animals. But when she got here, to Dover, she knew she had to be with him, so she went back. I have heard nothing of course. I can only hope they are safe. I think of them.'

* * *

There was no moon but it was a luminous summer night with the roofs of the blacked-out town showing pale and the sea glowing. They walked along the promenade and sat on a bench looking coastwards, above the skating rink. 'It was amazing, crazy,' said Giselle. 'When I came here with my mother at the Dunkirk time there were soldiers, English and French, everywhere, walking about like lost ghosts. They were in Woolies — Woolworths — buying some things, like sweets or toys for their children. Others just treading anywhere, or sleeping on seats like this one.' She nodded towards the skating rink. 'There were even some soldiers skating.'

Hendry looked that way, then narrowed his eyes. 'There's somebody down there now,' he said. 'Skating in the dark. Looks like kids.'

Together they unhurriedly rose and walked down the sloping path between the municipal shrubberies towards the low gate of the rink.

Harold saw them coming first and spun to a stop. Boot collided with him. Spots ran into the fence.

'Bit late for skating,' said Hendry.

'Just practising,' said Harold. He saw they were interested. 'Want to have a go?'

'Do you skate?' Hendry asked Giselle.

'On the ice,' she smiled. 'But it is not so different.'

The airman said to the boys: 'Where did you get the skates?'

'We only borrow them for a bit,' said Harold. 'The rink is closed now. Because of the war and that. We always put them back. Spots's got the key.'

'We lock it up after,' Harold said. 'If we don't the council bloke will know and they'll take the skates away somewhere. They're rotten spoil-sports.'

Boot said: 'Worse than Hitler.'

'Shush, mush,' Harold warned him. Seriously he peered through the dimness. 'Voices travel at night.'

'Let's get some skates,' suggested Hendry to Giselle. 'Have a try.'

The boys' delight was visible. 'Yeah, get some,' said Harold. All three turned eagerly towards the dark hut and it was Harold who returned with the first pair of skates. The other two boys carried one skate each.

'Maybe they are big for me,' said the French girl.

'There's a way you can make them smaller,' said Harold. After a glance at Hendry he performed a short awkward bow towards Giselle and she sat on a wooden bench at the side of the rink. Then, continuing the gallantry, he knelt in front of her with a skate held ready. Hendry grinned and motioned for the other skates. Boot and Spots were watching Harold and the French girl and held out the skates to him almost absently.

Giselle was wearing a summer dress. She lifted the hem to her knee, slipped off her left shoe and teasingly offered the foot to the boy. Again Harold glanced at Hendry who was adjusting his skates, and then at his entranced friends. He muttered: 'I'm only helping.'

The twelve-year-old was sharply conscious of the nearness of her shin. The rim of the dress was next to his nose. He fumbled with the skate and, without daring to touch her skin, fitted it to her foot. Then the second skate. She adjusted the ankle straps herself. Harold rose like a pageboy. 'Don't you fall off,' he warned with a croak.

Hendry tested out the skates. He offered his hand to Giselle. Harold hesitatingly offered his too. The young Frenchwoman, taking both, stood unsteadily between them but soon with confidence. 'The same as ice,' she said.

They were grouped in a semicircle next to the fence. She released their hands. 'All right,' said Harold, 'let's start.'

They set off easily around the oval rink. Giselle giggled and held out her left hand to Harold, then the other to Spots who grabbed it. Boot looked at Hendry and shrugged: 'I'm always last.'

They had made three circuits of the rink, the rollers purring, when voices came from the path above. They braked with their toes and Harold guided them into the shadow beside the ticket hut. 'It's the Home Guards,' he whispered.

A group of shadowy men stopped on the raised path. The skaters crouched in silence.

'Nice night for fishing, George,' they heard one man say.

'Aye, would be one time,' came the reply.

Harold put his finger to his lips in the dark. The men moved on.

'They'd shoot anybody,' said Spots. 'Soon as look at them.'

'We'd better go,' said Harold grumpily.

Regretfully they all removed their skates. The boys put them back in the hut and carefully locked the door. 'We're here most nights,' said Harold to the couple. He began tucking something into his snake belt.

'What have you got there?' asked the airman.

'Catapults,' said Harold. 'All of us.'

'And ball-bearings,' said Spots. He showed a handful of shining steel balls.

Harold glared at him but said: 'Go through any German, they would.'

'Make holes in them,' said Boot.

* * *

They walked, uncertainly and a little apart, along the esplanade towards the hotel. The night remained close and calm, the sky purple. 'War can be so very peaceful,' Giselle said.

‘It’s been fairly noisy recently.’

‘Are you very scared . . . frightened . . . when you are flying your plane and there is fighting?’ She paused. ‘You could die.’

Hendry gave a short laugh. ‘That has occurred to me. But there’s not much time for anything. Even dying. Sometimes, you know, I feel almost sorry for them, the Germans. The bombers are so slow, you can pick them off, and the Messerschmitts, good as they are, can only hang around for a few minutes before they have to turn back to avoid running out of juice.’ He waited thoughtfully. ‘And sometimes they send the bombers without the escorts. Sitting ducks.’

She moved close to him and put her arm around his waist. ‘These are not good times,’ she said, ‘for young men.’

They strolled, comfortably now, in silence until a single file of men appeared, progressing along the gutter with a dogged tread. The leading figure halted, raised a heavy sporting gun towards them and the rest of the men came to a ragged stop. One dropped a brass bed knob and picked it up coyly. ‘ ’Alt,’ demanded the leader. ‘Where d’you think you’re off to?’

To Hendry’s surprise it was Giselle who answered. ‘Bed,’ she said.

There were some murmurings among the men. Hendry guessed they were the same patrol from which they had hidden at the skating rink. The leader continued to direct his bulky gun towards them until Hendry said: ‘I am an RAF officer. I order you to point that thing somewhere else.’

The barrel was reluctantly lowered but only a few inches. 'More,' said Hendry with authority.

The man complied sulkily. 'It's for shooting ducks,' he said.

'We don't quack,' said the RAF man. 'What did you want?' His eyes travelled along the ragged line. The leading man was wearing a steel helmet and peered balefully from below the rim. The man who had dropped the bed knob had three more slung about his neck like grenades. The one behind him was in a First World War soldier's coat with a stiff peaked cap, and the last in the line wore a fireman's brass helmet glowing faintly in the uncertain night. There were two more guns — one of which was no more than an air rifle — a garden fork and a cricket bat.

'I'd like to see your papers,' said the man in the front trying to restore some gruffness to his voice.

'On what authority?' enquired Hendry. 'You can see I'm a serving officer.'

'We don't take no notice of uniforms,' argued the man, but uncertainly. Then adding: 'Sir,' he continued: 'There's spies everywhere.'

Hendry sighed and took out his identity papers. 'I'm a fighter pilot,' he said. 'I shoot down German planes.'

'Good for you, sir,' said the Home Guard, handing back the documents but not seeming overimpressed. 'You keep downing them. We'll round up the swines down 'ere.' He seemed about to ask for Giselle's papers, but he desisted, and looked behind him as if to ensure the others were still present. The man with the brass helmet had taken it off but now put it on again and the leader said: 'Section forward.' They shuffled off.

'Christ almighty,' muttered Hendry.

'These brave men would not frighten the Germans, I think,' giggled Giselle. 'Even the one with the big gun.'

'The bloke with the brass hat looked like the old German Kaiser,' laughed Hendry. They held each other's waists and went towards the darkened hotel. Giselle produced a key and opened a side door saying: 'This is the secret way.'

In the lobby, shuttered with heavy blackout curtains, a small night-light flickered in a saucer of water like something left for the cat. They turned and stood against each other as they embraced and kissed. When they parted she went quietly behind the reception desk. There was one key remaining on the board behind it, and she removed it and returned to him. 'Your key, *monsieur*,' she said with a droll expression. He took it but she then held out her hand and he returned it to her. 'I will show you. The stairs are dark.'

'I'm afraid of the dark.'

They mounted the staircase carefully. Hendry could scarcely believe what was happening. Halfway up, vibrations of a deep snore followed them. 'Charlie,' she whispered putting a pale finger to her lips. She pointed down to the lobby.

They reached the landing and then went up a second flight. Outside his door she kissed him again, touching him with her body, and gave him the key. He found the keyhole. She came close

again. 'It is a pity not to use a double,' she said.
He smiled in her face. 'A complete waste of three quid.'

* * *

Within the room an insipid light filtered from the window. He made to draw the heavy curtains but she touched his arm. 'Do not,' she whispered. 'There is too much dark.'

They stood, Hendry suddenly clumsy, Giselle faintly smiling, at the foot of the large shadowy bed. There was enough light for him to study her face, its pert lines, and the slender silhouette of her upper body. 'How old are you, Giselle?' he asked.

'I am old enough. Twenty. Why do you ask me?'

'Just . . . well, conversation . . . I'm a bit lost for words.' He paused. 'I am twenty-four.'

'*Merci*,' she said. 'Thank you for telling me.' With confidence she began to unbutton his smooth air-force tunic. She put her finger against her nose and gave the airman's wings a kiss. 'To bring luck,' she said. 'Take your tie off yourself, Toby,' she added like a mother. He did so and she took his hands and placed them on her breasts.

'They . . . they are very nice,' he mumbled. She laughed quietly and moved his hands to press the nipples. 'Ah . . . ' he said. 'That's how you do it.' He could see her smile clearly now.

'You can continue,' she invited. 'The buttons are down the front of my dress.'

'I spotted them.' His voice had become gravelly. With care he undid the small buttons, feeling the mounds of her breasts against his knuckles. Almost impatiently she shrugged away the top half of the dress until it fell, revealing her naked to the waist. He smiled suddenly, happily.

'I am running out of underwear,' she said as if in explanation. 'English underwear is for old women.'

'You're right,' he nodded. 'Absolutely right.'

He reached for her and held her naked top against his shirt and they kissed again, fully, then parted a little as his swift mouth travelled down her neck until he was kissing her breasts. 'Don't forget you have a tongue also, darling,' she prompted.

'Ah yes,' he remembered putting it out and against a nipple. 'Thank God you're French.'

Her hands were fiddling at his waist and, like a trick, when she took them away his uniform trousers fell down. 'So easy,' she said.

Hendry thought he was going to faint with enjoyment. Holding him she eased him towards her and, dropping to her knees, as gently as a handmaid, she put him to her mouth. There was an explosion.

It shook the whole fabric of the hotel. The sash of the window fell. Dust from the bedroom floor rose to meet falling flakes of plaster from the ceiling.

'Bugger it,' said Hendry.

Giselle said: '*Exactement*. Bugger it.'

* * *

There came bangings on the bedroom doors as Charlie ran around the landings. Hendry called out: 'I know, I know.'

'Down in the cellar!' shouted Charlie. 'Everybody!'

Giselle was standing in a corner of Hendry's room, among fallen plaster and floating dust, pulling her dress up over her shoulders. 'That Charlie,' she muttered. 'He should run the war.'

As if he suspected he might be in the right place Charlie shouted at the door: 'Miss Plaisance — she ain't in her room!' Hendry opened the door an inch. Charlie was in a collarless shirt, sagging trousers and toe-less bedroom slippers.

'She'll turn up,' mumbled Hendry. 'Probably gone for a walk.'

Charlie backed away. 'At one in the morning?' He was heading for the stairs.

Hendry closed the door. Giselle was putting on her shoes in the gloom by the wardrobe. She put her finger to her lips. 'You first. Then me a little after.' She moved quickly forward and kissed him on the cheek. 'Maybe another time.'

The airman went briskly along the landing and down the stairs. Other doors were open but when he reached the cellar only a sulky woman was there, clutching a cat in an open basket. Charlie came in with a fuzzy-looking man wearing a suit but no shirt, and a middle-aged couple with eyes downcast from either sleep or guilt. Then Giselle appeared. 'What is the trouble?'

Hendry grinned in the flickering light.

'Trouble? Trouble?' said Charlie. He glanced towards Hendry. 'Oh, there's no trouble, dear, except we could die any minute and it's the manager's night off. Didn't you hear the bang?'

Giselle looked surprised. She shut the door behind her and keeping her eyes from Hendry murmured: 'I sleep so well.' Absent-mindedly she stroked the cat in the basket and said: 'Nice pussy.'

The woman almost tugged the animal away from her. '*Pardon*, Mrs Wilberforce,' said Giselle sweetly.

'This,' said Mrs Wilberforce angrily, 'is so much nonsense. Dover used to be such a nice town.'

Nobody argued. The cat went to sleep and the humans sat down and began to loll against each other. There were no more detonations. There came a jangling of the hotel's front doorbell. Charlie went out and they could hear conversation. When he returned he said: 'It was a mine washed up. It went off right on the beach. One of ours they reckon, though I don't know who went to look.'

He opened the door and as they all trooped out he called: 'Goodnight. Sweet dreams,' to them before making for his cupboard below the stairs. Hendry went up towards the landing. He heard Giselle following carefully. The lobby was empty below. She kissed him tenderly on his cheek. 'Tomorrow . . . today . . . you must fly your aeroplane,' she said. 'You must rest. We love some other time.'

* * *

At four fifteen in the first light of the summer morning the famous cliffs of Dover stood like pale ghosts. From the bridge of his wooden minesweeper Lieutenant Commander Instow surveyed them as the vessel came about and began the journey back after the final sweep of that night. At sunrise the cliffs became gold.

It had been an uneventful night. Minesweeping was often like that, although not always. The Germans sometimes sent seaplanes to sow the mines at dusk along the approach to the port. It was like a game — the minesweeper's crew often tapped the old wooden hull for luck and gave thanks that there was no danger from magnetic mines. Those who could, often worked in stockinged feet; boots were heavy if a man ended up in the sea.

At times like this, the first wedge of the morning, as they made towards harbour, Instow struggled to keep his tired and middle-aged eyes alert. He often thought about his wife Roz, who remained distant in Cumberland. He had told her he was glad she was somewhere safe, but he knew by her letters, and his, that their lives were inching apart. It was as if the war had been the excuse, not the reason. When he was recalled to the navy he had urged her to expand her life without him and she had done so. For women, war had opened up so many doors, so many exits, so many excuses. With an energy he scarcely recognised she wrote of her work with the Women's Voluntary Service, the Civil

Defence, the Dig for Victory Club and, recently, the Allied Officers' Club in Workington.

That night there had been three minesweepers in the operation. One was steaming back to Chatham and one to Folkestone. Instow thought he was probably too old for the dangerous routines of war. It was not the first time.

The familiar unfolding of Dover town began. It unravelled like a tapestry. He could navigate now by the spires of churches. Signals began blinking from the defences ordering that the vessel identify itself although its shape was easily familiar. Other signals came from the onshore batteries where, he suspected, they might be tempted to open fire through sheer opportunity. He took the minesweeper through the one negotiable harbour entrance. The second entrance was barricaded by a sunken block ship. Most of his crew were on deck, some still without boots. Full daylight was spreading across the town now and he could see people and some vehicles moving in the streets. They tied up and he sent Sub-Lieutenant Mancroft to naval headquarters with the written report of the night's uneventful activities.

The cook brought him a cup of tea and a wad of toast. He took off his outer clothes and lay on his bunk where he fell at once to sleep. It seemed only moments later that the young Mancroft appeared beside him with a square of paper. 'Signal, sir. Something big's on. 'Prepare for sea, prepare for action, await further orders.''

* * *

In half an hour they were once more pushing out of the harbour in the foaming wake of two destroyers speeding towards mid-Channel. The morning was still bright and the French coast stood out clearly. Instow rubbed his sore eyes.

He assembled the crew on the deck below the bridge. Only the chief engineer was left below. The steward appeared at the door of the mess, his white coat splashed with egg and with an empty HP sauce bottle in his hand.

Instow believed in telling his crew what was happening — or what he thought was happening. There were twenty on deck. 'There's a convoy, a big one, coming through the Strait on a westerly course,' he said. 'They think there's a chance it will be heavily attacked by the enemy, by aircraft and surface vessels, probably E-boats — and you already know E-boats can do forty knots.'

He saw some of his men look towards the pom-pom, almost as toy-like as its name, and the pair of ex-army Lewis guns. They just provided sound effects. 'Any questions?' he asked.

A cockney gunner, who always had something to say, asked: 'When will we be getting shore leave, sir?'

A few of them laughed.

The two destroyers had cut their speed and were now lolling in the sea. Instow's vessel caught up and lolled alongside them. An upper-crust voice blared through a megaphone. '*Petrel*, keep to our leeside,' it ordered. 'You'll be safer there.'

'If they wanted us to be safe why bring us

out?' said Instow to Mancroft standing on the other side of the bridge. The young sub-lieutenant was tense. He never looked like someone in whom you could confide. The man at the wheel smirked. 'Looks like our convoy is coming up astern,' said Mancroft as if glad to say something. 'There's enough of them. Dozens. You wouldn't think they'd risk bringing them through all at once would you, sir, all bunched together like that.'

'Destination USA, I expect,' said Instow instead of answering. 'From London. Short of going around Scotland and risking it off Norway it's the only way out.'

Through his binoculars Instow could see the ships now spread like a forest over the English side of the Channel. He said: 'Maybe we want to encourage Jerry to come out and fight.'

'What will they think of next?' muttered Mancroft.

⋆ ⋆ ⋆

Hendry just made it to the gate of the aerodrome with steam rising from the bonnet of his little car. The corporal of the guard sniffed. 'That's cooking nicely, sir.'

'Thought I'd never get it here,' Hendry said. 'Bloody thing.' He kicked the car, but without venom, and regarded the corporal pleadingly. 'Deal with it for me, will you, corp?' he said. 'I'm going to be flying this morning and I can't worry about it now.' He leaned in and switched off the engine but the car continued to sizzle quietly.

'Bloody thing,' he repeated.

'I'll see to it, sir,' said the corporal amiably. He was fifteen years older. 'When the workshops have done with yesterday's mess, I'll get somebody to look at it.'

Hendry thanked him. 'I hope they've put my prop back,' he said. Quickly he started across the grass and then the tarmac to the workshop hangar. His plane was in there with three others, a Spitfire, a Hurricane full of holes and an Autogiro, yellow as a canary, the first helicopter. 'Where's my prop?' he demanded pointing at the bare nose of his plane.

The mechanics looked up almost guiltily from their oil. A sergeant came over. 'Not come in yet, sir.'

'Christ,' said Hendry dismal as a child. 'They said *today*. They damned well *promised*.'

'Jerry's bombed the factory in Southampton, sir. They're trying their best.'

'They said *today*,' repeated Hendry sulkily. 'And I bet there's not a spare crate anywhere.'

'Not one, sir. If they're in one piece they're flying.' He glanced at the bright Autogiro. 'Unless you'd like to fly that little novelty.'

'Thanks, I'm not *that* keen.'

He went to his billet, threw his overnight bag on to his bed, then turned and strode over to the operations hut. The pilots of the squadron were sprawled outside, on the grass in the sun, as if at a picnic. Their fighter planes were waiting. An armourer wearing no tunic, his trousers held up by braces, was feeding belts of ammunition into a magazine. As Hendry neared the others laughed and cheered. 'Have a good night, Toby?'

'Wonderful,' he grunted. 'Like the films. My crate isn't ready.'

'Should look where you're going, son,' called one of the pilots. 'That tree looks a bit sick.'

Greville, the wing commander, came out of the operations hut. 'Right, chaps,' he said briskly. 'Something's brewing.'

Like eager boys they got up from the grass and jostled into the operations hut, tugging their Mae West life jackets with them. They sprawled randomly on the chairs of the wooden room. Hendry stood at the back. He knew Greville was ignoring him. He ground his teeth.

The wing commander unrolled a map on the central blackboard. It was like being in a schoolroom. 'We've got a whacking great convoy, up to a hundred ships, plus escorts, about to go through the Strait of Dover, heading on a westerly course,' he pointed. 'The Germans will already have sniffed them out. They're in a poor way if they haven't. They'll attack with aircraft and surface craft.' Hendry turned and walked disconsolately out of the door. He stood smoking against the wall, again like a schoolboy. The door opened and the pilots clattered noisily out. 'Flap your arms, Toby,' one of them laughed. 'Maybe you'll take off.'

'Bollocks,' muttered Hendry. He watched them race towards the planes. The mechanics had already started the engines and the propellers were spinning. Greville came slowly from the operations room. 'Bad luck, Hendry,' he said watching the other pilots. 'We haven't got a kite for you.'

'I know, sir,' said Hendry. 'You wouldn't think it would take so long to get a spare prop.'

'Delayed by enemy action,' murmured Greville. 'Perhaps it will turn up later. There are no spares. We can't even cannibalise anything. There's nothing to cannibalise.' He patted the young man on the arm. 'Why don't you sit in a deckchair and enjoy the sunshine,' he suggested. 'It's going to be a nice day.'

* * *

The lean fighter planes were revving, emitting puffs of oily smoke, and spinning in tight circles before they followed each other in an eager line to the tarmac runway. Hendry watched them miserably. As each of the eight took off he gave it a resigned wave and some of the pilots waved back. 'Bollocks,' he grumbled again.

It was a perfect day for being in the air, a perfect day for a flying battle, the sky blue and peerless. Where he stood the sun was warm, as warm as any peacetime sun he could remember. The grass waved with buttercups; when all the squadron had gone he moodily kicked at them. He watched the southern horizon hopefully but nobody was coming back.

He went into his wooden billet and then into the adjoining mess, vacant of airmen except for the stiffly white-coated steward who looked up from a cup-strewn table and said: 'Coffee, sir?'

The telephone on the wall rang as he accepted

the cup. The steward picked up the receiver and said: 'Yes, he's just here now.' Hendry went towards the proffered earpiece eagerly. Perhaps they had found a plane for him after all. Maybe his propeller had arrived.

It was his mother. That morning she was using her impatient voice, up a notch or two: her deafness varied in degree, usually depending on what was being said to her.

'Toby,' she stated severely, 'you must come home at *once*. *Today*. I insist. Your father is not at all well again. His usual trouble. He may have to go to hospital.'

Hendry let out a sigh that became a grunt. 'Mother,' he said, then carefully spaced the words: 'This is not boarding school. It is the Royal Air Force. I *can't* just come home.'

'That is *most* tiresome,' she returned. 'Surely you can get leave? Lots of servicemen get it, some seem to be off most of the time. What do they call it, compassionate leave?'

'I can't get leave just like that. Remember we're fighting a war . . . '

'The war, the war, everyone seems to use the excuse of the war. There was not a farrier to be found yesterday.'

As she was calling to him down the telephone he became abruptly conscious of two swift shadows across the mess window. 'Duck, sir!' bellowed the barman who was already doing so himself. There came a series of explosions: the wooden walls of the mess trembled and the coffee cups on the table shivered. A pane of glass dropped into the room. Hendry fell flat on the floor, engulfed by clouds of rising dust. The earpiece of the telephone swung close by. He could still hear his mother blathering. He caught it and called into it: 'Wait! Wait a moment, Mother!'

Her pained protest came back: 'There's no need to shout!' she shouted.

After two minutes with no further detonations the steward rose from behind the table. He shakily rearranged a single cup and then made cautiously towards the door. As he opened it one of the hinges collapsed and it sagged outwards. He pushed it aside and surveyed the scene. 'They've hopped it, sir, I think,' he called over his shoulder to Hendry who was sitting on the floor. 'Dropped a stick of bombs on the runway by the look of it.'

Hendry caught hold of the earpiece and said: 'Hello?' He hoped she had gone but she was still there.

'What was that hammering?' she asked petulantly. 'I heard hammering.'

'Bombing, Mother,' he corrected. 'The Germans.'

'They're so fidgety,' she said. He could hear her hurt, deep breath. 'Now are you coming home? Your father looks quite terrible.'

'I'm sorry about Dad.' Then he lied: 'I will ask, but it's doubtful.'

'Don't be a chump, Toby. It's the least you can do,' she whined and the line went blank.

Hendry replaced the receiver on its hook. 'Mothers,' he groaned.

'Mine keeps sending me socks,' agreed the steward. He stopped rearranging the cups and listened. 'Someone's coming back,' he said. 'One of ours by the sound.'

Hendry followed him to the door. The steward attempted to push the broken hinge back into place. Above them a solitary Spitfire circled the airfield. 'Taffy Lewis,' said Hendry seeing the aircraft's number.

Together they watched the plane lose height. 'I hope he's spotted those craters in the runway,' said the steward.

The Spitfire came in over the trees at the distant end and made a bumpy landing on the grass. 'They told him,' said Hendry.

There was a bicycle leaning against the mess wall. Hendry caught hold of it and jumping over the crossbar pedalled towards the landed aircraft, its propeller still spinning. 'Every sodding time, they pinch my bike,' grumbled the steward.

The station fire engine and ambulance were already alongside the plane as Hendry bumped on the bicycle over the grass. The wing commander's little car was busily dodging the craters in the runway, tooting its horn as though ordering them out of the way. Hendry braked the bike, dismounted and flung it on the grass. They were lifting Lewis with difficulty from the cockpit. He complained they were doing it the wrong way. They took off his flying helmet; his face was like paper. 'I'm leaking bloody blood,' he croaked. He saw Hendry. 'You wanted a kite, you can have this one,' he said. 'The kite's all right. It's me that's been pranged.' There were bullet holes in the fuselage.

Dumbly Hendry watched as they carted Lewis, dribbling blood, to the ambulance. Wing Commander Greville spoke with the injured airman before they lifted him into the ambulance. He came towards Hendry. 'Poor fellow,' he said. 'Full of holes.'

'I know, sir,' said Hendry flatly. 'I saw.' He looked directly at Greville. 'But the crate is all right, more or less in one piece.'

The wing commander climbed on to the Spitfire's wing and grimaced as he looked into the tight cockpit. 'Take it if you want, once the mess has been cleared up,' he called down. 'They need as much help as they can get over the Channel.'

'Yes, sir,' said Hendry. Inside he felt the excitement rising. Swiftly he looked about him.

A sergeant said: 'Fifteen minutes, sir. We'll refuel and try and mop up this lot.'

The sergeant turned to get in a fifteen-hundredweight truck beside the driver. 'Give me a lift, will you?' said Hendry. 'I'll get my togs.'

Hendry jumped into the open back. He could feel his heart drumming. The small truck started across the airfield bouncing around the craters made by the bombs. They dropped him outside his billet and he rushed in and picked up his flying helmet and his uninflated yellow life jacket. Struggling into them he waited for the truck to return. It was on its way when the steward came to the still sagging door of the officers' mess. 'Your mother's been on again, sir,' he called. 'She said will you ring her back urgently.'

The blue truck was approaching. 'No!' called Hendry as he jumped into the back. The vehicle bucked across the grass towards the plane now ringed by ground crew, armourers and men feeding hoses from the refuelling bowser. The sergeant and the driver jumped out. They had rolls of towelling and a pile of newspapers. 'Quickest way, I reckon, sir,' said the sergeant as he climbed on the wing to get into the cockpit. 'We'll soon wipe it up.' He threw one of the newspapers aside. 'That's today's *Mirror*.'

'Do it quick,' urged Hendry. 'Blood doesn't worry me. Not Taffy's blood, anyway.'

He stood almost stamping his foot with impatience. Greville was approaching, on foot this time, at a lope. A map was flapping in his right hand. 'Pretty straightforward,' he said puffing a little. He spread the map on the grass and he and Hendry got on their hands and knees. 'You'll only have to get to fifteen hundred and you'd have to be blind to miss it. It looks like one hell of a scrap. Ships, planes, the full house.'

'I'll fly towards the smoke, sir.' said Hendry.

A ground crew man was handing the blood-soaked towels and newspaper pages down to the sergeant who rolled them and threw them on the grass. The armourer shouted: 'All ready, sir.'

The fuel hoses clattered out and the bowser moved away. The man in the cockpit, his face taut, handed over the last of the reddened towels, then leaned over the side of the plane and threw up his breakfast. 'I'm glad he didn't chuck that lot up inside,' Hendry said climbing on the wing, fastening his flying helmet and strapping the life jacket.

'I'll just spread these on the seat, sir,' said the sergeant holding more newspapers. 'It's still a bit sticky.'

'Good luck,' called Greville a little lamely. Hendry swung himself into the paper-draped cockpit. He could smell Lewis's blood. He gave the thumbs-up sign. Two ground crew swung the propeller and it clattered, then flew into noisy life. He moved the plane in a half circle and, pointing it along the grass, urged it forward, faster then faster, easing away from the ground, up over the trees and into the warm morning and the empty sky. He felt a huge surge of excitement and exhilaration. At a thousand feet, he saw the distant smoke of the battle and, still climbing, headed that way.

* * *

By eleven o'clock the fight was spread over eighty square miles of the English Channel, the merchant ships pushing stoutly west, some with barrage balloons hanging above them like bemused onlookers.

On the bridge of his small minesweeper it seemed to Instow that the balloons were laboriously towing the ships. German planes came in formations, the speedy Messerschmitts, the fighter-bombers and the operatically screaming Stukas. They curled in the smoke-hung sky with the Spitfires and Hurricanes fighting them like dogs. Every few minutes an aircraft would turn away from the battle as though in disgust, leaving a bent feather of oily smoke as it fell.

The destroyers and smaller escort ships fired salvo upon salvo, almost convulsed in the water by the force of their own gunfire, lost in their own smoke. The speedy German E-boats had joined the action, wriggling joyfully among the ships loosing their torpedoes and their gunfire. Two merchant ships were hopelessly sinking and one of the destroyers blazed at the stern.

⋆ ⋆ ⋆

At the Marine Hotel, chambermaids were standing on tiptoe on the window sills to watch. Almost every vantage point in the town was crammed with spectators, men with rolled-up sleeves (some with knotted handkerchiefs protecting their heads from the sun), women in bright print dresses, children jumping with excitement. It was a thrilling free show.

At the hospital, Sister Nancy Cotton was again trying to get patients away from the windows and back to their beds. She tried pulling down the blackout blinds but in a moment they were raised again. Women in labour dragged themselves from the maternity ward not wanting to miss a moment. The cliffs were thicker with people than on a peacetime July day; people pointing, lining the precarious paths, others standing on benches dedicated to the memory of citizens who had looked out from there on blameless afternoons. The town's buses had stopped and spectators were crammed on their upper decks.

The battle, fought out to sea, was fleetingly visible through the smoke, and deeply audible. Sometimes a pall of smoke would entirely obscure the spread-out fleet and the crowds would set up a great groan until a breeze cleared the sky and the ships emerged once more, guns flaring.

On his bridge, Instow was beginning to wonder why they were there if it was not to make up the numbers. His gunners had small chance to identify enemy planes. Just sighting them was difficult enough. He was hoping the E-boats would not search them out under the lee of the destroyer. 'Captain,' called Sub-Lieutenant Mancroft from the edge of the bridge.

'Yes, son?'

'I'm scared.'

'So am I,' Instow shouted back.

As he said it a low, darting E-boat, triumphantly flying the streaming pennant of the German navy, rounded the stern of the destroyer — as close, it seemed, as a peeling knife on a potato. Instow yelled orders to the gunners and attempted to slew the minesweeper sideways. The pair of Lewis guns and the pom-poms made a shattering noise even above the din all around, but did not hit anything. He thought he saw the German captain laughing.

The E-boat turned almost in its own length,

like a Brighton speedboat, and came back at the destroyer. It fired a single torpedo, aiming for the warship but brutally hitting Instow's minesweeper on her wooden bow and almost lifting her clear of the sea. Alarms screeched, there were shouts and howls and curses. Instow picked himself up from the bridge and straightened his steel helmet. He saw Mancroft sitting oddly in the corner against a bulwark, his face bloody, his mouth screaming without making a sound.

Instow didn't need to look to see if the bow was still there. He knew it was not. The vessel began to nosedive. 'Abandon ship!' he bawled unnecessarily into the megaphone which seemed to appear conveniently in his hand. 'Abandon ship!'

Men were scrambling and slithering across the tipping deck. Some were in the water, their arms raised as if in surrender, crying out for help towards the destroyer. A sailor on fire jumped into the sea making a small cloud of steam. 'Abandon ship!' bellowed Instow.

The ship was abandoning them. It was tipping sideways; he could not have stayed on the bridge even if he had decided to do so. Falling to his knees he crawled towards Mancroft who was now lying in a bundle, as if sheltering from the cold, against the bulkhead. He attempted to shake him but there was no life. The blood-smeared face fell to one side. Instow said: 'Poor lad.' He realised he was still clutching the megaphone. Lying against the bulkhead, next to the dead Mancroft, he bawled through it again, uselessly: 'Abandon ship!'

He somehow got down to the tilting deck. It was awash and vacant, the pom-poms swinging playfully. Closing his eyes and taking a deep breath he slid over the side into the chilly sea.

He spat out the salt water but his life jacket kept him afloat. He kicked his legs and splashed his arms. There were other men in the water around him, some moving, some floating and stiffly still. Shouting came from above, abruptly drowned by the noise of the destroyer's guns, and he saw sailors on the rail. 'Here! Here!' Instow called almost politely. They had already seen him. The warship had lost speed and was now lying nearly calm, continuing to fire at the low, droning aircraft. He looked about him from the water, stretching his neck and wondering if the E-boats had gone. Nets were being thrown over the side and he went towards them at an ugly paddle. He arrived at the soaring grey hull and grabbed the net at the same moment as another man. He realised it was his steward, still wearing his white jacket. 'After you, sir,' the man spluttered indicating the net.

'You go, son,' said Instow. 'Get the bloody coffee on.'

Sailors were scrambling down the nets to help. The tubby steward was almost dragged from the water. Instow half-climbed behind him. Hands grabbed him and tugged him the rest of the way.

He was safe and in one piece. He had even managed to get to his feet when a young midshipman ran to him and said: 'We'll get you fixed, sir. Come with me.' He put a blanket and a protective arm around Instow and introduced himself: 'I'm Parsons.' All around, the guns were flashing, detonations splitting the air. The young man helped him through a hatchway and into a dim cabin.

Instow sat gratefully. 'I'm soaking this bunk,' he said to Parsons.

'That's all right, sir. Smith wets his bed anyway. I'll rustle up some coffee.'

'Put a drop of Scotch in it, will you?'

'That's how it's served.'

He went out and Instow fell back exhausted against the bulkhead. He wondered how many of his crew were safe. Mancroft had been right to be afraid.

The door opened and a rating appeared with a bundle of clothing. 'Get your togs off, sir. You'll catch your death. Try and get into some of these.' Immediately behind him came the midshipman carrying a can of coffee.

He drank the coffee, grateful for the lace of whisky, then used the blanket as a towel and climbed into the rough-and-ready clothes. The midshipman returned and Instow said: 'How many of my men did you pick up?'

'I believe it was six, sir.'

'That's not enough,' said Instow.

'Other vessels may have picked up some more.'

'I'd like to see my chaps.'

'I'll take you.'

The ship was still shuddering, pitching so violently that they needed to hang on. Parsons opened a steel door and Instow walked into a medical room almost the width of the ship. Men were lying on stretchers being treated by doctors and navy nursing orderlies, bowed as if in prayer. The resounding outside noises had a descant in the sobs and groans of the wounded men.

'Next door, sir,' said the midshipman. He led him through. In the dull lamplight he saw them, most on stretchers. One man, Sims, was sitting in a chair moaning for his mother. 'Sir, captain,' he said as if Instow would do instead. 'We're being slaughtered. Where's the others gone, sir?'

Instow tried to say something to him but it was hopeless. For Sims, for the others and for himself. A Liverpool man, from the engine room, asked if he could please arrange to send a five-shilling postal order to his wife for her birthday. Instow said: 'As soon as I can get to a post office.'

As they went out again Parsons said: 'If you're feeling up to it, the captain said perhaps you'd like to go up to the bridge.'

'Yes,' said Instow. 'Thanks. I ought to try and see what's going on. I've lost my tin lid.' He glanced about him as if he expected to find it.

Parsons said: 'We'll pick up one on the way.'

He handed a helmet to Instow as they reached the hatch to the deck. There was a dent in the crown. Instow fixed it on his head and followed the young man out. The ship was being flung about in all directions, its guns silent only for moments. He choked in the acrid smoke. Two planes came in low and droning, passing quite slowly, indolently across the bow. He could see the German crosses. 'Where's our planes?' he called to the midshipman.

'Up there somewhere, sir. They've been doing all right. Downed plenty of Jerries. This is a lot quieter than it was.'

He led the way up to the bridge. Two blanketed men were lying on one side of it, neither moving. 'Get these casualties moved,' ordered a tall officer with a long face. His steel helmet seemed jokily small. He saw Instow: 'Ah, jolly good, welcome aboard. Glad you could come. I'm Jock Wilson. I'm Scots.'

'Yes, sir,' said Instow. 'I understand.'

They shook hands. 'How many of your crew got away with it?'

'Six at the moment. There may be others.'

'It's an absolute bastard. We've been lucky. *Connaught* over there has three fires.'

Instow could hardly see the neighbouring warship for smoke. 'How is it going?'

'Going? Well, it's going. We've just about won this round. The merchant ships, minus a couple, are still on course. Soon they'll be out of reach of the Stukas, anyway. Their E-boats have been swines, but it seems like they're pulling out. They've lost one or perhaps two.'

He was casting around through heavy binoculars. On the windward side the smoke had cleared. 'Take a wee peep,' he said handing them to Instow. 'To port.'

Instow did so. He was astonished. The French coastline, five miles away, was picked out easily by the powerful glasses. He could see lines of watchers. 'Christ,' he said. 'Grandstand seats.'

'It's the same the other way,' said Wilson. 'Dover looks like Saturday night at the Glasgow

Empire. On the roofs. The British, the Huns and the Frogs have all come out to see the fight.' He paused then said: 'Aye, like a Roman holiday.'

* * *

Even in a battle there are peaceful places; at times one of them is in the sky. Hendry had decided to take the Spitfire up to seven thousand feet. From there, he calculated, he could see the extent of the fight and pick out where he should join it.

At seven thousand there were some unruffled clouds, big and yellow, so slow and lumbering in the light air that they almost seemed to be resting. He had the sensation of being utterly alone, flying in a nicely decorated dream. There were wide breaks, lakes of blue, and flying the plane into the spaces he could look down on the Channel battle, scattered over the reflecting sea, moving slowly as the convoy of merchant ships pushed on bravely to the west. There was smoke, thick in places, but at that height, no noise. He could see two ships on fire, one of them a warship, and the wakes of others feathered the sea as they tried to avoid the E-boats which he could clearly follow by their white tracks. Aircraft moved over the fretwork of ships but, at that height, he could not distinguish between friend and foe. At the edge of the scene one was peeling away with a tail of smoke, thin as a pencil line, behind it. Then the uncertainty was settled for him. He flew into an enveloping custard-coloured cloud and a few moments later emerged into open sky to see in front and a little below a chugging German bomber, a Dornier, sneaking its way back towards the French coast. No fighter escort was in sight. Hendry could scarcely believe it. He eased the Spitfire to port as if he needed to be even more sure, and saw the crosses black on the flanks of the fuselage.

Then the Dornier saw him. He could almost see it tremble and he closed in to cruise alongside it. He moved ahead, turned to port, and went back. He was so close he could see the frightened faces and the rear gunner frantically turning his cumbersome guns towards him.

Hendry curved the plane away. He still could not credit it. It seemed almost unsporting, like assaulting a doddery old man. Then he pictured Lewis barely an hour before, carried streaming blood from the very cockpit of the fighter he was flying. 'Sorry, chaps,' he muttered into his mask. 'I've got something for you.'

From the rear and from below he attacked. So far he had not shot down an enemy plane. He had a share in one which another squadron claimed. This would be all alone, undisputed, his first.

From under the belly of the bomber he rose like a fish and fired a brief burst from his eight wing-edge guns. He banked away and came back from the other direction. He could feel his face harden. His target was attempting clumsy escape, yawing awkwardly, haplessly trying to keep out of his way. Bigger, straggling clouds gave it some sanctuary but it had to emerge sometime and he was waiting. Then again it managed to vanish. It went head on into a great bank of cream cumulus leaving him like a thwarted dog.

He banked the plane one way and then the other, turned in a loop and a circle, cursing his luck and theirs. Then he saw it, a mile distant and still plodding through the sky. 'This time,' he promised to himself. 'This time you've had it, old boy.'

From the tail and a little above he attacked. The first burst of the guns in the Spitfire's wings went straight at the gunner trapped in the turret. Hendry saw him fall forward over his guns; the first time he had seen a man die. Smoke began streaming from the rear of the Dornier and small polite puffs of flame. He lay off for a few moments. His chest felt tight. The Germans were trying to get out of the cockpit, with such clumsiness that he involuntarily wished he could help them. Two men jumped and he saw the parachutes open below. But no more.

As though to end any speculation the bomber was abruptly riven with an explosion that seemed to stagger along its whole length. Flames came from its carcass and it dropped from the sky, helpless, disintegrating, finished — another figure on that day's scoreboard.

Suddenly Hendry was consumed with exhilaration. 'Whoopee!' he shouted like a schoolboy. 'Got him, Mum! I got him!'

He calmed himself and sent his report to base in what he hoped was a subdued, matter-of-fact tone. 'Downed a Dornier,' he said into his mouthpiece. 'Confirmed. Crashed in flames.

Some crew ejected.'

A crackling voice came back: 'Good show, son. Go and find some more.'

Excitedly he began to throw the plane around in the sky. Another aircraft came towards him at such a rate they almost collided, a Messerschmitt 109. That was trouble.

But he never saw the fighter again. He dropped down below the fluffy clouds and saw the ships still savagely in the battle. Three were now burning, one still firing its guns. There were skeins of smoke and the water was patterned with wild lacy wake. He tried to sort out friend from foe. There were aircraft dashing all over the sky. Who was who?

Then he saw two Stukas falling towards one of the merchant vessels. It was like a separate scene, a cameo at the side of a stage. He watched one hurtling down towards the ship, unload its bombs, and then climb its slow, arthritic climb. *That* was the time to get them. The high second Stuka bent over as if it were at the top of a fairground ride and fell towards the ship. The vessel seemed to be covered with spray and smoke but kept moving.

Belatedly Hendry recognised the moment. He pushed the Spitfire to port and then came in on the struggling Stuka's rising flank. 'Got you now!' he exclaimed. 'You . . . ' The word would not come and he merely said: 'Rotter.' He fired as he came in but he never knew whether he had scored because as he pulled out of the manoeuvre his plane struck the cable of the ship's barrage balloon which he had failed to observe. It took the wing-tip clean off. 'God help me,' he said quietly. Suddenly he wanted someone to be there with him. Even his mother. He was frightened and alone.

* * *

That afternoon the sirens howled and Dover's children were imprudently sent home from school, running below the anti-aircraft fire to their homes. Three German bombers flew swiftly low along the whole length of the town, east to west, and dropped bombs which demolished a row of houses and an off-licence.

Streaming through the streets the children shouted with juvenile excitement when the shadows of the bombers flitted across them. People were tumbling back into rooms from their window perches. The chambermaids at the Marine Hotel tipped like skittles into the upper corridor.

People ran shouting from their houses and pulled the children to shelter. The town's anti-aircraft guns were firing madly and ineffectually for the bombers were too low. The pavements were scattered with lethal shrapnel.

The entire row of houses and the off-licence were demolished by a single stick of bombs. The detonations were loud and frightening. The walls and roofs fell sideways, smoke and dust rose in a huge cloud and there were screams from the wreckage. An old man came from a front door like a cursing ghost, covered in dust. Four people died among the bottles and barrels of the off-licence and another three on the pavement. A pram was turned on its side, the wheels spinning with the surviving baby still strapped inside it, not even crying as it had been asleep. The mother, dirt coating her face and clothes, was crawling towards it, weeping, calling on God to help her. Then she shouted again, more loudly, as if He might not have heard first time.

4

Cartwright had never felt more helpless, more unneeded. 'A spare prick at a wedding,' he snarled to himself in the chalk cave. There was a stone balcony and he could go out into the pleasant sunshine and uselessly view the battle on the summer sea. All around men were manning guns, not firing because with the distance and the smoke, there was nothing they could fire at.

Cartwright had asked the battery commander if he could do something useful. 'Not a single thing, old fellow,' the officer replied casually. 'We're not terribly busy ourselves. We're never going to hit an E-boat.'

Cartwright again swore quietly and walked down the chalk gallery into another. The gunners were grouped around the silent guns. A despairing bombardier suddenly shouted: 'For Christ's sake, let's shoot at somebody!'

There came a huge detonation from the next position in the cliff. Every man on the gun where Cartwright stood stiffened. Five minutes later an officer almost wandered through the tunnel, saw Cartwright and said conversationally: 'You're the ancient-monuments chap, aren't you?'

Cartwright only nodded. 'A great lump of the chalk has fallen down in there, in our gun position,' the officer said. 'Nearly hit me. But behind it there's a whole wall of ancient brickwork. Might be in your line.'

Cartwright could hardly believe the moment but, glad to do something, he hurried along the gallery as if he were on some rescue mission. Beyond the gun, the floor was thick with chalk and behind it, in the wall, was what he recognised at once as a Roman doorway. He stood with a sort of embarrassment. What did it matter? The officer who had told him about the wall reappeared from the tunnel. 'They're looking for you, captain,' he said. 'Houses have been bombed in the town and there are people trapped. You're an archaeologist — they need somebody who can dig.'

⋆ ⋆ ⋆

Swiftly he turned and hurried, his service boots echoing, along the dull white chalk corridors. At the main tunnel entrance the full afternoon sun hit him in the eyes. Two sentries outside saluted. One nodded towards the downward slope where there was an army truck, its engine vibrating. Soldiers' faces lining the tailboard were turned nervously towards the sky. An uneasy-looking corporal was standing in the road.

'We was supposed to be going to dig spuds . . . potatoes, sir,' he said forgetting to salute. 'But they've diverted us.'

'We're going to dig debris instead,' said Cartwright climbing over the tailboard. Each of the men had a spade. 'At least we've got the tools.'

A dozen soldiers were in the back, Pioneer

Corps most of them but with two Royal Engineers. The driver said he would head for the smoke and in ten minutes they were there. Before them, like an opera scene, were the demolished houses, with fire engines and ambulances clustered together. There was a small, silent crowd. There were always spectators.

Cartwright jumped from the tailboard and almost fell before springing to his feet, desperately trying to appear confident. An engineers sergeant strode towards him.

'Who's in charge?' asked Cartwright.

'You are, sir,' said the sergeant.

'Oh . . . Right. What's the situation, sergeant?'

'Three small kids, sir. Trapped under this one house . . . ' He indicated with his thumb over his shoulder. 'At least one of them is alive by the sound of it. There's crying.'

Cartwright began peeling off his battledress blouse. He tightened the chin-strap of his steel helmet. 'Let's get them out then,' he said.

'One drawback, sir. I've only just found out.'

'And what's that?'

'UXB, sir. Unexploded bomb.'

'Fuck,' said Cartwright thoughtfully.

'That's what I thought, sir. How touchy it is, I don't know. I've sent for the disposal squad, but it could go up any second.'

Cartwright surveyed the unmoving crowd. 'We've got to get these people out of the way at once,' he said. There was a group of helmeted policemen. He called over to them.

A sergeant detached himself and strode over.

He was sucking his teeth. 'What can we do, sir?'

'Get rid of these people. There's an unexploded bomb.'

'Fuck,' said the policeman. He gave his teeth another suck.

'That's what I said.' Sharply he turned towards the wrecked house, a pyramid of debris, with the engineers sergeant following him. 'Let's have a look,' he said. 'What's your name, sergeant?'

'Dunphy, sir.' Then, as if an explanation were required: 'I'm Irish.'

'I'll remember it.'

They had reached the edge of the wreckage and the air was thick with a smell of cement and explosives. A single doorpost seemed to be holding up a twenty-foot pyramid. There was still the shattered remnant of the door and a few feet of exposed passage. Fearfully Cartwright stepped in. At once he heard a child cry, but not urgently, a lulling sound. An inch at a time he eased away a plaster wall still hung together by flowered wallpaper and went, one small step following another, along the passage. 'Where is it?' he asked Dunphy. 'This bomb?'

'Right ahead, round the corner, sir.' They stepped gingerly. 'There.'

Cartwright felt himself go pale. The bomb was standing on end, like a hot-water tank, two of its fins and half its body visible. 'It's ticking,' he whispered.

'I hear it, sir.'

Like a reminder they heard the whimper of the child. Cartwright realised they had no tools. As if reading his thought the sergeant said: 'Best with our hands. Less disturbance.'

They advanced along the corridor, the smell filling their noses. Much had caved in but there was still a narrow way. In their path was a bicycle propped against the wall. As Cartwright moved it its bell rang and they jumped. 'I'll try not to do that again,' he said.

'I'd appreciate it, sir.'

It was ten feet but it seemed ten miles. With every inch they were more aware of the bomb. They could even see the number on its side. Dunphy produced a torch because the way had turned at another angle and it was suddenly dark. With a huge shock Cartwright saw a little girl in a dirt-covered red dress lying and not moving, almost at his feet. He beckoned the sergeant on and they tenderly stepped over her. 'God bless her,' whispered Dunphy. They removed rafters and bricks as they went, as painstakingly, as slowly, as they could. They had made a space when they came across another dead child, sitting in a high chair, with a dish of food coated with dust and blood. Cartwright choked and he heard Dunphy grunt. Then came the cry again.

'That way,' whispered the sergeant. 'Shine the torch, sir.'

'You've got the torch.'

'So I have.'

Dunphy pointed the beam in the direction of the sound, now silenced. They moved forward with extreme caution. The ticking of the bomb was succinct, like a clock in an empty house. No tock, only the tick.

In the wavering light of the torch he could see the sergeant's face sheened with sweat. Sweat was dripping from his own chin. With minute care Dunphy eased a thick wooden beam aside, standing back as a fall of plaster followed. It diminished and stopped. They edged forward again, their heads bowed, and shuffled sideways into what had been a room. A cry came from the darkest corner and the torchlight lit up a crouching figure, looking no bigger than a cat, hiding in the bottom cupboard of a dresser. Some of the plates were still in place on the shelves. 'We're here, love,' said Dunphy.

Cartwright said: 'We'll take you to your mother. Don't be frightened.'

The girl clutched a dust-covered rag doll. For a moment the ticking of the bomb seemed to have ceased. 'Come on, lovey,' said the sergeant. 'What's your name?'

'Margaret Meadows,' recited the girl with childish formality. 'I'm four and a half. This is my golly.'

'Let's get you out of here,' said the sergeant. He handed the torch to Cartwright and in its light lifted the little girl in one movement. 'All mucky, I am,' she said. The soldier turned in the confined space and handed the small body to Cartwright. His face pressed over her, he began, an inch at a time, to back out, Dunphy inching after him. They reached the bomb.

'What's that thing?' asked the girl.

'It's a boiler,' Cartwright said.

‘It’s ticking.’

‘It’s a ticking boiler.’

The men could scarcely breathe for fear. The air was still loaded. When they were closest to the bomb Cartwright said quietly: ‘Sergeant, I’m going to sneeze.’

‘Count to twenty,’ suggested the little girl in his arms. Dunphy somehow wriggled around his side and pressed a filthy finger below Cartwright’s nose. The sensation receded and Cartwright nodded his thanks. Daylight appeared at the end of the wreckage and they made towards it. First Cartwright with the child, then Dunphy reached the open air. They staggered into the sunlight, into the cleared space before the house. A policeman and a fireman were first to them. The little girl was lifted from Cartwright’s arms and, as though she had been a great weight, he fell forward on his knees. Dunphy helped him up.

The crowd had been pushed back two hundred yards but they were still there and people began to clap and cheer. ‘They’ll set the fucking bomb off,’ grunted the sergeant. A policeman with a megaphone shouted: ‘Silence! Shut up, everybody!’

‘Christ, now that’s *bound* to set it off,’ moaned Dunphy. He ran forward almost dragging Cartwright with him. They had reached what remained of the off-licence when the bomb-disposal squad arrived in two platoon trucks. A Wolseley police car followed them.

A woman in a pinafore got out of the police car and stumbled towards the man holding the child. Sobbing, she took the girl and embraced her so fiercely that the dust fell from her clothes.

'The others,' she mumbled through her tears. 'The other kids. We left them with a girl. Their mum and dad are on the way.'

The child began to wriggle and cry. Her mother kissed her roughly. 'It's all right, it's all right.' Guiltily she turned to face the policeman, Cartwright and Dunphy. 'We only went down to the cliffs to see the excitement.' She began sobbing again. 'And then all this upset happens.'

⋆ ⋆ ⋆

The words came crackling: 'Toby . . . Toby . . . Hendry . . . Toby Hendry . . . Are you receiving me? . . . Are you receiving me? . . . Where the hell are you?'

'Yes . . . Yes . . . Receiving you now loud and clear. Didn't before. Mayday, mayday . . . '

'What's the ruddy mayday about? Where are you?'

'Christ knows . . . Up in the sky somewhere . . . I'm buggered, boss . . . '

'Where are you, for God's sake?'

'The instruments are buggered as well . . . and the steering. It's all up the creek, sir. I can climb and I can lose height. But she won't turn corners. I'm at about four thousand, heading due east, for Holland I expect. I'm still over the sea and the juice is running low.'

'You'll have to ditch, Toby, or end up in a prison camp.'

'Are there any nice prison camps?'

'And soon by the sound of it. Try and come down where you can be retrieved.'

'Yes, sir. I'll start taking her down now.'

'Toby.'

'Yes, sir.'

'Listen now. Remember there are rescue buoys. A whole line of them below where I think you are now. Brandy, blankets, everything there, old boy.'

'I hope I can locate one of them. Tell Lewis I'm sorry I ditched his plane.'

'Lewis won't mind. He's no longer with us.'

Hendry closed his eyes and said nothing but: 'Here goes,' to himself. He put the nose of the Spitfire down keeping the angle shallow. The sea reflected the pleasing afternoon light. All the ships and the smoke and the battle had gone, far behind him now. The sea looked empty. There was plenty of room. He took off his flying boots.

It was no use trying to spot the rescue buoys. But, when the plane was at only five hundred feet, he saw one ahead, unmistakable, brightly coloured, bouncing like a toy in the mild waves. He cheered wildly, then braced himself. He released his body straps and inflated his Mae West.

The plane smacked down on its belly. The force of the impact threw him against the roof of the cockpit so that he found the release handle for the canopy first time. He pulled at it while the plane bounced and banged over the water's surface and he was crying out.

He cut the engine but there was no need — a cloud of obliterating steam told him it had done the job itself. There was no fire. He thanked God. The plane skidded for fifty more yards then settled quietly. It floated, rocking gently, waiting to sink. Shouting with relief he climbed through the open cockpit roof and tumbled into the sea. The water hit him coldly but no more than a hundred yards away he saw the capsule of the rescue buoy.

Clumsily he began to swim towards it. The plane was gurgling behind him as it sank. He lifted his head to see how far he had to go and realised with a shock that the capsule was already occupied. The side flap was down and framed not just a frightened face but also the muzzle of a gun.

'Hands oop!' called a high and nervous voice. 'Hands oop.'

Hendry attempted to tread water. His life jacket felt like a hindrance. 'I'll sink!' he shouted back. 'You born twat!' He spat salty water.

The man lowered the weapon. 'Okay, okay,' he called. '*Komm, komm*.'

Hendry reached the side of the capsule. The man had put down the gun and now reached over to assist him. Water cascaded from the British airman as he rolled into the aperture. He lay front down on the floor, gasping. The other man, who was also wet through, studied him and eventually helped him to turn over and into a crouching position. Hendry fell back on to the seat opposite. He was still breathless but he held out his hand and said: 'Thanks.'

'*Bitte*.' The man now produced the gun again and repeated: 'Hands oop.'

Hendry sighed. 'Don't be a twit, Fritz. We're three miles off the English coast and this is a British rescue buoy. You're the prisoner. That gun is waterlogged anyway. It won't work.'

The other man turned the revolver towards himself and peered down the muzzle. '*Kaputt*,' he agreed.

'Haven't you found the brandy?' Hendry leaned behind him and opened a small locker. There was also a signal pistol which he brought out and pointed.

'This would make a hole in you, old boy. A big hole.' He translated: '*Grosser* hole.'

'*Ja, ja*,' said the man agreeably. He held out a hand and Hendry shook it, saying: 'Toby Hendry, Royal Air Force.'

'Hans Hubert, Luftwaffe,' said the other man with a defeated sigh. He had a long face, streaked with oil. 'Please — what is 'born twat'? What is 'twit'?'

'Brandy,' said Hendry ignoring the question. 'There's brandy in here.' He continued to rummage in the locker. 'Blimey, and a game of draughts. And writing paper and pencils. They've thought of everything.' He pulled out the bottle. 'There's enough here for two,' he said. 'They've even put in a little cup.' He took the cup and handed it to the German, filling it with spirit in the next movement. He took a swig from the bottle himself and felt it burn down his inside. He lifted it in a toast and the German lifted his glass. 'Cheers,' he said sadly.

'Hans Oop,' laughed Hendry. 'That's a good name.'

★ ★ ★

Through the morning and into the long afternoon, lying in the long grass above the town, the three boys had grumpily witnessed the widespread Channel battle. Armed with their catapults, bows and arrows with metal points, and a new meat knife which Boot had lifted from the refugee hostel kitchen, they felt thwarted, left out.

They had witnessed the distant fight unfold, like a film at the Plaza. Their catapult fingers were itching and they aimed hopelessly at the remote aircraft attacking the ships and fired a few frustrated ball-bearings at passing gulls.

'Can't even hit a bleedin' bird,' complained Spots. 'We're just wasting ammo.'

The others did not disagree. 'We're after bigger stuff than seagulls,' grunted Harold unconvincingly. 'Messerschmitts.'

When the three German aircraft turned inland and dropped their bombs on the houses and the off-licence in Dover they jumped up and down in a ditch, daring the raiders to turn towards them. Just once.

Then, when the action was receding and they were ready to go down to see what damage the bombs had done, they suddenly saw an aeroplane coming low towards them. It was losing height and trailing smoke. They almost choked with excitement. 'It's a Jerry!' shouted Harold standing up and throwing his arms wide as if to greet it. 'Let's get 'im!'

Wobbling only a little the plane could not have

presented a better target. At no more than two hundred feet it roared towards them. Harold shouted: 'Shoot 'im down!' and three loaded catapults swung towards the aircraft's fuselage. It was right above their heads. They could see the face of the pilot. 'Fire!' shouted Harold and all three unleashed their elastic-powered missiles.

The Messerschmitt flew on. 'Got him! Direct hit! We got him!' They shouted in glee leaping out of the ditch and back in again. Then they stopped jumping and looked inland. A spiral of smoke was rising above the hedges three fields away.

'Come on,' panted Harold. 'Let's get there first.'

Their bikes were no use so they left them and rushed and fell over the stile opposite, charging across a stubbled field, over another fence and on to where the thickening smoke was rising. They reached the hedge of the third field, halted and peered through.

The plane was sprawled in the middle, smoke drifting from its body.

'Look,' whispered Spots wide-eyed. 'He's sitting over there.'

The German pilot was squatting cross-legged at the side of the field three hundred yards from the aircraft. He was puffing at a cigar.

'L . . . L . . . Let's capture him,' stammered Harold. 'Take him prisoner.'

The other two regarded him tentatively. 'Be better to wait until somebody turns up,' suggested Boot. 'The army or somebody.'

'And let them get the glory?' muttered Harold

narrowing his eyes towards the distant man. 'Come on. Let's capture him. Go around the side of the hedge. He's probably armed.'

'Christ,' said Spots. 'We could be in trouble.'

'Come on,' ordered Harold. 'Or I'm going to get a medal by myself.'

He set off, creeping along the fringe of the hawthorn hedge. After a moment the doubtful Boot followed him and then, reluctantly, Spots. 'Keep your weapons loaded,' whispered Harold.

It took them only five minutes. They dropped behind cover scarcely twenty yards from the quietly puffing pilot, and Harold lifted his catapult. 'I'm going to let him 'ave it,' he said. The others raised their catapults also.

Then the pilot waved his cigar easily towards them. '*Kamerad*,' he called mildly. 'Prisoner of war.'

'We've captured him,' whispered Harold. 'By ourselves.' They lowered the catapults.

They approached the man an inch at a time. He encouraged them with a flapping hand. When they were only feet away he invited them to sit on the grass, patting the field in invitation. His aeroplane was burning three hundred yards away, amiably as a garden fire. The German's cigar was long. They stared at it. 'Cigarette?' he invited.

He produced a packet from the pocket of his flying jacket. 'France,' he said offering them around. Each boy accepted one and he produced a lighter and lit them. None of them spoke. The Messerschmitt was mildly shaken by two explosions, as if it were coughing. 'Bang,' said the pilot.

They saw the police car arrive at the end of the field and three men stand and stare towards them. 'It's that copper bloke,' said Harold. 'Cotton.'

The German pilot nodded as if he thought he might know him and repeated: 'Cotton.'

Cotton stood with the others at the far edge of the meadow, the burning plane at its middle. They could clearly see the four sitting figures at the other extreme and the points of light that were the cigarettes and the German's cigar.

'Christ,' muttered Cotton. 'Now I've seen everything.'

⋆ ⋆ ⋆

By nine o'clock that evening the fighting was finished; most people had gone home, the smoke had drifted away and the convoy was continuing stoically west. It would be a warm night with a warm moon.

The sea had maintained its summer rhythm, rolling beneath the Channel moonbeams. Everywhere had become quiet.

In Dover the hospital was busy as were Mr Palfrey and the other undertakers. But there was a dance at the British Legion Club, and another at the Maison Dieu dance hall, two cinemas were open, and at the Hippodrome theatre a lady called Chesty Peploe, billed as the possessor of 'Britain's Biggest Bosoms', revolved on a glittering tub under smoky lights. Many people had been afraid that day but it was the law which petrified Chesty: she was not permitted to move, even to twitch. At the same performance was a duet, a married couple who often bickered during their love songs. There was also a comedian who joked about Hitler's impotence, and a man who should have had a pigeon act; his pigeons had been humanely released during the bombing and had not returned, so instead he recited a monologue.

The unexploded bomb remained trapped below what was left of the houses a mile away and the spectators who had gone especially to view the debris that evening were kept at a distance. Others enjoyed the evening sun on the promenade and on the cliffs, listening to the muted sea and feeling the balm of the evening air.

Frank Cotton drove his small car up the slope to the hospital. Nancy was waiting for him on the steps. In her uniform she looked small and hunched and he could see she was exhausted.

'I want to go home,' she said as soon as she got into the car. He kissed her on the cheek. 'This is the fourth coat I've had to put on today.'

'It's been nasty,' he said as he turned down the hill. 'People don't seem to realise. They're walking around Dover as usual.'

'Nasty,' she echoed. 'I've never imagined anything like it. That bombing . . . and the sailors from the ships. Christ, Frank, only a couple of weeks ago I was dealing with broken wrists and kids with boiled sweets stuck in their throats. Now . . . well, I'm so . . . '

'You've been there since early,' he said.

She moved to be near him. 'Were you all right?' she asked wearily.

'I'm okay,' he said. 'The most difficult thing was keeping them away from that unexploded bomb. One bloke asked if he could go and give it a tap. It's still down there, ticking.'

'Two of the children were dead when they brought them in. The one they pulled from the wreckage was as sprightly as anything. She was happy her golliwog was safe.' Nancy was silent and thoughtful. 'I've seen dead children before. Diphtheria, measles, fits, all the usual things. You do when you're nursing. But these tots were . . . well, were so battered. It was terrible, Frank, just bloody terrible.'

* * *

Instow trudged up to the destroyer's deck and marvelled at the late tranquillity. Dover enclosed dozens of ships in the embrace of its harbour, the sky fading blue, gulls crying as if demanding information. At the start of the battle they had prudently flown inland and sat on walls and roofs until it was done.

He felt wrecked. Even sleep would not help now. He had lost his ship, such as she was, and his crew, some dead, some wounded, had been carried ashore. Survivors remained below decks as though unwilling to come out. The casualties from the destroyer had also gone, and the ship was almost clear of debris; one anti-aircraft gun was still manned in case the Germans came back but two of the crew were asleep against its barrel.

He felt he had to tell someone. There was a red telephone box on the pier. He walked to the gangway and went down. There was a sentry who saluted him and a petty officer who appeared as he walked towards the telephone. 'It's all right to use it now, sir,' said the man. 'They wouldn't let the crew use it. It would have blocked it up for hours.'

'Their wives won't know they're safe,' pointed out Instow.

The man smiled seriously. 'The families wouldn't have known anyway that they'd been in action,' he said. 'Only when you're a casualty they get to know. Then they tell them.'

Instow walked towards the box. It was dusty but undamaged although one wall of the building next to it had been demolished. He dialled 'o' and the operator answered after half a minute.

'I'd like to make a trunk call, please.'

'I'll connect you to the long-distance operator.'

She did it quickly. 'Operator,' said Instow. 'Would you connect me to Otway 437, please. It's in Cumberland.'

'I'll try. The lines are very busy. It must be the war.'

'I expect it is,' he said.

'Ah, it's ringing. You're lucky.'

The ringing tone went unanswered. It sounded empty. He could imagine the telephone, sitting black and upright, on their hall stand. She was not there. The operator's voice returned:

'I'm afraid there is no reply.'

He left the box disconsolately and turned to walk back to the ship but then changed his mind, paused, and went in the direction of the town. It was getting dark. Outside the dock gates a young girl was sitting on a bench.

'Would you do me a favour?' she asked.

'What is it?' said Instow.

'Buy me a drink. A port and lemon will do.'

'All right,' he smiled.

The girl smiled too. 'My name's Molly,' she said. 'We could be friends.'

5

Doris saw the police car drop the three boys off at the bottom of the road. She went hurrying to the front gate, muttering: 'Now what's he done?' The trio were jumping with excitement, laughing and telling the tale to each other.

'Harold,' she called as they came up the hill. 'I've been worried to death. Where have you been?'

The three stood smugly at the gate. 'In action,' boasted Harold. 'We been in action.' He produced a cigar stub from the pocket of his short trousers. 'We captured a Jerry.'

'All by ourselves,' said Spots.

'We got him,' said Boot lifting his hands in surrender.

'You just stop this,' Doris told them. 'You . . . ' She pointed at her son. 'You are coming with me to Northampton. We're evacuating. And throw away that dirty cigar.'

'But we captured this German. We *did*.' He looked at the others. 'Didn't we?'

'Stop making these things up! You're coming to Northampton, Harold.'

All four turned as a car came slowly along the road. Cars were not frequent in that street. It pulled up a few yards away and a tall fair-haired man with a notebook climbed out.

'Ah,' he said, and pointed. 'You're the ones. You're the boys who took the Jerry prisoner. I'm from the *Daily Herald*. Reg Foster's my name.'

Doris thought she was going to faint.

* * *

Cartwright had a meal of pie and mash and tea with Sergeant Dunphy and the bomb squad, standing around the Women's Voluntary Service canteen which was parked a careful distance from where the unexploded device was still ticking. Whenever there arose an emergency a refreshment canteen swiftly arrived on the spot, at times before the fire engines. 'If that thing doesn't explode tonight we'll have to think again about what to do,' said the bomb-squad sergeant. 'That'll be up to the brass. My feeling is that it will go off. Everybody will wake up at the same time.'

Cartwright felt drained. 'Just as well they're not bombing at night,' he said.

'They will soon enough.'

Eventually Cartwright put his cup and plate on the counter. 'I'll come back tomorrow,' he said.

The sergeant saluted and then they all shook hands. Dunphy looked apologetic. 'You were the only officer available, sir — and a sapper.'

'Glad to be of use,' said Cartwright sincerely. 'I've nothing better to do.'

An army van pulled up and he climbed in. 'There's a brave man,' said Dunphy sinking his teeth into another meat pie. 'And he don't realise it.'

'You went in as well, sarge.'

'I don't know any better either.'

Cartwright got out of the vehicle and showed his pass to the sergeant at the entrance to the cliff tunnels, then despite his tiredness walked up three levels to where the chalk had fallen from the wall revealing the Roman brickwork. There was an aperture slightly larger than his head. He moved cautiously closer and sniffed the stale air. A gunnery officer came and stood by him. 'What do you think it is?' he asked.

'Won't know until we get inside,' said Cartwright. 'Some sort of bath place, I expect. A latrine maybe.'

'Anybody in there, d'you think?' The officer laughed at his own joke.

Cartwright did not want to climb into any more holes. 'I'm not going to look tonight,' he said.

* * *

'Bosoms,' argued the sailor. 'That's all wrong. She only can have *one* bosom. Two tits equals one bosom. Four tits, two bosoms.'

The soldier insisted: 'It says it on the ruddy placard. 'Chesty Peploe — Britain's Biggest Bosoms.'' He drank his beer. 'All I know is when she's going around perched on that tub on the stage, she *moves*, son, she *moves*. You can see 'em wobbling . . . '

Toby Hendry came through the pub door with Giselle. At the bar were four airmen. They raised their glasses. 'Long debriefing?' said one.

'Longish.'

One of the young officers bought the drinks.

'Hear you brought back a prisoner.'

Hendry laughed soundlessly. 'It was a toss-up who captured who. It was our navy that turned up first.'

Giselle turned and looked deeply into his face. 'You have been . . . ? You did not tell me any of this.'

Hendry shrugged. 'I forgot.'

'You have been flying . . . and fighting.'

'Swimming as well,' said one of the airmen.

'You were in the sea?'

'In the soup,' said one of the others. They laughed.

They raised their glasses. 'To Taffy Lewis,' they said together.

Giselle looked from one face to another. 'Lewis?' she said. 'What has happened to Lewis?'

There was a pause until one of the young men said: 'He's gone for a burton.'

'He's dead,' said Hendry touching her arm. 'He just died today.'

At that moment the unexploded bomb exploded. It was a mile away. Dust rose and fragments of plaster fell from the old ceiling. The clock slid from the wall behind the bar. Everyone crouched. Hendry put his arm across Giselle's head. The other men put their hands over their tankards.

* * *

Summer skies continued blue and warm along the English Channel coast. There was scarcely a puff of cream cloud from Cape Cornwall to Broadstairs on the nose of Kent. Fields were green, the sea docile, beaches, hung with barbed wire, lay empty. In Dover, when the Germans were not overhead, red-faced people sat outside the open door and boarded windows of the Sunshine Creamery, licked away the dwindling supply of ice cream and drank fizzy lemonade. Elderly men in caps huddled on the promenade watching the dainty sea without comment.

But now halfway around Britain from the Isles of Shetland to the Isles of Scilly waited a ring of enemy armies. From Norway to Spain the German army waited for further orders. In the southern counties of England there was excitement, there was tension, there was even some fear, but there was also an odd exhilaration and enough to talk about. In Dover the town council called an emergency meeting.

As the aldermen and councillors, soberly aware of their responsibilities, approached the town hall at ten to six on a Monday evening they were greeted by Latin American music. The bowler-hatted mayor, Alderman George Bell, was the first to the interior door and without ceremony he pushed it open. Twenty-five couples, some in uniform, danced stiffly on the oak floor. An old gramophone played through a horn extended like an exotic pink flower, and a woman with skinny shins and a feathered hat over a long face sang out instructions: 'Take your partner now to the left . . . hesitation . . . and then bend her over your arm . . . '

'What's this?' demanded the mayor stoutly

from the doorway. The aldermen and councillors crowded behind him, trying to see.

'The tango,' responded the tall woman half turning with the rhythm. 'The Argentinian tango.' She held out her thin arms. 'May I?'

'No, you ruddy mayn't,' responded the mayor backing away into an alderman. A soldier, his partner caught in mid-bend, stared at them and let the lady slip slowly to the floor. The dance ended in disarray.

'Turn it off,' ordered the mayor removing his bowler.

'I refuse,' responded the instructress standing tall. 'This is not Nazi Germany — not yet — and we book this room every Monday until six.'

A man with smooth hair, coat and trousers appeared, the town clerk. 'She is Polish, Your Worship,' he said gravely as if that explained everything. 'And she pays a month in advance.'

The mayor muttered unhappily: 'Hitler is on the doorstep, about to strike any minute and we have to wait for a ruddy fandango.' Stamping his feet he led the councillors into the chamber where they sat grumpily waiting for six o'clock while the alien music drifted from the next room. 'It's called 'Jealousy',' said a woman member. 'This song.'

Silence came as the town hall clock struck six. The sounds of the dancers making for the exit came through the door. 'Those army boots will ruin our floor,' grumbled the mayor. As always his official attendant approached proffering the shining and ornate chain of office used by mayors of Dover since 1606. He arranged it around the mayoral neck and Bell rested its weight on the table in front of him. 'I call this meeting to order,' he said. There were forty councillors and aldermen in the chamber. They were worried.

'At this emergency meeting we have before us a proposal that Dover should be evacuated of all civilians,' said an alderman. 'Forthwith. Some people have already left but this council can issue a statement saying that everybody should leave the town at once. We can expect more air raids and goodness knows what else. Invasion, gas attacks. The question is *should* we evacuate?' He paused, rattled his aldermanic chain on the table and looked belligerently around the faces. ' . . . Or should we stay and face up to Hitler? Show the Hun we're not afraid.'

Evacuation had always been an emotive subject. After the solitary German bomb had landed on Christmas Eve 1914, blowing a householder from a tree, there was an order for the entire town to be evacuated *at once*. Notices were posted, trains and buses mobilised, but the dumbfounded inhabitants refused to leave. Not at Christmas.

Evacuation plans at the outbreak of the Second World War in 1939 had been confused. Dover was the recipient of more than four hundred evacuee children from London, many of them howling for their mothers.

Soon afterwards trainloads of elderly residents were evacuated to the West Country where many of them ended in a Somerset lunatic asylum. Men and women were strictly separated, silence was imposed and the old people were issued with institutional uniforms. It was only when one who could walk far enough reached a distant telephone box that the error was exposed.

During the bombardments of the town in that summer of 1940 many people fled; the population diminished from forty thousand to twelve thousand. Almost a thousand children remained, however, sheltering in the caves. The schools were closed and their pupils, who became known as the Dead End Kids, ran wild through the town and its tunnels. The cinemas were bedlam every afternoon, crammed with children who rioted when the air-raid siren sounded and they were ordered to leave. Often the manager surrendered and let them stay despite the risk of a direct hit from a bomb.

It was an air-raid warning which halted the council meeting. Councillors strode out into the evening still angry and arguing. Councillor Walker, known in the locality as Darkie, who earned his peacetime living as a boatman, protested: 'Dover is where I belong so I'm not moving. How can I be a boatman miles inland?'

Darkie Walker did what he often did when he was disturbed; with his small dog he walked down to his boat on the foreshore. They had been telling him it must be moved. He strode over the shingle towards it. At his back a solitary German plane came towards him. The dog began to bark.

⋆ ⋆ ⋆

Doris walked irresolutely from her house, down the bay-windowed street towards the telephone box. Sandbags had been piled against three of its sides. By habit she scanned the area for any sign of Harold.

She had a shilling's worth of heavy pennies in the pocket of her pinafore. Her intention was to telephone her sister in Northampton but when she reached the bulwarked telephone box her steps slowed. All around the Dover evening was flat and peaceful as it had ever been, with a cluster of pink sunset clouds. She remained outside the box. A young girl came up the hill. 'Somebody in there?' she asked. She raised herself on her toes to peer through the protective tape on the door.

'Nobody,' said Doris.

'You waiting for a call?'

'No, you carry on.'

The girl looked puzzled but pulled open the door and went in. Doris, her mind made up for her, turned and retraced her steps.

She heard an explosion in the distance while she was sitting, still undecided, in her living room. Again she worried about Harold. She made a cup of tea and sat for another half an hour trying to read a month-old copy of the *Daily Mirror* which had been pushed beneath the settee cushion. It would come in useful for fish and chips. The headline read: 'HITLER FEARS RUSSIA'. There was an advertisement for Camp Coffee with a drawing of a Scottish army officer, heavily kilted, being served by a turbaned Indian servant.

She would have to make a decision and she knew what it ought to be. It was now eight o'clock.

Taking the cup into the kitchen she turned resolutely, went to the front door, and hurried down the hill towards the telephone. They would have to go.

Her sister did not want them. 'Well, you know we don't have much room, not for two,' she said. 'Somebody's going to have to sleep on the couch.'

Doris said: 'Ena, we've got to do something to get out of here. It's getting very dangerous. We'll just have to manage.'

'We'll be getting bombed here soon,' put in Ena, as if she knew something others did not. 'Army boots are made in Northampton, you know.'

Doris was firm: 'You had some nice holidays down here, didn't you. You and Eric. We made room for you. I want to bring Harold up there tomorrow.'

'Oh, all right,' sighed her sister. 'God knows where we'll put you.' She laughed sourly. 'Maybe Eric can clean out his old pigeon loft.'

Doris replaced the phone and moodily walked back towards her front door. From behind she heard a call and turned to see her son running frantically up the slope, his bare and skinny knees going like pistons. 'Mum! Mum! The Jerries dropped a bomb on the beach and killed that man called Darkie — the one who hires out the boats.'

* * *

Between them they hauled a single bulky suitcase, scuffed brown leather with two thick straps. Harold was sulking on the bus and kept his face turned to the lower-deck window. At the station Doris saw his two everyday companions, Boot and Spots, lurking behind the newspaper stand. 'Go on, Harold,' she said. 'Say goodbye to your pals while I get the tickets.'

'I don't want to go to rotten Northampton,' he glowered. 'It pongs. What's wrong with Dover?'

'Dover is being bombed and Northampton isn't,' she replied. 'Go on, say cheerio.'

'Grammar school cissies say that,' he said scornfully. 'Cheerio.'

Doris bit her lip and turned towards the ticket office. She asked for one single and one half-single to Northampton.

'Clearing out, are you?' said the man behind the aperture. 'Don't blame you myself. I would if I could but then there wouldn't be anybody here to give the tickets to those that is clearing out.' He laughed, a single 'hah', at his little joke and nodded towards the platform. It was thick with people waiting for the next London train. 'You'll be safe up in Northampton. One pound ten shillings please, missus.'

She counted out the money, leaving only a little more than a pound in her purse. She picked up the tickets and turned. Harold had gone.

'I'll kill him,' she muttered. 'Kill the little bugger dead.'

Tugging the suitcase she went outside the

station and looked swiftly both ways. She thought she would cry; she left the case and went on to the platform, working her way around the people and their belongings. There was no sign of Harold. Now she was in tears. A policeman, peacefully pacing, asked her why. 'I can't find my boy,' she said. 'He doesn't want to go to Northampton.'

He raised his eyebrows below his helmet. 'Northampton? Never been there myself. Not that far north.' He surveyed the platform. 'Here's the train now. You might find him when there's not so many on the platform.'

Doris began calling over the heads of the people. 'Harold! Harold! Where are you, Harold? We'll miss the train!'

They missed the train. It steamed in and then steamed out, crammed with evacuating people. Doris stood forlornly, tears wetting her cheeks, and watched it go. 'I'll murder him,' she sobbed to herself.

The policeman appeared sedately. Only a porter and Doris were on the platform now. 'He didn't turn up then,' he said as if he had solved a mystery. 'So you've missed it.'

'I'll have to go home,' she said. 'And I've locked everything up.'

'Next train is twelve thirty,' said the man.

'It's too late,' she said but only half sadly. 'Perhaps it was meant to be.'

'Some things are,' said the policeman. He began to rock slightly on his heels. His helmet slipped and he righted it. 'Northampton could be bombed as bad as here. Them bombers will always get through.'

She regarded him as though he had inside information. 'And this invasion business,' she shrugged.

'The invasion as well. That won't be long.' He patted the huge, polished revolver holster at his waist. 'I'm ready for them.' He seemed to extract himself from his thoughts. 'I don't know about your boy,' he said. 'He'll turn up. We can't go looking for him, not with the war situation. We're too busy all round.'

Doris sniffed. 'I can't just stand here waiting for him.'

'I've only got my bike,' he said. 'Or I'd give you a lift to the police station. Why don't you leave your suitcase and go down on the bus. There's no harm in reporting him missing. What's he called?'

'Harold,' she said bleakly. 'Harold Barker.'

Studiedly the policeman took out his notebook, licked the end of his pencil, and wrote in it. 'Age?'

'Twelve.'

'Address?'

'Twenty Seaview Crescent.'

When he had finished he closed the book with a snap like the conclusion of a job already well done.

She took her brown case to the sandbagged left-luggage office. She wondered who they thought would attack a left-luggage office. Disconsolately she walked from the station and boarded the bus outside, going to the top deck and lighting a steadying Woodbine.

She thought how different Dover looked now. There were gaps in the bombed buildings affording new views of the sea. The barrage balloons, twenty of them, floated like fat fish over the town, serene and unthreatening, and she wondered what good they did. She thought of the dead boatman they had called Darkie.

Inside the police station door, piled about with more sandbags, she almost walked into Frank Cotton.

'That Harold,' she sighed. 'He's bunked off somewhere. We were at the railway station, just about to go up to Northampton, evacuating to my sister's, and he just vanished. Cleared off somewhere with his mates.'

'So you missed the train.'

'Yes. I wasn't sure about going anyway.'

Cotton said: 'I'm just going off duty. We'll have a cruise around and see if we can spot him on the way. The car is at the back.'

Doris was unaccustomed to getting into cars. She peered from the window nervously. 'You're a kind man,' she said as they drove from the police yard.

'He's an unusual kid,' he said. 'He should have got in the papers. Some bright spark in London decided that if the story was published about three boys capturing a German airman it would not be good propaganda because the enemy would say we were recruiting children to fight.' He drove on. 'When did you say his father was coming out of jail?'

'Not too long with good behaviour,' she said wryly. 'First time in his life he's ever behaved any good. But I'm married to him. One of my worries about leaving Dover was that I was leaving him down here, locked up.'

She thought she was going to cry again. 'I don't know what to do with Harold,' she confessed. 'What's going to become of him?'

'A world leader, I expect,' said Cotton flatly. Their eyes were still searching the street.

'You've been kept busy,' she said eventually.

'Spies,' he replied. 'Everybody's a German spy — or so everybody else thinks. Spies and rumours.' They drove slowly, still searching. 'And some thieves, down from London, have pinched all the lead from the church at Stephen Street — the one that was bombed. It was all left in a nice pile for them by the men cleaning the site. And there's been a bit of looting . . . '

He interrupted himself and braked. 'There he is. See the kids playing cricket.'

'Thank God,' she said seeing him.

Cotton pulled the car over. Harold spotted it. There were half a dozen boys on a cleared area by a demolished house. They had chalked a wicket on a blank wall. Doris got from the car with Cotton and Harold looked as if he was thinking of making a dash for it. Cotton called: 'Come over here, son.'

The conciliatory tone halted the boy. He turned and said something to Boot and Spots. 'Come here, Harold,' called his mother firmly. 'Now.'

'I'm batting next,' said Harold.

* * *

At the top of the street Doris and her son got out of the car. Harold stood disconsolately on the pavement tugging at the top of his khaki shorts. He undid the snake buckle of his belt and did it up again.

'Thanks,' Doris said to Cotton. 'That's very kind of you. Again.' She hesitated. 'I'm glad you didn't drop us outside the house. Neighbours talk. You're a kind man.'

Harold sniffed and said: 'Thanks, mush.'

Cotton replied: 'Now you listen to me, mush, don't you cause your mother any more bother by running off and all that. It's very worrying for her, especially the ways things are and . . . ' He hesitated. 'And your father being away.'

'All right,' said Harold. 'I won't any more. I just didn't want to go to that crummy Northampton, that's all.' He looked at his mother. 'And she didn't neither.'

Cotton drove away with a wave. Doris said again: 'He's a kind man.'

'For a copper,' said Harold.

Before they reached the gate he asked: 'Where is my dad, anyway?'

She halted and stared at him. 'In the army,' she said. 'In Africa.' She glanced about them, pushed him forward and unlocked the front door.

'Whereabouts in Africa?' he persisted when they were in the passage.

'Somewhere,' she said. 'I don't know exactly.' She sat sadly on one of the wooden chairs and he, as if he knew a moment had arrived, sat opposite, his bony elbows on the table. She went on: 'You're not allowed to know where. Somewhere fighting.'

'I had a fight with a kid,' he said showing her skinned knuckles. 'Down the town. I missed his head and hit a wall. But I got him the next time. He said my dad was in prison.'

She felt the shock fill her face. 'Prison? Why . . . why would he say that? Your dad's in Africa. In the army.'

'Terry Bannister reckons he's inside Maidstone,' he told her calmly. 'That's why I punched him. His father's been in there and he says he saw my dad there. His old man's out now.'

Doris said faintly: 'He's lying . . . your father is fighting . . . for his country . . . ' She halted and put her face in her hands. 'He's in prison,' she confessed. 'I didn't want you to know.' She lifted her damp face.

He said: 'You should 'ave told me. I've always wanted to 'ave a look inside a prison. What's he in there for?'

'He did a burglary.'

Harold's face lit up. 'Crikey, did he! Did he get much?'

'Three years.'

'Can I go and have a look?' he asked eagerly. 'Is he behind bars, in a cell?'

'They won't allow you in there. You're not old enough. I wouldn't want you to see him anyway.'

She stood and went to fill the kettle. She took a slice of cake from the tin and handed it to him. He bit out a big piece. 'Not old enough,' he groaned, cake crumbs falling from his chin. 'I'm not old enough for *anything*. We wanted to fight against the Jerries but we're not old enough. I can't get in the prison. Not old enough. There's nothing I'm old enough for. Not even women.'

'Women!' She was about to eat a piece of cake herself. 'What do you mean . . . women?'

For once Harold looked embarrassed. 'Well, girls.' He tugged at his belt and then his khaki shorts. 'I want some long trousers,' he said. 'Next time I want some long trousers. I'm nearly thirteen. My willy hangs down the leg of these.'

'I'll get you some more underpants. You know we haven't got much money, Harold. The train fare cost me one pound ten and then we didn't go. I suppose they'll refund it.'

He brightened. 'We're definitely not going to Northampton after all?'

His mother sighed. 'No, I suppose not. Your auntie will be glad.'

'Uncle Eric won't. Last time he was here he kept sticking his hands up my shorts. And he niffs of pigeons.'

6

Outside the Priory station Sergeant Dunphy stood at ease, stainless as always, glancing down at his brasses, moving a few inches so that he was reassured by them catching the Dover sun. He took off his beret and — as if it might have somehow gone out of shape — scrutinised the Royal Engineers badge before repositioning it exactly on his close-cut hair. He was a deep believer in first impressions, especially with young soldiers. He checked his H. Samuel Everight watch. Soon they would be there, his new recruits green from the training depot.

He was at attention on the platform when the train steamed in but his heart fell as they began to empty from the carriages. 'Jesus,' he said softly as a prayer. 'What a gobbin' sight.'

There were twenty of them, pasty-faced to a man, some not even upright, almost falling off the train like shipwrecked sailors desperately reaching a shore. They flung their kit before them. The sergeant stamped along the platform. The porter looked sympathetic. 'They don't look much, do they, sarge. Like they've been struck.'

Dunphy snapped an order but there was scarcely any response. The trembling men stood clutching the Southern Railway green iron ornamental columns holding up the roof. Dunphy picked out a lance-corporal, taller it seemed, though bent almost double on one of the benches. 'It's the hab-dabs, sarge,' the man muttered. 'Last night's grub. It's been murder on that train.'

Some men had found the station lavatories and were crowding desperately into them like men pushing in to a football match. 'They can use the ladies,' said the porter considerately before frowning. 'As long as they aim straight.'

'I'll send a fatigue party up,' promised the sergeant. 'What's your name, son?' he asked the soldier.

'Ardley, sarge.'

Dunphy said: 'I'd better get some ambulances here, Ardley. They can't march through the town in this state.'

'Everybody would laugh,' nodded Ardley.

'A bus maybe,' decided Dunphy. He waited until the new arrivals had gradually reappeared from the lavatories and, whey-faced, stood in a crooked rank. 'The runs,' he told them, 'is not good for morale. But it goes eventually. I am going to commandeer a bus to get you to the unit. You won't need to march. Try to control your bowels, men.'

Getting the bus took only half an hour. By then the men seemed calmer, sitting wordless on the station seats. Two by two the lance-corporal directed them to collect their kit. Packs and rifles were piled on the platform. The Dover Corporation bus drew up outside and the soldiers filed shakily but gratefully aboard. 'Crack troops,' said the whiskered bus driver studying them.

'Something like that,' said Ardley. He sat next

to Dunphy as they set off towards the town. 'Not too fast, driver,' the sergeant called. 'And don't go over any bumps.'

After half a mile Ardley muttered: 'It pongs, sarge, doesn't it.'

'I've served in India, son,' said Dunphy.

The bus drove through the town, among the bombed shops and houses and the people on the pavements. Abruptly there was a hoarse call from the back followed by another. 'That cook's going to swing for this,' grunted Dunphy.

The man who had cried out was staggering down the aisle, his agony setting off the others. One followed, then another and another. More men tried to rise groaning from their seats. 'Stop the bus, sarge,' suggested Ardley. 'Get them off quick.'

The driver looked around in alarm. 'Stop the bus!' ordered Dunphy desperately. They were driving by the promenade where a line of coloured beach huts was set against the sea wall. Some workmen were preparing to lift a beach hut on to a lorry. Dunphy stepped briskly from the bus and confronted them: 'I'm commandeering these huts,' he said. 'Part of the war effort.'

The council workmen stared at him and then at the writhing crocodile of soldiers following along the pavement. 'There's no keys,' the foreman said practically. 'They're all locked.'

'Get something to open them,' said the sergeant. 'Or there'll be a disaster.' The foreman took a pickaxe from a parked lorry and ordered two of the others to do the same. While the whey-faced soldiers waited they broke the locks from the beach huts. The men rushed in. Others waited agonisingly. 'We've got some newspapers on the lorry,' said the foreman helpfully. 'Yesterday's, so it don't matter.'

'Thanks,' said Dunphy. 'They'll be useful.'

He and Ardley took the newspapers and opening each of the sagging, brightly painted doors tossed them in. Then the air-raid siren sounded.

* * *

'Which one of them beach 'uts was you in?' asked Tugwell dolefully.

Sproston said: 'The yellow one.'

'Brown,' said Tugwell. 'Matching colour.' They were sitting on the sides of their iron beds. Men were unpacking their kit. The section was occupying two caves in the cliffs.

'One of those 'uts was rockin',' said Jenkins, a small Welshman. 'Then the sy-reen went . . . '

Sproston said: 'They could 'ave bombed me, I wouldn't 'ave cared.' They all felt better now. Tugwell looked about him. 'We ought to be safe down in this 'ole. Not much would get through this.' He tapped the chalk wall and a piece fell away.

Sergeant Dunphy, although he was not a tall man, had to crouch as he came through the door. 'Stand by your beds,' he ordered. The ten men in the cave stood. 'Sit down,' he sighed. 'We don't want you hurting your heads.' He surveyed them. 'The other men are up the passageway. They've got a higher ceiling but it's further from the latrines.'

Lance-corporal Ardley came in. 'I think everybody's all right in there, sarge,' he said. 'All feeling a bit better.'

Dunphy said: 'Right. Good.' He studied the men's faces. 'Everybody fit in here now?' he said. There was a mumble. He laughed quietly, shaking his head. 'Dover Council won't be pleased about their beach huts,' he said. 'But there's a war on. They'll know all about that because most of the war's been down here. Any questions?'

Sproston said: 'What's happened to that killer cook, sarge?'

'The commanding officer has been in contact. The cook is on sick leave.'

'I'm not surprised,' said Ardley.

Dunphy still did not know all his squad. He asked each of the men his name. When he got to Jenkins the small Welshman said: 'Ardley's teaching me to read.'

Dunphy said: 'It's very useful.'

Ardley said: 'He knows what he's doing with explosives.'

'He just can't read the instructions,' added Sproston.

'We'll be having training exercises, schemes,' said Dunphy. 'Plenty, I expect. But tomorrow you're all on trench digging. Then it's a matter of waiting for the Germans.'

'And when they turn up?' asked Tugwell.

'You shoot them, son,' replied the sergeant.

★ ★ ★

Ardley marvelled at the solid calmness of the Dover people. On that bright morning they busied themselves about the shops, a few sat outside the Creamery over cups and glasses, and the more elderly occupied the ornamental benches and stared out of habit to the fresh blue sea. As the soldiers dug the trenches, sweating in the promenade sun, a bow-legged man with a dog stopped and surveyed their work.

'What's that for?' he enquired.

'To bury the dead,' replied Tugwell.

The man sniffed and the dog cocked his leg before walking on.

Their original training camp had been in the north where it was colder but safer. Up there they had never experienced an air raid. Now, as they were digging, the siren sounded. Lance-corporal Ardley ordered the squad to take cover and then looked about for somewhere to do so. There were two municipal promenade shelters, curled iron and glass, with open fronts, occupied by unmoving old people. They reluctantly made room for the soldiers.

'We're not used to all this,' explained Ardley to the people sitting in the shelter. The soldiers peered worriedly at the sky.

'It *is* a bit crowded,' said a tubby woman.

'I mean air raids,' said the lance-corporal. 'We've just come down from Yorkshire.'

'It's not an air raid, it's only a warning,' said a man puffing at a fuming pipe. 'They don't always turn up.'

'Look,' said Sproston pointing out to sea. 'Planes.'

The soldiers threw themselves down to the concrete floor. The local people observed them with curiosity. 'They're heading inland,' summed up the man with the pipe. He blew a foul cloud of smoke. Some of the old people coughed.

Shamefaced the troops gradually stood. Ardley shielded his eyes against the sun. A man with a holey red pullover said: 'He won't bomb the harbour because he'll be needing that when he invades.'

'If he ever does,' puffed the man with the pipe. 'He's dropped leaflets, ain't he, saying he wants peace.'

'He'll come,' said a woman. 'If Hitler says he'll come, he will.'

She rose and went out to walk along the promenade. 'I've got my cat to feed,' she said.

Jenkins, keeping his eyes on the sky, came into the shelter and found Ardley who was standing near the open front. 'I've done a letter,' he whispered. 'All on my own.'

Ardley said: 'That's very good, Welshy.'

'Look, if you want,' said Jenkins. From the top pocket of his tunic he took a folded piece of lined paper and modestly gave it to Ardley. It was written in capitals. 'DEAR MUM AND DAD AND DORSI.'

'Good start,' nodded Ardley. 'Nice name, Dorsi. Is it Welsh?'

'Doris,' said Jenkins looking ashamed. 'It's Doris.'

'Your sister?'

'No, the dog.'

The all-clear siren sounded across the sea

front. 'He went home the other way,' said the knowing man with the pipe. 'Over Folkestone.'

* * *

The cave was dimly lit, patterned with shadows. Some of the soldiers were already asleep. Jenkins sat upright in his bed, Welsh eyes wide, and began to read aloud, ponderously. In one hand he held a gnarled paperback book and in the other a torch.

'.......'*Hell-o, Big Dick,*'' he declared loudly. ''*Want to buy a puss-y cat?' She led him up the street to her room. It was hot and dim* . . . '

'So are you, Welshy,' groaned Tugwell. 'Shut it, will you.'

The men began to stir irritably. 'For Christ's sake . . . stop 'im, somebody . . . Welshy, pack it up, you bugger . . . '

Jenkins ploughed on flatly. '*She took her pant-ies off. Her big breasts shone in the* . . . ' He stopped and handed the book to Sproston who was leaning on his elbow. 'What's that say?'

'*Luminous moonlight*,' said Sproston wearily. He handed the book back.

Jenkins looked discomfited but then compromised: '*Moonlight*.' Continuing: ''*What big tits you have got*.''

Men began to sit up, dull-eyed, half asleep, one by one. 'Pack it in, Welshy,' pleaded one.

'Don't stop him,' said another. 'I'm getting a hard-on.'

'I'm on bonk as well,' whispered Jenkins lifting his blanket and shining the torch into the space.

'I'm glad I can read now.'

⋆ ⋆ ⋆

Cartwright pressed the 'A' button and the coins dropped clumsily. 'Hello, is that the US embassy?'

'This is the Embassy of the United States of America.'

The forceful voice made him move a fraction away from the telephone. The box was at a bare crossroads on Romney Marsh. 'Oh, right. I'm glad I got through.'

'There's a war going on,' said the American.

'So I understand. I'd like to speak to Mrs Sarah Durrant, please. She's in the Archives Department. I'm in a public telephone box.'

Sarah picked up the telephone at once. He heard the operator say: 'It's a man who's in a booth somewhere.'

'God knows where,' said Cartwright.

'Robin!' Sarah said. 'Oh, am I glad to hear you. I thought they'd send me back Stateside before we spoke.'

'Is that likely to happen soon?'

'It could just have been. But I've been smart. I've got myself a new job. Somebody did go home. She got scared here because of the bombing, so I got her job.'

'You've had bombs near you?'

'Not yet.'

'Sarah, I'll have to be quick. Can we meet up?'

'It would be fine. I don't work weekends.'

'On Saturday then? I can't get to London. Can

you get a train to Tunbridge Wells station? By say noon.'

'I'll be there. I can hear the bleeps going. Your pennies are running out.'

'See you Saturday.'

* * *

The train came in punctually at ten minutes past twelve. Cartwright was waiting on the platform and he saw her at once, in a slender summer dress, stepping towards him happily, her hair caught by the station sun shining through the steam. She wore a neat hat which fell over her forehead as she hurried. She laughed and straightened it. They shook hands and then impulsively embraced, the first time they had held each other.

'I was so glad to get through to you. The war gets in the way, doesn't it,' he said. 'They've given me a new job. Let's go and have some lunch.'

She smiled her clear smile and took his arm. 'I've been reading up on Tunbridge Wells,' she said.

They walked across the quaint street. 'They've had some raids,' he said. 'A few bombs.'

Sarah looked about her. 'All these cute shops and walkways.'

'And,' he said pointing, 'a restaurant.'

It was called the Brass Lantern and there was one hanging outside the small curved-paned windows, swinging a fraction in the early August breeze. There was a pink-faced waitress on the pavement, blinking at the sun.

'You're the first for lunch,' she said encouragingly. 'Everything you see on the menu, today, we've really *got*.' Her accent was Scots. She opened the door for them. 'We had two landmines yesterday,' she said smoothing down her white lace apron. 'Only up the street. Three dead.'

They chose a table in the window but the girl looked doubtful and indicated one in a further corner saying: 'You never know, Jerry might be back. It was lunchtime yesterday.'

They moved to the other table and each had a glass of wine. 'I was evacuated down here,' said the waitress determinedly. 'From Scotland. My folk thought it would be safer in the south.'

'Do you want to go back?' asked Sarah glancing up from the menu.

'Och, no,' the girl laughed. 'I'm having too much fun. The Polish airmen come in every night to the pubs. They're a hoot.'

After she had gone Cartwright said: 'By the time this war is finished half the population will have been transported somewhere else. People who once didn't even own a suitcase.'

Sarah looked gently over her glass at him. Her eyes were deep, her hair showed below her small hat. 'They keep trying to send me home,' she said. 'And I just don't want to go. The others think I'm crazy. They think there's going to be a lot of bombing.'

'But you're keeping one step ahead?'

'So far.'

'Well, at last the army have found a job for me,' he laughed quietly. 'I didn't know where I was or what I was supposed to be doing. There's not a lot of call for archaeology just now or guided tours for American ladies. They've sent me out to look at some churches.'

'That sounds peaceful enough.'

'The authorities are worried that some of the old church treasures in this area, from here down to the coast, the screens, communion plate, relics and suchlike will be in danger of destruction or looting if the German invasion happens. And not necessarily from the Germans. I've got to get around and, because I have a history degree, advise on their removal or protection. It's a weird job. Precious stuff has got to be removed and stored somewhere. Fortunately there are plenty of caves in Kent.'

'Where will you start?'

'On Romney Marsh. It's a strange part, very misty, very mysterious. It used to be a favourite place for smugglers and it's still a bit like that. Lots of tales. It's south-east of here towards the coast.'

Sarah said almost shyly: 'I copied the poem 'Dover Beach'.' She opened her handbag and took out a sheet of paper. 'I've almost learned it,' she smiled. 'Sitting in my bed. It's the middle words that are so beautiful.' She took a sip of the wine and spread the written lines on the white tablecloth.

In her soft American voice, but unselfconsciously, she began to read:

'Ah, love, let us be true
To one another! for the world, which seems
To lie before us like a land of dreams . . . '

'Och, poetry,' said the young waitress abruptly appearing and leaning over. 'I write poems. I've written hundreds.'

They regarded her soberly. 'Only yesterday I began one.' She politely examined the lines laid on the tablecloth. 'Did you write that?' she asked Sarah.

Sarah said: 'I'm afraid not. It's by Matthew Arnold.'

'What did I write last week now?' said the girl. 'Something like . . . oh yes . . . '

She smoothed her hands down her apron.

'The moon shines down on Tunbridge Wells
And there a lot of people dwells.'

'But I can't remember the rest. Would you like to order now?'

* * *

Even on the late summer afternoon the marsh looked shadowed and secret. He drove the small khaki-coloured car through lanes where the overhang of trees closed out the sky. 'England,' Sarah said, 'is really strange. In a small country who would know that there could be such differences, all in a few miles.'

'People even talk in different ways,' Cartwright said. 'And they're almost neighbours. Here on Romney Marsh some speak like their great-great-great grandfathers spoke.'

He eased the small car to a stop at a crossroads and checked a map. 'Had one heck of a job getting hold of this,' he said rustling it. 'If you ask for a map they think you're a German spy, even if you're in uniform. I convinced the Dover library I wasn't one. The army didn't have any maps spare.' He looked both ways. The lane was empty, punctuated with sharp-edged black shadows. Crows flapped over the trees, their calls cracking the silence. He turned left and after three hundred yards and three more corners said: 'This looks like it.'

The church was almost buried beneath its yews. The graveyard smelt of mildew; it was deep, green and unkempt except for two tombstones which had been kept clear and on which wild flowers had been placed in jam jars. One jar had toppled on to its side and as they entered through the gate Sarah stepped aside and righted it. She said: 'That's me. House proud.'

Inside the wooden porch of the church they stood for a moment. It was dim under there and the wood smelt rotten. Sarah moved a step towards a noticeboard.

'*Village Dance*,' she read aloud. '*In aid of the War Effort*.'

'Every little helps,' grinned Cartwright.

'*Reading Circle*,' she continued, '*Gardening Club and Knitting for the Forces*. Life goes on.'

One of the notices was faded. '*Bell Ringing Practice. Cancelled for the Duration*.'

'Unless paratroops drop,' continued Cartwright. They pushed the grunting church door and at once they heard a voice.

It echoed from the pulpit, raised above the pews, shiny and empty. There was a strong smell of flowers and furniture polish. In the pulpit, his head just above the rim, was a gesticulating man. He called to them: 'Be down in a minute.'

They waited in the aisle and watched him descend carefully. 'I find it even more difficult climbing up,' he said cheerfully. 'God knows how I am going to ascend into heaven.' He took on a thoughtful smile. 'But I imagine He does.'

He knew why Cartwright was there. They shook hands. 'Bernard Cowling,' he said. 'I am the vicar. Referred to in the parish as the Old Vic.'

He motioned them to sit in the front pew. 'On Saturdays I come in slyly to try out my sermon for Sunday,' he said. 'A sort of dress rehearsal from the pulpit itself.' He shrugged and waved his hand at the empty pews. 'We don't get many more people than this anyway.'

Sarah said: 'So many people are away right now.'

'And many will stay away, I expect,' sighed the clergyman. 'Who would want to come back to Romney Marsh once they've seen Cairo or Singapore?' He glanced at Cartwright. 'You want to see the church treasures,' he said. 'How we can stop Hitler getting his thieving hands on them.'

'Yes, that's the idea,' said Cartwright. 'We don't know what they might do.'

'Snaffle the lot, I expect,' said the vicar. Sarah smiled towards him. He added: 'I bet the Bayeaux Tapestry is in Berlin by now. And *Mona Lisa*.'

'The story is that the Germans have allowed the French to move the tapestry to a place of safety,' said Cartwright uncertainly. 'I don't know about the *Mona Lisa*.'

'Still smirking, I expect,' said the vicar. He waved towards the altar. 'Well, as you will have doubtless already perceived, the screen here is nothing to shout about. Victorian and very ordinary, local carpentry. Nobody would want to swipe that. But we do have quite a nifty communion set, plate, chalice and everything. Come, I'll show you.'

They followed him up the spongy red carpet to the altar rail. He gave a short bow to the cross as if greeting an everyday acquaintance and then opened a cupboard below. 'It's quite decent,' he said. 'Fifteenth century. I don't think it started out in this church. We probably offered to look after it for another parish during the Civil War.'

Carefully, but without reverence, he took the chalice, the silver plate and the smaller dish from the cupboard and, oddly like a salesman, set them out on the altar. 'There,' he said. 'Not bad, eh?'

'Beautiful,' said Sarah. The afternoon light, changing colour as it came through the stained windows, touched the silver. 'It is wonderful that you can leave these in a closet in the church.'

The vicar handed the chalice to Cartwright and half-turned to Sarah. 'A *locked* church, I have to emphasise. These days the insurance company insists. A few years ago we would not have found it necessary but churches in Kent have had things taken during the recent bombing and shelling. Quite often it's their roof.'

He looked pensive, then said: 'I will show you where we can hide it so the Germans won't sniff it out.'

They went down the aisle. Sarah let her eyes move along the ancient memorial panels on the wall. ' 'The rude forefathers of the hamlet sleep',' quoted the vicar. 'Quite how rude they were,' he paused near the font at the door, 'we can only guess. Would you mind signing our visitors' book?'

They both signed. It was a thick, aged book. 'It goes way back,' said the vicar a touch proudly. 'There's even a highwayman in there.' He turned back the discoloured pages. 'There,' he pointed. 'Davie Hawk. See.'

They leaned forward as he pointed to the brown scrawl. 'Davie Hawk, he signed that when he took sanctuary in the church,' said the clergyman. 'Not that it did him much good. They took him out and hanged him anyway.'

He emitted a strange chuckle. 'The things they did in those days. Almost as bad as now.'

They followed him into the churchyard overgrown with wild flowers. The sunlight was coming in fingers through the yews. Mr Cowling looked up towards the sky fragmented by the trees. 'Jerry hasn't shown up today,' he said. 'Not over here. It's strange how you can stand below these yews and listen to them fighting in the sky. You can tell our planes from theirs, just by the sounds.' He patted one of the yew trunks. 'The village men used to cut these for their bows at one time. Our Home Guard, as they call them rather hopefully, have asked if they can cut a few branches for the same reason.' He shook his head: 'They want to oppose the Third Reich with bows and arrows. But now, some rifles have turned up — from your country, madam.' He gave Sarah a short bow like the one he had offered to the altar. 'They arrived covered in twenty years of grease. The wives have been boiling them out. The stench from the Women's Institute is powerful.'

'Let's hope there's some ammunition as well,' said Cartwright.

'That, I understand, is on the way. I personally can't make up my mind, as a man of God, whether I should attempt to mediate with the invaders or shoot the swine. I have a 12 bore in the vicarage.'

He stopped his walk along the shaggy path by a tombstone almost leaning against the church wall and hung with honeysuckle. 'Here it is.' He tapped the stone politely like a man knocking on a door. 'After they'd hidden the chalice and the other pieces from the Roundheads they were not discovered for some time — about two centuries, in fact. 1845. Whoever concealed them probably did not survive the Civil War.'

He leaned towards the wall and, with a brief grunt, firmly pushed the gravestone from its right-hand edge. It obediently eased over as if it were hinged. An opening appeared. Sarah put her hand to her mouth.

'We're rather proud of it,' nodded the vicar. 'But nobody, not even the churchwardens or the parish council, will be told that the communion silver will be put into the hole again if the invaders come.' He pushed his hand inside the oblong aperture and moved it to show the space. He regarded Cartwright. 'I think it ought to be safe in there, don't you, captain?'

Cartwright agreed. 'And nobody will even guess,' said Mr Cowling. 'If they did, and they told, they would have to deal with me. And my shotgun. In some circumstances England must come before Christendom.'

He made to push the stone upright again. Cartwright moved forward and unnecessarily assisted him. 'I can say in my report that things have been taken care of,' he said. 'Precautions taken without going into detail. Eventually the Germans may read it.'

They shook hands with the vicar and he returned to the church saying: 'Must finish my sermon rehearsal.' He paused and half-turned. 'I wonder if the Germans would come to church? Might do them the world of good.'

Sarah put her arm through Cartwright's as they walked to the car in the lane. Carefully he asked her: 'What time must you go?'

'I don't have to go at all,' she said without looking at him. 'I have my toothbrush with me. I think I'll be staying. It's an interesting place.'

* * *

A low wind moved by night across the marsh, grumbling along lanes and ditches, sighing among roofs. There was a three-quarter moon, robed in clouds, that came and went across the window of their room, below the thatch. She lay close to him, his arm embracing her warmth. They were both awake. Sarah, almost submerged by the bedclothes, began a muffled giggle. 'That landlord,' she said. Her face appeared as a sheet of moonlight crossed the bed through the bare panes. 'He said that if the air-raid warning sounded to put our heads under the pillows. Sounds like fun.'

'It's not in the air-raid precautions manuals,' Cartwright agreed. He kissed her face. 'But at present the Germans also seem to prefer their beds.'

She turned close, her breasts moving against him. A cat began to yowl outside. They both laughed. Then she said quietly: 'Again? Are you okay for again, darling?'

'I am okay for again,' he said folding her to him. She was wearing a slip and he felt the incitement of its silk against his naked groin.

'I figured you might think I'm being greedy.'

'I am greedy too. For you. I'll be there soon.'

'I'll know.' He moved into her; she drew in a sharp, deep breath and said: 'You are.'

They eased together under the moonbeams. The cat continued to howl throughout. He pulled the straps of the slip over her shoulders. Her breasts rose to meet his mouth. Their movements made sweat run on their bodies. When she reached her climax it was with a cry not unlike the cat's. They lay, eyes shut, breathing against each other's faces. The cat was wailing outside the window, its face against the glass. Dozily Sarah opened her eyes. 'He's on the window ledge,' she said. 'He's looking in.'

Cartwright saw the fluffed outline, the bright eyes staring into the room. 'We'd better let him in,' he said.

'I'll do it,' she said. 'You're naked.'

'The cat won't mind,' he laughed. 'But I'm sure he'd prefer you.'

A touch primly she adjusted the straps of her slip and slid from the big bed. The cat stared at her through the glass. Sarah playfully put her face close so they were only an inch apart. The cat expected to be let in. The woman eased up the latch and opened the window. With a half-grunt, half-purr, the cat dropped into the room. 'Now where?' asked Sarah.

The animal softly jumped on to the quilt. It padded up and down, allowed Sarah to return beneath the sheets and blankets, then sniffed casually at Cartwright before settling to slumber in the folds of the foot of the bed. 'Seems like we've got a cat,' said Sarah.

The animal curled and dropped effortlessly into a deep, purring sleep. The lovers lay against each other. 'My husband,' she said, 'was blind drunk when he was killed.'

He said: 'That worries you.'

'He wasn't like that,' she said. 'In the States I had never known him take a drink, maybe just at

Christmas, and because he didn't I didn't either. But he was drunk when the taxi hit him. They said at the inquest.' She laughed bitterly. 'Imagine coming to London and being killed by a cab in the blackout. He came over from the US before me and in weeks he had changed. It was like he'd thrown away everything he had believed in. God only knows why. He was a different guy.'

'People become different,' he said. 'This war's made them.'

'I know he went with other women here. They weren't even lovers, just pick-ups. He went to clubs in the West End,' she said. 'When I arrived it stopped him for a while, but then he began it again. It drove me crazy. Lies, double-crossing . . . ' Her voice had softened to a whisper. 'And now I am here with you.'

'It's all that matters,' he said.

She put her fingers on his hair and kissed his neck. The cat began to snore. 'I'm very glad,' she said, 'that we wrote our names in that old book in the church today. Whatever happens to us from now, just imagine, our names will be there together for years and years.'

7

Each evening as darkness came down over the Strait the war finished for the day. The long daylight hours of British Summer Time afforded enough time for battle. Sometimes a late enemy raider would drone across in the dusk but it would turn and be back in France by dark. British Hurricanes and Spitfires took their rest like boxers between rounds.

There were sly movements by sea on both sides of the Channel and to the hazards of darkness were added the dangers of shoals and mines. Cargoes, some of them odd, continued to be moved. A British coaster was lost while transporting a hundred tons of cement, another with a cargo of pit props; a German barge was sunk loaded with cattle whose lowing gave away her position.

But along the English southern coast there was always relief as another dangerous day drained away; meals were cooked and eaten, sentries posted, and wireless sets tuned in to the news followed by the evening comedy programme and dance music on the BBC. In Dover the theatre was unlit, but inside there were gas lamps and the shows went on, brightly optimistic and with an attempt at glamour; the three cinemas showed Hollywood films with a change of programme on Wednesdays. There was a dance in or around the town every night except Sunday.

'One thing you can't deny,' said Tugwell profoundly, 'Dover is loaded with crumpet.'

'All shapes and sizes,' agreed Sproston. 'But all definite crumpet.' They were polishing their boots. Boots had to be worn even to dances.

'It's no use moaning about how women look,' said Tugwell. 'There's a war on.'

'These Land Army girls are big,' said Ardley.

'Strong, like carthorses,' said Jenkins.

There was a bus to the darkened village and the dance. Servicemen did not need to buy a bus ticket. It was a shadowy straggle of houses but they located the hall easily by the blare of the band. An old man, chewing on a charred Woodbine, was collecting the sixpences at the door. They pushed back the thick blackout curtain and went expectantly into a cavern of smoke, heat and discord. 'We're late,' said Tugwell. 'There won't be any kyfer left.'

The band was doggedly attacking the new dance, 'The White Cliffs of Dover'. It was a greatly popular song, frequently on the wireless and played on people's pianos at home, promoting widespread sales of sheet music. The dancers revolved around the floor in an anticlockwise direction.

'Let's get to the bar,' said Ardley. 'Who's got any money?'

'I'll buy you boys a drink.' The voice was deep but softly female. Ardley, who was looking down towards his trouser pocket, took into his view a pair of corduroy leggings. His gaze travelled up to a green, comfortably crowded, woollen jumper, to a brown neck and a tanned, optimistic face framed by copper hair.

'Oh, thanks,' he managed to mutter. He glanced at the surprised trio.

'Yes, thank you,' they chorused.

Tugwell added: 'Ever so.'

'Pints?' she asked.

The soldiers' faces beamed. They nodded and mumbled. No one could think of anything to say to her but Ardley eventually came out with: 'You look smart tonight.'

'Women's Land Army,' she said as if they might not know. 'WLA.' She laughed. 'We Lie Anywhere.' The pints travelled across the bar. She finished: 'But I don't.'

'People say brainless things,' said Ardley. 'Are you drinking?'

'I've got a gin and orange,' she said reaching for it. 'There's no tonic.'

Then she said to Ardley: 'Would you like to dance?' He swallowed and almost choked. With a grin at the others he followed her on to the floor.

'Well, Ardley's a big bloke,' said Sproston to Tugwell.

'He's that,' said Tugwell. 'They'll fit nicely.'

It was a romantic waltz, 'Moonlight and Roses'. Her big bosom lay against his battledress. 'I was milking until half an hour ago,' she said. 'I didn't have time to change. Anyway, nurses and ATS girls come in their uniforms. Why not the Land Army? We don't all niff of pigs.'

Ardley revolved her enjoyably. 'I'll say not.' He sniffed at her cheek. 'You smell good.'

'Chickens,' she laughed. 'My friends are over

there.' She nodded to a collection of green jumpers in a corner by the band. 'We're up to our necks in animals and cow shit most of the day,' she went on. 'While you're watching out for the Germans.'

'That's all we can do,' he shrugged. He was conscious of her breasts rolling as he moved her. 'Just watch, dig holes and pretend we're blowing up bridges.'

'Somehow I don't think Jerry will turn up,' she said. She hummed the tune of 'Moonlight and Roses' and Ardley softly sang some of the words. 'It doesn't seem real, this war, does it?' she said. 'Where do you come from?'

'Buckingham,' he said. 'There's a limerick about it.'

She said: 'I don't live that far away from here. I work on the farm next to my father's house. I came over on my horse. He's a working horse. Lovely and big. Three evenings a week I go out with a couple of the other girls. We ride across country, patrolling. Looking out for German parachutists.' She sighed regretfully. 'We've never found any yet.'

Ardley had his damp face adjacent to her rosy cheek. He closed them together. 'What would you do if you captured these Jerry parachutists?' he asked in her ear.

'God help them,' she whispered.

He saw Sproston dancing with a girl with bare shoulders, holding a courteous handkerchief next to her skin. Tugwell was surveying the opportunities over his beer, his nose almost resting on the rim of the tankard. Jenkins was making the landgirls laugh.

The band, called Kentish Fire under its leader Raymond Swing, was not very good, but they rallied and joined in the Gay Gordons, the Hokey-Cokey and 'Underneath the Spreading Chestnut Tree', the music almost drowned by the exuberance on the floor. Fuelled by Kentish beer the musicians attempted a *paso doble* but soon clattered into chaos and had to be halted by Raymond Swing.

'He's called Ernie Benbow really,' Rose told Ardley as they stood aside. 'I used to go to Sunday school with him. He pinched his name from that American who reports on the wireless, Raymond Gram Swing, is it? He even tries to speak like an American. I remember in Sunday school he wet himself.'

He smiled at her. They had been together the entire evening. Her lips looked damp and her face flushed. 'Can I take you home?' he asked.

She said: 'I came on the horse, remember. I've got to go home on the horse.'

'Is it far? Could I walk at the side?'

'It's not far, but enough. What time do you have to be back in camp?'

'Midnight. Well, twenty-three fifty-nine. One minute before.'

'You can ride on his back,' she said.

He laughed, then said: 'All right, I'll try. I'll tell my mates.'

'And I'll tell mine. See you at the door.'

Kentish Fire was fairly confidently playing the national anthem. Everyone stood to hushed attention, although some swayed with the beer.

Once the final notes had staggered away there were some catcalls in the direction of the musicians and everyone made for the door.

Ardley eased Rose out into the grey quiet night.

'He's around the back,' she said. 'You're sure, are you? There's no saddle.'

'As long as the horse doesn't mind. I've never been on one. The nearest thing was a donkey when I was a kid, and I wasn't so heavy as now.'

'He's strong,' she said. 'He's not one of these little trotters. He pulls a muck cart on the farm.'

The backside of the horse made a rounded silhouette against the pale sky. He was standing against a fence and he snorted as she moved towards him. She whispered against his head: 'We've got a guest tonight, Pomerse.'

The animal half-turned its head. 'I'm lighter than I look,' said Ardley to the horse. He eyed its back. 'Mind, I don't know how I'm going to get up there.'

The horse snorted and Rose snorted back at him. 'He says he can manage,' she said. 'I'll get aboard first and then you climb on the fence and get up that way.'

She was going to ride bareback and she mounted in a single easy heave.

'Stay put, Pomerse,' she asked as the horse moved. She studied Ardley through the dimness. 'Just climb up the fence and get your leg over,' she said. 'But don't fall off the other side. He'll think you're larking about.'

Sproston and Tugwell appeared like shadows. 'The bus'll soon be here,' said Tugwell. Jenkins came out and began to waltz by himself.

Ardley told them: 'I'm going on this horse.' He said to Rose: 'I'll be all right. As long as Pomerse is.'

The others watched with amusement as he climbed carefully to the second rung of the fence and then eased himself ponderously across the horse's back. The smell of the animal invaded his nostrils. He almost slid across the other flank but the horse moved obligingly to balance his weight. Rose half-turned and put her arms out to help him.

He was fit enough. Drill and digging had achieved that. He became upright by degrees and put his arms around the young woman's accommodating middle. 'No galloping,' he said. 'Please.' She gave a deep giggle which was echoed by the horse. Ardley hung on to her woollen waist, warm and reassuring. She spoke to the horse and turned it in the yard. They headed for the country road. Tugwell and Sproston waved doubtfully. Jenkins continued to waltz.

Ardley was trying to keep in time with the regular bounce of the horse. His thighs were already hurting. He lay forward against the girl saying: 'I feel much safer like this.'

Although it was a pale night there was no moon. They plodded into the black shadows of trees. 'How far is it?' asked Ardley anxiously.

'About another mile,' she said. He could feel his spread legs aching. When they reached a roadside cottage and she said: 'This is it,' he could scarcely get off the horse. He slid sideways and his knees buckled as he reached the ground. She helped him to his feet. 'I want you to meet my father,' she said. 'You've got time.'

* * *

Two oil lamps glowed warmly in the low room. What appeared to be a very old man was sitting in the corner of the cottage clutching a knobbed stick, his eyes bright above it. Rose said: 'Spatchcock, I've brought a soldier to see you.' She whispered aside to Ardley: 'He's always called Spatchcock. He's not as old as he pretends.'

Narrow and fierce, the eyes moved sideways. 'A soldier?' It was like a groan. 'On our side?'

Ardley smiled weakly and gave half a bow. 'I hope so, sir,' he said.

'I'm no sir,' said the man. 'I was only a private soldier.' His face moved as if he were trying to remember.

'Spatchcock was in the Boer War,' said Rose. She said to her father: 'Weren't you.' Ardley noticed a blackened hole in the ceiling as if a stove-pipe had once been there.

'Spion Kop,' said Spatchcock. 'Them Boers was crafty. They wore khaki so we couldn't see them. Cheating that is. That chief of theirs, Smuts was his name, we used to call him Smutty . . . ' His train of thought seemed to drift away. His eyes dimmed.

'He's on our side now,' offered Ardley. 'General Smuts. He's the South African prime minister.'

'I've got a gun,' said the old man pointing. 'It's

in the corner there. I'm ready for them Huns.'

Rose was making a pot of tea. 'And it's going to stay in the corner,' she said to Ardley. 'He's already fired the thing accidentally.' She pointed to the hole in the ceiling, then poured the tea into three mugs. 'Sugar?' she asked Ardley.

He nodded: 'Two, please.'

'It's rationed, you know, sugar,' said Spatchcock. 'We're all going to starve. Like the Hun wants. That Smuts on *our* side? And he was a Boer bugger. Next thing they'll say the Germans are our friends. It don't take long.'

He took one of the mugs and sucked at the tea powerfully. 'Now *my* father was in the Crimea,' he said. 'We been in wars all over the place but it ain't got us anywhere.' He cocked his ear. 'That's the last bus,' he said.

Rose put her hands to her mouth. 'He's right. It is.' She hurried to the cottage door, opened it two inches and called out into the night, but then came back into the lamplight of the room.

Spatchcock put his cup down and grinned wickedly over the top of his stick. 'You can't stop 'ere,' he said to Ardley. 'Not enough beds. Not unless you snuggle in with me.'

'Thanks for the offer,' said Ardley. 'But I've got to get back to camp. Midnight.'

Spatchcock remembered: 'Twenty-three fifty-nine.'

Rose touched Ardley on the arm. 'Sorry,' she said. 'We've got to get you back. You've got an hour.'

'You'll be AWOL,' said Spatchcock with satisfaction. 'On a charge.'

Ardley said: 'I'll run. It's all downhill.' He returned the touch on her green woollen pullover.

'No, I'll get old Pomerse back out. He won't be asleep yet.' She made for the door. 'Finish your tea,' she said over her shoulder. 'Pomerse won't mind. I'll let him lie in tomorrow.'

Ardley said goodbye to Spatchcock. 'Keep them Hun bastards away,' said the old man knocking his stick on the floor. 'That's my advice. Stop 'em landing.'

Ducking under the door the soldier went out into the empty lane. Rose was in the yard cajoling the horse, shoving him gently. Ardley waited as the two shapes came towards him in the dark. 'He's more or less happy,' Rose said. 'He was only dozing.'

Ardley was so stiff that she had to lever him up on to the animal's back. He groaned as he spread his legs. 'I'll have to report sick,' he said. 'The MO won't believe me. Riding a horse.' Eventually he was seated, straddling the warm rug of the animal's back.

Rose climbed nimbly in front of him. He put his hands about her waist and she patted them. 'I bet this is the first time you cuddled the bum of a land-girl,' she said.

She gave a short tug at the reins and Pomerse snorted and began to nod down the hill towards Dover. They could see searchlights out in the Channel. 'It won't be long,' said the girl. Ardley thought she was talking to the horse.

On the outskirts of the town they were halted

by two air-raid wardens in a small car. 'Off to Ascot?' asked one.

'Going to Cliff Camp,' Ardley called down to them.

'We'll take you.'

'Thanks.'

'It might be better,' said Rose. 'We'll be getting stopped all the time.'

Painfully Ardley slipped from the back of the horse. Rose smiled dimly down to him. While the wardens watched she leaned over. He reached up and with difficulty they kissed and said goodnight.

One of the wardens said: 'Give the 'orse one for me.'

* * *

In those late summer days in Dover it seemed that the war almost went by the clock. Early mornings were placid, often rosy, with the sun colouring the sea, the green land and the white cliffs. People got out of bed and made themselves ready for work; those children who had not been evacuated, or who had returned to the town, played in the caves.

Some of the Dover caves had been excavated in previous centuries. There were few cellars in the town because the sea crept in but the chalk was readily worked and they had been used, originally by smugglers, then as warehouses and stores. At the start of 1940 one cave was used for growing mushrooms and when it was taken over to shelter civilians the crop was quickly harvested by the new denizens. On pleasant evenings the aroma of fried mushrooms, eggs and chips pervaded the cave entrances.

There were ten caves, the longest at Priory Hill which could accommodate 1,400 people. Athol Terrace could take 725, Barwick's Cave 700 and Travaion Street 686. The smallest was Launceston Place where 75 people could shelter. The cave in London Road was outside the Regent Cinema and 200 patrons had been known to scurry from a war drama and out into the open air and the real thing. When the film was riveting they often stayed in their seats.

Inside the caves ran ranks of wooden bunks, chemical lavatories and primitive washrooms. Some families camped there even when there was no emergency, men, women and children sitting outside enjoying the summer air, in the evening, before blackout, cooking on campfires and formed in convivial circles on wooden chairs, deck-chairs and old armchairs and sofas. They drank beer and lemonade and sang songs as the daylight diminished. It was like a gypsy life.

Many of the Dover children ran wild like feral creatures. For more than a year the schools were closed and there was anxiety that an underground generation was evolving. In the town some shops and offices, standing shakily among the debris and gaps where others had been destroyed, carried on an uncertain business. The barber's door was among the first to open of a morning and his parrot in a coloured cage was placed outside to enjoy the safe early sun and the attentions of passers-by. The bird, which had once cursed the Kaiser of the First World War, now squawked insults about Hitler. Milkmen did their plodding rounds, their horses circumnavigating half-filled bomb craters, and delivering pint and half-pint bottles to the doorsteps. Sometimes there were only doorsteps; the houses were gone and wives came from shelters to collect their milk. Resourceful postmen took trouble trying to locate people. The blast-resistant iron pillar boxes from which they collected letters were sometimes the only objects remaining upright in the street. There remained a calm air about the town, although its inhabitants went about their lives gingerly.

Above Dover floated the soft barrage balloons, silver and smooth. Small children would try to reach for them. German fighter planes shot them down for fun. There were air attacks almost every day; sometimes enemy aircraft came in relays and dropped their bombs seemingly at random. One thousand houses and other buildings were destroyed, more than two hundred civilians lost their lives and seven hundred and fifty were injured. There was a lingering acrid smell about the streets.

The cliff-top caves of Dover were occupied by soldiers and guns, some of the guns so old they could have been in museums. Soldiers emerged into the morning to echoes of bugles from all over the town. Seagulls screeched in chorus. Ardley rolled aching from his blankets. 'What was she like then?' asked Sproston sitting on the edge of the next iron bed.

'Lovely,' said Ardley. 'And lovely with it.'

'Liked the woolly jumper,' said Sproston. 'Must have been like cuddling your mum.'

Ardley groaned as he went towards the latrines. Jenkins was trying to read aloud as he laced his boots. 'What's this word, Ard?' he asked.

Ardley said: 'Spell it, will you. I can't walk.'

The Welshman spelled it. It was Tugwell who answered: 'Vagina.' He sighed. 'Ugh, first thing in the bloody morning.'

'What's it mean? Vagina?' asked Jenkins.

'Cunt,' said Sproston.

'And you,' returned Jenkins in a hurt way. 'I'm only trying to learn.'

⋆ ⋆ ⋆

They were in the lorry park half an hour later, twenty men drawn up in three ranks. Ardley still could scarcely move. Sergeant Dunphy studied him, first from the front and then sideways. 'Lance-Corporal Ardley, I said *attention*. You remember what attention is? Feet and legs together.'

'I know, sergeant,' answered Ardley miserably. 'I came back on a horse last night. I can't get my legs together.'

Dunphy rarely said anything in a hurry. 'That goes for a lot of soldiers. If you can't march you could be on a charge. Self-inflicted wound.'

'I'll march, sergeant, I'll try.'

Dunphy started the squad down the hill. At first every step caused Ardley's long face to crease with pain, but as they marched he moved more easily. As the tallest man he was in the centre of the squad.

As they tramped up Seaview Crescent three boys in short trousers began capering alongside: 'Left right, left right, left right.'

'Piss off,' said Ardley fiercely.

Harold, Spots and Boot continued. A woman in a flowered apron came from a house and called the boys. 'I'm going to be out until tea-time,' she said to Harold. 'There's some sandwiches. And some cherry pop. Don't drink it as soon as I've turned my back.'

She returned to the house. The soldiers had marched on up to the main road. 'Where's she going all day?' asked Boot.

'Maidstone prison. To see my old man.' Half the town knew by now.

'I wouldn't like to be stuck in a cell,' said Spots. 'Not in the bombing.'

'It's not very safe,' agreed Harold.

Boot said: 'They ought to let the crooks out.'

'They wouldn't come back,' said Spots.

Doris Barker appeared from the house again. 'I've got to get the bus,' she said. 'What are you going to do?'

'We're goin' down the caves, Mum,' said Harold. 'We'll take the grub with us.'

She sighed. 'Don't get into mischief.'

Harold regarded her steadily. 'We'll be patrolling,' he said.

* * *

The sunshine of that summer was almost mocking. Cloudless skies, warm afternoons and dusky evenings formed the backdrop to the battle in the air: fighters fighting, guns firing, smoke and explosions and always, somewhere, death.

But there were interludes when suddenly, and with contrary innocence, summer would spread itself across the southern coast and countryside. Gladly people came from close rooms, sat on kitchen chairs in small gardens, adjacent to air-raid shelters, and congratulated each other on the lovely weather.

Dover children roamed in brown-faced gangs across the stubbled fields, running through the town's streets, playing hiding games in caves and shelters, and clambering through the new landscape of destroyed buildings.

Harold, Spots and Boot had pledged to stick together and not to join other gangs and alliances. The vow was sealed in blood, each having pricked his thumb with a pin. They had secret codes and passwords and referred to the metal-skinned Anderson air-raid shelter in Harold's garden as 'headquarters'. There, sprawled on the bunks, they made plans to blunt the first invasion by the Germans. 'We are a small but deadly force,' said Harold. On fine nights, with the permission of their mothers, they often camped out in the shelter and were early on patrol the next day.

Some children helped with the harvest, alongside bronzed soldiers pleased to be released from tedious defensive positions. At first the three boys had volunteered with enthusiasm but they found the work demanding and dusty, and instead spent their time with the farm dogs, chasing rats and rabbits. They drank rough cider with the men who swung scythes or drove steam harvesters. They fell asleep under hedgerows.

Guards kept them away from the positions of the big guns, and the anti-aircraft batteries, but they were tolerated on the barrage-balloon sites where each of them had had a turn sitting beside a winchman in his cage as he paid out the cable and the balloon rose into the sky.

But it seemed to the eager trio, armed with their bows and arrows and their secret catapults and ball-bearing ammunition, that the enemy would never pluck up the courage to face them. Each had acquired a semblance of a uniform. Harold wore a discarded steel helmet with a hole in its bowl which he boasted had been made by a bullet. Spots had a threadbare beret and Boot, with a touch of chagrin, wore a cap last used by a conductor of the East Kent Bus Company. Sprawled on their stomachs one afternoon on a bank of coastal dandelions, they were practising with the catapults, using a Peak Frean biscuit tin as a target. Sometimes they hit it and enjoyed the metallic crack as the ball-bearing struck.

Perhaps a bird or a rabbit, and occasionally a fox, would present itself as a target; the first of the trio who spotted it would shout: 'Action stations!' and they would fan out, and open fire at Harold's order. The drill was necessary: once Boot had fired a ball-bearing which struck Harold's steel helmet just above the hole.

The afternoon seemed to have become even hotter when the languidly flying pigeon appeared. There were German aircraft out of range in the distance. 'Action stations!' shouted Harold. He stood, his skinny knees projecting from his grubby khaki shorts, trying to right his steel helmet. It slipped over his eyes but the pigeon remained hovering. Harold and Spots both fired their catapults but Boot, for once, took steadier aim. The pigeon was invitingly poised and the ball-bearing hit it full in the chest. There was a small explosion of feathers, the bird gave an affronted jump and then fell heavily. It bounced as it hit the stubble. The boys were dumbfounded. Then each shouted: 'I got him!'

'*I* got him,' insisted Boot firmly. He was not accustomed to triumph. 'I shot last.'

'All right, all right,' said Harold irritably. 'But it was a unit action.'

They were already running towards the grey tuft, the breeze ruffling it. It lay with its wings spread, eyes tightly closed, the wound clearly outlined by a red stain on the breast. The trio stood around it.

'What a shot,' said Boot in a subdued voice.

Then Harold pointed. 'It's got a ring on its leg.' He and Spots looked accusingly at Boot. 'It's a carrier pigeon.'

Looking as if he were going to cry, Boot pointed out: 'It was a unit action.'

Harold picked up the dead pigeon. 'Let's get out of sight,' he said. They ran to the hedge. Harold leaned over the bird and managed to unclip the message ring. He took out a flimsy oblong of paper. 'It's in code,' he said hoarsely. He looked at the others bleakly. 'Probably Top Secret.'

⋆ ⋆ ⋆

They waited until dusk. It had begun to rain and the town was subdued. The Germans rarely flew in the rain but Harold knew his mother would become anxious and start looking for him. She did not like him getting wet.

Going down the hill in single file, the way they always moved, they skirted the main streets and eventually established an observation position in the soaked and overgrown garden of a damaged house opposite Dover police station. Boot had the dead pigeon and its message. The street was damp and vacant. The police station windows were blacked out.

Harold looked up and down the road once more, then gave a sharp order to Boot: 'Now!'

The Polish boy straightened up and, looking both ways also, made a dash across to the police station where he dropped the dead carrier pigeon on the pavement in front of the main door, then scuttled back to the wet and weedy garden. The three boys crouched and watched in the diminishing light. Then Spots whispered: 'Coppers,' and they dropped even lower as two policemen, talking like mates, trod down the street. They almost fell over the pigeon. The boys tensed.

'Look at that, Oswald,' said one of the constables.

'A pigeon,' deduced Oswald. 'Probably the bugger that's been eating my beans.' He gave it a push with his foot and, with its coded message, it slid into the gutter. His colleague patted him on the back as if he had achieved some feat and they tramped into the police station.

'They'd fall over a pig,' said Harold sourly.

'Look,' said Spots. 'A cat.'

It was a large, prowling cat and it saw the pigeon at once. Spots drew his catapult but Harold restrained him with his arm. 'No more bloodshed.'

Helplessly the trio watched. The cat sniffed at the pigeon in the gutter, cuffed it, then picked it up in its teeth and dragged it, with no great difficulty, along the street until it pulled it through a hole in the hedge.

'We won't get it back now,' said Boot.

'Or the message,' said Spots.

'This,' muttered Harold, 'could cost us the war.'

* * *

The soldiers strode out of town, past the damaged houses, shops and churches: windows and doors were nailed up, roofs yawned, and there were open spaces where walls had once been. It was August.

On the open ground above the cliffs at the western end of the town the squad was digging gun emplacements. 'Can't see any sense in digging bloody 'oles,' grumbled Jenkins, 'if no bugger knows how big the guns are going to be.' He had a new confidence now that he could read. He read aloud every word he could see: posters, notices, things in shop windows, only regretting that, because of the war situation, all road signposts had been removed.

Sergeant Dunphy called the sweating men to stop. 'Now isn't this a beautiful day to be doing a bit of delving by the sea,' he said. 'Like when you were little boys.'

To the east, over the lip of the green rise, Dover curled like a comma around its harbour, its cherubic barrage balloons suspended above. From that distance the destruction in the streets could scarcely be detected for they were still threaded with morning mist. In the port the many ships lay orderly against the jetties and against each other. Even the block-ship — the *Sepoy* — scuttled to protect one side of the harbour entrance looked a comfortable part of the scenery as the morning sea broke unhurriedly around it.

The soldiers had stripped to their waists and gulls swooped for worms in the newly-turned earth. Sproston unearthed a big worm and tossed it up for a grateful gull to gobble. 'After the war,' he said, 'I might go in for animal training.'

They dug on stoically for an hour. Then they heard a breathless engine climbing the hill and leaned on their spades and cheered as a shuddering canteen van appeared over the crest. 'Not yet, not yet,' Dunphy warned his men. 'Wait till I give the order. I'm first.'

The van stuttered to a halt where the road became grass. It disgorged three jolly women and a fat driver who made the soldiers laugh because he wore a steel helmet sitting like a pimple on his head. The women briskly donned aprons while the man puffed as he pushed up the shutter at the side of the vehicle.

'Dig! Keep digging!' ordered the sergeant. 'Make more holes. Without the holes there'll be no guns. Hitler will win. Dig!'

After a few minutes reassuring steam began to issue from the open hatch of the canteen van. The colours of the women's aprons stood out in the interior dimness. They had cheese rolls and jam rolls and home-made cakes too. One signalled Dunphy with a pale, podgy hand. He made sure he had his mug filled and a cheese roll in the other hand. Then: 'Squad,' he called behind him. 'Fall out.'

There was a scramble. 'Nothing,' said Dunphy leaning back expansively, 'is superior to the British army char and a wad.' He bit into his roll, then turned and said to the woman framed by the canteen hatch: 'You're a sitting target up here, missus.'

She was unconcerned. 'Jerry won't touch us. We've got a red cross painted on the van's roof.' Her face changed to annoyance as the air-raid warning warbled from the town below. 'Oh, bugger it,' she sighed. 'It gets us so behind. I have to get home for my husband.'

All three women were plump and pink-faced.

One said: 'The noise of those things.' She tried to imitate: 'Ah-aaaah, ah-aaaah . . . Why didn't they choose a nice tune like 'The Blue Danube'.'

Dunphy took out his field glasses and, standing in the open, swept the horizon. He abruptly stopped the movement and wheeled back. 'ME 109s,' he said. It was almost a whisper. 'Three of the bastards. Coming in low . . . ' His voice rose. 'Well, for God's sake, look at that, they're shooting up the balloons!'

'Aw, not our barrage balloons,' said one of the tea women.

'They're so pretty,' said one of the others.

'Like little elephants,' said the third.

The soldiers were standing watching amazed. The German fighter planes, as though enjoying a game, swerved and curled over the town, loosing their machine guns at the benign barrage balloons. 'Typical,' sniffed Tugwell. ' 'Armless and 'elpless.'

Dunphy stood astonished. Up there, at the summit of the rising ground, they were almost on a level with the height of the balloons. He pushed his helmet back on his head and said: 'Now I've seen the bloody lot.' One of the fighters continued on its course until it was thundering above them. Some soldiers flung themselves flat, others jumped down into the trenches they had been digging; the women pulled the hatch of the canteen down with a resounding bang. One of them tumbled from the door at the back and pointed angrily at the roof of the vehicle. 'Red Cross!' she bawled shaking her fist at the sky. 'Ruddy Red Cross!'

The plane curved away and joined the others. Four of the balloons above the town were now burning and staggering downwards, their cables hung slack. The anti-aircraft guns were firing like sledgehammers. Then, with a final joyful swoop, the planes came in and loosed their machine guns into the two silver elephants hanging half a mile from the hill.

One of the balloons exploded without fuss, no more than a puff of smoke and a sizzle of flame. The cable below it fell clear. The fresh breeze, coming from the east, blew the other blazing balloon towards the hill. 'Christ,' said Dunphy, placing his mug of tea on the grass. 'It's coming at us!'

Low and fiery it ambled threateningly towards them. The soldiers began to scatter. Men ran into each other. The women clambered back into the canteen.

The swollen silver bag came across the lip of the cliff, like a mythical fire monster, touching the grass and rolling as it roared. The soldiers in its path ran away, wildly shouting. The balloon skimmed the ground again and bounced. It settled, like a massive hen on a nest, on the only obstacle in its path — the canteen.

There came an almost soundless mushroom of flame. Dunphy clambered to his knees and bawled to his men. He ran over the springing grass. The air was full of burning smoke. The soldiers came running. 'Get the ropes!' shouted the sergeant. 'Get the bloody ropes! Pull it off!'

They caught the trailing cables and pulled, forcing what was left of the burning balloon sideways. But the van was on fire. Dunphy rushed to the rear door and threw it open. He climbed in. It was burning hot and black, the smoke was choking. Two of the women were crawling like fat children. ‘Out, get out!’ he shouted. Some of the soldiers came in the door and dragged the women out. ‘Come on, love. Let’s ’ave yer.’

The third woman, the one who had been in charge, was sprawled below the smoke, her clothes and her hair on fire. Dunphy, breathing red hot air, bent and picked her heavily from the floor, half-carrying, half-dragging her through the open door.

‘Help! Help me!’ he shouted. His men rushed, taking the woman from him, trying to beat out the flames with their hands. Dunphy stumbled with them. ‘Roll her — roll her on the grass!’ he choked. He fell on his knees.

The soldiers put the woman down and rolled her in the grass. They rolled her down the slope. ‘Watch it! Watch what you’re doing!’ shouted Dunphy sitting on the ground. Smoke was coming from his mouth. His hair was singed. ‘You’ll roll her over the fucking cliff!’

They almost did as the surface dipped. But they stopped and stood up, each one gasping. The woman lay senseless between them almost without clothes, her face burned black. The man who had driven the van hauling the canteen appeared. He looked at her, turned and went back to the van. Without hurry he came with a clean tablecloth. While the soldiers watched, shocked and stunned, he opened it and carefully placed it across her body. He adjusted the edges. The German planes had gone and the sky was a summer morning blue. 'Bastards,' he said.

8

Cotton did not want to immediately alarm the old couple; they would have enough cause for it, he thought, when they realised why he had come. So he left the constable in the car at the foot of the brief hill. The young policeman, Gates, had been rejected by the army because his feet could not be trusted, so he had opted for the police and now spent hours on the beat trudging the streets of Dover. He was grateful for the respite, sitting in the police car. Cotton said to him: 'These people are harmless. The old boy used to have a second-hand bookshop in Stargate Street. They'll have a fit if they see you in uniform coming to their front door.'

'Like the Gestapo,' suggested Gates.

Cotton sighed. 'They've got to be told they're going to be interned under the Emergency Regulations. Suspect aliens. And strange lights have been reported up here.'

It was only a short path up to the house but it was steep and open to the wind, and he wondered how they managed it. He paused at the top and, nudged by the stiff breeze, turned and viewed the town in its defile in the cliffs — the curve of its beach cluttered now with gaunt barbed-wire coils — then over the harbour and its thin grey boats and ships, and beyond the breakwater and the block-ship, out to the glinting Channel. The French coast lay like a frieze across the horizon.

The house was a chalet, built in the early 1900s for the view. It had not been painted since years before the war and its woodwork was peeling so badly he was tempted to pull a piece of paint away. It was next to his nose. But he left it. The windows were draped with unwashed lace curtains. Cotton took a preparatory breath, knocked, and sensed rather than heard the shuffling approach within. The door was opened with such difficulty that he helped by giving it a push. Eventually it was rattled away and an old wispy lady in a Bavarian apron stood uncertainly blinking through rimless spectacles. 'Not today, but thank you,' she said.

She made to shut the door again but he gently held it. Her eyes brightened with concern and she said: 'Vot?'

'Mrs Heine, I would like a word with you and your husband,' said Cotton carefully.

He produced his warrant card which she examined with her eyes only an inch away, but then again said: 'Vot?'

'May I come in please? I am the police, you understand.'

She examined him, his appearance. 'No clothes,' she said pointing at his sports jacket. 'The Gestapo always had clean uniform.'

'I am not the Gestapo.' He decided to shock her. 'We've had reports that somebody in this house has been signalling with a torch to German submarines.'

It sounded ridiculous, these things always did. But he had to make a report. The old lady considered it, then stepped aside. Cotton saw that the hallway and the room beyond were crammed with books, piled ceiling high like an inner defensive wall. Scarcely any light seeped into the passage and only a little more into the room where he now found himself. There was a low window, the sun seeping in almost at floor level. Books climbed every wall. There was a smell of leather and old grime.

Cotton had seen the old man before, standing outside his dishevelled Dover shop as if determined to prevent anyone entering. Now he was sitting in a round chair, reading a book, sunlight bathing his slippers. He was wearing wiry glasses like his wife's and he stooped as he sat as if to get a better view of Cotton.

It was the wife who spoke. 'This man asks if any persons have been signalling to German submarines *mit* a torch.'

'Maybe,' shrugged the old man. 'But it is not us. You are employed by the authorities?'

Cotton introduced himself fully and displayed his warrant card again. 'You are, I take it, Mr and Mrs Heine.'

'Gustav and Marie,' said the man. He smiled thinly but fondly at his wife.

Cotton got to the point. 'There have been reports to the police in Dover of a light seen flashing up here, at night, possibly signalling an enemy vessel, a submarine or some such ship, offshore.' Again looking at them, their helplessness, he thought how unlikely it sounded.

Mrs Heine took some books from another rounded chair and brushed it, briefly but enough to send up voluminous dust, before inviting him to sit down. The old man looked calmly at Cotton. 'We could be shot?' he said.

'No, no, no.' Cotton held up his hands. 'Nobody is going to be shot. Have you been outside with a torch at night? It is against the blackout regulations for a start.'

'Our little dog, Hermann, we let him out at night,' said Mrs Heine.

'So he does his business,' her husband added apologetically. As if he had heard his name an elderly dachshund, dull eyed and dusty, wriggled to Mr Heine's feet. 'Then he gets lost in the dark,' the old man said.

The old lady gave a quaint, obedient curtsy, said: 'I will bring you coffee,' and shuffled from the room.

Cotton took from his pocket a document. 'This is your aliens record,' he said trying to sound authoritarian. 'You have been in this country since 1937? Is that correct? Why did you come here?'

'It was not to see the Coronation,' said Mr Heine. He nodded as if pleased with the joke.

'Why did you come?' repeated Cotton patiently.

'To keep away from Hitler. Every Jew was getting a knock on his door. So we came here.'

'Why Dover?'

'It was the nearest place when we left the ferry boat.' He looked about him as if for help. 'We had much luggage, books, so we did not go anywhere further. But I would not signal submarines. Just because we have a foreign name, and our voices, does not mean we would do that.' He paused as if considering his next words, then said: 'Last year, at the beginning of the war, we were taken away from here, you understand — as they say, evacuated. With many other old people from Dover.'

Mrs Heine reappeared with the smallest cup Cotton had ever seen, like something from a child's teaset. He had to hold the handle with the tips of his thumb and first finger. 'And they sent us to the *Krankenhaus*,' she put in heavily.

Cotton was wondering how he should drink the black coffee and not swallow it all at once. Mrs Heine had only brought in one cup. 'The what?' he asked.

Mr Heine said: 'The hospital, a lunatic asylum.'

'A madhouse,' said his wife. 'In some place.' She shook her head as though trying to dismiss the memory.

'One hundred people from here, from Dover,' continued her husband, 'all getting old, like us.' He demonstrated with his hands. 'They put the women in one place and the men in one place and made us wear the uniform. It was like the Nazis.'

'How long were you there?' Cotton felt helpless.

'Twelve days,' said Mr Heine. 'Then they left the gates open and we got out.' He made a walking movement with his fingers. 'It was easy. We walked out, went to a station on a bus and came back here. It took a long time to find our way.' A bleak look took over his face. 'Now, I think, we will be sent away again.'

There was no point in lying. 'It will not be like before,' Cotton promised unsurely. 'Not the *Krankenhaus*, nor any place like that. You will be sent to a nice holiday spot called the Isle of Man.'

Mr Heine said glumly: 'Will they keep us away from each other?'

Cotton shook his head. 'No. They won't do that again. You will all be together. It is a very nice island, so I've heard.'

'Not a concentration camp?' Both pairs of pleading eyes were fixed on his.

'No,' he said. He finished the tiny drain of coffee in the cup and thanked them for it. He handed it back. She smiled with real fondness at the cup and saucer.

Mr Heine said: 'Perhaps we will find friends there.'

'Very probably.' Cotton made to go, nodding towards the dachshund. 'Don't go looking for him at night,' he said.

'If we go to this place of Man as you call it, and women also, can we take Hermann?'

'I expect so,' said Cotton unsurely. 'Put him in a basket and cover him up.' He rose from the hard round chair and, in an almost quaint ceremony, the old German couple each shook his proffered hand.

'You mean us well,' said Mr Heine with a stiff short bow that made his spectacles slide down his nose. Without hurry, he adjusted them as his wife smiled hopelessly and made another small curtsy.

'Someone will come to see you,' said Cotton. 'I will have a word with that department. I'll make sure that when you leave everything will be safe here.'

Mrs Heine gave a tight puff that showed the veins in her cheeks. 'We do not worry,' she said. She looked about disparagingly. 'This stuff.'

'We have lost everything before,' shrugged her husband.

'The authorities will arrange everything,' said Cotton hoping they would. 'I will write a report so that they look after you properly. The Isle of Man is an interesting place. Lots of history. Even mountains. You might like it.'

'We will try,' said the man.

His wife brightened a touch. 'Maybe they will like us.'

They moved towards the front door, down the tunnel-like passage lined on both sides with books. Cotton was trying not to sneeze with the dust. He lifted the latch gratefully.

The bright day was framed in the doorway, glaringly after the dimness of the interior. Cotton thanked them again and told them not to bother to come out. But the old man followed him below the sagging porch.

As they moved out into the sun, on the overgrown path, Cotton sensed there was something strange. The old man knew it at once. 'The birds,' he said looking at the sky. 'None of them sing.'

Cotton was suddenly alarmed. Even the town's insistent gulls were silent. Mr Heine crouched where he was standing and caught the policeman's shoulder in a feeble attempt to pull him down. A shattering explosion flew from the centre of the town, and ran up the hillside. Then another. Both men were left crouched on the path. A clump of hydrangeas flew by as if in a wind. Twin columns of smoke rose from the town. There was a cry from behind them, slightly apologetic, and through the open door they saw that the old lady was buried in books, her startled face above the pile with dust and grit rising all around. She began to sneeze violently and her husband struggled to his feet. Cotton got to her first and the two men threw the books aside and pulled her, gasping, from the pile.

Mr Heine began feeling her limbs as if he knew what he was doing, but she pushed him away spiritedly. 'It is too late for them to wound me,' she said.

Her husband pushed some more of the books aside with his foot and Cotton pulled away others. 'So heavy, books,' Mr Heine puffed. 'All books one day will have paper covers and the world will be safer.'

'God knows what that was,' said Cotton going out into the garden again. Smoke was still rising in two columns from the town. They could hear the bells of the fire engines. 'There was no air-raid warning.' He looked into the empty sky. 'No planes.'

Mr Heine sniffed at the air. 'A shell,' he said confidently. 'Artillery shell.'

Cotton realised he was right. 'Shelling us from France now.'

'The birds keeping shtum told me and then

the sound in the sky, like whirr . . . ' said Mr Heine in an oddly pleased way. 'In the First War I was in the artillery.' He glanced in a shy way at Cotton. 'The German artillery, you understand.'

* * *

Three more high-explosive shells burst in Dover that day, killing four people and demolishing a bicycle shop and a bagwash. Sheets from the bagwash were strewn across the street and were used to cover the dead bodies. The attack caused consternation in both low and high places. England had never before been shelled; the land had never been within range of an enemy gun.

'I still intend to sleep in my own bed,' said Nancy that night. 'Who knows if you'd be any safer in the shelter? All I can say is the Germans must have some very large guns.'

Cotton said: 'This is about as far as their range is. Just another couple of miles of English Channel and we'd be safe.'

He got up from their supper and they both began the familiar ritual of clearing the table. 'There's no time to hide with shells, is there,' she said running the water into the sink. 'I wonder how long they take to shoot over here, over the Channel?'

'Seventy seconds.' Cotton picked up the tea towel. 'But you need to see the flash and then start counting.'

'And running,' she said.

'The Germans can't know what they're aiming at. You need a spotter plane, or better aiming aids anyway, to know that you're not just wasting ammunition. Maybe it's just to terrorise people. And if too many of those things land around the harbour then they're cutting off their nose to spite their face. If they do invade they're going to need that harbour.'

She stopped washing. 'Do you think they'll come?' she asked looking directly at him.

Cotton put his arms about her and they hugged briefly. He said: 'Only God and Hitler know. The question is *how*? If he'd got together some sort of invasion right after Dunkirk, followed us back over the Channel if you like, then, with parachute troops capturing airfields, he would have had a decent chance. We were in disarray, all over the shop. But he didn't. Now it's getting late. He's given us the best part of three months to pull ourselves together a bit. We're still weak but we'll be ready for him after a fashion.'

'He's got to get across that water,' she said. 'It's like a trench, a ditch, isn't it.'

'It's a big ditch. The navy can't wait for him to try.'

The telephone rang. It was late. She picked it up. 'Are you sure, Brenda?' she said. 'No, of course you're not. You can't be. Frank's here. I'll put him on.'

She offered the receiver to Cotton. 'It's Brenda,' she said. 'She thinks she's seen a spy. He came into the pub. She wouldn't serve him because it was after hours.'

* * *

‘Everyone keeps seeing spies,’ grumbled Cotton as they drove east, two miles to the village. ‘Kent is apparently crawling with them and we’ve not found one yet. You’ve only got to have a funny eye or a lisp and somebody thinks you’re a Nazi agent.’

‘Well, Brenda is frightened and she *is* my sister. She wouldn’t want to look silly which is why she rang for you. You know she’s very sensible, she wouldn’t just raise the alarm for nothing.’

The customary Home Guard patrol, mooching along the coastal road, halted them. The four damp men recognised him readily but still demanded his police warrant and examined Nancy’s identity card by a pinpoint torch beam.

‘Where you going this time o’night, then?’ asked a man who was a fishmonger in Dover. ‘If I may ask.’

‘Going to nab a German spy,’ said Cotton blandly. ‘He called in for a drink at the Merry Mariner at St Margaret’s. After hours.’

The Home Guard men laughed and waved him on. ‘If I’d said Hitler had swum ashore they’d still wave us on,’ he said to Nancy as they drove.

‘I hope it isn’t Hitler,’ said Nancy tiredly. ‘I don’t think I could face Hitler at this time of night.’

It was deeply dark but they navigated the steep, curling lane towards the coastal village, foot by foot, guided by the tight slits in the cowls masking the car headlights. They stopped in front of the inn, got out and Cotton knocked. An anxious answer came through the letter-box.

'It's us,' Nancy called back. Bolts were drawn and Brenda's pale, tight face showed.

'He's gone,' she whispered as she let them in. The windows were heavily curtained and a single oil lamp burned behind the bar. 'He asked for cider.'

Patiently they sat. Cotton placed his big torch on the table. 'Frightened the life out of me, I can tell you,' she went on. She could see they were unconvinced.

Cotton leaned forward and patted her. 'Maybe it was just a tramp,' he said.

'With a German accent,' she said. 'Well, a foreign accent.' Blinking timidly she sat opposite them.

'Tell me what happened — slowly,' said Cotton.

'It was just on closing time. Everybody had gone, even Bert who helps out. He'd just gone up the lane, home. I was locking up when this face appeared at the door. Frightened me stiff. He had a five-pound note and asked me for cider. He looked in a poor way. He smelt like he'd been in the sea, salty, and his eyes were all sore and sticking out. I slammed the door and pushed the bolts and shouted that it was after ten.'

'Where did he go?'

'Towards the church, I think. I watched through the window but it's so dark out there. I couldn't be sure. Maybe it *was* a tramp. We still get them. I'll pour you a drink.'

She measured out a Scotch from the bottle

behind the bar and Cotton took a drink. 'Shouldn't, on duty,' he said. With a sense of embarrassment he drew his large revolver from its holster beneath his jacket, then said: 'I'll pop over to the church.' As if trying to help Brenda silently handed him his torch.

It was only three hundred yards. He went through the dark, rustling churchyard without turning on the torch. A bat flew out from behind the roof of a family tomb and startled him.

In the church porch he stood and listened. Someone was playing the organ. 'Christ,' said Cotton to himself.

He touched the ancient door and shone the torch on the iron ring handle. He turned it and the door creaked open. There were no further organ notes. He drew his revolver.

The lancet windows of the church were uncovered, letting in a faint light. The pews stood hunched and black. He could discern the bulk of the raised pulpit, and there was the touch of a glow from the brass eagle on the lectern.

Carefully he advanced down the aisle. His shoes squeaked. He was almost at the chancel steps when a shape rose from the organ loft. Cotton almost fell backwards.

'Goodnight to you,' said the man.

Cotton shone his torch with one hand and raised the revolver with the other. The intruder was bulky but bedraggled. He was encased in a waterproof coat and was eating something.

'What are you doing in here?' demanded Cotton.

'Eating this sausage,' replied the man holding it up.

'I am armed,' said Cotton.

'Me also,' returned the man still munching at the sausage. 'Also drunk. I found a bottle of wine here in the church.' His words were succinct with an edge of accent. 'I will pay.'

'Throw your firearms to the floor,' ordered Cotton. A heavy pistol clumped and bounced on the aisle carpet. The man in the organ loft finished the sausage as if he thought it might be confiscated. Then he held his arms above his head.

⋆ ⋆ ⋆

It was his fifth cup of coffee, lukewarm by now, and it was four thirty in the morning. Birds were beginning to stir outside the window of Dover police station. Two military police captains with a driver and an escort had arrived two hours before and after them two men in important civilian clothes. They had gone down to the cells where the prisoner was being held.

Sergeant Wallace, the duty officer, came into the room. 'All this,' he grumbled. 'As if we didn't have enough trouble with this war, Frank, let alone spies. They been in there with 'im for hours.' He dropped a newspaper on the table. 'Thought you might like a read, if you can keep your eyes open. I'll put another kettle on soon.'

Cotton picked up the *Dover Express*. Its reporting of the bombing and shelling that the town was suffering daily was so fogged by censorship that it might have been giving news of some distant foreign war. Even the name of Dover had to be omitted although its readers knew the location of every obliquely mentioned street. He turned the page. The rugby club had enjoyed its annual meeting at the Grand Hotel. Its pitch was covered with sharpened stakes to trap gliders. His eye went down the small advertisements: 'Pram for sale.' 'Children's books wanted.' 'Congratulations Grandad on your ninetieth birthday.' 'Puppy lost Thursday. Answers to Adolf.' Cotton half-grinned.

The door opened and the two men in important suits came in, followed by the military police officers and Sergeant Wallace with a decent tray holding cups and a silver coffee pot which Cotton recognised as being an exhibit in a burglary case.

The men sat down wearily. 'Can't say I think much of the calibre of current German agents,' said one of the suited men in a public-school voice. He addressed Cotton and then remembered that they had not been introduced. 'Henry Liston-Smith,' he said. They shook hands across the table and the other man said: 'George Parry-Jones.' The other officers simply nodded and Cotton nodded back.

Liston-Smith said: 'He tried some cock-and-bull story that he was Dutch. I suggested he meant Deutsch and he nodded. He's had enough. He came ashore from a small boat with another man who went over the side and vanished, apparently couldn't swim because he was from the mountains.'

Liston-Smith grunted: 'In Holland.'

'It confounds me why they send these incompetents,' said Parry-Jones. They drank the coffee gratefully. The military police officers sat bolt upright and as if feeling they had to add to the conversation one said: 'We'll be taking him in,' and the other said: 'Tonight.'

'This morning,' corrected the first officer and the other said: 'Yes, this morning.'

Parry-Jones glanced at them with no affection and stated: 'The Boche have sent half a dozen so-called agents over now, every one a joke. One got caught up a tree in Dorset and fell out almost on top of a chap from the Somerset Light Infantry.'

Liston-Smith said to Cotton: 'This chappie just about speaks English. He and his pal got absolutely plastered on the way over. After the other man had vanished over the side this one got ashore and hid in some sort of cave until after dark when he came out and went to the pub for some cider. Cider! Christ, where do they get them?

'His belongings included a Luger pistol, a German camera, a map of airfields in Wales — he landed a long way from them — and five hundred and fifty-seven quid in sterling notes.'

Parry-Jones said: 'And the sausage. Well, the wrapper anyway.'

'He ate the rest,' confirmed Cotton.

'Made in Frankfurt,' Parry-Jones shrugged. 'So the wrapping said.'

Liston-Smith said to Cotton: 'I don't think you need to hang about any more. We'll need to come back to you, of course.'

'What will happen to him now?'

It was Parry-Jones who answered: 'Oh, there'll be a trial. Quite a quick one, I imagine. In a couple of weeks. You'll be required to give evidence.'

'Then what?'

'After that? Well, they'll take him out and shoot him, I expect. They usually do.'

* * *

Cotton shook hands with them, left the police station and wearily climbed into his car. Could the Germans be that incompetent, that amateur?

He drove through the town, past the dawn silhouettes of the Hippodrome and the Plaza cinema, the streets with gaps where the houses had been destroyed.

Nancy heard the car and came down to unbolt the door. Her hand went out to him. 'Do you want a cup of tea?'

'I'm full up with coffee,' he said. 'I just want to sleep.'

'What did they do to him?'

'Asked him a few questions.'

'Poor man. Fancy sending someone like that as a spy.'

'Apparently, they keep doing it. It's probably a way of getting rid of their head cases.' He began taking his clothes off, sitting heavily on the bed.

'What will happen to him now?' she asked.

He looked directly at her in the dimness of the room. 'They're going to shoot him,' he said.

* * *

A solitary afternoon Heinkel, wandering almost idly above Dover, had dropped a bomb directly on the East Kent bus station, killing nine people. The attack had happened as office staff were going home to their tea. Men were still digging without hope through the rubble the next morning.

People walked with a resigned politeness around the warning barriers which now bordered the site. They shrugged as they walked; something which had been part of their lives, an ordinary place, was now levelled to wreckage. People paused, some whispered and passed on. By nine o'clock that morning the final silent blanket had been carried out while double-decker buses arrived and departed according to the usual timetable.

The café opposite opened its doors and the woman there put on a big clean white apron. There were no windows left in the café. She went inside and brought out a wide tray of tea for the men who were digging. 'Nothing to pay today,' she called as she carried it to them.

Giselle, holding a brown paper bag, boarded the bus, went to the upper deck and looked through the window. She was glad when they began the journey. The conductor, a spotty boy, took her fare. He had a band of black material around his hat. 'They never 'ad a chance,' he said. 'Didn't know what 'it 'em.'

She was conscious of her fresh summery dress,

brightly coloured silk with buttons down the front.

'Due at work I was, ten minutes later,' said the conductor and added, like an odd boast: 'I was born lucky.'

The sunlight coming through the window lit her hair. 'How long till it all ends?' she said.

'I 'ope not before I get in the army,' said the spotty youth. 'I want to kill them Jerries.' He made as though plunging in a bayonet.

'Of course,' she replied.

The bus was heading out of the town, driving under the lee of Dover Castle, the union flag stretched out over its battlements.

The youth said: 'Fancy coming to the pictures with me?' It was as if turning the stony corner into a new scene had prompted him. 'Wallace Beery's on at the Granada.'

Giselle blushed. 'I am sorry,' she said. 'I cannot. I have a boyfriend.'

The conductor said: 'Well, you would. You're foreign. Where you from?'

'France.' From her seat she could see the smudge of the French coast across the Channel. 'Over there.'

'We'll get you back there before long,' he promised extravagantly. They were out in the country now, on the climbing Kentish road, among the farms and fields. A dull explosion came from the distance behind them. The conductor looked out of the back window and Giselle's eyes followed him. A ribbon of black smoke was rising from Dover.

‘’Ere we go again,’ said the conductor. ‘Just got out in time.’

* * *

Toby was waiting for her at the bus stop. He had two rustic bicycles, supporting one in each hand. She moved between the handlebars and they kissed. The conductor watched from his bus as it moved off.

‘The bus station was hit,’ she said. ‘There were people killed.’

‘I know.’ He paused. ‘I brought a bike for you.’

Giselle kissed him once more and he eased one of the bicycles towards her. He said thoughtfully: ‘It’s bloody disgraceful this war. I’ve seen enough of it this week.’

His face seemed to have aged in a few days. He was wearing his blue shirt and air-force trousers with grubby plimsolls. ‘You have been flying every day?’ she asked.

‘Every day would be easy,’ he said. They began to wheel the bicycles. ‘It’s been three times a day. One day it was four. I’m shagged out.’

‘How long have you got for leave today?’

‘It’s hardly leave. Six bloody hours.’ He grinned apologetically. ‘It’s not long, is it?’

‘Six bloody hours,’ she repeated.

‘They can’t spare us, any of us,’ he said. ‘We’ve lost three pilots, good chums. There’s replacements coming but they’re half-trained. They don’t know what they’re doing. I only got off this morning because I told the medical officer I was going mad.’

'So you have six hours to get un-mad,' she said. 'Let us find a field with flowers.'

It was a gently climbing lane but he puffed. 'Too much sitting on my bum,' he said. 'Thank God you don't have to pedal a Spitfire.' They stopped and looked about. There was a stile and a path rising into a buttercup meadow with a bramble hedge and a big tree at its summit. 'A field with flowers,' Toby smiled at her.

They kissed across the bicycles. Gently he put his hands against her dress. 'We'd better hide the bikes in the ditch,' he said. 'People will pinch anything these days. One of our pilots had his flying boots stolen in a pub. While he was resting his feet. He got back in his socks and now the RAF wants him to pay for the boots. He sniffed: 'It's hardly worth dying for your country.'

They hauled the old bicycles over the stile and dropped them into the bordering ditch. The buzzing field was loaded with flowers and the scents of summer: nettles, cow parsley, overhanging elderberry. Hand in hand the two young people walked to the top. A hare made a sudden dash causing them to exclaim and stumble out of the way. They laughed and held on to each other. 'Scared by a rabbit,' he said.

'*Le lièvre*,' she corrected. 'A hare.'

They sat on the thick grass at the rim of the outspread tree, then fell together and held each other close. He kissed her forehead. 'I knew this week couldn't be all bad,' he said.

She smiled almost against his face and said: 'I have brought some French wine.' She lifted the bottle and the sun shone through it. 'From the cellars of the Grand Hotel.'

'You pinched it,' he laughed. 'Did you bring a corkscrew?'

'*Naturellement*.' He took the cool bottle from her and sitting up against the tree eased out the cork. 'And glasses,' she said taking them from the bag. 'Also pinched.' She poured the pale wine. 'The wine and the glasses can go on the insurance claim. There has been a lot of damage.'

Sitting close, their bodies touching, they toasted each other and drank quietly.

'Even six hours is something,' he said. 'Now, every time I go up in the sky I'm frightened. I used to love it. Not long ago.'

Her solemn face was light brown, her neck smoothly rising from the summer dress. Carefully she put her glass down, took his empty glass away, and pushed him easily back on to the springy grass. The profound and smothering feeling of summer was all around them: the thick air, bees and other creatures almost grunting in the flowers and long grass, birdsong sounding.

Giselle rolled above him and teased his face with a stalk of grass. They kissed, the grass trapped between their lips. Then a high sound came from the sky.

His body stiffened. She half-left him and looked up also. 'Dogfight,' he said flatly. 'See the trails.' They stared up from the meadow to the swollen clouds standing against the blue and picked out the tiny fighting planes. Echoes of machine guns filtered down to them, the planes rolled like insects. 'One's going down,' he said.

The fighter curled away and they could hear the engine screaming, smoke trailing as it turned and began to fall. 'Jesus,' he said flatly. 'Oh, Jesus.'

Giselle moved on top of him again. 'Do not look any longer,' she whispered. 'Forget about up there. Under my dress there is nothing.'

She straddled him and hitched up her silken dress. She began to unbutton it beginning between her thighs. 'One button,' she smiled. 'Two buttons . . . '

Toby reached up and caught her fingers. 'I'll do the rest,' he said. 'I can count.'

Firmly and gently she pushed his hand aside. 'I am counting now,' she said. 'Three . . . four . . . five . . . and six.'

The final button opened and the dress slid away exposing her fawn breasts, the nipples full and pink. Impatiently wriggling she pushed the dress aside.

'You're lovely,' he responded. 'Such a lovely girl.' He held on to her desperately.

Behind them, high in the sky the dogfight continued, the roars and the crackle of the gunfire sharply defined. The field murmured around them. When she bent to kiss him she saw he was crying. She pressed his face into her body and felt his tears on her skin. 'What a fucking life,' he sobbed.

* * *

Wing Commander Greville looked an old-fashioned figure, his face puffy, his hair, dark but fading, slightly greased. His manner was serious, like a doctor with bad news. He stood with his back against his desk, as if he needed its support. 'We're going to lose this battle,' he confided to Hendry. 'Or at least there's a good chance we'll lose it. Today or tomorrow, or next week. Believe me, we're up against it.'

'But we're downing them left right and centre,' said Hendry. 'This bit of England is strewn with crashed German planes. You can hardly move for them.'

'And a lot of ours,' put in Greville. 'Don't believe all the figures, son.' He paused and took a breath. 'The fact is we're losing pilots faster than we can replace them. Some dead, some wounded, some gone in their heads.'

'I've noticed,' said Hendry. 'In the mess.'

'Mess is the word,' said the wing commander. 'I wish Churchill could know the mess we're in. It's all very well his fine words, his speeches. 'Never has so much been owed by so many to so few.' They probably keep the unpleasant facts from him. They're giving bomber pilots, transport pilots, army people who fly little spotter planes at the best of times . . . they're giving them crash courses in flying Spitfires, Hurricanes. Crash courses, that's the right phrase. And there's still a million civilians unemployed. Doesn't seem credible, does it?'

Hendry guessed: 'You want me to go up again today, this afternoon.'

'In a way. Not quite the usual. You'll find it easier, I imagine. It's escort duty.'

The young man looked up. 'Escorting what, sir?'

'Bombers. A squadron. They're going to bomb the Jerry invasion barges.'

The young man said: 'They've got barges ready?'

'All along the French coast, Calais, Boulogne, according to the photographs.' He half-turned and picked up a large brown photographic envelope from the desk behind him, opened it and produced an aerial reconnaissance picture, then another. He handed them one at a time to Hendry: 'It's like Henley Regatta.'

The pilot took the photographs one at a time. 'I wondered how they were going to get across the Channel,' he said. He handed the pictures back. 'And we're going to bomb them.'

'We're going to have a go. You're the escort.'

'Me? Just me?'

'Only you. We can't spare another plane. Or pilot. You'll have to fly up and down. Try and look like a squadron.'

'When's the briefing?'

'Half an hour. The show is timed for seventeen hundred hours. You'll be home before the pubs open.'

Hendry rose wearily. 'Right, sir. Half an hour.'

As Hendry turned towards the door the wing commander said: 'Your mother's been phoning the Air Minister. She wants you taken off flying.'

Hendry stopped as he was stooping under the door and turned back into the room. 'She's what, sir? She's done what?'

Greville shrugged. 'She *knows* people apparently. She knows the Air Minister. Which is more than I do.'

Bitterly Hendry said: 'The old bat.'

'In any event, once you've done this jaunt they're transferring you. Somewhere a bit more peaceful.'

Hendry turned for the door again. Then he stopped. 'Where would that be, sir?'

'God knows. But it's bound to be better than this, son.'

* * *

He rendezvoused with the Whitley bombers over Newhaven. The battles seemed over for the day, the sky was clear, everyone had gone home. He could see the beach and the two piers at Brighton.

The Whitleys did not keep him waiting; there were three flights of three. He radioed them and the formation leader, who was called Humphrey, replied languidly. It should be a picnic. 'Bit of flak, old boy,' he told Hendry. 'Only enough to warm your arse. Not much more.'

Hendry had little idea of escort duties, especially how one small fighter could protect nine bombers. He had asked this question at the briefing and the officer had appeared just as unsure and said: 'Well, just be around them. In the vicinity, as it were. Let them know you're there. Jerry shouldn't be much bother. He's had a hard day again today.'

He began to feel a touch elated. If it was a

piece of cake, he was ready for it. He set the course and flying at ten thousand feet began to think of his mother. He laughed out loud. The daft old bat might get him a transfer. Perhaps it would not be too remote and he would still be able to see Giselle. In only minutes the shaky line of the French coast came into view. The evening had settled fair and visibility was for miles. Just a few angelic clouds. The bombers moved below him, travelling at half his speed. He had time to circle several times and count them.

The leading formation banked to starboard on cue and he drew off like a sheepdog eyeing the turn of a flock. He could see the geometry of the harbours and then, following the Whitleys across the target area, he could see the barges like piano keys against the jetties. He wondered where the Germans had got them, how they had assembled them and, more to the point, how they were going to get them across the Channel. It would not be easy.

The first flight of bombers moved in. Below him he saw anti-aircraft fire, like sudden sprays of bright flowers. He had plenty of experience of enemy fighters but enemy anti-aircraft fire was something new. He decided to keep well above it.

Below him the Whitleys were spread across his view like a pattern of dark crosses. Fighter planes rarely kept such formal formations. He saw explosions on the harbours below, some straddling the barges. One of the barges was quickly on fire. It seemed so remote he began to feel much happier. Soon, perhaps, he would be out of all this. It was only so long before it became your turn to die, before your number was up. Good old Mum. Crazy old bat.

Then he saw a Heinkel below him, a solitary, chugging Heinkel bomber, which had not spotted him. He banked away to get a better look. The German pilot was busy eyeing the bombers. Toby went after him. It was almost too easy. He came in on the tail and he guessed that his opening burst from the machine guns in the wings was the first time the German pilot had been aware of him. It was not a fair contest but there were no rules. His tracer bullets on the German plane homed in. It shuddered as though kicked, a snort of black smoke came from the fuselage and then a small red circle, no bigger than a snooker ball, expanded and exploded. The aircraft wobbled and turned sharply towards the earth. Toby shouted into his mouthpiece: 'Got one, got one! Heinkel 105, he's tipping over. He's going down. Nailed him first time!'

He saw one of the German crew baling out, his parachute opening in the smoke, and being overtaken by the plunging plane. 'Good luck, Fritz,' he said. 'Happy landings.'

Then his Spitfire bucked like a car heavily going over a bump in the road. Anti-aircraft shells were bursting just under the belly. He had been careless. 'You chump!' he muttered. 'You utter chump.' He pulled the plane into a steep climb. To his astonishment the propeller flew clean off and zoomed, spinning like a boomerang, over his cockpit. The engine let out a howl of pain.

The aircraft seemed to thread itself through the spread bombers and the random flak before it flattened out and began to glide almost sedately. Below were flat French fields, evening green, with patches of houses and a straggle of roads. Now he was frightened. He tightened himself and knew it was his turn to bale out.

He reached for the catch of the cowling above his head. It refused to open. He swore and jabbed at it again. Sweat streamed down his face and into his eyes. It was dripping off his chin. 'Oh God!' he cursed. The cockpit cowling opened. 'Thank you, God,' he breathed.

The wind screamed about his ears. He pulled away the harness holding him to the cockpit and somehow managed to stand. He checked his parachute and with a grunt heaved himself through the aperture and jumped.

The plane spun away from him. It was the last he saw of it. He seemed to tumble in the sky, then pulled the rip-cord and, to his huge relief, felt the chute open above him and arrest his fall. He looked up at it; it seemed beautiful, like a silver flower. He had never made a real parachute jump before.

Now he even had time to look below. The fields were spread out like a quilt, a finger of peaceful smoke was rising from a chimney. Abruptly he remembered to look directly below and saw with alarm that he was descending on to a big red tiled roof. There was no way he could avoid it and he hit the roof, knocking the breath from his body, and slid down, dislodging tiles until a rain gutter stopped him falling over the edge. He stretched backwards, trying to regain his breath. He could already feel the bruises. 'Now I'm fucked,' he said aloud. The parachute was draped over the roof. He disengaged the harness.

Then he saw a man pedalling a bicycle across the meadow, a man who stopped and stared up at him with a red face.

'*Alors*,' said the man. '*Ça vas, monsieur?*'

'*Je suis* fucked,' said Toby. 'Will you get a ladder?'

The man nodded his head understandingly. Another man on a bicycle, a policeman, was coming across the field. He stopped alongside the first man who pointed to Toby on the roof and said: '*Il est* fucked.'

They studied more than stared. Then they turned at the splutter of a motorcycle, bumping across the grass, contorted their faces and said together: '*Les Boches*.' There were two German soldiers, one in the sidecar. They carried rifles and ambled anxiously towards the scene after leaving their machine alongside the bicycles. They wore steel helmets and, as Hendry could see, uncertain expressions. The French policeman reported to them: '*Le pilote Anglais. Il est* fucked.'

'Fucked,' said the Germans to each other. Then again: 'Fucked.'

'*Absolutement*,' said one of the Frenchmen.

Between them they got a ladder, running with it like comic firemen. The Germans refused to mount it but the French policeman reluctantly did so and tentatively helped Hendry on to the top rungs. He went painfully to the ground. All four men shook hands with him and congratulated him on his escape, the Frenchmen first, the Germans following. Then one of the Germans produced a camera and handed it to the policeman. They ranged themselves around Toby and the policeman took two photographs before handing the camera back to the German and replacing him in the group. They took six photographs in all. They asked Toby to smile and he tried.

9

As a symbol of Dover the Hippodrome Theatre was only just short of the fame of the sturdy grey castle and the wide white cliffs. In that early wartime year of 1940 it represented a cheery and unusual defiance: despite bombs, shells and the everyday threat of invasion it only closed its doors for one week, and that was because its windows were blown in and the touring company which was billed to star there failed to reach the town due to the disruption of the railways.

It was part of the last generation of music halls and variety theatres throughout Britain, stretching back to the Victorian age and before. Home-grown stage stars such as Arthur Askey, Old Mother Riley and Her Daughter Kitty, Two-Ton Tessie O'Shea, and G. H. Elliott the Chocolate-Coloured Coon, familiar to millions through their wireless sets, drew crowds six nights a week and for matinees. There was standing room only for Max Miller the Cheeky Chappie.

They were wandering stars and at some time they all appeared on a weekly variety bill at the Hippodrome, as did some more exotic acts including a donkey which had to use the main entrance since it was too wide for the stage door, and a fully grown lion which nibbled a piece of meat from the trembling stomach of a chorus girl.

There were less than syncopated dancing girls, wearing massively darned stockings, and decorous striptease artistes, even the illustrious Phyllis Dixie, much in demand as the armed services crammed into the town. During the Dunkirk evacuation, when half the surviving British army had trudged from the harbour, the evening shows at the Hipp, as it was known, were a haven for soldiers who only hours before had escaped from the deathly beaches of France.

The theatre orchestra had once consisted of five musicians but the percussionist left, and the others played on without him through the most dangerous days and nights of German attacks. The drummer was never replaced, one of the other players leaning over to crash or rattle the instruments as required.

A recurring and popular act was a lady contortionist called Carmen from Havana, who lived in Folkestone. She could tie her body in knots, sing and whistle as she did so, and athletically play the piano. Servicemen would tussle for front-row stalls, and urge her to perform her most convoluted tricks, in her brief and sparkling costume, at the edge of the footlights.

'Just look at that gusset,' breathed Tugwell.

Jenkins the Welshman asked: 'What's a gusset?'

Tugwell sighed. 'Don't you know anything? It's the bit there, look, there between her legs.' He pointed. 'Right in front of your face.'

'Very nice indeed,' agreed Jenkins leaning

forward. 'Have all women got them?'

'Most of them,' said Tugwell. 'But they're hard to see.'

* * *

The grand circle at the Hippodrome, where the seats were deeper velvet, was reserved for officers who were severely discouraged from mixing with lower ranks. A government pamphlet suggested that no officer should ever treat a non-commissioned rank to a drink, even if the man were his brother or his father. 'It will save embarrassment for both.'

Instow sat in the grand circle with empty seats around him. In the lower stalls the audience was tight; soldiers sometimes had rifles and always carried gas masks, and the upholstery was tattered. At the end of the performance the servicemen often clambered over the seats to reach the public houses before they closed.

He was not sure why he was there. There was a bar but the view of the stage was more remote. The aching tones of the orchestra drifted up through the cigarette smoke.

Instow left early. He felt he was plodding through a cheerless and useless life. Now that he had been posted ashore to a movements office, his pedantic work seemed remote from the war.

He was in the foyer when he heard the scratchy sounds of the national anthem. As he came to the salute his eyes went across the lobby and met those of a girl selling ice creams. Molly. The tray was still around her neck as she stood to attention. Recognition lit her eyes and she winked.

He smiled and as soon as the anthem was finished she came across to him. 'Too late for a Walls, I suppose,' she said.

'A bit,' he said. He touched her hand holding the tray. She had neat dark hair.

'Will you wait for me outside?' she said. 'I won't be long. About a quarter of an hour.'

Instow felt a small warmth. 'I'll wait,' he said.

'Sure you won't have a Walls? You can have it free.' Her young face clouded. 'But I don't suppose they'll let you eat it here. Being an officer.'

Outside the theatre it was so dark that he had to watch carefully for her. The audience had cleared in ten minutes.

'The blackout's good sometimes,' she said taking his arm. 'Nobody can see you with me. Or me with you.'

'Where are we going?' asked Instow.

'My place,' she said giving a giggle. She turned on a bicycle lamp. He could just see the profile of her face. 'I don't actually live there. I live in one of the caves. It's cheap and it's safe.' As far as they could tell there was nobody else on the street. A wandering cat began a lament. 'That's how I feel sometimes,' she said. 'Do you remember my name? I bet you don't.'

'I remember it,' he said. 'Molly.'

'That's good.' Their footsteps were loud on the empty pavement. 'Not many men would. It's been weeks. What have you been doing? Out there in the Channel. Fighting and that?'

Instow sighed. 'Unfortunately not. I've not even got a ship now. I'm stuck in an office on the quay.'

'But it's got to be safer,' she said. 'You've got to make sure you're safe, as much as you can in this war.'

'It's not what I came back to the navy for,' he said.

'Last time . . . the first time . . . I saw you, you were in a terrible state,' said Molly.

'Lost my ship and half my men,' he said. 'Good men.'

'I don't suppose there's much difference, good men or bad men in war. They die just the same,' she said. They turned down a stony hill, the bicycle lamp a ring of light on their feet. At the foot was a terrace of houses all but demolished by the bombing. 'This is it,' she said uncertainly. 'It will be a surprise.'

The end house remained standing and she went up a brief flight of steps and put a key into the lock. 'I've got my own nook,' she whispered. 'It's very nearly romantic.'

He smiled at her in the dark. They went into a black, warm passage. He felt along the wall and when they went into a room he collided with the arm of a chair. His hand reached another chair. 'I don't use the downstairs,' she said. 'Not the time I'm here.' She shone the light briefly around the walls. There were some paintings and photographs. The windows were boarded. 'This way,' she said. 'Up the wooden hill.'

She went first and waited for him on the landing. It was the first time that night they had been close together. He felt her full breasts against him and her arms came out and looped about his waist. He kissed her cheek. 'Hello, officer,' she said. 'Again.'

By the unsteady beam of the bicycle lamp they went into a bedroom. 'It's very handy and quite safe. I mean, the place isn't going to fall down on our heads or anything.'

'Who does it belong to?' he asked keeping his voice low.

'There's no need to whisper. There's nobody for miles, well, a good distance anyway. Come to me.'

In the darkness, he moved against her. 'I should be ashamed of myself,' he said.

'And me,' she giggled. 'But I'm not.'

'You're twenty-two,' he said. 'You told me.'

Molly said: 'Twenty-one. In a couple of days. I lie about my age. Put your hands back on me, will you.' Slowly he raised the palms of both hands; she caught them and placed them on her almost motherly breasts. 'Bit on the big side,' she said. 'But maybe you like that.'

Instow said: 'I just feel guilty.'

'About me? About your wife? Don't worry about either of us. The only thing is I'm here and she isn't.'

She was still wearing the uniform of the theatre usherette which had brass buttons down the front and metallic epaulettes on the shoulders. 'I'm like a ruddy solider,' she said, beginning to unbutton her tunic. 'But they make you.' She studied his silhouette. 'Don't you think you ought to take your cap off?'

Instow laughed. 'I hardly know what to do with you. I've never met anybody like you. And I'm twice your age.'

She said: 'In that case you ought to know how to go about things. You could start by undoing my blouse.'

He fumbled with the small buttons and the front of the blouse fell open. 'I'll do the next bit,' she said. 'Otherwise we'll be here all night.' She had continued to hold him lightly around the waist but now she took both hands away and her fingers undid her brassiere. It fell away and he could see the faintly luminous breasts. He bent to kiss them and she misunderstood. 'Here,' she said. 'You'll see them better with my bicycle lamp.' She turned the switch and the faded beam illuminated first one breast, then the other.

'Molly,' he sighed resignedly. 'You're lovely.'

His hands went to her still-illuminated bosom and she moved the lamp obligingly. 'I get used to it as an usherette,' she said. 'Pointing a torch this way and that. I bet you've seen plenty like this.'

'Not by the light of a bicycle lamp,' he told her.

She giggled and placed his hands over her breasts. 'Warm hands,' she said. 'Mine feel quite warm too.' She lowered them and deftly undid the buttons on his fly.

She released the catch of her skirt and it dropped to the floor. She was a little plump around the middle and her white knickers glowed in the dark. 'Take the lamp,' she said. 'If you'd like to see me.'

He turned the switch of the lamp and shone it on her.

She leaned and kissed him on the forehead. 'You're a gentleman,' she said. 'Just what I would expect. Pull them down . . . go on . . . pull them. I double dare you.'

Close as they were they could scarcely see each other's faces, only the points of their eyes. They embraced with temporary gladness. 'I could get really worked up about you,' she said. 'I'm not like you think. I wouldn't say this to everybody. I don't go with just any bloke. But you remind me of my dad.'

She moved towards the bed, climbing over her clothes on the floor. 'My uniform,' she said. 'Better fold it. They like you to be smart to sell Walls.' She glanced towards where he stood. 'You'd better fold yours up too. You'll be in trouble.'

They both did so with strange formality. Then she rolled on to the bed stretching her legs with a pleasant sigh. He looked down at her pale shape. Naked he climbed against her.

He lay alongside her and she enjoyably snuggled against him. He kissed her with tenderness. 'I still feel guilty,' he said.

'About your wife?'

'About you.'

She kissed his ear. 'Don't worry about me. I'm going to enjoy it. And I'm getting paid.' She eased her face away. 'I suppose so anyway.'

'Of course, Molly,' he said.

'I want you to pay me in National Savings stamps,' she said firmly. 'Or a savings certificate.

You can get one for fifteen shillings, if you don't think that's too much.'

Instow laughed deeply. 'I can't get over you. Yes, it's all right if that's what you want.'

Molly said: 'I do go on talking, don't I.' She put her plump arms about his neck and he stroked her comfortable breasts. 'Let's make a start,' she suggested.

He could feel her in every sensual movement of her body from her rolling breasts to her opening and closing thighs. Their knees collided gently. At the end they clutched each other and then drew apart. 'Not bad for somebody your age,' she said.

* * *

They sat on the bed in the dim and anonymous room, their bodies cooling, now half-familiar. 'There's still some running water in the house,' she said conversationally. 'We could have a wash before we go.' She leaned back, her breasts and her round face in dark profile. She held his hand. 'I'm going to have a fag,' she said. 'Do you smoke?'

'A pipe,' said Instow.

'Got it with you?'

'The pouch is in my pocket.'

She found her cigarettes and a box of matches. 'Why don't you smoke your pipe?' she suggested climbing back into the bed. 'There's no rules against it. Not here.'

Sliding from the bed he took the pipe from the pocket of his uniform coat. Molly lit her cigarette. 'Is it loaded?' she asked tapping it as he returned to the bed. 'My dad always kept his loaded, as he put it.'

'I did it before I came out,' said Instow. He almost laughed at what was happening. He climbed on to the bed again and they sat naked against each other, their shoulders damp. 'I can light it,' she offered. 'I used to once but I might be out of practice.'

She struck a match and held it to the bowl of the pipe. He put his hand across the bowl, puffed two puffs, and saw it was glowing. They sat in darkness and temporary contentment. 'I loved my father,' she said eventually.

'I can tell.'

'What sort is your tobacco?'

'St Bruno.'

'He used to smoke Digger Flake. My mother cleared off when I was eleven and, by her reckoning, old enough to look after myself. So my dad and me stayed together. I was like a housewife. I'd go to school, do the shopping on the way home, and keep the house for him — better than she ever did. Nobody thought it was strange. Where we lived in south London nobody took any notice, nobody reported you to the council and that. There was lots of unusual arrangements going on. But people minded their own business.'

'Where is he now, your father?'

The end of the cigarette glowed as she drew in, then puffed. 'In heaven. He'd better be, anyway. If he isn't there's been a mistake.'

She was still and for a while silent. 'Me,' she

eventually said. 'I thought he'd be there for always. So did he. But he got pneumonia and just pegged out. Two days after the war began. He was talking about joining the air force.'

She locked the door with care when they left and went down the front steps into the blacked-out street. 'The old couple who lived here got evacuated and they lent me the key. I said I'd keep an eye on the place. It'll probably collapse when they knock these other houses down.'

She turned on the doorstep and they kissed briefly like real lovers. 'Back to my cave,' she said.

'What's it like?' They were walking down the cobbled hill. She switched the bicycle lamp on intermittently. Ahead was a faintly luminous segment of sea. All was silent.

'It's just a cave,' she said. 'With hundreds of people living in it, well, sleeping in it. Snoring and farting. Most of them are on bunks, up against the walls. And there's lots of caves like it. It gets a bit niffy down there, damp and not much air and too many people. But it's shelter and it's safe and it's cheap.'

'Do they mind what time you get in?'

'I get a few grumbles if I have to step over people when I come in, and a few sideways looks in the morning, but it's mostly all right. They know I work at the Hipp so that's a good excuse.' She glanced at him in the darkness. 'And I'm not out all the time. Don't think that. Just now and again. Only if I like somebody.'

She put her arm in his and said: 'Will you have

any trouble with the guards and that?'

He patted her hand. 'Nothing. I'll probably go into my office. Sometimes I do if I can't sleep. What about the savings certificate? I may not see you for a while.'

'Next time,' she said hugging his arm. 'There's no rush. You might think it's a bit odd, but I'm saving up for my future.'

He thought he had ceased being surprised by her. Then she said: 'What's your name, by the way?'

'Paul,' he said. 'Paul Instow.'

'That's posh. Sorry, I forgot to ask.'

He left her and watched her shadow walk up the short slope to the Trevanion Cave, then turned smiling, shaking his head, and went down towards the harbour. He had no trouble at the gates. There was always someone on duty in the Naval Movements office and he went up the stairs.

Inside, under the dim lights, there were three men bending over desks, but with no urgency. A jug of just-warm coffee was on a table and he poured himself a mug. He went to his desk and picked up a sheaf of orders. 'One of them's for you, sir,' said a rating walking by with another wad of paper. 'The one on top.'

'For me?' Instow could scarcely believe it. He used the tips of his fingers to pick up the order. He was to join the destroyer HMS *Carnforth* in Dover the following day.

The night duty officer wandered over. '*Carnforth*,' he muttered. 'First World War. She's getting on.'

'So am I,' said Instow.

★ ★ ★

At this twenty-first century distance it seems highly bizarre that part of the German plans for invading the south coast of England was the landing of eleven thousand horses; four thousand on the first day and the rest with the second wave of the attack. The British army had disposed of its horse transport before the war.

Like the conquering William, whose first objective, after getting his army ashore and winning the battle at Hastings, had been to capture meadows so that his soldiers' horses could graze, the Germans' attack plans in the summer of 1940 had mapped out for immediate occupation not only defensive redoubts, airfields and harbours, but also the lush pastures of Sussex and Kent.

Despite the dreaded and irresistible Panzer divisions of heavy tanks, the screaming squadrons of Stuka dive-bombers, and the powerful artillery at its disposal the German army had a long tradition of harnessing horses as transport for troops and haulage of heavy guns and equipment. There were also formations of bicycles.

At the start of September in Dover and the surrounding threatened countryside, ill-equipped and scarcely trained troops, some with only five rounds of rifle ammunition per man, awaited the massive assault which a Dover fortune-teller firmly forecast was only hours away. No one argued, not even the War Office, and confident of her own prediction she then boarded up her kiosk and left for Scotland.

The Home Guard now numbered a million men in disarray. Some were armed with the donated American rifles which had been preserved in thick grease since the end of the First World War. There were thoughts that these over-enthusiastic volunteers were a liability; they shot and killed or wounded more than two hundred motorists, some of them deaf, who failed to stop when ordered to do so at arbitrary roadblocks; there were also reservations about arming some men who might be criminals rather than patriots. A chief constable was shot dead in dubious circumstances. There were other civilian casualties. Lord North was killed while walking on his estate near Dover. He trod on a land-mine.

The English Channel tides would be suitable for an invasion for the first three weeks of September. The defenders of the British Isles declared themselves relieved to be alone without the handicap of uncertain allies. While they waited they indulged in football and cricket, public-bar brawls, church parades, housey-housey and baffling manoeuvres. There was an unwarranted airy optimism. Each officer, and in effect every man, knew the national coded warning which would tell them that the invasion was imminent. It was only one word: Cromwell.

★ ★ ★

'It's 'Cromwell',' confided Frank Cotton.

'I know,' Nancy said. 'Everybody knows. The cleaners at the hospital know.'

When the telephone rang it was Cotton who picked it up. A hoarse male voice said: 'Oliver.'

Cotton said: 'Who's Oliver?'

'You know, the code word. The invasion. *Oliver*.'

'Don't you mean Cromwell?'

'Oh, that's right. Cromwell. Silly me.'

Cotton replaced the telephone wearily and said: 'Christ.'

Nancy was studying him. '*Was* it Cromwell?' she asked. She was gathering her nursing cloak and her bag for the hospital.

'He *meant* Cromwell,' sighed Cotton.

They regarded each other seriously. 'They'll be sending a car for me,' he said. 'We can drop you off.'

They moved towards each other and embraced tightly. 'You be careful,' said Nancy. 'I don't want to see it's my husband they're carrying in.'

Cotton grinned and kissed her. 'I'm relying on the Home Guard.'

'Thank God we've got a navy,' said Nancy. She heard a sound in the lane. 'It's here,' she said. 'At least that's worked according to plan.'

He buckled on the cumbersome revolver in its shiny holster, they put the lights out and suddenly both wondered if it might be the last time. They went out of the door with their arms around each other's waists.

'Looks like he's on his way then, Hitler,' said the police driver. 'I don't know what kept him.'

'Seems like it,' said Cotton. 'Could we drop my wife at the hospital?'

The constable hesitated. 'Against orders,

sarge. No unauthorised passengers.'

'I'm authorising it,' said Cotton sharply and the man nodded. He began to drive.

'Them parachutists will be dropping soon, I reckon. They come in all disguises, like fancy dress, so some bloke on the wireless said. They even come down disguised as nuns and bus conductors.'

'Easy to recognise then,' said Cotton. 'A nun on the end of a parachute.'

Despite the fact that the Wolseley was clearly a police car and had a dimly lit sign on the roof saying so, they were stopped at roadblocks manned by Home Guards. 'We're going to the hospital, then the police station,' said Cotton stiffly at the third block. 'There's an emergency on.'

'Don't we know it,' said the thin sergeant with the long wet moustache who came to the window. A vacant-looking lad came to his side. 'Trevor here saw your sign saying 'Police' but he thought it said '*Polish*' because he don't read very well. He reckoned you might be foreigners.'

'The Poles are on our side,' said Cotton heavily. He pointed to a large barrel standing on end at the side of the road. 'What's that?'

'The vat? That's petrol. Filled up fresh from Campbell's garage in Deal. If you'd have been Germans we would have chucked that all over you and set you alight.'

They continued down the hill to the tranquil-looking town. 'Those silly sods will set themselves alight,' said Cotton nodding back to the Home Guard roadblock.

'And petrol's on ration,' said the driver.

Nancy left the car at the hospital. She and Frank kissed each other's cheeks. She watched the car as it drove away wondering what was going to happen that night. The medical director of the hospital had almost the whole staff already assembled in the lobby. Nancy crept in at the back.

'We will be treating both Allied casualties and German casualties,' said the senior doctor. 'We will treat both equally. Except we'll treat ours first.'

⋆ ⋆ ⋆

That September evening there was a tangible crackle of excitement, almost of exhilaration, along the English beaches, cliffs and coastal towns. Never had the Channel been watched so sharply and with so little to see. There was half a moon but it lit only the backs of indolent waves.

On land, uniforms moved in the darkness; the army shuffled to its prepared defences, the navy was aboard its ships and either at sea or ready to sail, pilots sat in their billets inland waiting for the call to their planes. The eager and often elderly eyes of the Home Guard peered from the slit holes of concrete pillboxes, many of them willing the Germans to come, daring them to try it. Just once.

Among the uniforms assembled as the light retreated were the green jerseys of the Dover Cub pack. They sat in an obedient circle in a church hall at the centre of which, on a stool too small to safely accommodate her backside, was Akela, their cheery leader, who in civilian life was Olive Parsons of the municipal library.

She looked up floridly but without consternation as the door to the hall sounded dramatically and in strode two police constables, trying to look businesslike, followed by Cotton who was in plain clothes.

The dozen small boys looked around expectantly and Olive clasped her hands to her blue-bloused bosom. 'Oh, it's only you. I rather thought it might be the Germans.'

'We're ready for them, Akela,' said a boy with the yellow bands of a senior sixer on his sleeve.

'They'll head straight for here,' forecast one of the policemen. 'Objective number one.'

'Right from the beach,' said the other.

'How exciting,' breathed Olive unconvincingly.

'They'll think you've been signalling them. You've got enough light showing through that blackout curtain to attract the Waffen SS.'

'Oh, really,' said Olive spinning with surprising agility on the stool. She peered towards the sagging top of the old curtain. 'I can see,' she admitted. 'I can see what you mean. It's fallen down again. I keep pinning it up. The parish council say they can't replace it until the war's over.'

Cotton moved from the door. 'Akela,' he said seriously, 'I think you ought to send the lads home. Just for tonight it might be a good idea.'

'Right,' said Olive as if instantly obeying orders. She addressed the boys: 'Pack,' she giggled, 'pack up.'

The Cubs rose and faced her expectantly. Three fingers on each boy went up in salute. 'We'll do our best,' they recited. 'We'll dib, dib, dib. We'll dob, dob, dob.'

As they made for the door Cotton asked: 'Do they have far to go?'

'Not at all,' said Olive. 'A few yards most of them. The Nazis won't catch them.'

'They'd have to move fast,' said the senior sixer.

The policemen went out into the dim churchyard. Olive put out the lights in the hall. 'There, *now* the invaders will not be able to find their way,' she said confidently. 'Goodnight, officers.'

The three policemen stood on the church path. 'I wonder how Hitler would deal with Olive,' said one.

'Wouldn't lay a finger on her,' said the other. 'If he's wise.'

As he said it a loud, hollow and ominous clang came from the church bell tower.

* * *

The church door was an inch ajar. Inside, they found the bellringers standing in a circle, their ghostly shadows thrown up the ancient walls by a single oil lamp placed in the middle. They were staring up into the bell tower and scarcely more than glanced at the entering policemen.

'Young Jamie is up there,' said a heavy man Cotton recognised even in the dimness. 'Jamie Ernshaw.'

Cotton left the talking to the constables. 'What's he doing up there?'

'Checking on the bells. Cobwebs on them, I shouldn't wonder. We just gave one a little pull.'

'Don't ring them any more before the order comes,' said the policeman.

'Until the parachutes begin to drop,' said the man as if he knew the strategy by heart. The others in the circle nodded solemnly. To Cotton they looked strangely like the Cubs. The oil lamp trembled.

The chief bell-ringer seemed to think that Cotton might know something. 'Why does Mr Churchill want us to ring the bells anyway? There's no sense. If there's thousands of them parachutes coming down surely it would have leaked out by then, the word would've got around.'

Cotton said he had not been informed of Churchill's war plans. One of the other men in the ring said: 'I 'eard that they parachuters is given a pill, a fog pill they call it. They pops it in their mouth and a cloud like fog comes around them so you can't see them.'

Cotton laughed. 'Did the same man tell you that the Jerries have dug a tunnel under the Channel and are coming up from it any moment?'

'Where d'you reckon they'll come out?' said the man seriously. 'We ought to be there waiting for the buggers.'

'They're all just tales, fairy stories,' said Cotton soberly. 'As long as you know what you're doing with the bells.' A skinny youth began to descend from the void at the top. They waited for him to reach the ground. He touched his cap, knocking it sideways. 'They look all right,' he said. 'I counted them.'

'We know what we be about with the bells,' said the chief man. The others murmured and nodded. 'We're going to ring a Plain Bob Major, ain't we, boys. Better than any steeple in Kent.'

Cotton led the other policemen out into the night. They were on their way to check the isolated houses above the beach to the east of the town. 'There are times,' said Cotton as they got into the car outside the church, 'when I wonder if this whole country is not gone stark raving mad.'

* * *

Cartwright sat in the Roman latrine in the cliff tunnel on a stool placed in front of a collapsible table, a heavy Underwood typewriter before him and a voluminous notebook open on the floor. The odd scene was lit by a single bulb on a lead slung from the chalk passage outside that cast black shadows on the damp, tiled walls and concave ceiling.

'Nice and cosy in here, sir,' said a corporal appearing in the rough entrance Cartwright had opened in the wall.

'No choice,' said Cartwright. 'I've been turfed out of my office by some gas squad.'

'There's everything and nothing going on, sir.' He put an untidy bunch of letters on the table beside the Underwood. 'Charging about, staring out to sea, saying that Fritz is on his way. But there's no sign of Fritz.'

He regarded with interest Cartwright's notebook and the paper in the typewriter. 'What they got you on, sir, something dead secret?'

'Not really, corporal, unless you can call the ancient contents of Kent churches a secret. I've had to write them down in case the Boche takes a fancy to them. When he eventually turns up.'

'Sounds like a useful job,' said the corporal. 'And there's not many useful jobs around at the minute. Everybody's rushing around doin' nowt.'

'It's not useful yet. But it may be. Like that gas squad.'

'You could be right, sir, you could just be. I'll be on my merry way.'

He saluted and left. Cartwright picked up the small wad of letters. He knew they would be mostly detailed returns from vicars, church wardens or parish councils. They were impressively conscientious. But there was also an envelope stamped: 'Embassy of the United States of America.'

'*Darling*,' Sarah had written. '*I've been desperately trying to get in touch with you . . .*'

He had been trying to reach her too, only to have his calls rejected by the embassy switchboard. He read on:

> *I don't know how long I am going to be able to stay here. They are sending people home and when they tell you to go, you have to*

go. So we must meet again soon. Some days I go to a little café for lunch. I'll go every day next week so if it is possible for you to phone between 12.30 and 1.30, then I'll be able to pick up the call. It's Belgravia 429 — the people say they don't mind as long as we're not spies! I love you.

'I love you too,' murmured Cartwright thoughtfully.

⋆ ⋆ ⋆

Despite Britain being a confined island there was ample room for panic. The code word 'Cromwell' was known through the military chain of defence and had filtered easily through to the civilian population. Like many well-prepared strategies, however, and basic and simple as it was, it was widely misinterpreted. It *meant* that an invasion was thought to be imminent but many believed it signalled that an invasion had *already begun*. Few people believed that anywhere apart from the obvious south coast would be the target of a German invasion from the sea but, once the code word was out, areas of remote Scotland and the safely quiet borders of Wales were thrown into confusion.

Even in a front-line town like Dover the response was garbled; some had received the 'Cromwell' call, some had not — and those who had frequently misunderstood its warning.

At the twice-nightly Hippodrome the early-evening performance was getting into its stride with community singing. On stage a flushed soprano and a man in a baggy brown suit led the songs, and the four-man orchestra played with their customary shortcomings, the violinist at almost appropriate moments leaning over and giving the untenanted drums a crashing blow.

Community singing was always popular. Songs were dredged back from the days of the Boer War, songs such as 'Goodbye Dolly, I Must Leave You' and 'There's a Long, Long Trail Awinding', and a popular chorus from the hungry thirties, 'I Do Like Potatoes and Gravy'. The servicemen in the audience robustly joined in bawling the Lambeth Walk while the two performers on stage strutted like cockneys and everyone shouted 'Oi!' in the right places. There was a novelty song, 'I'll Rasp Right in the Führer's Face', in which the word 'rasp' was invariably changed to a spit-spraying raspberry. Then the lady performer took a red boa and sang 'My Old Man Said Follow the Van' and joined with the florid man in 'The Old Kent Road'. The good time was so much enjoyed, that the confused young messenger bearing the emergency word 'Cromwell' was ignored and, being one of the few not knowing the importance of his mission, gave it up as a bad job and joined in the singing.

It was not until Carmen from Havana was at the high spot of her contortionist act, rolled into a ball, her face to the audience and her legs tied around her neck, that the message was repeated by telephone and the manager, straightening his bowtie, strutted on to the stage, hushing the orchestra with his arms. They halted to a slightly hurt silence. Carmen was left tied in her own knot at the front of the footlights.

'This is a priority coded message,' the manager intoned while the contortionist rolled her eyes. 'The warning 'Cromwell' . . . repeat 'Cromwell' . . . has been given. All servicemen must return to their units at once.'

There was a rush for the exits by sailors, airmen and soldiers, some with rifles, all with gas masks. They were gone in three minutes leaving a scattering of civilians remaining in their seats, including a small man in a collar and sober tie and with a bowler hat placed on his lap, almost face to face with the convoluted Carmen. She looked him in the eye from the footlights. 'I don't know why I bother to do this,' she said.

* * *

There were troops everywhere. Half-trained, half-armed, they waited in their dugouts, staring out at the vacant sea, or drove along the Kentish roads and coastal lanes, on a fruitless search for an invading force. But it was a nice evening, the Channel was as calm as the land in the dusky light, animals grazed and men not in uniform went to inns, and drank beer under low beams.

'We can set the sea on fire,' boasted a man. Everyone knew this was true. A pipeline, assembled in Dover, had been quickly laid just offshore along the entire south coast of England. Thousands of gallons of oil could be pumped through it. 'All we got to do is to light the match,' said the man in the pub, 'and let they buggers cook.'

A mile away Sergeant Dunphy was urging his men aboard a truck. 'Look, a brand new lorry,' he said smacking its side. 'Mind you don't get it dirty.'

'There's nice, fancy getting a new one,' said Jenkins.

'We haven't got many old ones,' said Ardley.

Once the dozen men were aboard the driver called: 'Here goes,' the vehicle coughed and with a grating of gears began the journey through the shadows of the almost deserted town. More than two thirds of civilians had left by now. It looked ready to be invaded. They drove through the lanes. Cows looked over hedges at them. A pub appeared, almost buried in a tight valley.

'Right, lads, this looks a likely place to conceal parachutists,' said Dunphy. 'Hold it, driver!' The lorry pulled into the yard. There were chickens pecking around some bicycles.

The landlord seemed unsurprised to see them. 'Half-price for defenders of the realm,' he said. 'Be in the mob myself but I've only got half a foot from the last war to end all wars.'

'I've got more than half a thirst,' said Dunphy. 'Come on, boys. We can't be looking for the mortal enemy all night without a beer. Anyone got some money left from pay day?'

They dug into their pockets and counted out the coins. 'Half a pint of ale to each man,' decided Dunphy. 'And a pint for me.' He looked around challengingly. 'I have to make the decisions.'

Two old men, string tied around their moleskin trouser legs, caps over their foreheads, played darts.

The soldiers stood and drank the Kentish ale. A local came in and sang a short song. The landlord gave him a shandy. 'We're all ready for the Jerries here,' said the landlord. 'Look at Jem and Harry there. Deadeyed with the darts even if they're gone eighty.'

One of the old men sniffed and paused with his dart poised. 'If 'Itler comes, me and Jem 'ere, we're goin' to give ourselves up.'

Dunphy drank with appreciation. 'A man has to have a drink, no matter what state the world is in. The last time I was decent drunk was in Ireland, the Feast of the Immaculate Conception. Some piss-up.'

They trooped out after ten minutes when the singer tried another song. Outside, Ardley recognised the surroundings. They drove on and he said: 'This is where we came to the dance. When I got a lift home on a horse.'

Ahead he saw the cottage. 'Worth looking it over, sarge?' he suggested.

'Why not,' said Dunphy. 'There's nothing else to search around here.' He banged on the driver's cab.

They pulled up close to the house. There was no movement, only some worried ducks in the yard. 'I'll go, shall I, sarge?' said Ardley. 'I know them.'

Dunphy nodded. 'Front door,' he said. 'Let's screen this properly now. There might be Storm Troopers hiding inside.' He pointed to Tugwell and Sproston. 'You two go around the rear. Don't let the ducks scare you.'

Ardley stepped forward. 'Shall I knock, sarge?'

'Not too loud,' said Dunphy.

As the soldier was about to knock, Tugwell and Sproston reappeared around the flank of the house with their rifles raised above their heads and their faces ashen. 'Sarge,' said Tugwell his eyes rolling. 'This old bloke's going to blow holes in us.'

'That's what he says,' said Sproston trying to look over his shoulder.

Ardley recognised the grey man holding the shotgun. 'Spatchcock,' he recalled. 'Spatchcock, sir. Do you remember me?'

The man lowered the shotgun and shuffled around the soldiers. 'Now who's that calling me Spatchcock?' he demanded.

Ardley stepped forward diffidently. 'Me, sir. I was here not long ago. I came here with Rose.'

Spatchcock said: 'Ah, that Rose.' He did not interfere when Sproston and Tugwell lowered their rifles and crept around the back of the other soldiers. 'All the blokes be after 'er. She's well developed, that's why.'

'She took me home on her horse,' said Ardley.

'Could be.'

Dunphy said: 'Mr Spatchcock . . . '

'There's no *mister*. It's just Spatchcock. I been called it for years.' He nodded at Tugwell and Sproston. 'I thought they was Jerries dressed up, like disguised. They reckon they parachutists sometimes dress like nuns, you know. I like nuns.' His haggard face came up for a moment, challengingly. 'Nuns do a lot of good.'

The soldiers were silent, standing in the darkening garden listening as though they had found someone wise. 'When do you think Hitler will come, Spatchcock?' asked Dunphy. 'They think he's coming tonight.'

The old man ruminated, sitting himself on a broken wooden seat. 'I don't reckon he's coming at all,' he said. 'Not never.'

'So we're all running around for nothing,' said the sergeant.

'Like rabbits,' nodded Spatchcock. He stood and went into the house. Although his shoulders were bent he still had to crouch beneath the lintel. 'I'll show you something,' he called from the dim interior. 'I'll find it in a minute.'

The dusk was becoming heavy now, closing like a grey hand over the countryside. They could hear solitary birds piping in different parts of the fields. It was warm and peaceful. The old man returned ducking through the door and holding a square of paper.

'Right now, sergeant,' he said to Dunphy. 'Have you had a sight of this?' It was a leaflet dropped by German planes. 'Bought this at the church fête,' said Spatchcock. 'Cost me five bob.'

The printed page was headed: 'A Final Appeal to Reason'. It was a statement by Adolf Hitler to the British People asking them to order Winston Churchill to stop the war immediately.

The squad crowded around. 'I can read that,' said Jenkins eagerly. 'Can't I, Ardley?'

Ardley said: 'Have a go.'

He glanced at Spatchcock. 'I've been teaching him to read,' he said privately. 'He's Welsh.'

The old man nodded as if that were understandable. Jenkins took the leaflet and with faltering words and Celtic accent recited Hitler's proposals. The others listened. The Welshman finished with a flourish. 'Signed Adolf Hitler,' he said. Then he threw up his right hand in a stiff salute and proclaimed: 'Heil Bloody Hitler.' Everybody laughed as he handed the document back to Spatchcock.

There was a movement on the other side of the wall. Spatchcock said: 'It's that Rose.'

She appeared at the gate with a shotgun in one hand and her big horse in the other. 'Not a German anywhere,' she said.

'I know,' said Sergeant Dunphy. 'We can't find any either.'

'Ah, it's you,' she said seeing Ardley. 'I gave you a lift on my horse back to camp. Never heard from you again.'

Ardley said: 'Sorry, Rose, but we've been busy getting ready for Hitler.'

'Digging up Kent,' put in Jenkins. 'I saw you come by the camp on your horse,' he added. 'Beautiful.'

'He is,' she replied.

'We'd better get back to defending England,' announced Dunphy. They moved towards the front gate.

Ardley said quickly to Rose: 'I really do want to see you again.'

'All right. As long as Jerry doesn't arrive first.'
Spatchcock said to them all: 'I don't reckon that Hitler will ever set a foot here. And you know why — because he's windy. He's scared of us.'

10

Number three company of the Dover Home Guard had been taken on a seventy-mile route march the previous weekend, a long walk for men many of whom were over-age and suffered with their feet. Captain David Price, the unit commanding officer, had not made the march himself since, as he openly explained, he was engaged on tactical matters at headquarters which was established in the classrooms of the junior girls' school, the pupils of which had been evacuated to Wales. Grown men had sat at small desks and listened intently.

The route march had been exhausting even for the most active men. They returned so fatigued that many were unable to go to essential war work on the Monday. Blistered feet and aching joints were treated by the local doctors on standby to treat military casualties. Captain Price said the march was a show of strength.

In the late dusk of the placid evening after the Cromwell warning, he led a patrol of number three company, those who could still walk, through the streets in the segment of the town his men had been assigned to defend.

There had not even been any German air attacks to add realism that day. A few shells had hit open country at the back of the cliffs, white and sunlit, which presented the only target. The bombardment was desultory. There had never been a time that seemed so unlikely for an invasion.

The Home Guard captain, who was manager of a Dover carpet shop, was determined to go about the task of screening the streets efficiently and his hobbling recruits were encouraged to knock on doors and search gardens and outhouses. There was some doubt and confusion. 'Sir, when they answer the door what shall we say?'

One of the younger men, a school teacher, interpolated: ''Good evening, have you by chance noticed any German invaders?''

The captain glared in his direction and muttered: 'Well, just . . . just say 'Home Guard. Everything all right?''

They split into sections and began their search. Between the back gardens of two sloping streets was an alley with entrances into the gardens. Taking one side at a time they climbed fences or went through gates. There were rabbit hutches, pigeon lofts and Anderson air-raid shelters among vegetables and clumps of flowers.

They reassembled after twenty minutes.

'Anything to report?' asked the captain. Hopefully he regarded their vacant faces. 'Anything?'

A few men shook their heads. He asked: 'What happened when you knocked on the doors?'

'One bloke said he was listening to the wireless.'

'A woman asked if we could look out for her lost dog . . . it's called Spot.'

'Most people said: 'Sod off.''

The captain coloured. 'These are the same people who'll be wanting protection soon, perhaps within a few hours,' he said. 'Let's try the other set of gardens.'

* * *

Tommy Handley had finished his weekly comedy wireless programme. Harold sat back disconsolately. 'Now what do I do?' he called to his mother. She was washing curtains in the kitchen. Because of the emergency she had told him to stay in the house. 'Read something,' she called back. 'Haven't you got the *Dandy* or something?'

'It's *Beano* week,' he said. '*Dandy*'s next week.'

He brightened and scanned the outside street through the window. 'I could swap,' he shouted to her. 'I've got some comics I could swap. I'll go along the street to Spots's home.' He rolled from the chair.

'Don't you stay out,' she warned. 'Come back right away. There's a big alert on.'

'I know. And I'm stuck in here.'

'Come back as soon as you've swapped the comics.'

'All right.'

Slyly he moved towards the passage, picked up his catapult from its hiding place below the stairs, and went to the front door. He knew where the boys would be waiting.

They were. 'Where you been?' demanded Spots. 'We been 'anging around hours.'

Harold screwed up his face. 'She wouldn't let me out.'

'Mine had to go and take her dancing class,' said Boot. 'That got rid of her.'

Spots said: 'I just went out the back door. My mum was having her fortune told in the tea leaves. She 'ad her 'ead in a cup.'

'Those Home Guard twerps are around,' said Harold. 'Looking for Germans.'

'We ought to defend something,' said Boot with unusual conviction. 'They reckon Hitler will be here tonight.'

Harold said: 'Tell us news, not 'istory, mush.'

'What will we defend? All the best places have been nicked by the army and the Home Guard,' said Spots. He glanced along the street. 'What about the phone box?'

Harold did not like others having good ideas. 'Yes, I thought about that,' he said. 'It's got sandbags, so it's supposed to be defended.'

'And it's . . . comm . . . communications,' said Boot.

Reluctantly Harold said: 'You're dead right, Booty, mush. If a Jerry parachutist landed in this street he'd be in there like a shot. Ringing up.'

Spots said: 'They've probably got a special bag of pennies.'

'Come on then,' said Harold. 'Into action, men!'

Crouching, they ran to the telephone box. Boot flung open the door and they jammed into the tight space inside. 'Somebody's been havin' a piss in 'ere,' said Spots. 'A big one.'

'You probably,' sniffed Harold. 'Right. We can

just see over these sandbags. Keep your eyes skinned. Take one side each. I'll do the door as well.' There was criss-crossed adhesive tape on the door.

They could just see through the late dusk. Spots whispered: 'There's the enemy. They're coming from the gardens at the back.'

The three boys crowded to see. 'Armed,' said Harold. 'To the fucking teeth.'

'Let's go 'ome,' said Boot.

'Stay where you are,' ordered Harold. 'It's only those Home Guard nuts.' The group of ten men emerged into the street from the alley. They had rifles and crept along the privet hedges.

'Somebody's in that phone box,' said one of the men. Captain Price held out his hand and the men who were able to crouch did so. Others flattened themselves against the hedge.

'I've got a rope,' said another of the volunteers. 'I found it in somebody's garden.' He beamed as if he expected instant promotion. 'Why don't I creep up and tie it around the phone box there. They won't be able to get out then.'

The captain looked towards him disdainfully. 'What will we do — starve them out?'

Doris Barker strutted belligerently from her front door. 'You!' she said pointing a finger.

'She means you,' said the captain to the man with the rope.

'Yes, missus?'

'That's my spare clothes line. You've stolen it.'

Harold heard his mother's voice and he pushed open the door of the telephone box calling: 'Mum . . . Mum . . .'

The Home Guards looked in the direction of the voice. Doris marched towards it leaning over to recover her spare clothes line as she went. 'Harold?' she called outside the box. 'Harold, are you in there?' She opened the door forcefully and the three boys almost fell out.

'We was defending it,' said Harold miserably. 'Then this lot turned up.'

'Get home!' ordered Doris. 'And you two . . . get home.'

Harold slouched towards his garden gate and the others walked, then ran down the hill. 'Playing soldiers!' shouted Doris at the Home Guards. She turned on their commander. 'You should stay in that crummy rug shop of yours.' She lashed at him with the rope and turned hitting out at the nearest men, missing both. 'You're like a load of kids.'

* * *

At Chatham, Portsmouth and Plymouth, British warships lay rocking gently, prepared to put to sea. It was a grey, lean, formidable fleet, composed of cruisers, destroyers, submarines and others, patiently waiting. Somewhere in the Continental ports were enemy ships, their numbers and spirits diminished by losses off Norway in the battles of the previous autumn. The German army had occupied whole landscapes but the navy had suffered heavily at sea. Fast E-boats were hiding in French ports but they were the only support that an invading

German army, with its slow, rolling barges, could expect for the adventure of invading Britain. It was not much.

The old destroyer *Carnforth* had left Dover before dusk. At seven o'clock the German battery near Calais had opened fire, the shells sending up fountains of sea half a mile beyond her stern.

'That's as near as they'll get,' forecast Captain Bertram Elphinstone to Instow. 'Unless we're really unlucky. They've transported those guns miles, put them on railway tracks. But they've got no gunnery radar, so they haven't a clue where they're aiming.'

Instow, now second in command, felt happier than he had been for months. 'She's a bit of an old bag this,' said Elphinstone.

'I remember her well,' said Instow. 'First time out.'

'Ah, of course. You were in Dover then.'

Instow said: 'I served in her for six months, sir. It was the days of the Dover Patrol.'

Elphinstone slapped the rail. 'It's terrific you've come back,' he said. 'The Dover Patrol, the Zeebrugge raid.'

'Zeebrugge,' acknowledged Instow. 'All a bit of a shambles but we came out all right in the end.'

'And here we are years later, still fighting the Hun,' said Elphinstone. 'When will he ever learn.' He sniffed over the side of the bridge. The air was light, the sea moderate. 'Nice night for an invasion.'

'Do you think they'll come?' asked Instow. 'It all looks a bit empty.'

'Never saw the sea more unoccupied. Not even in the Indian Ocean,' agreed Elphinstone. He swung his binoculars along the horizon. 'You married?'

'Yes. As far as you can be married in a war,' said Instow.

'Absolutely. That's one of the good things about it. It keeps marriages together by keeping the participants, the marriage participants that is, apart. Personally, I know by instinct when it's time to go back to sea. It's when she starts hinting that the lawn needs cutting.'

Instow laughed quietly. 'Well, I've been a civilian since the Great War. I've hardly seen the sea in twenty years.'

'Get on all right with the wife?'

'It's gone a bit quiet lately. She's doing war work up in Cumberland.'

'It's like that. Just take a look at the faces of this crew when the ship's paid off, see the expressions. A lot of them don't look happy about going on leave. We had one stoker who got himself taken into hospital rather than face his missus and kids.'

He revolved through ninety degrees with the binoculars again. 'Miles of bugger all,' he muttered.

'Those barges in Boulogne and Calais,' said Instow. 'Most of them will have to be towed across. Even those with their own power won't raise much more than four knots. It will take them all night. It's not a river crossing.'

'I think the whole thing is propaganda, bollocks on both sides,' replied Elphinstone. 'If they'd managed to get across right away after Dunkirk, with paratroops as well, they might have had a decent chance. But not now. Hitler's quite literally missed the boat.'

A call came from the lookout: 'Vessel ahead, sir.' He gave the bearing. The captain and Instow went to the side of the bridge. They both searched with their glasses. 'Christ,' said Elphinstone. 'That's a small invasion fleet. A fishing boat.'

He ordered the ship to slow and manoeuvred her so that the darkened fishing smack came under the hull of the destroyer, rolling in the swell. 'Ahoy! What the hell d'you think you're up to?' he called through the loud hailer. There were three men in the boat.

'Evening,' came the gentle response. 'We just came out 'cause there's a nice bit of dab and pollock about. Would you like some for your supper, captain?'

'With chips, sir,' called another of the men. 'Lovely.'

* * *

Which peal of bells sounded first will for ever be a mystery; but peal they did, and the ringers of Kent and Sussex, and then of Hampshire and Surrey, were swift to grasp the ropes that for months had remained hanging as if dead. Bells echoed across the wide night-time of southern England, one melody beginning another. People waited under their roofs, anxious more than afraid, for German parachutists to fall into their fields and their streets and to trample their gardens; they took up defensive bread knives, kept pots of scalding water on their stoves, de-chained bicycles, removed the rotor arm from any car, and hid horses. They also listened close to the wireless. There were barricades on every road. But the night sky remained the calmest place for miles; there was a theatrical wedge of moon, small unhurried clouds and no sounds of aeroplanes nor any sight of parachutes.

Cotton and two constables reached the sandbagged coastguard station overlooking St Margaret's at Cliffe and its undisturbed sea. Below the post they could see coils of barbed wire snaking into the distance. 'Any news, Fred?' asked Cotton.

'Only rumours,' sniffed the coastguard. 'Fancy a cup of tea?'

Cotton left the constables with the assistant coastguard staring out at the anonymous view and went through the low adjoining door into the cottage.

'Margaret's took herself off to bed,' said Fred Wansey. 'She says if the Huns come, to wake her up in time to take her curlers out.' He looked straight at Cotton. 'You heard anything?'

'Nothing. Except the church bells,' said Cotton. He accepted a mug of tea.

Almost as an afterthought Fred poured in a splash of whisky. Then he sat down, his expression serious. 'There's a rumour that Pegwell Bay is floating with Jerry corpses,' he said. 'I heard it down the line. Thousands. And they've landed at Deal and been fried in our petrol trap.'

'It's all been done very quietly then,' shrugged Cotton. 'You would think there might have been the odd bang.'

'You would that,' agreed Fred. 'Some excitement or other.'

There was a brisk knock on the door that made them both sit upright. With trenches full of soldiers only a hundred yards away it was unlikely to be an enemy. Fred got up and called: 'Who's there?'

'Woolly,' came the shout from outside. 'Woolly Woolford from Pegwell Bay.'

Fred pulled the two heavy bolts. 'I know you're from Pegwell. I know'd you thirty years, Woolly.'

A big man wearing a jersey around him like a coil of rope, and with a badged cap halfway over the back of his head, came through the door with heavy caution. He went straight to the blacked-out window and inched the curtains apart. 'All quiet then.' He sounded disappointed.

'Hear a pin drop,' said Fred. He handed Woolford a mug of tea and without asking added the whisky.

'We got a report . . . well, just a rumour really, not a report . . . that there was hundreds of Jerries floating in the sea down here,' he said. 'Don't seem to be true.'

'Is that the same lot of bodies who were floating around in Pegwell Bay?' asked Cotton.

Fred said: 'That's the rumour we got.'

'Nothing happening there,' said Woolford.

'We're all ready for 'em but they 'aven't turned up.'

The latch on the black inside door of the cottage clicked heavily and the three men looked up to see Margaret Wansey coming down in a sagging red dressing gown and with paper curlers in her hair. 'Hello, Frank,' she said. 'Hello, Woolly. We've got all the top commanders here then.'

They laughed. 'Any sign of Hitler?' she asked.

'He's not shown hisself yet,' said her husband with some regret. 'Here, nor anywhere else by the look of it. Even the bells have stopped now.'

'Bretton church was the last to stop,' said Woolford.

'County champions just before the war,' said Margaret. 'They would be last. It was nice to hear them ring again, weren't it. Anybody like a sandwich?'

Each man said he would. She rolled up the sleeves of her dressing gown, set about frying in the pan and laid out three plates on the table. She gave them fried bread and bacon sandwiches and made another three mugs of tea.

'Pity they didn't come,' said Fred. 'They sank the lightship. Been a chance to get even.' They had settled around the table, the oil lamp light dwelling on their faces. It was now one o'clock. 'Well,' said Cotton, 'they haven't turned up. I'll be getting back.'

'Spoilsports,' sniffed Margaret.

* * *

Air attacks on the town became sporadic and, to the inhabitants, almost incidental. The howling of the air-raid warning attracted little more attention than a change in the wind and few people went into shelters or caves until there were aircraft overhead. Enemy planes flew over on their way to inland targets — airfields and RAF control centres now — and eventually to London. For much of the time Dover passed beneath their wings.

Shelling from the French coast persisted, haphazard bombardments, fired blindly and in brief spells. Housewives were able to do their shopping while the enemy was reloading. Dover's shops still closed for lunch.

British guns fired back just as blindly. There were no targets unless enemy ships conveniently appeared against the distant shore.

This aimless bombardment from both sides prompted a question in Parliament: if British guns promised to stop firing would the enemy agree to do the same? Winston Churchill growled a dismissal but went to Dover to see the guns for himself. There he ordered bigger guns. The aimless battle continued. Enemy high-explosive shells demolished buildings and killed people in the Dover streets; one fell in the middle of a football match between the army and the navy, killing two players and a man tending his nearby vegetable plot.

Cartwright was driving to Dover Priory station. Sarah was due on the London train. When he was a mile away two shells exploded, and columns of smoke rose from the station. He reached the yard at the front; air-raid wardens and policemen were erecting barriers. The clanging bell of the fire engine announced that it was on its way. One shell had hit carriage sheds and there was a fire burning. He hurried through the barrier saying to the air-raid wardens the first thing that came to his mind: 'Headquarters.'

'Ah, right, sir. Right you are. Watch out for some more. Jerry's got the range now.'

Smoke was whirling around the platforms. The waiting room and the refreshment room were on fire. Three elderly porters were tugging fire buckets towards the fires, spilling much of the contents and shouting to each other, and another two were trying to pay out the hose of a flimsy stirrup pump.

Another man was struggling to right a milk churn which was rolling around the platform. Cartwright helped him. 'Where's the London train gone?' he asked.

The sweating man looked up but with no surprise. Between them they steadied the churn. The man said: 'She's gone back in the tunnel, sir. It's safer in there.'

Cartwright followed his nod. He almost laughed when he saw the nose of the engine half-projecting from the hole of the tunnel. 'Thanks,' he called back.

'Don't mention it,' said the station man touching his forehead and allowing the churn to tip over again. Cartwright heard him curse. Somewhere dogs were barking. The first fire engine had reached the station yard.

An incongruous sheet of smoky sunlight, like

stage lighting, was illuminating the opening of the tunnel and the round nub of the railway engine. Cartwright ran towards it, jumping down on to the line and stumbling across the wooden sleepers. He reached the tunnel. The locomotive almost filled it but along its sides, against the sooty walls, were ranks of crouching people. One woman from the refreshment buffet had a tea towel draped over her, another held a tin tray above her head. There was a small but clear explosion from the direction of the platform. The woman with the towel said: 'There goes our tea urn.'

'Make room,' some man shouted. 'Make way for an officer!'

'Thanks, thank you,' mumbled Cartwright as he pushed along the crowd. 'Headquarters . . . headquarters.'

They fell back to make way for him. The driver was still in his cab with the fireman. 'We're going to be late,' he called cheerfully.

With difficulty Cartwright climbed into the first green carriage. He slammed the door behind him and hurried along the corridor. Passengers stared out of the compartments. A woman politely asked if the invasion had started.

He found Sarah sitting calmly alone in a first-class compartment. She jumped up to greet him and they held each other. 'What happened?' she asked. 'We came out of the tunnel and then straight away came back in.'

'A shell's hit the station,' he said. 'We may be stuck for a while. I'm so glad to see you.'

They kissed each other. 'I brought your

package,' she said holding out a brown paper parcel. 'My excuse for coming.'

'Good.' He took it. 'Now I won't be court-martialled because you're here. Somebody had to bring it.'

'It was no trouble,' she grinned. 'I went to the military police office at Waterloo station and they couldn't have been sweeter. A guy with a red armband even saw me to the train.'

Sitting on the opposite seat Cartwright opened the package.

'They had it waiting for me at Church House,' Sarah said.

He had taken off the wrapping. The book was old and scuffed. 'Look at that,' he said. '*Kentish Churches Since the Reformation*. Just what I need.' He looked at her quizzically. 'It must seem absolutely mad doing this, worrying about churches and their stuff, when we're under shellfire and waiting for the Jerries.'

'Not at all. Your history is something you're fighting for.'

He put his arms about her and said: 'It's not as though we're *doing* any fighting. Everyone's been on the alert, day upon day, night after night, but you can only stare at the English Channel for so long. Everybody is having a good time, going to pubs and dances. Spelling bees and raffles, for God's sake. The army is trying to keep itself occupied by marching up and down.' He paused. 'And there's always the shelling.'

* * *

September afternoon light drifted through the browning leaves of the lime walk over the path leading to the church door. Other shadows moved unhurriedly across the stones of the path. They sat on a mossy tombstone drinking tea from cups and saucers. It was very peaceful.

'Old Jeffrey Baines won't mind,' said the vicar tapping the tomb. His name was Henry Francis Lyte and he proudly told them it was the same as the curate who had composed the words of 'Abide With Me'.

He was sitting on the tombstone on the opposite side of the path. 'Been there since 1743,' he said. 'The Baines family still live here in the village. Every Sunday, if it's fine, some of the older ones sit here, keeping Jeffrey company, until it's time to go home for lunch.'

'Everywhere is so quiet,' said Sarah. 'For a war.'

'Some people are even a touch disappointed,' said the vicar. He was a round, youngish man, with a good smile. 'I'll show you our treasured books.'

He led them towards the rectory, smothered in trees. He opened the heavy door and casually moved a shotgun from the hall stand. 'For shooting rooks,' he said. 'They're a real pest. Not that I've ever hit one. That's why they won't have me in the army.'

They went into a room full of untidy papers and cushions, with a settee and two heavy armchairs. He pulled the curtains wide to let in the sun, sending up thousands of dust particles. 'That's what an airborne invasion would look like, I imagine,' he said standing back and studying it.

He moved piles of parish magazines and newspapers so they could sit down. 'You tried to join up then,' said Cartwright.

'I thought I had to,' shrugged the vicar. 'But they wouldn't have me because I can't see very well. In any case, I would want to be a soldier, an ordinary, real soldier. There are too many chaplains, padres or whatever.'

He sat on the edge of a worn armchair. 'That's a terrible job anyway, a chaplain. I went down to Dover hospital when that first convoy was attacked in July. I thought I was going to pass out. All those poor fellows, asking me about heaven, what it was like.'

He became suddenly silent, crushed. 'Who knows what it's all for.' Then he straightened up. 'The books,' he said to Cartwright. 'That's why you've come.'

'It is,' said Cartwright. 'It seems like an odd occupation just now. Making lists of books.'

Mr Lyte shook his head. 'It's a good sensible thing,' he said, 'guarding what we have.' He rose. 'I'll get them. They were kept in the church for centuries but I thought it might be a good idea to bring them over here.'

He went from the room and returned with difficulty carrying a dark wooden chest. Cartwright apologised and helped him to put it on the oval table. It was locked and the clergyman took the key from a vase on the mantelshelf and opened it. 'Now, let's see what's here,' he said. 'If I recall there's . . . ' He paused with only a little embarrassment. ‘Oh, *Lady Chatterley’s Lover*.’ His visitors both laughed. ‘Haven’t read it since my days at theological college,’ said the vicar. ‘I was making a special study of sin.’

★ ★ ★

They stayed at the same inn on misty Romney Marsh as they had the first time, in the same big old bed in the same room, but with a new moon. It floated as though behind gauze outside the open window as they lay close together in the dark. The same cat climbed over the sill and, folding itself up familiarly at the foot of the bed, began to purr.

‘This could be the last time,’ Sarah said deeply sad. ‘We may not see each other again until after the war.’

He knew. They were lying on their backs, naked but a little apart, only their fingers touching. ‘It doesn’t seem fair, does it,’ he said. ‘But then nothing does.’

‘In love and war,’ she murmured.

‘And there’s no way out? No way you can stay?’

‘Only by marrying,’ she said. ‘And I don’t think there’s going to be time for that.’ She gave a sorry laugh. ‘They’re getting rid of everybody they don’t think of as essential. There are security checks every day. There was a clerk, a cipher clerk, arrested last week. Passing coded messages on to some pro-German group.’

She turned to him so that her breasts were against his ribs. His arm took her in. ‘It will probably be next week,' she said. 'Or soon after. They're sending groups back to the States by way of Southern Ireland. Then you take an American ship from Cork,' she said. 'And keep your fingers crossed.'

They said nothing more for several moments. Then she turned on to her naked back again and stared at the shadowed ceiling.

'*Ah, love*,' she whispered, '*let us be true, to one another!* . . . '

He picked it up: '*For the world, which seems, to lie before us like a land of dreams* . . . '

She continued: '*So various, so beautiful, so new* . . . '

Together they spoke in the dark: '*Hath really neither joy, nor love, nor light* . . . '

Sarah rolled on to him. He pulled the sheet over her. She was crying now.

They made love again. In the end she remained above him. He felt for the tears on her face and wiped them with his fingers. She was still for a while, then she began to giggle. 'Oh, darling,' she said, her wet face against him. 'This cat is walking up and down my back.'

* * *

The East Kent Company's evening bus arrived in Dover at precisely seven o'clock as it had done since the days when it was drawn by horses. Bombing, shelling, the threat of invasion, the deaths of its staff and the destruction of its own bus station made no difference to the timetable. It was a matter of pride.

Ardley met Rose at the bus stop and they kissed with a touch of formality. 'Plaza then?' she said.

'That's the best bet,' he answered. They walked arm in arm towards the cinema. Two land-mines had been dropped by parachute that morning demolishing shops and houses in the eastern part of the town and causing five deaths.

At the Plaza cinema there was a comedy with Ethel Revnell and Gracie West. The main film was a war drama starring Marlene Dietrich, who people still regarded with suspicion since she was from Germany and sounded like it.

There was also a Ministry of Information short film called *Mrs Smith Answers the Door* in which a resourceful Englishwoman finds an enemy paratrooper on her front step. She has already deflated the tyres of her bicycle and hidden the pump. The German is at a loss.

It was the *Gaumont-British News* which provoked the biggest reaction from the audience. The King and Queen, visiting war-wounded in a hospital, were clapped and Churchill was cheered violently. Then came some film of Hitler with Hermann Goering, his fat air-force commander, looking across the Channel from the French coast. A mass outcry of booing and hissing lifted from the audience. Goering was pointing across the Strait of Dover as if Hitler, with binoculars, might not know in which direction England lay.

Through the booing and hissing the servicemen began to sing lustily to the marching tune 'Colonel Bogey':

'Hitler 'as only got one ball,
Goering 'as two but very small,
Himmler's got something sim'lar,
But poor old Goebbels 'as no balls at all!'

When the main film began Rose settled back with Ardley's arm around her shoulders. They were wreathed in blue cigarette smoke and almost silence. Ardley waited for the opportunity to place his fingers on her breast beneath her woollen cardigan and she placed her fingers on top of them.

They walked, arms about each other's waists, to the bus stop. They kissed and then kissed again. 'Do you feel this is getting serious?' said Ardley close to her face.

'I think it is, a bit,' said Rose. The bus arrived and the conductor stood watching wryly.

'Goodnight, love,' said Ardley.

'Goodnight, love,' said Rose.

Rose got on to the platform. Ardley said: 'See you Saturday.' She smiled and waved and the bus drove away with her still waving. 'Bloody hell,' said Ardley to himself. He performed a brief jig on the pavement. 'I'm in bloody love.'

* * *

Twice he had been to the low house in the village hollow. On the first evening Spatchcock had poured him cider from a stone flagon and told him more about the Boer War. They sat each side of the September evening fire, low in the grate, while Rose was putting her horse to bed. She had come in grumbling from her patrol. 'We ride and we stop and we search the sky and not a solitary Hun,' she said. 'Maybe the rumours about them being invisible are right.'

'Churchill was a prisoner of Johnny Boer,' said Spatchcock. 'But he escaped. Some said he broke his parole, but I don't know. It wouldn't surprise me. He's never been somebody you can trust.'

'We're trusting him now,' pointed out Ardley.

Spatchcock scratched his big nose. 'He's a good actor and he can talk,' he said. 'He talks better than Hitler. And a lot slower.'

'There's plenty of hands helping with the harvest this year,' Rose said. 'Half the British army.'

'Keeps us occupied,' said Ardley. 'What else would we do? We march, we pretend to blow up bridges, we train as much as we can, but there's a limit. They're talking about roping me in to help a chap from the Education Corps to teach the men reading and writing. Most of them can add up. And he's giving them lectures on citizenship and suchlike.'

'Depends which country they're going to be citizens of,' said Rose.

They went from the house and walked towards the village but she did not tell him where they were going. She halted outside the village hall where they had met at the dance. Ardley could hear a vocal chorus sounding. Carefully Rose opened the door and put her finger to her lips. 'It's practice night,' she whispered.

There were a dozen women and four men, one

in fireman's uniform, another with a black eye patch, grouped around a big woman almost engulfing a piano stool as she pumped the keys. She stopped playing and everyone turned towards the open door. 'Sorry,' said Rose. 'I had to muck out.'

'Hope you've had a wash, girl!' exclaimed the man with the eye patch and everyone laughed.

Rose introduced Ardley. 'My friend,' she said. 'Who's in the army.'

'Unless he's in disguise,' said the one-eyed man.

The large woman rose from the piano and the stool creaked. 'I'm Polly Mason,' she said. 'This is our first autumn get-together, merely a tune-up. And one or two are missing. But in November we are going to put on a glorious Gilbert and Sullivan evening.'

She had water-filled blue eyes and she looked challengingly around the group before manoeuvring herself on to the wide piano stool again. 'Right,' she said brightly. 'Let's have some lung openers. Some really good singing.' Rose joined the end of the half-circle.

She thumped the keys resoundingly but just as the singers opened their mouths for 'Old Uncle Tom Cobbleigh and All' she stopped and turned like a fairground roundabout towards Ardley who had seated himself on a chair against the wall. 'Do you sing? Or play?'

Ardley stood and walked towards the group. 'I bang the piano a bit,' he said. 'We have one in the front room at home and we've sometimes had a Sunday night sing-song around it.'

'Oh, good, good,' enthused Polly. She lifted herself from the stool. 'You take over here, young man. This thing is going to collapse under me before long. I can feel it going.'

Ardley took her place. He was a good everyday piano player and he launched into 'On Ilkley Moor Baht 'At' and they quickly joined in, singing with spirit and some tune. Then Ardley played a chord and began to sing by himself, unselfconsciously, 'Rose of England'.

The village people fell to silence while he sang and applauded with surprise when he finished.

'How wonderful,' Polly's large face beamed. 'Perhaps you could join us in our Gilbert and Sullivan evening. November fourteenth.'

'I don't know where I'll be,' said Ardley truthfully. He glanced at Rose and saw how happily flushed she was. 'By that time I could be in Berlin.'

⋆ ⋆ ⋆

That Saturday the village dance was lively, only one of four dances throughout the Dover region, plus an Olde Tyme Ball at the town hall and an amateur talent contest at the British Legion. That day the German guns on the French coast had laid out a bombardment more prolonged than usual, but without improved accuracy. Every one of the high-explosive shells fired towards Dover fell well short of the town and even the projecting harbour. By six o'clock fishermen were scooping up hundreds of fish killed by the explosions and floating on the surface of the water waiting to be collected. Over the whole town that evening lay the aroma of fried cod and hake. With chips.

There was no air of desperation at the village dance, no urgent sense of having a carefree and abandoned time before it was too late. Instead there was a feeling of release, release from the working-class restrictions of pre-war days when only the wealthy could misbehave and get away with it. Now there were freedoms, often from wives, husbands and families, and there was some available money. Nobody very much cared what you did. Invasion, battles and death might occur next week.

The band, the Channel Swingers, had to be wedged in a corner because of the number of dancers. The caretaker had newly chalked the floor so that after the opening foxtrot shoes and boots appeared to have a light dusting of snow.

The bar was wedged in the opposite corner to the band. The squad had clubbed together for a pint of Guinness for Sergeant Dunphy. Ardley was dancing with Rose, and Sproston was sent to collect his contribution. He came back and said: 'You'd need a chisel to prize those two apart.'

Tugwell asked: 'Have you ever been married, sarge? Or thereabouts?'

'A few brushes,' admitted Dunphy. He looked as if he had trouble in remembering. 'There was a lady in India,' he said squeezing his eyes to assist the recall. 'Beauteous and aromatic. I went through some form of ceremony with her.'

'Was she . . . er, dusky, sarge?'

'Just a touch,' said Dunphy. 'Anglo-Indian,

and they're beautiful people. All of them. Name of Gloria. I don't know whether it was legally binding. It was more symbolic.'

Everyone joined in the novelty dances: the hokey-cokey, the Gay Gordons and the Dashing White Sergeant. Two bulging land-girls had a fight over a thin airman during the ladies' excuse-me waltz.

Ardley and Rose danced together all night, hardly an inch between them. 'Shall we go out?' she suggested. 'It's getting stifling in here.'

They eased the blackout blanket aside and, having let it drop into place again, opened the door and went out into the placid air. There was a wall behind the village hall. It was lined with embracing couples. 'Let's stroll up the hill,' Rose said. 'They'll bring down that wall.'

It was a short rise with a wooden seat at the top, near the dark church tower. They sat on the seat. 'How long do you think you'll be here?' asked Rose.

'In Dover? God knows.'

She looked prudently across the back of the bench. 'Nobody's listening,' she said. 'They tell you walls have ears, don't they, and so do hedges. Everybody thinks they know everything around here. They even thought they knew the date of the invasion.'

'All over the country they thought they did,' he said. 'We've been building bridges, when we're not digging trenches. Building them and pretending to blow them up. How long we're going to be pretending, I don't know. Maybe Jerry will make up our minds for us. If he comes, then he comes. If he doesn't, then God knows, we could be hanging about for years. Not that I mind.' Their arms encircled each other. 'I've met you.'

He waited, then said: 'Rose, will you marry me?'

Rose seem unsurprised. 'When?' she said. 'You'll have to ask Spatchcock.'

'I'll ask him,' said Ardley. 'What about next Saturday?'

⋆ ⋆ ⋆

On the day before the wedding an enemy shell exploded in the field next to the church killing a cow, wounding another, and sending the rest of the small herd in a headlong panic over the crumbling churchyard wall and through the graves. They were rounded up cowering and ululating under the roof of the lychgate. That night a homeward-bound Dornier dropped two spare bombs into an orchard not far from the village, bringing all the apples down at once.

'I was assured that this was a safe parish,' complained the vicar to Spatchcock. He was new and nervous. 'Out of range of the guns and of no interest to the Luftwaffe.'

'Been quiet enough up to now,' said the old man. 'They never tried to bomb the Reverend Hodgekinson.'

'Well, I'm not the Reverend Hodgekinson, I am the Reverend Kenneth Hands,' said the peeved vicar. 'I'm from Worcester and I'm too close to the Germans for my liking.'

‘I saw your name in the paper,’ Spatchcock assured him. ‘Give it time. The Huns might go away.’

They were standing at the vicarage gate. ‘And look at the churchyard,’ complained the priest. ‘All churned up by those mad cows.’

‘Turned old Bertie Shanks’s grave right over. Never thought I’d see him again.’

⋆ ⋆ ⋆

Rose’s bridal gown was white silk. Ten days before it had been a parachute supporting a Messerschmitt pilot on his long drop to the ground. The German manufacturer’s number was still on the hem. The village women had used a pattern from *Home Notes* magazine, cut it out and sewn it within a week. Rose tried it on only on the morning of the wedding. It was, she said, perfect.

Spatchcock produced her mother’s bridal veil. ‘I kept it when she went,’ he told Sergeant Dunphy in the church.

‘Now that’s a nice thing,’ said Dunphy. ‘If only she could come back and see it.’

The vicar’s florid face still betrayed his pessimism. His gasmask case was slung across his vestments and his steel helmet was looped on his shoulder. He approved of special licences even less than he approved of enemy action. ‘The Church has ordained that the banns should be called for three weeks before the ceremony,’ he intoned. ‘But in these troubled and dangerous times this has been changed, not necessarily for the better. Today the bride and groom have given less than a week's notice to the Church and to God. I must therefore ask this congregation if there is anyone present who knows just cause or impediment why these two people should not be joined together in holy matrimony. Speak now or for ever hold your peace.'

The only sound in the ancient church was the brushing of the trees outside and the mooing of the cows apprehensive in their new field.

The Reverend Hands was not comfortable. He stumbled through the service and Rose, kneeling beside Ardley, whispered: 'He's windy.'

Then as Dover's siren howled distantly, the vicar stiffened. 'The air-raid warning has sounded,' he announced unnecessarily. 'Enemy action is imminent.'

A distraught voice came from the church door. It was the new clergyman's wife wrapped in an oriental shawl. 'They're coming!' she bellowed. 'The bombers are on the way!'

It was all the priest needed. 'To the crypt!' he exclaimed waving his arms at the full congregation. 'We will continue the service in the crypt.' He placed and adjusted his steel helmet firmly above his pink face and went at a trot up the aisle. The astonished parishioners watched him exit. They went out into the pale and locally peaceful afternoon and then filed into the dark space of the crypt. An embarrassed verger lit two oil lamps and the vicar stood between them spectrally, his shadows crossing. It was more crowded than it had been for three centuries.

‘What’s in them boxes, sarge?’ whispered Sproston.

‘Dead bodies,’ answered Dunphy. ‘Old ones. Have yer never been in a crypt before?’

‘One is moving,’ muttered Jenkins. ‘I can see it.’

The vicar was incanting the service. Rose whispered to Ardley as they knelt: ‘Not many people have a wedding like this.’

‘I bet,’ he said.

Jenkins persisted. ‘There’s something moving. Behind them coffins.’

A shadow materialised. Jenkins gave a moan. A black cat slid between the old caskets, pushing through the cobwebs. ‘They’ve even got the well-known cat in the crypt,’ said Dunphy. ‘Who crapped and crept out again.’

* * *

‘You looked beautiful in your dress, Rose,’ Ardley told her.

‘Good stuff this parachute silk,’ she smiled. ‘You looked pretty smart too. Even down in that crypt I could see the toes of your boots shining.’

They were in the village hall. There was the aroma of a large side of beef being roasted on a spit. The cow killed by the bomb had been a touch of fortune. The Ministry of Agriculture inspector would not arrive for several days.

There were sixty people in the hall. A man had come along and offered to play the spoons and another had his handbells; rung fully they were used as a warning of a poison-gas attack, so he played them softly.

'The sergeant polished my boots,' said Ardley to Rose. 'All the boys mucked in. They pressed my uniform. It could stand up by itself.' He fingered the creases on the sleeve saying: 'You could cut your finger on that.' She felt the crease carefully. 'And they polished my cap badge and my brasses and blancoed my belt. Welshy even scrubbed up my ammunition pouches. Who wears ammo pouches at his wedding?'

Rose said: 'Let me have a smell of your toecaps.' Ardley lifted the boot and she put her nose close to it. 'Smells like something I know. When my horse has a pee.'

Ardley laughed and lowered the boot. 'You could be right. Something Dunphy learned in India. Spit and urine.'

Spatchcock came across the room. 'You looked better than your mother did,' he said reflectively. 'Mind, it was a long time ago.'

Rose was suddenly forlorn. 'She would have liked to have been here today, wouldn't she, Dad.' She turned to Ardley. 'I hardly remember her. I was only five when she died.'

Spatchcock said: 'She's not dead.'

Rose almost fell from her chair. 'Not . . . not dead? But you've always told me . . . '

The old man was scarcely embarrassed. 'Well, I had to say something to explain why she wasn't here,' he said. 'It seemed easier . . . more straightforward.'

Rose put her face forward into her hands as though she were crying. 'My God,' she said lifting her head. She was laughing. 'My father!' She looked directly at Spatchcock. 'Well, if she's still alive, where is she?'

'Don't know,' he shrugged. 'She went off with some motor dealer, years and years ago, to . . . what's that place that sounds so wild . . . ?'

'Timbuktu,' suggested Rose. Now she had tears on her cheeks.

Her father said: 'No, not as far as that. In this country . . . in England . . . It's called . . . Leighton Buzzard, that's right, Leighton Buzzard.'

One of the village girls brought over a tray with filled wineglasses, red and white. They each took a glass. The old man seemed to think some further explanation was needed. 'She went off with this chap in a Daimler . . . it wasn't his, he was just selling it. But she left that headdress behind and I hid it. I'm glad I did. It suits you, Rosie.' And he kissed her.

* * *

At ten o'clock the truck arrived to pick up the soldiers. They were full of beer and beef and Sergeant Dunphy had to be helped up over the tailboard. It had been a glad occasion. There had been dancing to piano music with the rhythm of spoons and hushed handbells. Everyone agreed that they were unlikely to enjoy a meal so much until the end of the war. Spatchcock made a speech which few understood and then slipped slowly but spectacularly beneath the table taking the cloth and everything that was on it with him. Ardley played the piano and they sang.

Between them the bride and groom helped Spatchcock to his bed. 'Now,' said Rose. 'I'll show you our wedding bed.'

She took him by the hand and led him out of the house. 'We're not sleeping with the horse,' he said.

They held each other in a full and happy embrace in the night-time farmyard while the clouds moved heavily overhead. Somewhere an aeroplane groaned but it was far distant. 'I've moved Pomerse to the far corner,' she said as she began to open the barn door. 'And it's all warm and clean. I cleaned it up myself.'

He helped to open the door and they closed it behind them. There was a candle in a jam jar on a shelf behind the door and Rose lit it. The glow filled her face. 'There,' she said. 'Our marriage bed.'

They walked tenderly towards it, a mattress laid on straw in one of the stalls. It had white sheets and pillows with two blankets folded at the foot of the bed. They undressed and lay on the bed with the jam pot still gleaming and making great shadows in the roof of the barn.

'Nobody's ever had a wedding day like mine,' whispered Rose.

Ardley said: 'Except me.'

11

Said the sailor to the soldier: 'After this war's over you'll be able to go to the doctor, or have him come to your house, for *nothing*. Not a penny. No more saving up two and a tanner to go to him if you're poorly. Hospitals, everything, will be free.'

Said the soldier: 'I'll believe that when it happens, mate. Where's all the money going to come from?'

'The government pays. And rich people. Every bandage, every bit of cotton wool if you've cut yourself bleedin' shaving. All free.'

'I've heard promises before. Plenty of 'em.'

'Oh, you might have to pay summat. A shilling a month or summat. And there'll be proper pensions as well for everybody. Not some measly ten bob a week and the means test.'

Giselle came into the bar and looked to the side where the RAF crews congregated. No one was there but an air-raid warden in an oilskin gazing deep below the surface of his beer.

She went immediately to the sailor and the soldier. 'Where are they gone?' she asked. 'The air-force boys.'

'Spent their pocket money, I expect, love,' said the soldier. 'Want a drink?'

'Thank you, no.' She stared about the bar again as if someone had performed a trick. 'All gone,' she said.

The sailor said: ‘I bet they’ve moved them. Out of harm’s way.’

‘But where?’

‘God only knows, dear. And if you go around asking in that foreign accent they’ll arrest you for a spy.’

The barman, greasy-faced from the cellars, came from the door at the back. Giselle turned to him. ‘I’m looking for Toby . . . Toby Hendry the airman. He is usually here with the others.’

‘They’ve vanished.’ He hunched his shoulders. ‘Done a flit somewhere. The planes flew off this morning. I heard them, one after the other.’

She looked at the faces of the men, turned decisively and left walking briskly towards the bus stop. It was still early evening. Ten minutes later she was on the bus. She got off at the stop by the RAF station. ‘All flown the roost,’ said the conductor as she was about to leave the platform. ‘Gone with the wind.’

The gate of the airfield was closed, and the field behind was unoccupied, now just a field. Hung on the gate was an Air Ministry warning to trespassers, but the sentry post was unoccupied. She walked in. The airfield was ghostly, a wind parting the grass, the huts and buildings standing dumb. A metal door banged repeatedly. There was only one aeroplane to be seen and that was nose up at the end of the runway. She walked to it and called: ‘Toby,’ up to the empty cockpit but softly, not expecting a response.

Sadly she turned and walked slowly towards the buildings. A door opened and two RAF officers came out. They saw her immediately. She went towards them. 'Where is everybody gone, please?' she asked.

'Who would like to know?' enquired the senior of the two men.

'I am Giselle Plaisance . . . Giselle . . . from the Marine Hotel.'

'Yes, I recognise you.'

'I am the friend of Toby Hendry.'

'I know that too,' he said. He pushed open the door behind him. 'Come in and sit down.'

His tone gave her a heavy heart. She followed. The room was bare except for a scarred desk and two chairs. The officer motioned her to take one. He sat behind the desk and the second officer said from the door: 'I'll make myself scarce.'

When he had gone the senior officer said: 'I'm Squadron Leader Gidman. I'm locking the place up.' He moved his hands about. 'It's odd to have an empty desk.'

'What has happened to Toby?' she asked directly.

'Missing,' he said miserably. 'Missing in action. He could be a prisoner.'

Giselle continued to regard him steadily. 'But you think he's dead.'

'No, no. There's always hope. But he was operating with another squadron, bombers, and nobody saw him go down, no sighting of a parachute. If he'd been with his chums they would have followed him down and we would know. But bombers are not so manoeuvrable. And they didn't know him.'

'I cannot believe it,' she said, stone-faced.

He sat embarrassed behind the desk until he thought of something to say. 'His mother is his next of kin and she's quite cheerful about it. She says he's had good luck all his life. Something about a motorbike crash when he was seventeen.'

'This is an aeroplane crash,' said Giselle.

'I know, I know.' He decided to tell her. 'We are moving to a new air station in Essex. Hitler is going to start bombing London in earnest and we need to be on the spot.' He looked up. 'Toby's car is in the workshop hangar,' he said. 'I was wondering what to do with it. I can't see his mother coming down to collect it.'

'I will take it,' said Giselle quietly. 'I can put it in the hotel garage. There is not much in there. I can look after it for him. Until he comes back.'

The officer seemed relieved. He stood. 'I'll show you,' he said. 'And I'll get somebody to drive it down there.' Giselle went out in front of him. He pointed towards the upturned plane at the end of the runway and tried a joke. 'Wouldn't like to take the pranged Hurricane, would you?'

Giselle smiled wanly. 'There is not enough room in the garage,' she said.

'We've got to get it taken away. The army are coming in here and they moan like fury if we leave any litter.'

He was talking for the sake of it. He led her to the workshop and opened the door with a key. 'There,' he said. 'In the corner.'

'I see it,' she said. The place was otherwise empty and the car stood in a patch of light coming through a grimed window. They walked to it and she touched the driver's seat. 'I cannot drive,' she said. 'So if you can make that arrangement I would be grateful. If you will give me the number, I will telephone Toby's mother and tell her I have the car.' She turned and gravely shook his hand. 'I must go. My bus is due.'

'I hope to have better news soon,' he said. 'I will have to tell Mrs Hendry first, of course.'

'She will tell me,' said Giselle. 'I am sure.'

* * *

A pink-cheeked RAF corporal brought the car to the hotel the following morning and Charlie opened the doors to the garage. 'Handy little runner that,' said the airman to Giselle when he had the vehicle parked in a dim corner. There was only one other car in the wide gloomy space, a Rolls-Royce with a sepulchral sheet over it.

'That's not bad either,' he laughed picking the edge of the covering from the Rolls-Royce. 'Whose is that?'

'Mussolini's,' said Charlie his face unmoving. 'Left it here last time he stayed.'

The airman gave him a joking push and let the sheet drop back into place. He nodded at Toby's Austin Seven. 'It'll be after the war till that's on the road again. Who knows, we might all have to drive ruddy Kraut cars by then.' He saw the expression on Giselle's face and added: 'But I don't reckon so. I can't see anybody in this country driving a German car.'

When he had gone and Charlie had followed

him Giselle stayed with the car. Tenderly she ran her hand over the door and polished the handle with her handkerchief. Then she opened the door and sat in the tight passenger seat. She leaned forward and closed her eyes. Please God, make him be safe.

She did not stay praying long. She went up to her desk in the lobby of the hotel and picked up the telephone. 'Fogmoor 235, please,' she said to the operator. 'I don't know where it is.'

'Nor me,' said the man. 'But it's not the worst one this week. Somebody wanted Dunkirk and I thought they was joking, naturally. But they wanted Dunkirk that's near Canterbury. There . . . Fogmoor's ringing for you.'

It rang for a minute before Toby's mother picked it up. She sounded so deep and formidable that Giselle almost replaced the receiver. 'Mrs Hendry?' she said instead. 'Toby's mother?'

There was a slight alteration in the voice at the other end, a touch of anxiety. She said: 'It is. Who is this speaking?'

'I am Giselle . . . I was . . . I am a friend of Toby. I work at the Marine Hotel in Dover. I have his little car here.' She paused. 'Is there any news?'

'Not yet, young lady,' said the older woman firmly. 'But I have alerted the Air Ministry. They will tell *me*. But I am quite sure he is safe. His father was posted as missing three times in the Great War and he turned up each time. Just like a bad penny, as they say.'

'I pray that Toby will be like a penny also.'

'Don't worry, I have the greatest confidence in him. You are French?'

'Yes.'

'Not Belgian or anything like that? Worse still, Flemish.'

'No, I come from northern France. I can almost see my house from here on a clear day. My mother and father are still there.'

'I am sure they'll be quite all right, dear.'

'Yes, of course.'

'You say you have Toby's car.'

'Yes, it is in the hotel garage here. It is quite safe. The air force have moved to somewhere and they let me have the car to look after. I cannot drive but I can keep my eyes on it.'

'Well done. You sound a sensible gel. Not like some today. Flibbertigibbets.'

'No, I am not one of those.'

'Excellent . . . now what was your name?'

'Giselle. Giselle Plaisance.'

'What a nice name. The telephone number, please.'

Giselle told her and with an airy farewell Toby's mother rang off. Giselle sat staring across the lobby. Outside the door three boys were climbing on each other's backs. She thought they were the same boys as had been at the skating rink on the night she first met Toby. When they all skated together in the dark. The telephone rang, startling her.

'Marine Hotel. How can I help you?'

'By opening a bottle of champagne,' said Toby's mother triumphantly. 'I had scarcely put the phone back when it rang again. My friend at the Air Ministry. Toby is safe. He is unhurt and is a prisoner of war. They treat them well. Geneva Convention rules.'

'Thank God,' said Giselle deeply. She thought for a moment, then said: 'I can write to him and send him food parcels.'

'Yes, indeed. I told you, did I not? He will be home when this idiotic war is over.'

'I will wait.'

* * *

In the third week of September the tides, the winds and weather, and the ominous expectations all began to change. The soldiers remained in their trenches and emplacements and surveyed the ever-vacant sea. Some army units still only had enough ammunition to carry out sporadic fire for fifteen minutes. There were special church services in Dover at which the clergy prayed that the invasion would not come while the Home Guard prayed more fervently that it would.

The contrary sun had shone benignly to the end of one of the most perfect summers England had known. A military barber set up shop on the promenade below the swooping gulls and the troops lined up to have themselves shorn, watched with amusement by old soldiers who occupied the municipal benches. There had been a strong debate in the council chamber over whether those benches should remain in place, since they might provide resting places for attacking troops, but in the end nothing was done to remove them. Some of the retired men had their trousers decorously rolled up to the knee and others had knotted handkerchiefs shading their elderly heads. Their wives methodically shopped as they had always done and the shops closed for a punctual hour at lunch-time. A new rendezvous for afternoon tea and morning coffee had opened with the name of Front-Line Café.

German aircraft made hit-and-run raids on the town and the inhabitants instinctively found the nearest sheltering cave. There was also regular but random shelling from the French coast. Often the streets were filled with acrid smoke. A horse was killed in York Street and lay stiffly on its back with its legs in the air. A bomb demolished a wing of the Grand Hotel where the regularly visiting newspaper correspondents stayed. One American reporter, Guy Murchie of the *Chicago Tribune*, dropped three floors when the room disappeared under him, but he was unhurt. Because of the dispatches from him and others Dover had become famous throughout the United States and good wishes and food parcels were sent plus a surprise consignment of surplus First World War bandages.

In the evenings the formations of enemy bombers overflew the town, high in the pale sky, now heading for London. The roar went on beyond darkness, the raiders finding their way by moonlight reflected on the River Thames.

Along the coastal counties the military trained and exercised, fighting mock fights, blowing up imaginary buildings and bridges. Many troops had been divered to gather in the harvest and worked, bronzed and happy, among the corn, some of them town boys who had never stood in a field.

None of the thousand children who had not been evacuated from Dover went to school after the summer holidays; they ran wild in and about the caves. An attempt was made by the council to impose a bedtime on them: up to eight years, in their bunk in the cave by seven thirty, eight to ten years, eight thirty, all other children by nine thirty. The timetable was ignored.

Harold, Spots and Boot excelled in the freedom. They roamed the streets and meadows, and had secret dens in the woods, some of these shared with the military.

‘ ’Ere, what are you kids doing in our snipers’ nest?’

‘It’s not your snipers’ nest, it’s ours, mush,’ answered Harold.

‘Get out or I’ll ask our officer if I can shoot you.’

‘Bet you’d miss too.’

* * *

Some Dover inhabitants still felt that the artillery on both sides of the Channel were indulging in a game of tit for tat, firing at each other in turn. Winston Churchill was obliged to make a second visit to placate the Dover protesters. He wanted to know where the heavier guns he had ordered were.

‘They are not here, Prime Minister,’ an officer

informed him. 'The emplacements are prepared but the artillery has not arrived.' Churchill dictated a note to a secretary.

The Prime Minister, stumpy and pugnacious, inspected the bomb and shell destruction, cheered by people calling: 'Good old Winnie,' and waving Union Jacks from the pavement.

'You'd think he'd be a lot bigger,' said Doris Barker. 'He sounds bigger on the wireless.'

On the cliff tops the leader inspected trenches which had been specially dug for the visit; they had a limited view, no field of fire, but the ground was firm and mud-free for the Downing Street shoes. The soldiers occupying the trenches were up to their armpits in earth and their ankles in water.

The visit was not protracted. Lunch was served in the town hall where Churchill, never short of words or phrases, gave a speech that was both rousing and stirring.

Before he left, he was shown the two biggest guns on the Dover coast. 'They both have names, Prime Minister,' said the proud conducting officer. 'This one is called Winnie.'

'Splendid,' growled Churchill. 'It was not what I was called at my baptism, but I appreciate the tribute. And what's the other called?'

'That one, sir, is called Pooh.'

⋆ ⋆ ⋆

The first of the autumn gales came bounding up the Channel at the end of the month. The Straits were wreathed in rain. 'Perhaps he'll try it now we can't see him coming,' suggested Elphinstone. 'But I don't think so. He's missed the boat. If he ever intended to catch it.'

Instow was due on watch at eight. HMS *Carnforth* was unlikely to leave Dover in that weather and at six he went briefly ashore and walked, raincoat collar turned up in the squally street, to the theatre.

Molly was in a room off the foyer loading ice creams on to her tray. 'Last lot of Wallsies,' she said offering him one. 'Until the end of the war.'

He refused. 'I'm back on watch in an hour and a bit,' he said. 'Better keep sober.'

She laughed in her fruity way: 'It will be toffee apples next week, I bet, or that funny Spanish Root stuff, like wood tasting of liquorice. And they're talking of treacle on carrots. All that munching, they won't be able to hear a word from the stage.' She stopped suddenly and looked directly at him. 'You're on duty then?'

'Soon will be,' said Instow. He felt inside his tunic pocket. 'It's your birthday, isn't it?'

She said: 'How did you know?'

'You told me.'

'Big mouth I am. I'd never be any good as a spy.'

Quickly he glanced towards the door and kissed her on the cheek. 'I brought you a birthday card,' he said. 'It's a present as well.'

He handed the National Savings birthday card to her. Her face glowed. 'And I thought I wouldn't get a single one,' she said. She opened it and gasped softly. 'Five pounds!' She took the ice cream tray from around her neck and pressed herself to him and kissed him. 'What a kind man you are.'

'Well, you said you were saving for your future.'

★ ★ ★

At nine thirty that evening, with the storm in full gust, a message was brought to Instow on the bridge. He picked up the mouthpiece of the internal telephone. 'Sir, we've just received an order to prepare for sea.'

'Jesu,' grumbled Captain Elphinstone. 'In this lot? What's the excuse?'

Another slip was handed to Instow. 'It's just arrived, sir. There's a report of a submarine in the Goodwin Sands area. Something snagged the telegraph cable and the coastguard picked it up. And it's not one of ours.'

'Right, I'm on my way. Prepare for sea, Number Two. I'm sorry for anyone stuck on the Goodwins tonight, U-boat or not.'

Instow alerted the crew and they stumbled out on to the wet, windy deck and began their tasks. He felt the warm roar of the engines starting up. It would take thirty minutes to get under way. The captain appeared beside him. 'I was just settling down to listen to Arthur Askey,' he said. 'He makes me laugh, doesn't he you?'

'Very funny, sir,' said Instow seriously. 'Never miss him. *Davenport* is starting to move.'

'Her engines are not as clapped out as ours,' said Elphinstone. 'She'll get the glory, if there's any to be had.'

It was less than half an hour before they were casting off and heading for the barely discernible harbour entrance. The other destroyer had already passed through to the open sea. The Channel came to meet them, dark with white luminous edges, throwing itself powerfully against the outer breakwater and punching the hull of the block-ship at the other harbour entrance. Wind whistled as though through a funnel. 'It's no night to look for U-boats,' said Elphinstone. As if in response there came a deep, dull explosion, a depth-charge, followed by another.

Instow stood beside the captain on the bridge with the steersman and the gunnery officer, searching the smeary night through binoculars. There appeared the sudden shaft of a searchlight ahead. 'They may have dug him up,' said Elphinstone.

They could see by the beams lighting the sea ahead that there were four ships already searching. The single big searchlight continued to sweep the rough water. Another set of depthcharges rumbled and then flung the sea in massive spouts, leaping like sudden shadows in the night. 'If Fritz has got stuck on the Goodwins then nobody is going to tow him off,' muttered the captain. 'He'll have to get himself unstuck. His chums sank the lightship.'

'U-boat surfacing, sir,' said the gunnery officer quietly. He shouted an order down his voice tube: 'Prepare for action.'

'Not just yet, Guns,' Elphinstone corrected him. 'We're not going to plaster him while he's stuck on the sands. That *would* be unsporting.'

'Gun crews, stand down,' muttered the officer.

They slowed their engines. The other ships were in a circle two miles across. The searchlight gave another stab. 'There he is,' said Instow. It was almost a whisper. The conning tower of the U-boat was projecting above the waves. 'U-16,' said the captain. 'Like a rat in a trap.'

The gunnery officer glanced at him anxiously. The searchlight had the awash conning tower fixed in a circle of white light. 'Never seen a better target, sir,' he mentioned.

'I'm not in charge of this operation, Guns,' said the captain. 'The commander is, over there in *Davenport*. But if he's a sailor, and I know he is, he's not going to open fire on a defenceless vessel, even if it is a ruddy U-boat. Poor old Fritz is in enough trouble as it is.'

Instow said: 'Be nice to tow it into Dover in one piece.'

'What a prize,' breathed the captain. 'That *would* be a sight for a lot of sore eyes.'

The searchlight was joined by another. They pinned the conning tower at their apex. 'She's rolling,' said Elphinstone. 'Trying to get off the shoal. Some hopes. Odd situation. He can't get out, we can't get in or we'd be stuck too. And we can't open fire.'

'We could be here till Christmas,' said the gunnery officer adding: 'Sir.'

'Maybe Dover lifeboat . . . ' suggested Instow.

'They've been told to stay at home in their beds. They're not well disposed since the lightship incident. Even in daylight it's going to be an impossible job.' They watched and waited for another ten minutes. Then, in the white beam of the searchlights they saw a movement at the top of the U-boat's conning tower. 'They're abandoning ship. Or giving it a try,' said Elphinstone. 'Prepare the lifeboats.' Instow gave the order. Then the captain said: 'I don't intend to send them anywhere in this sea, but if those Jerries can get away just a few cable lengths there may be a chance of picking them up.' He sniffed: 'Although I doubt it.'

They watched. The wind screeched around the bridge and the sea rolled the ship. They kept their eyes on the submarine. There were figures moving on the conning tower. 'One, two, three, four, five,' counted the gunnery officer.

'And a boat,' added the captain. 'They're bringing out a collapsible. In this sea they'll be lucky if it doesn't collapse.'

The men on the submarine were attempting to launch the small white boat. Each time it was thrown up by the waves plunging across the shallow sandbank. The water was rising around the conning tower. The British watched their enemies make another attempt, and another. The Germans managed to right the small boat and ease it into the sea and they followed it, one after another, getting into the craft. Everything was lit by the searchlight. 'It's just like a stage play,' muttered Instow.

'I'm glad I'm not in it,' said the captain. As he spoke the white boat and its men were lifted by a long wave and swept right across the back of the barely submerged submarine. It turned over and the Germans could be seen briefly in the sea. 'God help them,' he muttered.

Now the U-boat was sinking fast. The water was halfway up the conning tower. No more figures appeared.

A lieutenant came to the bridge with a message: 'Type Two B. Launched 1936, thirty-eight crew.'

'Thank you, son,' said Elphinstone. There was silence on the bridge. Then he said: 'Don't like to see thirty-eight sailor men drown like that.'

Instow said: 'No, sir.'

'And she'd have made a nice prize. Pity.'

* * *

As a dull daylight spread across the choppy Channel the ship turned and made for Dover. They had searched but they knew there was little chance of seeing survivors.

Instow, his watch ended now, went to his cabin and was taking his sea boots off when a young midshipman knocked on his door. He was holding a letter. 'It came just before we sailed, sir,' he said. 'But what with all the excitement . . . '

He handed the letter over. Instow knew it was from his wife even before he saw the writing. It was her sort of grey envelope. The midshipman seemed reluctant to leave. 'That U-boat, sir,' he said. 'Will that go down as a kill to us? Or will we have to share it?'

Instow said: 'We'll have to share it with God, I suppose, son. It was God got the U-boat, not us.'

'Right, sir. Thank you, sir.' The boy went out. Instow sat looking at the envelope. He almost knew what she would say.

Dear Paul,

This war has kept us so far apart, and for months. I hardly know what you look like and I expect you have the same trouble remembering me.

One thing the war has done is to give people like us a chance to look at our lives and wonder where we are going — if anywhere.

Paul, I have met someone else and I am in love with him and I eventually want to marry him. He is Canadian, an army officer, and one day I want to go with him to Canada. So this will be the end of us.

I hope you understand.

Yours faithfully,

Roz.

He put the letter on his pillow and began to laugh without mirth. 'Faithfully,' he muttered.

12

The big windows of all the wards at the hospital were criss-crossed with wide adhesive tape to minimise the threat from glass should a bomb explode nearby. When it was sunny the rays shone through the diamond gaps and made kaleidoscope patterns over the walls and the counterpanes. Patients used the apertures as spyholes if they wanted to see what was happening in the town below.

There were twenty in the ground-floor men's ward: seventeen civilians suffering from common illnesses, two with injuries caused by enemy action, and one sailor boy, sixteen, with a round red face, who had fallen into the harbour and swallowed the water.

When the air-raid warning sounded it had no immediate effect on the men reading their newspapers in the lined-up beds; everyone was used to the undulating howl. But then came the hard impact of bombs and the deep din of aircraft. Several men left their sickbeds and peered through the spaces in the window tape.

'What is it, Mr Shadbolt?' called the young sailor apprehensively. 'What's going on?'

'Junkers,' replied Mr Shadbolt.

'Noisy bloody things,' said another patient.

'Is it time to get under the beds, Mr Dickens?' the boy asked the second man. The answer came from outside. A cracking explosion shook the hospital followed by a second which shattered the taped windows and made them billow inwards like sails on a ship. Every man tumbled under his bed, clutching at the floor, as another bomb sent violent vibrations through the boards and the dust rose in clouds. All the patients began coughing wildly and the boy sailor rolled from beneath his bed and staggered spluttering about in the middle of the room. One of the bedridden men called the lad over to him and began to pound the coughing boy on the back croaking: 'Nurse! Nurse!'

There were no more bombs. They heard the grunt of the planes receding. Two of the large windows were hanging by their tapes like ragged curtains and a third collapsed slowly inwards as the men edged from beneath the beds.

There were groans and splutterings. One man shouted: 'I've gone and piddled!'

All the men hooted wildly. The boy joined in.

The door opened and Nancy Cotton came in briskly followed by a nurse.

'Everyone all right?' she said. 'Anyone hurt?' She strode towards the boy.

'All right, Popeye?' she said.

'Bit of bomb dust that's all, sister.'

A doctor in a white coat came through the door and called Nancy over. 'The police station got a direct hit,' he said quietly.

She felt herself pale. 'Frank's on duty,' she said.

'We're sending two ambulances. You'd better go with them.'

She turned and hurried along the corridor

taking her cloak from its peg as she went. She could feel herself praying, telling herself to keep calm.

Outside the hospital was one ambulance with the door open opposite the driver. She climbed in. 'The other crew are gone,' said the driver. 'I thought you'd be coming. It got the full packet.'

'Perhaps Frank was out,' she said almost to herself. 'He's nearly always out somewhere.'

'We'll soon see, Sister,' said the driver. She heard the two other members of the crew climb in the back and slam the doors. 'We got no defence down 'ere. Nothing to stop them,' grumbled the driver. 'Where's the RAF? Defending London, that's where they are. Never mind about Dover.'

She sat upright and wordless. When they approached the police station her heart almost stopped. Smoke was hanging over it, a mound of wreckage and rubble. 'New only last year,' said the driver.

Nancy clambered from the ambulance. She had never seen a building so completely demolished. Even the Civil Defence rescue teams, the firemen and the air-raid wardens were standing around hopelessly staring. 'It's a job to know where to start,' said a man.

There was a confusion on the other side of the building and she hurried across, skirting the smoking pile. They were bringing out a figure from an aperture, calling for assistance. She ran towards them, conscious of the restrictions of her starched uniform. Someone was on a stretcher. 'Frank,' she mumbled. 'Frank.' It was not Frank.

But it was a dead body. Then another and another.

At the other side of the building there was a shout as the rescuers unearthed a different way in. She hurried there. They brought out a wounded woman, still in her canteen uniform, ragged and soiled. There was plenty of help. Anxious men were standing around waiting for victims. An ambulance crew took the woman away and another crew carried two more laden stretchers. The second was a policeman, barely recognisable, but conscious. She said: 'Do you know where Frank Cotton is?'

The man's eyes seemed amazed as if she had intruded on his nightmare. He shook his head. She was aware of all the people around her, now digging frantically, burrowing in to the rubble, panting, calling. 'Frank Cotton,' she kept asking. 'Anyone seen Sergeant Cotton?'

No one was paying attention. She resisted the strong temptation to shout. She hardly recognised anyone. Another stretcher would be carried away and she would hurry to see who it was. The ambulance crews came back from the hospital. No, they had not seen him in casualty. There were at least a dozen dead.

Nancy stood solitary in the sun. 'Oh, Frank,' she kept saying to herself. 'Frank.' She had always been so professionally capable but now she almost panicked with her indecision. She kept circling the rubble, no one stopping her in her nurse's uniform. The usual spectators were gathering and barriers were being erected. She felt she ought to try to help, but it all seemed as if it were nothing to do with her. She thought she was going to break down.

Then she saw a woman from the police station coming towards her, a woman she knew although she could not remember her name. She worked on the switchboard. 'I'd only just gone off duty,' she said. She was holding a steel police helmet. 'Is this your husband's?'

Nancy felt her fingers tremble as she reached out. Slowly she turned it over and saw 'Sgt. F. Cotton' on the inside rim. She folded herself over it, sobbing, trying to stop herself. 'Alf is going up your way,' said the woman. 'He'll give you a lift home. It's no good you waiting around here. It could be hours.'

An elderly man she did not know came from a few yards away and said: 'It's only a sidecar. But it's not far, is it.'

She hardly knew what she was about. There was no sense to it. She allowed herself to be led away from the destroyed building and, in her awkward uniform, helped into the sidecar. 'You might get some news if you go home,' said the woman closing the little door for her.

Nancy stared ahead. She had a feeling that she ought to be getting back to the hospital but then, inconsequently, she thought she ought to have a bath before she did. Perhaps someone would telephone at home. Alf started the spluttering motorcycle and set off with a jerk that threw her head back. There was no top on the sidecar and she felt the wind blowing at her. Lowering her head into her hands she wept. Alf stopped outside their house and she said to him: 'I don't know what I'm about.'

'A nice cup of tea will help,' said Alf. He guided her to the door but then, as if he wanted to leave her quickly, turned and got back aboard the motorbike. It roared in a cloud of smoke down the hill towards Dover. Trembling Nancy stood outside the door. Her hand was unsteady as she put her key in the lock and turned it. But the door was already unlocked. She walked stiffly into the house.

Her husband, covered in brown dirt, was sitting at the table and lifted his head as she came through the door.

* * *

'I swapped my tin hat with Bert Wallace,' said Frank. 'Weeks ago. Mine was too big and his was too small.'

Nancy held on to him and he put a gritty arm around her. He had walked out of the police station twenty seconds before the bomb had struck it. 'I woke up across the road,' he said. 'I came back here. I don't know why exactly. I got a lift.'

'So did I,' said Nancy. 'It's where we belong, I suppose. Those poor people.'

'Poor everybody,' he said. 'God knows how many. I'll have to go back down there soon.'

'And I'll have to go back to the hospital. You should come in, Frank, and see the doctor.'

Cotton said: 'I feel all right. Just shattered. I'll have a bath.'

'That's what I was going to do but I won't

have time. I'll run it for you. Then I ought to go.'

'How? I'd better get the car out.'

He went out of the cottage and took the small car from its shed. A sullen cloud of smoke was hanging above the town. Nancy came from the house. She had changed into a clean uniform. She got into the car and they drove silently down the hill into Dover. There were diversions around what had been the police station but they could see it from the end of the street, smoke rising from the rubble, vehicles and rescuers filling the scene. Still without saying anything Cotton followed the diversion signs and drove around the side streets. Some girls were playing hopscotch on the pavement, women were talking in the doorways, an old man walked his dog.

'Life goes on,' said Nancy.

'It's supposed to,' Cotton replied.

They kissed each other outside the hospital. An ambulance was following them up the slope. 'Take care,' she said as she got out of the car. 'I'll get home when I can.' She paused. 'I didn't leave the bath running, did I?'

He smiled. 'I hope not. We'll never get any help today.' He drove off, waving as he did so, then skirting the destroyed police station again and going up the hill. He put the car in its shed and went into the house. The telephone was ringing. He unhooked it from the wall and said: 'Frank Cotton.'

'Good,' said the man. 'Glad I've got you. Brian Morris, CID Folkestone, here. We've temporarily taken over your business. There's not much of your new station left, I gather.'

'It's a mound of rubble. We've had some deaths.'

'I heard. Sorry about that. And I'm sorry to bother you now, but on top of all this — you've got a murder.'

* * *

A detective sergeant from Folkestone was at the scene. 'My day off,' he grumbled to Cotton. 'They got me out of bed.' He held out a heavy hand: 'Don Breck.' Despite the closeness of the afternoon he was wearing a trench coat and a trilby hat. 'I hear you've had a bit of trouble today, at the nick.'

'A bit,' answered Cotton. He knew the man slightly and did not like him. 'It got a direct hit from a bomb. They're still digging people out.'

'Sounds nasty.'

'It is. Who's been murdered?'

'Some girl.' Breck pointed down the hill to the row of damaged and unoccupied houses. 'Found in one of these. We only got the guff a couple of hours ago. They switched it from Dover. Want to take a look?'

They walked down the damaged and weedy street. There was a uniformed policeman sitting on half a wall. He stood when he saw them. 'She's inside,' he said. 'Upstairs. 'Orrible.'

Breck stood aside and indicated that Cotton should go ahead of him. 'Your patch,' he said. He stood back a pace. 'Don't look too safe to me, this place.'

'I wouldn't touch anything, like the walls,' said

the police constable bringing up the rear. 'Don't bang your head or you could bring the whole house down, the whole street.'

'Got a torch?' Cotton asked him. The man handed it forward and Cotton went up the stairs into the dim room. There were crevices through which the afternoon sunbeams crept. She was lying white and naked on the bed with string tight around her neck. Her eyes were open and glassy. Her body was slightly to the left, her breasts were leaning that way and one hand was over her pubis. She looked stiff and cold. 'Christ,' said Cotton. 'You'd think there's been enough people dead for one day.'

'They're sending an ambulance, sergeant,' said the constable. 'But they're a bit on the busy side. I'm from Deal but I had some good mates at your station. Fishing and that.'

Cotton looked around but there was not much else to see. Her usherette's uniform was neatly folded on the chair at the bedside. 'Looks like she worked in one of the cinemas,' said Cotton. He went through the clothes. Her knickers were missing. Every time he paid attention to anything Breck followed suit.

'Only young,' the Folkestone man said with a hint of appreciation. 'No drawers. On the game, probably. Uniforms and that.'

'She might be . . . have been,' said Cotton. 'Part-time. This room looks as though it's been regularly used. There's a towel and some soap and some Player's Weights.'

'Well, she didn't come in here to smoke,' said Breck.

Cotton wished he would shut up. He edged around the bed. 'I don't recognise her,' he said.

Breck nodded. 'You get to know the tarts. And the bookies.'

They heard a vehicle outside and the toot of a horn. 'Ambulance,' said the constable.

'Tell him to pack up doing that,' said Breck. 'He'll bring the flamin' roof down on our heads.'

The man went out. Another vehicle sounded. 'The bloke to take the pictures,' called the officer who had gone to the ambulance.

'Send him in,' said Cotton.

'Carefully,' added Breck.

Cotton was still looking around. The other detective said: 'No need for me to be here now, is there. Like I said, it was my day off. I'm going to the pictures tonight. Abbott and Costello, my favourites.'

'No, you go ahead,' said Cotton relieved. 'Thanks. We were caught a bit on the hop.' Breck bent almost double to get out. The other men were talking cheerfully outside. Cotton sat on the end of the bed and looked at her dead, exposed young body. 'What a bloody world,' he said to himself.

* * *

Eight people, including Sergeant Wallace, had died in the bombing of the police station and ten more were injured. The dead included an old man who had been arrested for collecting illegal bets and was waiting to be charged.

Cotton sat at a teacher's desk in the school

which had been taken over as the police station. The only telephone was in a room down the corridor and a constable had been stationed there to answer it. Now the man poked his head around the classroom door. 'They've picked up a bloke on the murder, sarge,' he said. 'Asking after her at the Hippodrome. They're bringing him over. Navy, apparently.' He read from a slip of paper. 'Lieutenant Commander Paul Instow.'

Cotton sighed and said: 'Right.' They had already arrested a soldier.

A woman brought him a cup of tea. 'Not the facilities here,' she said. 'Not like that new kitchen at the police station.' She began to sniffle. 'I'll be glad when it's all over, the funerals and the like.'

'We've got to bear up,' he said inadequately. He thanked her and put the tea on the desk. The blackboard was covered with chalked swear-words. It irritated him. He picked up a duster and cleaned it. Some shapes were beyond the glass panes of the door and he turned to greet the new arrival.

'Sorry about this, lieutenant commander,' he said. 'But they had to bring you in. You're not under any suspicion. We already have a confession.'

They shook hands. 'Who was it?' sighed Instow. 'She didn't deserve that. Poor Molly.'

Cotton went to the desk and turned over some papers. 'A soldier. Went absent without leave and when they picked him up he blurted it all out.'

'What a bastard,' breathed Instow. 'She was only a girl, a nice girl. Decent in a special way.'

Cotton regarded him. He picked up a card from the pile of papers. 'Did you give her this?'

Instow reached out and touched it but did not take it. 'I did. It was her birthday and I gave it to her last week. At the Hippodrome.' He put his head in his hands. 'Why did he do it, this soldier?' He looked up.

'All the usual reasons,' said Cotton. 'Lost his head, he says.'

'Lost his head,' repeated Instow. 'And she lost her life.' He said again: 'Bastard.'

Cotton began: 'Was she regularly . . . ?'

'On the game? I suppose I can't deny it but it was just now and then. She was saving up for her future, she said. She had that room in the bombed house and I went there with her. I know I'm old enough to be her father and there's no excuse. She was good company and she wasn't . . . well, hard. I should be ashamed of myself. It just happened.'

Cotton regarded the naval officer. They were about the same age. 'Things do happen,' he said. 'More often than not these days.'

* * *

By the end of September the Channel weather began to fret and the British wondered what had gone wrong: day by day, night after night, they still watched and waited but there was no sign of invading Germans.

The sea had a blank expression, the land was untroubled; defence works, trenches, pillboxes, roadblocks had become part of the scenery.

There was only so much training an army could do, only so many exercises, only so many obstacles to be dug. The football games and cricket matches, the dances, and the gathering of a harvest provided occupation but there were no battles on the ground. Some people in the south began to feel a sense that was almost disappointment like a cast of characters, over-rehearsed, but with no sign of the curtain going up.

There was still activity in the air but now the bombers were flying high, so high their black crosses could not be distinguished, all heading for London and other places inland. In Dover there was still shelling but the diminished population, by instinct now, rarely strayed far from cover. There was usually a handy hole in the ground.

Military men began to eye the low horizon of France with speculation. If the enemy was disinclined to attack, why not attack the enemy? Churchill called for a new task force to strike at the kernel of Nazi Europe.

The reality was less dramatic. Even in the early summer of 1940 there had been attempts, verging on the amateur, to mount raids on the occupied coast which achieved nothing. The only casualty of one misadventure was to the officer commanding, who was wounded in the ear lobe. A raid on the Channel Islands was carried out from a submarine; a collapsible boat, purchased privately in Oxford Street, London, was assembled during the undersea voyage but was then found to be too large to unload through the conning tower. It had to be sawn in pieces and reassembled before entering the water. During this misbegotten muddle troops landed on the wrong island due to a navigation fault and one officer became wedged on a cliff and had to be rescued by the enemy. The tragic debacle of the raid on Dieppe with poor planning and unsuitable tanks, which resulted in mass casualties for the Canadian soldiers who were saddled with it, remained in the future.

In September 1940 there were rumours of a hardened Scottish unit, training for raids on the coast of Europe, which boasted its own bagpiper, a prospect viewed with deep concern by those whose lives depended on stealth and silence.

The prospective raiders, who with other formations became known as commandos, a term from the Boer War, were men selected for their toughness, bravery and resourcefulness and, to a man, they were volunteers.

* * *

'Volunteers,' pronounced Sergeant Dunphy. 'All volunteers.' Ardley, Sproston, Tugwell and Jenkins looked collectively surprised. The sergeant brought the order in his hand closer to his eyes. 'It says here. 'Volunteers'.' He sighed. 'In the army you never volunteer. For anything.'

They were on the parade-ground. It was drizzling. He stood them at ease. 'We didn't, sergeant,' said Ardley. 'None of us.'

Dunphy said: 'Well, somebody's volunteered for you, by the look of it.'

'Can we ask what we've volunteered for, sergeant?' ventured Jenkins nervously.

'It doesn't say,' said Dunphy staring at the order again but then looking up. 'But it requires special training. You're all going to Thorncliffe for an intensive course. And me as well. Three weeks. Maybe it's maypole dancing.' He paused. 'Anyway, somebody must love us. You've each been made up to lance-corporal. Ardley to corporal.' They cheered wildly. He stood smirking. 'And I'm promoted to staff sergeant. That's an extra twelve shillings.'

When he had dismissed them he said: 'See you in the NAAFI tonight. We'll have a drink in celebration.'

But as he strode away Dunphy guessed they were heading for trouble.

* * *

It was blackberry-picking time and, after such a summer of sun, the brambles were loaded. The three boys diverted from their normal patrol to gather and gorge on them. The patrols were, like those of the more adult and numerous army, becoming tedious. They gathered in Harold's air-raid shelter and made decreasingly enthusiastic plans. The usual time for the end of the holidays had gone by and there was no news of a resumption of lessons. Spots had even voiced the unthinkable: that school sometimes had its enjoyments. Harold had silenced him but Boot said nothing.

The best and fattest blackberries were to be

found on the sloping fields back from the cliffs and they climbed there, scrambling along the grass, harvesting the fruit, sitting down in the sun and eating the lush shiny berries, reminding themselves of their promises to take full jam jars home to their mothers.

Their route took them along the flank of the shelter-cave that was closest to the shore. The cavern was a favourite place to seek refuge because unfounded rumour had it that German guns on the French coast always overshot it, and it had suffered little damage apart from a fall of chalk and a burst water-pipe.

It was not a cave with which, for all their daily explorations, they were particularly familiar. It was inhabited by powerful women who worked in the war factories and in the dockyard. They had become almost an Amazon community with a reputation for aggression and for keeping intruders at a distance. They had captured a snoopy air-raid warden, stripped him, taken him to the harbour and thrown him in.

But the three boys saw no threat on this autumn morning as they harvested the blackberries. Some of the women had hung washing outside the entrance to the cave and they sniggered at the widespread knickers and big brassieres. There was no visible activity although they could hear voices echoing inside. The caves and tunnels were sometimes noisy with singing or laughter or fighting, the sounds floating above the town at night.

When they had easily filled the jam jars the trio turned down the slope and squatted, eating the blackberries, purpling their mouths and hands and looking towards France. It was clear that day, etched along the edge of the Channel; it seemed hardly out of touching distance. Harold put his jar on the grass and took out his catapult and a ball-bearing. He wound himself up and fired it into the air shouting: 'Take that, you Nazis!' The ball-bearing landed among some gorse down the slope. The other boys set aside their blackberries and took their catapults from beneath their shirts.

Boot fired first and the morning sun caught his missile as it flew. 'Take that for Warsaw!' he called.

Then Spots. His shot had a lower trajectory and had fallen before he could shout: 'And for Dunkirk!'

Harold looked a touch peeved, as he always did when the others thought of ideas first. He loaded his catapult again, deliberately, and fired it high and long. 'That's for . . . ' He faltered. He lowered the weapon and muttered: 'What's the bloody use.'

Below them was a single-track road, hardly more than a footpath, and they were surprised to see a military car approaching, going slowly and tilted by the incline of the land. Their interest increased when it stopped and three army officers got out of it. Two were French with distinctive flashes on their uniforms; the third was a Royal Engineers captain.

'This is about the best view at this time of day,' Cartwright said.

The French officers stood in the breezy

sunshine and looked towards their homeland. 'Calais,' said one. 'Poor Calais.'

Cartwright reached inside the car and the driver handed up a bulky pair of binoculars. It was only then that he saw the three boys. 'Hello, lads,' he called up the slope. 'What are you up to?'

'Eating black 'uns,' said Spots holding up his jam jar.

Harold scowled at him. 'Keeping watch,' he said pointing to France. 'Just in case they try something. The blackberries are just a cover.'

'I am from Poland,' Boot informed them stoutly. 'I want to kill Hitler.'

The men laughed. 'We also want that,' said one of the French officers.

Cartwright was focusing the binoculars. He wiped the lenses and handed them to the Frenchman nearest who, in deference to rank, handed them on to the other man. 'It's very clear,' said Cartwright. 'You can even see the town-hall clock.'

'It looks peaceful over there today,' said the Frenchman looking through the glasses. 'And very near. We could swim maybe.'

He handed the binoculars back to his compatriot who studied the distant coast. 'My uncle winds the clock,' he said to their surprise. The boys, standing in a line, got closer and listened intently. 'Every week,' said the man, 'he winds it. If things are okay then the clock is right; if they are so-so, then the clock is one minute fast. If times are bad then it is one minute slow.'

'And today?' asked Cartwright.

'It seems things are not so bad.'

They seemed suddenly aware of the riveted boys. 'Careless talk,' said Cartwright nodding towards the trio. 'You could get your uncle in trouble with the Germans.'

The Frenchman looked in a surprised way at the boys. 'These are Nazi spies?'

Harold was horrified. 'We're not spies!' he said. He turned to the others. 'Are we?'

'Nothing will go past our lips,' said Spots.

'We'd die first,' said Boot.

Again Harold looked aggrieved. 'Even under torture.'

Boot persisted: 'I am Polish. We are good at dying.'

All three officers laughed. The second Frenchman handed the binoculars to Harold and helped him to focus them on France. 'Cor!' he exclaimed. 'I can see the lot. I can see a Nazi lorry moving.'

Reluctantly Harold handed the glasses to Spots who was nudging him. Spots swept the coast then came back to the town. 'We could get over there,' he said. 'In a decent boat.'

He handed the glasses to Boot who kept them on the town then turned along the horizon. 'There are the roofs of the houses,' he said. 'We had a good house once.'

'We've got to be going, lads,' said Cartwright. 'Keep watch.'

'We will,' said Harold hurriedly before the others could speak.

'They will not come,' said one of the French

officers, reassuringly.

'The bastards cannot swim,' said the other.

* * *

The boys hurriedly finished the blackberries, so hurriedly that Spots pushed his face into a handful. Harold and Boot laughed. 'You got more spots now!' scoffed Harold and they rolled on the grass laughing.

''S not that soddin' funny,' Spots retorted. 'The doctor says they'll all be gone when I'm twelve.' Boot gave him a filthy handkerchief but he refused it. 'Don't want to get poisoned, mush,' he said. He picked some dandelion leaves and wiped his face with them.

Their encounter with the officers, especially the Frenchmen, had put a new purpose into their morning. Harold took a much-folded bicycling map from his pocket and spread it on the grass. It covered the coast from Folkestone to Deal. 'We've got to know *everywhere*,' he insisted as he always did when the map was unfolded. 'We've got to know every inch of ground. We've got to strike at the enemy and then like . . . melt away.'

As they crouched over the grubby map they heard a female sound, a laugh, then another, lighter. All three heads raised themselves. Harold put his finger to his lips. They stared about them. The scene was unchanged, grass and sky and sea. Then Spots pointed along the bank. A wisp of vapour was rising above the ground. Harold jerked his head sideways and they crawled in that direction. There was more female laughter.

It was fifty yards. They got there on their hands and knees and knew they were over the extremity of one of the cliffside caves. They crept to the top and saw two glass apertures, ventilation windows masked with hessian, now slightly open and emitting threads of steam. Eyes lit, Harold led the way. He lay on his skinny stomach and put his face close to the aperture, closely followed by Spots.

Down below was the shower room of the shelter. Boot crept alongside the other two and looked through the other open pane. His body stiffened.

The bare room was lightly wreathed in steam and in the steam were two naked young women, laughing and dancing on the wet floor. One was called Maisie Watkins — she lived in the same street as Harold and Spots — and they all knew the younger girl as Loopy Lovestock. She went to their school. The girls were streaming with steam and sweat. They were trying to dance the cancan.

'La . . . la, la, la, la . . . la, la . . . ' they sang kicking their bare legs high and throwing their hair back. The boys stared down at their glistening shoulders, exposed breasts and streaming stomachs. Spots edged Boot to one side so he could look too. None had ever seen such an erotic sight. The girls swung about and their steaming backsides were bent upwards. They stopped dancing through exhaustion but laughed and hugged each other. Harold's erection was digging into the loose ground and he shifted, sending a small shower of earth through the aperture in front of him. The two girls halted, transfixed. 'There's somebody up there,' said Maisie hoarsely.

'I can see 'is starin' eyes,' said Loopy.

'And another lot,' said Maisie. Both girls screamed and ran towards their towels.

Harold turned and ordered: 'Evacuate!' and the three boys scrambled to their feet and ran down the grass.

Voices bawled from below. 'Dirty sods! We know who you are! We'll tell the police!'

The trio kept running. After ten minutes they reached the bottom of Seaview Crescent and, not slowing, they scuttled up through the alleyway into Harold's back garden and down into the Anderson shelter. They pulled the curtain across and sat panting on the bottom bunks.

'That was good, wasn't it,' said Harold eventually.

'Both starkers,' said Spots rolling his eyes.

'What titties,' sighed Boot.

'Did I get a bonk-on,' said Harold.

'And me,' said Spots.

'I could 'ardly stand up,' said Boot. They all began to laugh.

Seriously Harold said: 'I liked that Maisie Watkins's big 'uns.'

Spots said: 'I liked Loopy's little ones.'

'I'll 'ave a really good wank tonight,' announced Harold.

The other pair stopped and turned, suddenly

serious, towards him. 'It sends you mad, you know,' said Boot solemnly.

'Turns your brains to milk,' confirmed Spots.

'That's bollocks,' said Harold. He studied the younger boys aloofly. 'If you've never had a wank,' he said, 'you 'aven't lived.'

* * *

Ardley caught the afternoon bus. The summer was dying on its feet; the sun had browned the fields and the trees on the country roads were golden topped, and they had begun to rattle. There was still no sign of the Germans.

'Can't understand it myself,' said a man with a shaking head on the top deck. 'It's like paying to watch a boxing match and one of the fighters don't turn up.' He appeared to think that Ardley, with his corporal's stripes, might have an answer. 'What do you think, soldier?' he asked almost belligerently. 'It's all been a bit of a let-down.'

Ardley said: 'All I know is it hasn't happened. There's still time. Maybe he's waiting for Christmas.'

The man gave him a withering glance. 'He won't come now,' he said. 'It's October.' It was odd how people referred to Hitler as if they knew him personally. Indicating that was his final word on the war situation the man stood up heavily and went down the curve of the stairs with a wave that might have been dismissive. Ardley did not care; he was eager to see his wife. The lanes looked different after a few weeks; the colours had changed and the sky between the trees had taken a different shade.

The bus driver stopped just short of the farm and waved to him as he clambered down with his pack. 'How's married life?' he asked opening his window. 'My missus did the flowers. The cows 'et them afterwards.'

Spatchcock was sitting on the old wooden chair in the sunny autumn garden, his shotgun handy. He squinted at Ardley coming through the gate and around the side of the farmhouse. 'Don't shoot, Spatchcock,' called Ardley. 'It's a friend.' He rounded the corner and shook the knotted hand. 'In fact, it's a relative.'

Spatchcock cackled. 'Is the war finished? Or have you deserted?'

'Forty-eight hours' leave,' said Ardley. 'Where's Rose?'

'Top field,' said Spatchcock pointing. 'Want a drink? She's got some up there if you can't wait to see her. She worries about you.'

Ardley laughed. 'She needn't do that. I'm quite safe in the army.'

'Safest place, probably,' said Spatchcock. He examined the sky. 'I reckon 'Itler's give up.'

Ardley dropped his pack in the kitchen and climbed the ragged track that led to the upper meadow. He could barely wait to see her, and when the land flattened out at the top he did. She was loading stooks of corn with half a dozen other land-army girls. He even recognised the horse now and it was mutual. From between the shafts Pomerse snorted as he saw him in the distance.

Rose stood and pushed her full, dark hair from

her face. She saw him and shouted delightedly. The other girls stopped working and waved. She ran to him and they embraced. Her body was hot from the work, sweat coated her cheeks. 'How long?' she asked at once. 'How long have you got?'

'Forty-eight.' He kissed her warm lips and her damp, brown face.

'I'm such a bloody mess,' she said. 'Why didn't you let me know?'

They put their arms around each other's waists and began to walk back to the working party. Again Pomerse snorted. Ardley went to him and patted his snout.

'Why?' asked Rose suddenly suspicious. 'Why did you get leave now? They're not sending you anywhere, are they?'

'It's a course. God knows what it's about. I don't. Sergeant Dunphy says it's probably maypole dancing.' He patted his new stripe.

'You're a corporal,' realised Rose. 'I'm Mrs Corporal Ardley!'

By now it was four o'clock. 'Look,' said Rose, 'we'll be finished here in an hour.' The field was mostly stubble with the corn stooks still to be loaded standing together like a small crowd. Again she looped her arm around Ardley's waist. 'You take a nap and I'll be done.'

He said: 'I could do with that. I'll stretch out here. Have you got a drink?'

'Cider,' answered one of the girls who had been watching them with affection. 'I've got some left. I'm not a guzzler like this lot.'

They all laughed. The sun was gentle and the

air still. Birds sounded in the hedges and the horse farted. The bottle was produced. 'I'm dry,' said Ardley unscrewing the top. 'Can I take it all?'

'Watch out, she's had a pee in it,' giggled one of the other land-girls.

The girl who had given the bottle pushed her. 'Would I do that?'

'I'll soon know,' said Ardley. Rose kissed him and he walked towards the side of the meadow. There were two bales of straw there, left as a lunch-time sitting place. He sat gratefully and drank half the bottle. It tasted all right. Then he stretched out in the sun, unbuttoning his heavy khaki battledress, and pushing his cap forward over his eyes. The warmth was good and he went to sleep.

* * *

He woke with Rose carefully pushing an ear of corn up his nostril. He smiled before he opened his eyes as he remembered where he was. The sun was lower, dusty and golden, and the shadows deeper. 'Wake up,' she whispered. 'I want your body.'

'You can have it,' he murmured. 'Any time.'

She eased herself beside him on the bales. 'I've even sent Pomerse home,' she said. They kissed deeply and he circled her with his arms. 'Unfortunately, I niff like a compost heap.' Her face was tanned, her cheeks red and her hair awry. 'We finished in record time,' she said. 'We'll probably get the Women's Land Army award for quickness.'

'Lie against me,' he said. 'Just lie there. I don't care if you niff.'

They held each other warmly. Then she said: 'Let's go to the pool.'

'Where's that?'

'Other side of the hill, where the stream comes down. It's not far.'

She helped him to his feet. 'Finished with the bottle?' she asked. She glanced mischievously at him. 'It *was* cider.' She undid the stopper and drank the rest. 'There,' she said.

Arms about each other they walked across the harvested field, the stubble crunching beneath their steps. A rabbit ran headlong and a startled pheasant dashed away. The countryside fell away around them, coloured and subdued, becoming misty at the edges. 'One day,' said Ardley, 'I won't have to go back.'

'One day,' she said sadly. 'This bastard war. We could just go back to the farm together.' She stopped at a thought. 'You *will* want to live here, won't you? I mean, it's never occurred to me. You might want us to go back to your own part of the country. I don't know.'

'I'll be happy here for the next hundred years,' he said. 'I'll have to learn about farming.'

She grinned. 'Spatchcock will teach you. He'd like that,' she said confidently. 'Not that he does much now.'

When they had reached the ridge he saw where they were going. Below them, like a scene in a fantasy, was a stream falling over a brief fall and into a pool that now reflected the bronze evening light.

Rose began to trot down the slope leaving him behind. As she went she began to peel off her clothes, her green pullover, her shirt and then her brimmed hat which she flung like a discus so that it whirled and fell accurately into the middle of the pool with a light splash. She turned towards him and threw off her brassiere. She stood in her rough land-army jodhpurs and her heavy shoes. Her neck was burned brown and so were her forearms, her breasts white as chalk, the nipples cherry-red. 'Come on, darling,' she called back to him. 'The water is lovely. It always is.'

In his bulky black army boots and cumbersome uniform he lumbered towards her. She waited until he was on the grass bank of the pool before she stripped away the rest of her clothes and her shoes, and jumped in feet first making a heavy splash and sending a moorhen squawking. Peeling off his clothes swiftly he stood as if to attention and then jumped in beside her, the water taking his breath away but then coolly engulfing him. They came up together, standing on the bottom, and held each other's nakedness. Rose put her hand down between his legs and pulled, laughing: 'Ding, dong!'

Up to their waists in the pool, with the small waterfall splashing behind them, and the stream running on its way, they embraced and nakedly kissed. 'We used to come here as kids,' she said. 'All through the summer. It was here I realised that boys and girls were made different.'

'When you were eighteen,' he joked. She

pushed him and he stumbled away. 'It's too shallow to swim,' she said. 'Not like when you're ten years old.'

They scarcely noticed the evening was closing around them. 'I'll only work half a day tomorrow,' she promised. 'I'm owed a lot of time. I'll work in the morning so you can have a lie-in. We've nearly finished, anyway.'

'What's next?' he asked.

'Sowing winter oats,' she said with a smirk. She clambered on to the bank. Her backside was firm as were the tops of her legs.

'You're beautifully made,' he called to her. 'Well put together.'

'I used to be a tub,' she said. 'A real fat thing. But all this wartime work has got rid of that. Can I dry myself on your shirt? The army won't mind, will they. I'll wash and iron it tonight.'

She climbed up the bank and instead of drying herself on the shirt, she spread it on the grass and lay back on it as if she were in luxury. There was a late skylark singing miles above. On his hands and knees he moved to her and putting his knees firmly on the shirt, closed his body with hers.

'What shall we call our first baby?' she asked while they lay together. The lark continued to chorus.

'What's the name of this stream?'

'Robertsbrook,' she said. 'Someone called Robert, or Roberts, must have owned the land years ago.' She realised what he meant. 'That's a good idea,' she said. 'I like the name Robert.'

'It could be a girl.'

'Roberta,' she said easily. He put his tongue against one of her nipples. 'Or something like that. Miranda, if you like. I don't really care at the moment.'

In her luxury she turned her head to one side and quickly whispered: 'We're being spied upon.'

Ardley turned. 'Pomerse,' he laughed uncertainly. The horse was observing them from the long crest of the meadow.

'Someone left the gate open,' said Rose.

'He's coming down!'

Rose sprung halfway up and grabbed at her shirt. 'Oh, God. He's never seen me without my clothes. He might not recognise us!'

Pomerse was gently increasing his trot and snorting as he descended the slope. 'He could do untold damage,' she said.

There was no time. Rose began shouting: 'Pomerse, Pomerse! It's us! It's me, Pomerse.'

The big horse neighed and pulled up ten yards away. It seemed to appreciate what had been going on and gave an ungainly but sprightly jump. Then it circled them daintily, loped over the stream and began drinking from the pool with long sucking noises.

13

Each time the dining-room windows of the Marine Hotel were replaced they were explosively blown out again. The room, in its semi-dark state, had put on a mysterious air, the windows boarded and blacked out with heavy curtains and electric light glimmering dolefully.

Cartwright chose a table from which he could see a segment of the foyer and hear Giselle's voice. Joseph Laurence, the onetime Giuseppe Laurenti, manager of the hotel, who now wore a small but bright Union Jack badge in his lapel, came from the foyer into the dining room and to Cartwright's table.

'Dining alone, sir?'

'My wife is a long way from here,' replied Cartwright.

'Like most men's wives,' said Joseph with a small touch of envy. 'I trust the fish was to your liking, sir.'

Cartwright said it had been.

'Came from the Channel only a few hours ago,' asserted Joseph. 'Courtesy of those German shells that fell short this afternoon.'

At the end of his dinner Cartwright remained until he was alone in the dining room. In his tunic pocket was a letter from Sarah. It had arrived from America that morning. He read it again with sadness. How long would it be before they met once more? She wrote that nothing seemed to have changed in the United States. She had. She felt like a stranger in her own country. The previous day he had passed the village where together they had signed the visitors' book in the church and he had gone in and looked at their names; almost as if to make sure they had been there, that it had happened. He doubted if they would ever see each other again. An ocean and a war were between them.

The two waiters, after eyeing him for half an hour, had given up and gone, and it was Giselle who came in to ask if there was anything further he would like.

'Would you have time for a talk?' he asked.

She was surprised: 'What type of talk?'

He smiled. 'A secret talk. Something of national importance. Tomorrow perhaps.'

She retained her calm demeanour. 'Of course,' she said. 'I can take the morning off tomorrow.'

'Good. I'm very grateful. My name is Robin Cartwright.'

She glanced at his rank. 'And you are a captain of the Royal Engineers.'

'So I am. I will call here for you at eleven. It will only take an hour. Perhaps the army may buy us some lunch.'

She grimaced. 'Not in the Marine Hotel,' she advised. 'Everybody knows me here. And the food is not getting better.'

He laughed and they shook hands. Hers was very slender. 'It sounds very exciting,' she said.

Cartwright said: 'It might be.'

* * *

When they were in the army staff car he said: 'I know you very well by sight. You have an RAF boyfriend, don't you?'

'Now he is a prisoner of the Germans. I will not see him until the war is ended. I have written three letters but there is none from him. He must wait and I must wait too.'

The journey was only a few minutes. She looked with curiosity from the window. They took the garrison road from the town to the castle on its abrupt hill. 'I have never been here,' she said. 'When I came it was all guarded.'

'You came with the troops from Dunkirk, didn't you.'

'You seem to know much about me.'

'A little. Bits and pieces.'

'Why do you want these bits and pieces? There is no trouble for me, I hope.'

'None at all.' She was wearing a pale dress with a short jacket, her fair hair deftly curled about her ears.

The car climbed the steep internal road until the driver called over his shoulder: 'We're here, sir.' They pulled up among the military vehicles on a square. There was an anti-aircraft gun against an ancient wall and two more nosing over the sea, their crews sitting around them playing cards or reading newspapers.

'This castle was built against the French?' asked Giselle.

'Among others,' said Cartwright. 'We've had a lot of enemies.'

'But nobody got here,' she said looking about

her. She laughed pleasingly. 'No French until me.'

'Some prisoners,' he joked. 'The trouble is getting out again.'

The sentry at a door into the thick wall let his eyes flick once towards the slim girl but swiftly switched them to the front again. They went beneath an ancient archway, Cartwright having to lower his head, and into a starkly lit chamber, wood-panelled but with white channels of chalk showing between the boards around the walls and across the ceiling. There were two desks with a spruce sergeant sitting at one and an ATS girl clattering an upright Underwood at the other. Giselle noted it was painted khaki. Why would they need to camouflage a typewriter?

The sergeant stood. Cartwright showed him a pass. 'You know where it is, sir,' said the sergeant. He took a moment to cast his glance at Giselle. 'Major-General Fisher is expecting you and the young lady.'

'It's a bit of a walk,' apologised Cartwright as they began down the tunnel in the opposite wall. 'But downhill, most of it.'

Giselle said: 'I am fit. I can run and swim.'

'You won't have to do that today.' He was trying not to get short of breath, leading the way through the deep passages under the glimmer of the bulkhead lights. The air was close. 'Are you nervous?' he called back.

'It is exciting, but I am not nervous. It is not every day I am nervous.'

It took ten minutes. Cartwright had to stop halfway under the pretence of consulting a wall chart. 'I should be fitter than I am,' he confessed. The tunnel eventually flattened out and led into another chamber, again lined with wood. Another sergeant sat at a khaki metal desk, rose and checked Cartwright's pass. 'General Fisher's in there, sir,' he said.

Major-General Philip Fisher was a short, firm man. Giselle wondered how someone so small could be a senior soldier. He was studying a wall map when they entered. Cartwright, who was still wearing his beret, saluted, and with a miniature smile Fisher came forward to shake Giselle's hand. She thought his hand was smaller than hers.

'It was very kind of you to come to see us, *mademoiselle*,' said the general. 'We don't have many of the fair sex down here.' The ATS secretary at her corner desk looked up sharply and Fisher saw her. 'As visitors, that is.' He rolled his eyes a little towards Cartwright, then said to the girl soldier: 'Thank you, Annie. You can take a few minutes now.'

The ATS girl stood and with the suspicion of a sulk left the cave. 'Being down here does them no good at all,' commented Fisher when the door had been shut. 'They get moody.'

There was a heavy door on the back wall and the senior officer moved briskly towards it. 'I should have offered you a chair, my dear,' he said over his shoulder. 'But I want to show you our view.'

He turned the brass handle and opened it letting in a hard, thin shaft of sunlight. When he pushed aside the second door it splashed across half the room. 'Come and see,' he invited.

Giselle moved forward and Cartwright followed her. They stepped on to an almost formal balcony in the flank of the cliff, like one in a country mansion, with a carved balustrade and figured coping. 'Nice, isn't it,' said Fisher tapping the stone. 'It's been here years, since Napoleonic times, I gather.'

Giselle said: 'Napoleon would have liked it.'

'Come and see,' invited Fisher with a wave of his hand. She stepped forward and saw the heavy binoculars mounted on a stand to one side of the veranda. 'See France, your homeland,' he invited theatrically. 'In close-up, as they say in the films.'

Cartwright moved forward with her. The Major-General was focusing the instrument. The French coast was spread clearly before them. 'There,' he said. 'You may need some small adjustment for your eyes. And they'll be at the correct level.' He gave a small laugh. 'If I can reach the eyepiece, anybody can.'

Giselle moved a little timidly and looked through the glasses. Startled, she stepped back before going close again. '*Mon Dieu*,' she said in a small voice. 'It is my house.'

* * *

'It's a bastard place, Thorncliffe,' said the driver of the platoon truck in a smug tone. 'Right on the edge, the weather comes straight off the sea. They reckon the rain tastes salty and they've had fish land plonk on the bastard barrack square.'

'Perhaps there'll be a late heatwave,' suggested

Dunphy with a sniff at the October air.

'You wouldn't want that either. All that bastard training, obstacles and running and that, you'd bastard fry.'

'Don't they fry the bastard fish? The fish that land on the bastard square?' asked Dunphy carefully.

The driver gave a wry snort. 'They ought to, staff. The grub's a bastard.'

It was the first time anyone had called Dunphy by his new rank. He had only the evening before sewn on the crown above his well-worn stripes.

Dunphy squinted to look through the window behind his neck. His four men were hunched in the back. 'Sounds more like a detention centre than a training camp,' he said.

The driver nodded unremittingly. 'Used to be a bastard glasshouse,' he said. 'And it's not much better now. At least if you end up going somewhere dangerous then it won't be so bad, will it.'

'Thanks,' said the staff sergeant. 'You've made me feel very much better.'

The driver grunted and said: 'Oh, it's not so bastard bad.'

As they drove so the rain began and thickened quickly. There were only military vehicles on the coastal road. Thorncliffe appeared like the backcloth to a melodrama, an elevated shadow, perched over the biting sea. 'There she is,' said the driver almost fondly. 'Home sweet bastard home.'

'Just get us there,' said Dunphy.

It was not the first time the man had ever been

cut short. 'I'll take it I have been bollocked?' he said.

'It's a bastard,' Dunphy grunted.

There was a portcullis gate, half-raised as if ready to be dropped at the first sign of an enemy. Two sentries stood, water channelling from their oilskins. They did not challenge the truck which the driver then took around the edge of the wide, wet parade-ground and parked alongside some bigger trucks. Dunphy got out and banged on the side of the canvas back. 'Come on, lads, we're here,' he called. 'Wherever it is.'

Ardley, Sproston, Tugwell and Jenkins groaned as they squeezed over the tailboard. They stretched their limbs. The staff sergeant was already looking around him with surprise. 'It's an Indian barracks,' he said. 'It's just like Meerut. Terrible place.'

The others stared through the rain at the roofs of the buildings, their wide verandas and arched doors. A dome would not have been out of place. A soaked Union Jack lolled against a flag mast.

'Built like Indian barracks,' confirmed the driver. 'Before the bastard war. They used the same plans. No money for the army then.' He had to have a moan. 'Just like now. It's a bastard.'

'All right,' said the staff sergeant to the four. They were all getting wet. 'Get your gear and form up under this roof. It was built for the monsoon.'

At the end of the building was a carved eastern door with 'Orderly Room' painted on a sign above it. He straightened his belt and beret and strode towards the door. They watched him go. 'What a pit,' whispered Sproston. 'What a bleedin' pit.'

In the distance, at the far side of the square, a platoon of troops in full kit and trailing rifles was marching at the double through the downpour. They could hear someone bawling at them. 'I'm not going to like this,' muttered Ardley.

'Let's go AWOL,' suggested Tugwell half-heartedly. 'Let's fuck off now.'

Jenkins said: 'It might be all right. They might have a nice NAAFI.'

* * *

The barrack room was dark and filthy. 'Not been used since right after Dunkirk, the very day,' said the corporal who had conducted them there. 'Three blokes bled to death in 'ere.'

He swept his hand around as if denying blame. 'It needs a bit of bullshit but at least there's bags of room.' He was tall and hard and looked as if he could be nasty. 'The assault platoons are in the Hindian barrack rooms which might have been all right in the 'eat of Hindia but are bloody draughty in Blighty.'

They were standing in dimness, a sort of internal dusk although it was still morning. He reached for a switch on the wooden wall and it came off the woodwork in his hand, the wires looping. It still worked. Three bare bulbs blinked to life at the far end of the room.

'Looks like you'll all 'ave to crowd in at that end of the billet,' the corporal said. 'Otherwise you won't be able to see to bull your kit. This CO is very keen on bullshitted kit even if you've been up to your arse all day in mud.'

He seemed to be searching for something optimistic to say. 'And the stove is that end, as you can see.' The four soldiers regarded a black boiler standing balefully. 'Bit of boot blacking on that and, if you can rummage up some wood, you could have a nice cheery fire.'

A nonchalant rat appeared and crossed the grim floor. It halted and stared at the men with abrupt consternation. The corporal moved with lightning swiftness, taking two steps and kicking the rat with his heavy boot and sending it against the stove. It lay on the concrete. 'Right you are then,' he said almost in the same breath. 'Any questions?'

The group stayed silent until Jenkins asked in his bright Welsh voice: 'What's the NAAFI like, corporal?'

There was no hesitation. ''Orrible, mate. They've even lost the table-tennis bat. It closes at nine anyway because there's nobody in there after that. Everybody's too shagged out. Off to their wanking chariots early. Not that they do much wanking either. Too knackered. Flat out by half past. One bloke got up and shaved when lights out sounded. He thought it was reveille.' He studied their faces ominously. 'That's funny, innit.'

They nodded miserably. 'We got a swimming pool,' he said. 'And you'll be spending a fair amount of time in it. It's not got any 'eat and it's filthy, just the same as the English Channel.'

'Corporal,' said Ardley with caution, 'do you know what we're going to do? I mean, when we go from here.'

'Don't you know, corporal?'

'No, corporal,' Ardley answered for them all.

'Well, I don't — nobody tells me. I 'spect some officer will tell you before you go.'

He considered his duty done and without another word turned and strode out into the rain. The four men sat despondently on the iron bedsteads.

'Christ,' said Sproston. 'I don't like the sound of this lot at all.'

'Nor me neither,' said Tugwell. 'Talk about being browned off.'

'Not even a decent NAAFI,' moaned Jenkins.

Ardley said: 'I can't swim.'

* * *

'You can't WHAT?' The dart eyes retreated into the puffed, professionally scarlet face. The voice drooped to an unbelieving whisper: 'You can't do *what*, corporal?'

'Swim. I can't swim. I never learned.'

The eyes widened as though a screw had been released.

'Corporal . . . what's your name? And number?'

'Ardley, sergeant-major . . . 1934682. Corporal Ardley.'

'Ardley.' The tone became soft, almost affectionately menacing. The four soldiers stood in a rank in front of the foulest swimming bath any of them had seen. The air was dank and the tiles around the walls ran with cold moisture. The men were wearing only baggy physical-training shorts. 'Ardley,' the sergeant-major repeated. 'And you can 'ardly swim!' He suddenly, madly, doubled up with coarse laughter.

'I can't swim *at all*, sir.'

The pointed eyes fell back into their slots. He pointed to his badges of rank. 'I am a warrant officer, class one, the top noncommissioned rank in the British army. But I'm called sergeant-major. Did you know that?'

'Yes, sir, I did, sir.'

'And I am addressed as 'sir'.'

'Yes, sir.'

'My name is Warrant-Officer Hunt, M. for Michael, Mike. And if I 'ear any of you giving me nicknames — like My Cunt, Mike 'Unt, get it? — 'is feet will not touch the ground.' He smiled unnervingly. 'We 'ad another Hunt 'ere,' he confided. 'Isaac 'Unt. And he was too.'

Only Sproston smiled but blankly. Jenkins did not understand.

Hunt regarded them caustically. 'By a long way I am probably the nastiest man in the British army, maybe the German army as well,' he said. 'Now, is there anybody else can't swim?'

The others shook their heads. 'No, *sir*!' bellowed Hunt.

'No, *sir*!' they shouted back. The shouts reverberated. Dunphy, wearing battledress, came into the building. His nose wrinkled at the smell. He strode to the group.

'This NCO can't swim,' Hunt said. He pointed to Ardley like an accusation. 'Is he needed?'

Ardley's eyes lit hopefully but Dunphy said: 'Essential, sergeant-major. He's the demolition-team leader.'

'And he can't swim. He can blow things up but he can't swim.'

'I didn't know that he couldn't, sir.'

'Nobody ever asked me, staff,' said Ardley to Dunphy.

Hunt wrinkled his forehead as if he were planning a battle. 'He's got to learn quick.'

Decisively he turned about and went through a door marked 'Latrines and Dressing Room', returning quickly clutching a huge pair of white-and-red, partly inflated water-wings. 'With these,' he beamed. The bulbous floats were rubber and they dangled like a dead body over his arm.

He held a foot pump in his right hand and quickly attached it to the water-wings. 'Found on the beach,' he said as he began to press with his foot. He spoke directly to Dunphy. 'I do a turn at the camp concerts,' he said. 'And I use this. Like a prop. The colonel loves it, pisses hisself.'

The white-and-red rubber balloons were soon inflated and he detached the pump. His bullying bluster had now calmed and he seemed to be enjoying himself. 'Right, lad,' he pointed to Ardley. 'Get 'em on.'

Ardley glanced at the others, then at Dunphy who gave him a nod. He struggled into the huge appendages and Jenkins stepped forward and helped him adjust the straps.

Hunt said: 'Stand to attention, corporal.'

Ardley did so, his back to the water.

'Swimming lesson number one,' barked the sergeant-major assuming his unpleasant tone. 'Enter the water.'

As he said it he gave Ardley a powerful push which sent him tumbling into the foul pool. The other soldiers stood dumbstruck. Ardley hit the green surface and plunged below it until the water-wings brought him up. He was spitting water and croaking. 'Well done, corporal!' cried Hunt. 'First-ruddyrate!'

Then the right side of the contraption let off a small fart and air began to emit. The helpless Ardley turned over in the water with his face half below the surface, his arms and legs splashing in panic.

'He's drowning!' shouted Jenkins. 'He's going to drown!'

To everyone's astonishment the small Welshman leaped into the pool and grasped Ardley. Sproston and Tugwell followed him, and Dunphy, in his uniform, went in with them. Hunt was shouting encouragement from the side, urging them on. 'Operate as a team!' he bellowed. 'Teamwork!'

He continued shouting but no one heard or cared. Between them they managed to get the big soldier to the side and lever him from the water. Dunphy climbed out first and began to drag Ardley's arms. He half-turned and said in his soft Irish voice: 'Could you lend a hand here, sir?'

The warrant-officer took a surprised step back but then, on a thought, went to Dunphy's aid. Between them and the men in the water they pulled Ardley clear and he lay on the cold edge of the pool, coughing water. The other men were doubled up, coughing, spitting and shivering.

Hunt said solidly: 'He'll never learn like that.'

Ardley sat up holding his ribs, his face angry. Then Jenkins said: '*I'll* teach him to swim. He taught me to read, he did. I'll teach him in no time.'

Hunt stared at the small man. The others did also. Hunt said: 'You're good at it, are you, Taffy?'

'Welsh schools champion, Cold Knap, Barry Island,' Jenkins said. Without adding to the statement he dived cleanly into the murky pool and while they all watched amazed he tore up the middle to the other end, performed a racing turn and ploughed his way back. He climbed from the water in one movement.

'All right,' said Hunt. 'You teach him.'

'But not in there, sir,' said Jenkins. He pointed accusingly at the bath. The water ran from his short, muscled torso. 'A week swallowing that muck and anybody would be in the fever hospital.'

'There's a pool at Maidstone,' said Hunt almost humbly. 'You could have transport there and back. But he's got to learn in ten days no matter how long it takes.'

Jenkins faced him. 'He'll learn. In ten days he'll be able to swim the Channel.'

Hunt looked thoughtful and said: 'He might have to.'

* * *

It was dusk when Dunphy marched towards the commanding officer's office; he went alone around the square, eyeing three distant platoons of soldiers still drilling. The harsh orders echoed through the dimness. He strode out smartly. You never knew who was watching. But for all his years in the army he had always thought marching by yourself seemed ridiculous.

'One of your men couldn't swim, I understand,' said the commanding officer mildly from behind his wooden desk. His name was Stelling and below his colonel's pips, crossing over his arm in an arc, was the word 'Commandos', the unit formed in June at Churchill's insistence for aggressive action on the Continent, from which the British had just fled in disarray. On the upper sleeve were the eagle, anchor and tommy-gun of Combined Operations. 'Why couldn't he swim?'

'He tells me they never asked at the basic training unit, Catterick Camp, sir,' said Dunphy. 'I've only been with these boys since they arrived in Dover. I should have enquired myself, I suppose, about the swimming, but all I was concerned about was that they knew how to handle explosives.'

'And he does?'

'Top class, sir. All the squad are, all four. One of them is teaching him to swim.'

'Good, excellent,' responded Stelling but

quietly. He looked weary. 'And you have to keep this particular squad together, that's essential?'

'They're a team, sir.' He was standing before the desk.

Stelling sighed and waved him towards a round leather chair. 'Sit down, staff. I'm played out. I need a drink, d'you want one?' Dunphy took off his beret and sat down. No officer had ever asked him to have a drink. 'I've got a drop of the Irish stuff here,' said the colonel. He opened a drawer and brought out two clouded tumblers, and then a half-empty bottle. He poured two drinks and they raised the glasses. 'Where are you from?' asked the officer.

'County Kerry, sir. Nearby Dingle.'

A brief smile touched Stelling's mouth. He took a drink. 'I know it well. When I was a boy we used to go down to the peninsula in the summer holidays. My father loved boats and islands. From the house we rented you could see the Great Blasket Island.'

Dunphy said: 'I've been across to the Blaskets many times, though not for a few years. When I was growing up the men would row me across in their currachs. I was always soaking wet.'

'Christ, I wish I were there now,' said Stelling sincerely. 'Just for the peace of the place.'

'It must be just the same, sir,' said the staff sergeant. 'The islands and the sea and the seabirds . . . '

'Shitting on your head,' said the officer.

'It's a long time for me,' said Dunphy. 'I don't have close family there any longer. I've been in the British army since 1932, in India and the Persian Gulf.'

'This dump ought to strike a chord then. Jesus, fancy having an Indian barracks here.'

They had finished their whiskey. Dunphy stood and Stelling said seriously: 'I've tried to make the NAAFI a bit more homely, if that is possible. I've indented for a gramophone and some records, dance music and so forth, and two table-tennis bats. Oh, and a ball.'

'I think that will be appreciated.' Dunphy hesitated. 'Do you mind if I make a request, sir?'

'Not at all, staff.'

'My lads are pretty fit. They've spent most of the last three months digging and drilling, or on exercises. But they're technicians. They're not assault troops. If one of them breaks an arm or a leg going over these obstacle courses here we'd have trouble doing our own job. It would be hard to operate. Each man depends on the others.'

'I realise that. You want us to cut out the rough stuff?'

'Parade-ground drill, physical training . . . swimming . . . are fine but charging over ropes and barrels and brick walls and dodging thunder-flashes, like your assault troops do, might put one of them out for good.'

'And then we're buggered.'

'Yes, sir.'

'If a commando breaks his neck there's always another to take his place, but not your lads.'

'As I say, they fit in together.'

Stelling stood. 'That's a reasonable suggestion, staff. As long as I don't find them loafing around the NAAFI listening to the gramophone.'

'They won't be doing that, sir. There's plenty of technical exercises.'

'Blowing things up. Maybe you could blow up the NAAFI.'

Dunphy decided to ask. 'I realise that everything is secret. But is there any notion what we're going to do? I think my boys would like to know.'

Stelling sniffed. 'So would I, staff. It's going to be an amphibious operation, that's for sure. And being in this country's situation, cornered, there's not many places it could be, although we could try and invade Norway again, I suppose. It didn't work last year, but we could give it another go — if we're completely mad. Other than that I haven't been informed. It will be a small job. The top brass will tell me when they're ready and then I'll tell you.'

'Thank you, sir. I appreciate it.'

'Staff, I'll tell you one thing. We're not going to Honolulu.'

Dunphy put on his beret and came to attention to salute. He went out into the dripping evening. The commandos were still drilling, their feet banging on the wet square. He went to the billet. Jenkins was on his bed reading the Bible. Ardley came from the latrines.

'It's a terrible place, sarge,' said Jenkins unconvincingly. 'Those council baths.'

Ardley said: 'A nightmare.'

'How are the swimming lessons?'

'I can do breast-stroke,' said Ardley. 'With only one leg on the bottom.'

Tugwell and Sproston came through the billet door, the rain running from their steel helmets. 'Christ, staff, we're done in,' puffed Tugwell. He saw that Jenkins was reading the Bible. 'What's that for, Welshy? Reckon you're going to die?'

'Easy to read, the Bible is,' said Jenkins. 'Most of it is short words. *Hath, hath not, unto, pass*.'

'What about *crucifixion*?' suggested Sproston. 'That's buggered you.'

'Not got that far yet. I'm still on the Book of Ex-o-dus.'

The two began to peel off their wet clothes. Tugwell asked them: 'Any crumpet at the baths?'

Dunphy interrupted: 'I've got some good news.'

'We're going home?' suggested Jenkins dropping the Bible on the floor.

'No. But I've persuaded the CO to cut out the assault courses in our case. It's all right for his commandos but we're technicians. Anyway, he agreed.'

'Christ, that's good,' said Sproston. 'Did he tell you anything else, staff? Like what we're on, what we're supposed to be doing?'

'I expect he knows but he says he doesn't,' said Dunphy. 'We're going somewhere. I'll tell you what my guess is.'

There was silence. Every face was on his. 'My guess is that it's right across the Channel. Us and those commandos. I reckon they want us to blow up those big Jerry guns.'

No one said anything. Slowly Jenkins picked up the Bible from the floor. Dunphy added: 'There was one other piece of good news. The colonel is getting a gramophone and some records for the NAAFI.'

'That's great,' sighed Ardley. 'That's bloody well great.'

* * *

At seven thirty on a chill morning Tugwell and Sproston were running on the spot, shivering in shorts and vests. Staff Sergeant Dunphy was in the misty distance going through a drill alongside a squad of commando non-commissioned officers. Ardley and Jenkins gratefully crept into the fifteen-hundredweight truck.

'Sod that for a game of soldiers,' muttered Jenkins surveying the parade-ground once they were in the back. 'Thank God you can't swim.'

They passed other squads as the driver headed for the gates. Rifle fire was echoing from a distant range. 'This place is busy,' suggested Ardley to the driver.

'Not so busy as the real thing, mate,' he replied.

The municipal baths in Maidstone were damp and run down but they entered happily. There was a café and they went in there and had a coffee and a cake each. 'Good skive,' said Jenkins. 'I can teach you in a week.'

'There's a telephone box outside,' muttered Ardley. 'I could ring Rose.'

'I'll go and get changed while you're at it,' said Jenkins. 'Don't be too long. There's a copper walking up and down. I've spotted 'im. Suspicious buggers, coppers.'

The telephone box was piled on three sides with sandbags and the door glass was crossed with safety tape, so if he lowered his head only a few inches he was invisible. He put two pennies in the slot and waited. Rose answered.

'Oh, darling . . . I was worried to death.'

'Sorry. They won't let us out of the camp and there's no phone box inside. I love you.'

'And I love you. When will I see you?'

'Don't know. We should be finished here in two weeks. It's just another army course. Something to keep us busy. And then we'll probably go back to Dover.'

'Thank God for that. I miss you. So does Pomerse. And Spatchcock. Please come back soon.'

'I managed to get to this phone,' he said. He paused: 'I'm leaning to swim, Rose.'

She half-shouted, half-laughed. 'Swim? Can't you swim?'

Trying not to sound offended, he said: 'Never learned. I was scared you were going to duck me in that pond the other day.'

'But you're learning now,' she said suspicion coming into her voice. 'Why? Why now?'

'You're supposed to be able to swim in the army. In case . . . well, it's a way to keep us occupied. I'm with Welshy. He's a champion swimmer and he's teaching me. It gets us out of camp. We've just had a coffee and a cake.'

He half-turned and saw a shadow outside the kiosk, an unmistakable shape with a domed helmet. 'I've got to go, love,' he said. Then his time was finished. 'The pips are going anyway.'

'Bye, darling,' she said before she was cut off. She meant to say: 'We're going to have a baby.' But there was no time.

* * *

He went back into the municipal baths. It seemed tropical after the October street. Jenkins was already in the water, swimming with an arrogant grace, strange in a little man. He was being watched by a thin ginger male and a group of schoolchildren.

Jenkins turned at the far end of the pool and cruised powerfully back to where Ardley was standing. 'All right? Did you get through?'

'Yes, I think I'll desert.'

'They'll only drag you back, boy. Put you in the bloody glasshouse. Get your togs off and let's get on with it.'

The thin ginger man shuffled towards them. He had crumpled clothes and a wan face. 'I hope you're not going to be taking up the whole swimming bath,' he said. 'This is booked for Maidstone Middle School. Ten until eleven.'

'This end is booked by the War Office,' answered Ardley before turning towards the dressing rooms.

'Yes, it is,' confirmed Jenkins from the water. 'Part of the struggle against the Nazis.'

'Oh, *that*,' sniffed, almost sneered, the man. 'In what cause, may I ask?'

'The army. You know, the brown jobs who are going to have to save your skin.'

The man took on a remote look. 'I don't agree

with armies,' he said.

'You'd probably agree with the German army,' said Jenkins. 'Argue with them and you're dead.'

'The children need to use this pool.'

'We need the shallow end for special anti-submarine exercises,' said the deadpan Jenkins. 'Keep your kids to the rest of it.'

'*They* can all swim,' the teacher said loftily. 'They eschew the shallow end.'

He shuffled away. 'What does 'eschew' mean when it's at home?' Jenkins asked Ardley when he returned.

'No idea,' said Ardley. He lowered himself into the mild water. 'Ask him.'

'I'm not asking that conchie cunt.' He climbed from the bath, went to a lifebelt lettered 'Maidstone Council' and took it from its hook on the wall. 'We'll use this today.' He dropped it into the water and followed it. 'Get your head and shoulders through the 'ole and we'll do the frog legs. Once we've got arms and legs right we'll try them together.'

The ginger teacher had gone into the changing room and reappeared in a pair of long bathing trunks. Two dozen schoolchildren, their noise amplified by the cavernous roof, came rushing to the side at the far end. 'Stop! Stop!' squeaked the schoolmaster whereupon half the children jumped into the pool. When he had eventually got their attention, he said: 'You must not go to the shallow end, because that man is learning to swim.'

'For his country!' Jenkins bawled back.

His vivid Welsh voice caused silence at the

other end of the baths. Then some of the children, twelve-year-olds with sagging woollen swimming costumes, advanced with curiosity towards the two soldiers. They watched as Ardley struggled through the water encased by the lifebelt.

One boy shouted: 'It's a hippopotamus! Look, it's a hippopotamus!'

The girls began to squeal and jump on the wet tiled side. They pointed and hooted as Ardley splashed haplessly to the other side. 'Hippo! Hippo!'

Jenkins climbed from the pool and steadily approached the teacher. 'Get these kids away or I'll bloody throw you in the water.' He reached and caught hold of the sparse red hairs on the man's chest.

What colour the teacher had ebbed away. 'Don't touch my hairs,' he said. 'I've been off sick.'

'Bollocks,' said Jenkins.

The children began to giggle. 'Class,' said the teacher in his strained voice, 'move to the other end of the baths. Leave these . . . warriors . . . alone.'

14

Some evenings were quite peaceful in Dover now, once the German bombers had groaned over on their nightly journeys inland. Sometimes, on their return course, they would rid themselves of unused bombs but most of these fell into the fields.

It was eight o'clock and the light was diminishing, the sea a pale, flat, grey, the air becoming edgy. Frank and Nancy Cotton walked up the lane towards their house. 'It's just like it used to be, like peacetime,' said Nancy holding on to his arm. 'Do you think the worse of it's over?'

'They still turn their guns on us when they feel like it,' he pointed out. 'Thank God they usually miss. Half the time they don't even hit *England*. We're stuck here for the winter, both sides, them and us. They won't get over the Channel now. Maybe they'll come in the spring.'

They turned the bend in the lane and saw a military car standing in front of their hillside house. 'They've come to get me,' joked Frank. 'They want me for the army.'

'You're too old,' she said. Then uncertainly: 'Aren't you, Frank?'

'A bit,' he said. 'I was last year.'

An officer and a civilian were standing by the car. 'I've got a sinking feeling,' said Nancy.

The men looked equally uneasy. They said

they would like to talk. Frank invited them into the house and they stood awkwardly while they introduced themselves: Major John Haines and Mr Percy Begrie, of Kent County Council, who had a bowler hat.

Nancy still had misgivings. She said: 'Would you like a cup of tea? We put the kettle on before we went out for our walk.'

'I think we should tell you why we've come,' said Begrie as if he thought the offer might be withdrawn. He tapped the crown of his bowler which he held before him.

He glanced at the officer who said: 'Yes, I'm afraid so.'

'Tell us,' said Cotton in his policeman's way.

'We are here to tell you that this house will have to come down.'

Nancy was pouring from the kettle into the teapot and she let the water run over the top. She jumped away. 'Come down from where?'

'From where it is at present,' said Begrie firmly. 'It must be demolished.'

'We need to put a heavy gun here,' said the major.

'Here?' said Cotton. 'Why here, for God's sake? This is our home.'

'It is an optimum site,' said Begrie. 'So the army tells us. You will be served with an order to quit.'

Nancy suddenly shouted. 'No! No! No!'

Both men looked startled. 'Everyone must make sacrifices in wartime,' said Begrie as if he had given everything.

'No,' repeated Nancy but more quietly. 'No,

no, no. If you demolish this house you'll have to demolish me with it.' She glared at them angrily. 'Don't you think we've had enough down here? Bombs and shells, people dying in the streets. Don't you think . . . ' She could not stop the tears.

'I understand your annoyance,' said Begrie. 'But . . . '

'Annoyance?' retorted Cotton but keeping himself under control. 'We're bloody furious. Why here? There's a hundred other places. There's enough guns perched up here at the moment. Every few days they fire. God knows if they ever hit anything.'

'We have to show caution in selecting targets,' said Haines uncomfortably. 'There are French civilians to consider.'

'What about considering the British civilians?' demanded Nancy.

Cotton said: 'From what I hear these guns can hardly reach France anyway.'

'That,' answered the officer pompously, 'is a military matter.'

Nancy had hidden her head in her hands. Begrie said: 'You will be compensated. In full, of course — after the war. And you will be provided with alternative accommodation.'

The army man said: 'These orders came right from the top. You will be aware that Winston Churchill came on a visit of inspection to Dover and he was not pleased with the way the guns were being deployed.'

'Bugger Churchill,' replied Cotton. He regarded them challengingly. 'You can tell him I said it if you like. Let them put me in the Tower.'

'Clear off,' said Nancy angrily. 'Go back where you came from, your offices. We'd get more consideration from the Germans. I thought we were fighting for freedom.' Her voice cracked. 'What kind of freedom is this?'

The two men left with mumbled goodnights, one behind the other, looking straight ahead. When they had gone Nancy wiped her eyes and made the tea. She stared at Cotton as she handed him his cup. 'What shall we do, Frank?'

'God knows,' he sighed. 'If they say we've got to go, we've got to go. It makes no difference to them what you're doing in the war.'

They held their cups as they went to the cottage door and stood in amazement. Over Dover the sky seemed to be on fire.

'The Huns have got a new secret weapon,' breathed Nancy. 'What next?'

* * *

There had been thunder lurking all day and that evening nineteen barrage balloons protecting Dover were struck by lightning.

'It's Hitler's secret weapon,' decided Harold. 'Look, they're all on fire. Come on, men!'

They ran, bare knees like pistons, through the streets towards their headquarters in the Anderson shelter, the balloons on fire in the sky above them as they ran. People rushed out of their houses. 'Five hundred quid each, they cost,' said a man crouching below his porch. 'We can't afford this war.'

As the balloons staggered down their cables clattered across the roofs and spread in the streets. It was as if Dover was being tied in a parcel of fire. The three boys jumped over the hawsers as they ran. Then a salvo of high-explosive shells were fired by the German guns across the Channel, encouraged by the red sky above Dover. As the boys ran up Seaview Crescent a shell exploded behind them bowling them over in the street. Harold's mother came to her door in her curlers and ran downhill shouting: 'Harold! Harold!'

Harold sat up propping himself on his hands. Spots had rolled into the gutter but pulled himself upright and squatted, shocked, on the kerb. Boot remained deathly still. 'They got him!' shouted Harold. Other people rushed into the street. 'They got Booty!'

A man knelt by the boy and carefully turned him over. 'There's a lot of blood,' he said.

'That's blackberries,' said Harold. 'He's been eating black 'uns.'

'This is blood,' insisted the man. 'In his head. I think he's copped it.'

Harold's mother and Spots both began to howl. Harold stood to attention and saluted. 'Get his mother,' called one of the dark, gathering crowd. Then Boot opened his eyes and said: 'Oh, my head hurts.'

* * *

Ardley viewed the far side of the swimming bath, ten yards away, as he might survey a distant shore. 'Do you think I can do it, Welshy?' he said.

'Easy,' said Jenkins. 'Take the ring off.'

Ardley had ceased being self-conscious about the lifebelt circling his middle. If the schoolchildren arrived to laugh, let them laugh. Now he pulled himself from it and again eyed the far side of the baths. 'It's not that far, is it,' he said unconvincingly.

'No distance at all,' encouraged Jenkins. 'And once you can do that, you can swim the length and then two lengths, then a mile. It's only a matter of staying afloat. Once you've got the confidence, boy, you'll do it.'

Ardley dropped into the pool, aromatic with chemicals at that early time in the morning. 'Before you try by yourself,' said Jenkins, 'I'll get in ahead of you and back away, holding the lifebelt out, a yard in front of your nose, and if you get in a panic you can grab on to it.'

Ardley said: 'I could put one foot on the bottom.'

'No, don't. When you're swimming somewhere, there might be no bottom. Just get hold of the ring if you need to.'

The squat Jenkins went into the pool and treading water like a turtle, held the lifebelt in front of him. Ardley launched himself clumsily on to his chest. He sank. His hands grasped for the lifebelt, he hung on to it and came choking to the surface, his feet seeking the bottom. 'Like an old woman,' said Jenkins.

'Sorry, Welshy . . . I'll do it next time.' He tried again with the same result.

Spluttering he hung on to the belt. 'Next time,' he said.

The next time he did it. He began spreading his arms on the surface of the water, extending and drawing in his legs. 'You're going!' exclaimed the Welshman in delight. 'You're bloody swimming, man!'

It was only three stokes before he floundered. 'It's a start,' encouraged Jenkins. 'And in only a couple of days, a few hours. That's good, bloody good.' Ardley retreated to the side of the bath again. 'If you think you can't breathe put your mouth on one side, just above the surface, and keep it out of the water.'

At the next attempt Ardley miraculously swam the width of the bath. He set out, his arms moving sideways, his legs extending and contracting, with Jenkins shouting: 'Big strokes, big strokes . . . that's it, man, big strokes.' Spitting water triumphantly he reached the far side. 'I did it!' he shouted in disbelief. 'Welshy, I can swim!'

Jenkins was joyful. 'You can! You did it! I taught you. Me! Now swim back. All the way.'

So engrossed were they that neither noticed the first influx of schoolchildren that morning. Six girls standing in an unspeaking clutch. Then, as Ardley made for the other side, they began to shout and cheer. 'Come on! Come on!' They jumped girlishly on the spot. Ardley scarcely noticed them. He struck out purposefully. He reached the far edge with the squeals of the schoolgirls filling the resounding baths.

'Take a breather,' said Jenkins. 'Then we'll try the length.'

As he said it he saw two red-capped military policemen enter at the far door. One pointed towards them and they strode forward on echoing boots, the girls moving nervously out of their way, and arrived at the edge of the pool where Ardley and Jenkins were sitting. They loomed over them. One was a sergeant and one a corporal. They surveyed the pair from beneath the sharply descending peaks of their caps. One consulted a pad. 'Corporal Ardley and Lance-Corporal Jenkins,' read the sergeant heavily.

'That's us, sergeant,' said Ardley.

'Is it trouble?' asked Jenkins carefully.

'Could be. We don't know. We just do as we're told. Orders. They want you back sharpish at Thorncliffe. Something's on.'

The pair hurried for the changing room. A woman teacher in a bulging swimming costume had joined the girls. 'Are they deserters?' she enquired of the MPs. 'Runaways?'

'Nah,' said the corporal. 'They're up for the Victoria Cross, missus.'

The military policemen had time for a cup of tea and a quick cake before Ardley and Jenkins reappeared. All four got into the army car outside and drove in twenty minutes to Thorncliffe. At the gate the sergeant of the guard pointed to a building at the edge of the parade square and said: 'Over there.'

They got out of the car and ran around the square to the hut, pulling up quickly as they entered the door. The room was already full with

Staff Sergeant Dunphy standing just inside and three officers sitting behind a table on a raised stage. There was a big map on a board behind them.

'Good,' murmured Dunphy. 'You got here.'

Colonel Stelling, who was in the middle of the table, looked up: 'Had a nice swim, chaps?' he asked amiably.

'Yes, sir, thank you, sir,' said Jenkins. 'We can both do it now.'

'Well done,' said Stelling genuinely. 'Let's hope you won't need to.'

Ardley and Jenkins moved to chairs at the back of the room, next to Tugwell and Sproston. 'This is it,' muttered Sproston keeping his head low as if under fire. There were two rows of chairs occupied by the commandos. From behind every man looked the same, square and still, with thick shoulders and a short haircut.

'Right, lads,' said Stelling. 'Now the bathing belles are back.' There was a slight rustle of laughter but nobody turned to look.

'My name, in case any of you don't know by now, is Colonel Stelling — Robert Stelling if you meet me after the war and wish to buy me a drink. You have been training here less time than intended but the show we're expected to put on apparently couldn't wait. Perhaps only the War Cabinet know and they haven't told me. Anyway, the objective remains the same and I know that we are prepared for it. It shouldn't take very long and we may get away with it. By next weekend you could all be on leave.' There was a slight cheer.

Stelling stood to the front of the stage like someone about to perform a turn. His voice, however, was formal and serious. 'This is an amphibious operation,' he said. 'A landing by a compact force — you, gentlemen — on the French mainland with the object of destroying, or short of that, disabling those big guns the Hun keeps discharging across the Channel. They haven't done much military damage because they are firing blind but they are annoying the population of Dover and, perhaps more to the point, annoying Mr Churchill.

'I intend to take a party of a dozen men ashore and advance about a mile to those guns where, we hope, our friends from the Royal Engineers will be able to blow the bastards up. Then we retire in good order to the boats.

'Reconnaissance suggests that despite the presence of the guns the Germans are not going about their defence duties particularly arduously. According to aerial photographs they took a month to dig a single trench. They obviously don't expect to be interrupted by an incursion from this side. I intend to show them how wrong they are.'

* * *

Cartwright picked up Giselle from the hotel at seven in the evening. 'This is becoming very exciting,' she said but doubtfully. 'A little mysterious.'

'They just want some more help from you,' said Cartwright.

'I am like a spy,' she laughed.
'The perfect spy.'
They drove to the entrance of the military caves and again went through the guards and tunnels. Beyond the final door was Major-General Fisher, standing like a small boy among other officers. There was a tray of sherry on the desk. The general seemed delighted to see her, like an uncle meeting a favourite pretty niece. He offered her a glass of sherry. 'We are pleased you have come,' he said as he handed it to her. 'Everybody was waiting for a drink.' He chortled at his own joke. An orderly appeared and took the tray around.

All the officers were army except for one in naval uniform. Instow studied the young Frenchwoman and wondered about her. He had difficulty in believing that he was there. Four days previously he had been ordered to report to a downcast-looking vessel tied up among the many in Dover harbour and to familiarise himself with it, to take her out to sea with her six crew and ascertain her capabilities. He was to be her temporary commander. Being a spare officer was an uncertain business. 'She's a crummy old ex-RAF thing,' said the officer who accompanied him into the Channel. 'But she floats and she turns to port and to starboard. And she's low in the water, so it's difficult to see her.'

Now he saw how increasingly uneasy the French girl was. She looked as if she were tempted to turn, make her excuses and leave. When she had almost finished her sherry and her small talk, the diminutive major-general took her by the hand, again as if he were her uncle, and led her to a table in a corner of the cavern. As they reached it a bank of lights was turned on.

Below them was a model of a section of coastline, a beach, rocks and gullies, a cliff and the immediate hinterland, paths and a road, and dwellings. She knew the place. She approached carefully. 'My father's house,' she pointed. 'It is exact.'

The general picked up a pointer. 'And you know this beach.'

'Of course,' Giselle echoed. 'All my life. I used to play on it.' She regarded him directly. She was a fraction taller than him. Some of the officers grinned. 'Why do you show me?' she asked.

Major-General Fisher did not answer the question. Instead he pointed. 'Do you know what this is? It's a sort of defile, a cutting in the rock.'

'Yes,' she whispered. 'It is a path. We used to say as children, it is a secret path. It goes to the top of the cliff. Then you can walk, or run maybe, to the small road that goes to my house.'

'There is a barn at your house.'

'That is correct.' She pointed. 'There it is.'

He sighed, the sigh of a man who was about to put all his cards on the table. 'Ma'm'selle,' he said. 'We need your help. It may be dangerous. But we need you to guide a group of soldiers from that beach up the concealed way to your house and then perhaps a little further. And we need to use the barn.' He paused as if uncertain whether he should say any more. Then he did:

'We are hoping for some local assistance, but we can't be sure.'

She stared at the model. 'Of course,' she said, her voice low. 'I will be able to see my mother and father again.'

There was an aching pause, then all the officers began to clap. Major-General Fisher looked surprised for a moment. Then he joined in. What could have been a sweet smile came on his small face. He hoped to God she would survive.

* * *

It was six in the morning and they could smell the breakfast as they left the chilly billet, the aroma of bacon drifting towards them in the seeping damp air. They hurried their first disgruntled pace, and arrived at the cookhouse to find the commandos resolutely piling their trays at the counter.

'We're always first at the action,' said one of them as Ardley and the others sat down with their hot plates. 'Especially at grub.'

'At least they give you a good breakfast here,' said Tugwell artlessly. He sliced into a fried egg and let the yolk run across the bacon.

'They 'ave to,' said the commando, half a sausage protruding from his mouth like a cigar. 'It's sort of a tradition with the cooks. Send you off full up to get fucking killed.'

Jenkins sniggered uncertainly. 'Makes you a bigger target with all this inside you.'

Ardley said: 'It's like before they hang you for

murder. You know, the condemned man ate a hearty breakfast.' He glanced at the commando as two others joined him. 'Is this going to be hairy?' he said.

''Airy as my balls,' said one of the new arrivals.

The first commando was not sure. 'We don't know. Because none of us 'as ever been under fire.'

'Only practising,' put in the third man. He pushed his plate away. 'I got no belly for that greasy stuff.'

When they had finished the four engineers went out into the wan daylight again. Dunphy was waiting for them outside the billet. He eyed Ardley aside. 'I'm going to tell the driver of a new way to get into Dover,' he confided. Ardley did not comprehend. 'Coming from the north a bit, past Spatchcock's farm. You'd better watch out for your wife.'

Ardley grinned. 'Sarge . . . I mean, staff, you're a great man.'

'I'll know by the end of the week.'

'Is it going to be dangerous?'

'Enemy territory usually is,' said Dunphy.

Ardley went into the hut and began to pull on his kit. Jenkins was stuffing the Bible into his pack. '*Thou shall not steal* — and I'm pinching this,' he said. 'But we might 'ave time on our 'ands.' Each man had his small and large pack, his belt, his bayonet in its scabbard, his ammunition pouches and his rifle. They had left their gas masks. There would not be time for gas.

As he went out, each man gave the interior of

the hut a final glance as if it had been his home for happy years instead of uncomfortable days. The truck was outside. Dunphy waited until they had climbed in the back and ostentatiously counted them. 'One, two, three, four.'

'All present and correct, staff,' said Sproston. 'At the moment.'

'You all stick together from now on,' said Dunphy seriously. 'Look after each other.'

They understood. The staff sergeant climbed into the front beside the driver. A pale sunrise was touching the roofs and walls of the curious Indian barracks. They went out on to the wet autumn roads of Kent. Nobody said much. They bounced with the truck. Sproston was burping and Jenkins asked him to shut up. After fifty minutes the vehicle pulled in at the side of the road and Dunphy climbed out and went to the back. 'In ten minutes,' he said to Ardley, 'we'll be there. You've got another five minutes after that and then we're off again. The driver's going to say the traffic was heavy.'

Ardley was ready. He felt the vehicle slow and pull in to the side of the country road. The others guessed what was happening. 'Five minutes,' said Jenkins. 'Not long with your missus.'

Ardley climbed over the tailboard and realised that they were almost outside the farmhouse. He ran bulkily across the road, pushing aside the wet climbing roses, and turned around to the back. Spatchcock was asleep in his chair, early sun filling his face. He awoke and started feeling for his shotgun. When he saw Ardley he said: 'On leave again?'

'Five minutes,' said Ardley. 'Where's Rose?'

'Over in the home field,' said Spatchcock. Ardley went through the gate at the rear and saw her immediately. She was riding Pomerse and she shouted excitedly and waved, turning the big horse, who recognised him too and, without need of urging, came clumping down the field towards him. Ardley began to stumble up the slope and almost collided with the horse.

'Whoa! Whoa!' laughed Rose. Her face was glowing with excitement. She took one foot out of its stirrup and Ardley used the stirrup to haul himself up to her. 'Stay there, darling,' he said standing upright on it. 'I've got three minutes left.'

He flung his leg across the horse's broad back behind her and Pomerse snorted with pleasure. Rose twisted round to face her husband and they embraced like that, deeply, kissing each other, holding each other.

'Three minutes?' she gasped. 'Why three minutes?'

'The others are waiting in the road,' he said.

She eased herself back and regarded his face closely. 'Where are you going?' she demanded.

'Dover,' he said truthfully. 'Then we're on some exercise. I'll be back at the end of the week.'

'You're doing *something*,' she said fearfully. 'Something dangerous.'

'We're not. We're just going somewhere. Probably the Isle of Wight.'

He could see she did not believe him. But she said: 'It's nice, the Isle of Wight.'

They closed with each other again. With a final deep kiss. He hugged her breasts to him then released her and began to climb from the horse's back. She hung on to his arms, trying to keep him for a few seconds. Then Dunphy's voice echoed over the hedge: 'Ardley! Corporal Ardley!'

'I've got to go, Rose,' he said. He reached the ground and backed away. She was crying as he turned away from her. He patted the horse's nose and went down the field, not looking back until he reached the garden gate and turned to wave.

Abruptly she called him. He stopped and she urged the horse forward down the sloping grass. 'Darling,' she said. He leaned up towards her. She took her foot from the stirrup and he stood on it and eased himself upright. 'Darling,' she said, 'we're going to have a baby.'

Ardley whooped and they kissed exuberantly. Dunphy's voice came over the hedge a second time: 'Corporal Ardley, you're AWOL!' Ardley kissed his wife again. She was weeping and laughing at the same time. He dropped from the stirrup and went through the gate without looking back. Now he would *have* to stay alive.

⋆ ⋆ ⋆

They tumbled from the truck at the dockside and found themselves looking down on a flat boat, grimy and grey, with a sailor on guard at the gangway holding a fixed bayonet, his deep blue and white uniform standing out against the drabness of the vessel.

Two motherly looking women were poised, as if ready for action, behind a tea wagon, and they began waving mugs towards the young men. 'Let's have a drop,' said Dunphy. 'Help us celebrate.'

They knew it would take more than tea but they each accepted a mug from the women who smiled sadly and kept saying: 'God bless you,' as if it were some sort of benediction.

'Is that it, staff?' asked Tugwell ruefully nodding down at the boat.

'I bet it is,' said Dunphy.

'Noah's Ark,' said Sproston. 'Ready for the monkeys.'

'All aboard for the Isle of Wight,' said Ardley, almost to himself.

A bossy-looking port officer arrived waving his arms. 'Staff, get your chaps on board. The combat unit will be here soon. One of their vehicles hit a ruddy lamp-post.'

'Any casualties?' muttered Ardley but too low for the man to hear.

They drained the mugs and handed them back to the two women who repeated their blessing with each return. Then the staff sergeant led them, unsteadily with their equipment, down the gangway like mules crossing a narrow bridge. The sailor sentry remained unmoved, his eyes fixed, although he said out of the corner of his mouth: 'Welcome aboard.'

The bossy port officer reappeared on the dock

above. 'Staff, once they've parked their kit get them ashore again and into that pub across there. The one with no roof.'

Dunphy led his men ashore again. 'Have you got a nice cabin, staff?' asked Jenkins. 'Ours is really cosy. We can all cuddle up in there.'

'Make sure you get nearest the door. It's no place to be seasick.'

He formed them in a file on the dockside and they marched to the roofless public house which still had its inn sign, 'The Sailor's Dream', sagging forlornly outside. There was no door and the bomb had blown out most of the interior fittings. The bare bar was still there. 'Just the place when you're browned off,' groaned Ardley.

They stood to one side of the room. A makeshift stage accommodated a large easel hung with a map illuminated by two spotlights. There was a screen and a slide projector. The squad looked at it uncomfortably. Then through the door came the commandos, a dozen of them, armed with Thompson submachine guns and hung with grenades. 'Here they are — the fighting men,' muttered Dunphy.

Following through the door came a padre, arrayed in church vestments, stiffly white, and holding a prayer book.

The four engineers regarded the commandos and the clergyman apprehensively.

'Nice tommy-guns,' ventured Jenkins.

'Shut up, Welshy, for Christ's sake,' said Tugwell. 'Slap-up fried breakfasts, tommy-guns and a vicar. I don't like the way this is going.'

★ ★ ★

In the darkness of the military car, Giselle and Cartwright sat silently, occupied by their thoughts. Once more she thought of Toby and he of Sarah. Would any of it matter after the next few hours?

The car bumped across the dockside and came to a halt on the cobbles above the boat. No one was visible on board apart from the naval sentry. Cartwright got out and opened the door for the slight and timid figure of Giselle. She leaned over to see the boat. 'It is this?' she said.

'It is this,' confirmed Cartwright. He went to the rear of the car and took his equipment from the boot. He was wearing his service revolver. Giselle looked at him strangely. 'You too are coming?'

'I am.'

'But you . . . you are not a fighting soldier.'

'We all are fighting soldiers in the end. My job is to look after you.'

Her hand came out and touched his. 'I will be safe with you, I know. You will come to my wedding.'

Cartwright replied: 'And perhaps you will come to mine.'

Instow came to the head of the gangway. Giselle was dressed in army dungarees with a khaki sweater. 'Welcome aboard, ma'm'selle,' said Instow. 'I am sorry it is not as luxurious as the *Normandie*.'

'The *Normandie* would be seen,' said Giselle quietly. Instow glanced at Cartwright. A young sailor appeared and took Giselle's lightweight bag from her.

'I brought only my toothbrush,' she said. She followed him along the deck.

Instow said: 'We have a cabin for the young lady. And you are right opposite, captain.'

'God knows why she has to come,' sighed Cartwright. 'Bloody madness.'

'A lot of things are,' said Instow. 'Would you like a cup of coffee?'

'I could do with a large Scotch but I suppose I'd better have the coffee.' He followed Instow below. The vessel smelt of oil and lavatories. 'You're right, commander,' he said. 'She's not the *Normandie*.'

They sailed before midnight edging through the harbour entrance and setting a southerly course. There was no escort vessel. The sky was starless and the sea thick and calm.

Instow was on the bridge. After asking, Colonel Stelling came through the companion-way holding a coffee mug. The steersman was forward and out of hearing. 'Funny sort of vessel, this,' said Stelling, careful not to offend. 'Have you been in command long?'

'Last week,' said Instow succinctly. 'She's like sailing a plank of wood.'

'Ex-RAF, isn't she?'

'They should stick to flying. But, so we're told, this is the best sort of boat available for this job. They sit low in the water so they're not easily spotted. There are only three of them in operation.'

Stelling gave a small grunt. 'Shortages,' he

said. 'I had to fight to get my men Thompson sub-machine guns.'

'They look very useful,' said Instow.

'In the entire country we've got twenty-two tommy-guns. Twenty-two.' Stelling hesitated, then said: 'This whole bloody thing is a travesty.'

'This operation or the war?'

'This operation. We've got the war, there's no getting away from that. But this lark is something that's been dreamed up by Intelligence, which is full of giggling ex-public-school boys concocting super wheezes and selling them to jolly generals who are old boys from their schools. Then they send the likes of my men, and yours, out to see if they work. And, in my opinion, commander, this won't work. That girl, what the hell are we taking her for?'

'She knows the way, so I understand.'

Stelling snorted again. 'Listen, it's one big idiocy and even if it fails and we leave dead bodies in France it will be broadcast on the BBC as propaganda, an uplifting bit of derring-do, and Intelligence will pat themselves on the back and say how well it went.'

'And you don't think it's going to.'

'If we put those guns out of action, or even one of them, it's going to be a miracle. The enemy keep them in caves and they're brought out only when they're being used. They have to trundle across two small bridges. They're only exposed, vulnerable, when they're on those bridges. But we don't know when that's going to be. And, of course, they are well guarded. The only thing in our favour is the surprise element.

The Hun thinks that even the British would not try anything so stupid as this.'

Instow said: 'What about the girl?'

'I'd thought of leaving her on board,' Stelling told him frankly. 'But if the Jerries spot you while you're waiting offshore she could end up floating in the drink. And I'd be court-martialled for disobeying orders. But the bright boys think it will add romance, it will look good in the papers. She'll probably get the Croix de Guerre or something. Besides a bullet. My boys could find their way up from that beach without her.'

He drank the rest of the coffee. 'Commander,' he said, 'I think we're in the shit.'

15

It was difficult to keep the engines of the RAF boat subdued. But somehow it was contrived, and almost as slowly and silently as a snail, Instow brought her to anchor under a low headland, no more than a hundred yards from the German-occupied shore. She was so close to the cliff that someone looking out from the top would not have seen her.

It was still dark. Cartwright knocked on Giselle's cabin door and took her a cup of coffee. 'You are like a mother to me,' she said. She had not been asleep.

'It's my job to look after you,' he repeated. 'And that includes early-morning coffee.' He handed her a small cardboard box. 'Make-up,' he said. 'Before you go on deck smear that on your face. It's thick and black.'

He went up to the deck and recognised Dunphy by his whispering voice. 'We meet at the most exciting times, staff,' he said quietly.

Dunphy's teeth gleamed through the black grease on his face. 'At least it's not a UXB this time, sir.'

Five of the commandos went ashore at a time, in a rubber dinghy with a man silently paddling. It returned to pick up Colonel Stelling and his sergeant, a studious-looking man with glasses, and Giselle. She was helped into the boat but she did not need to be. She turned and surveyed the dark form of her own country. almost in front of her nose.

Five more commandos made the third trip and then the squad of engineers under Dunphy. They stared at each other, black face to black face. Jenkins tried to blow his nose but Tugwell stopped him. They eased away from the larger vessel and in five minutes were standing on the beach. There was no sign of the soldiers who had gone before but then they began to materialise out of the deep shadows of the rocks. Giselle put her hand down to the beach and picked up some sand. Then they heard dance music.

Everyone melted away. Cartwright eased Giselle gently into a defile. Two of the commandos moved forward and the rest waited. After ten minutes the dance music ceased and everywhere was quiet except for the subdued washing of the waves.

Stelling came and beckoned to Giselle. Cartwright followed her. She led them, at first tentatively then confidently, to the left of the beach, sharply turning between rocks and boulders until they reached a narrow path, sandy at first but giving way to shingle and rock, which led steeply up the side of the cliff.

It reached a brief plateau, where they could feel the breeze, and then climbed again. Stelling was at the front with his bespectacled sergeant, and the girl with Cartwright behind them. The two men who had attended to the dance music remained on the beach by the entrance to the path. The commandos were three feet behind each other, each man's head bent a little, each taking a carefully measured pace, each tommy-gun at a set angle. Then, in front of them, they heard a dog growl, then bark.

Stelling swore under his breath. He made a motion and his sergeant moved like a shadow alongside him. He produced a knife. Giselle abruptly halted him with her arm. 'I think it is my dog,' she said.

Alone she went the few feet up the dark way and whispered: '*Pooky, Pooky. C'est moi, Pooky. C'est Giselle*.' There was an excited rush of earth and stones as the animal tumbled towards her. She embraced it in the dark and it licked her blackened face. Stelling, in the darkness, rolled his eyes and muttered: 'Fuck.'

She returned down the path towards them holding the tailwagging black mongrel by its collar. 'It will be okay, safe,' said Giselle. 'But I need something to lead him and some chocolate. He likes chocolate.' A bar of chocolate was passed to her. The dog snapped at it. '*Pardon*,' she said to the waiting soldiers.

The farmhouse was not far from the top of the incline. They let Giselle go through the gate first with the dog on a piece of cord. The men stood back in the shadows as she went to the front door and quietly knocked with her knuckles. The door was opened at once and her father stood in the frame. 'You are ten minutes late,' he said.

* * *

There were tears and embracings. Giselle's mother was crying into the front of her flannel nightdress exposing her bony shins. Giselle, kissing her, pulled the nightdress into place at the same time. Her father hugged her. Then Giselle waved her hand around at the men who shuffled into the low-beamed room and said: 'These are my friends. Some are also outside.'

Her father said: 'We were expecting them.' He spoke in French and Cartwright had to interpret.

Stelling said: 'Tell him that we must use his barn.'

The Frenchman gave a Gallic shrug and replied.

Cartwright said: 'He says there is a pig in the barn. Tomorrow he is selling it to the Germans. But we can use the place, providing the pig doesn't mind.' Dunphy, who was standing against an old dresser, turned to go out to his squad, dislodging a framed photograph which, without looking at it, he carefully replaced. He went out.

Giselle's father spoke to Cartwright who said: 'There is also somebody important he wants us to meet.'

The colonel said: 'It's probably the bloody local mayor.'

'The man is here,' said Cartwright after another sentence from the Frenchman. 'He's in that room.'

Giselle said: 'It was my room.'

Her mother, who was still dabbing her eyes, almost gabbled: 'Your cousins Elianne and Marie in Cherbourg are both well. Your old Uncle Gaston in Lille is dead.'

'I am sad for Uncle Gaston.'

Stelling had moved towards the room. Cautiously he opened the door and saw a thickset man with wild, black hair and a straggling moustache sitting upright in the bed. He was wearing striped pyjamas and drinking calvados.

Cartwright followed Stelling into the room, then Giselle. 'It is only Henri from the village,' she said.

The man politely said: '*Ma'm'selle*,' and she went out. Henri offered the two British officers the stained calvados bottle but they declined.

'You have some information,' said Cartwright in French.

'A little,' said Henri. 'You have come to blow up the guns, I understand.'

Cartwright translated, but Stelling had got the gist. 'Christ,' he said. 'Every bugger knows.'

Then the man said: 'One gun, number two, is in its cave so you cannot reach that. Number one is on the little railway bridge. It is stuck there because two trusted French railway workers, who have been helping the occupation forces with their maintenance, these men have not finished some work on the tracks that lead to the first cave. They have been very slow. So the gun is still there, on the bridge. Tomorrow the tracks will be in place again and the gun will move. That is all I want to tell you.' He raised the grisly bottle.

They returned to the main room to wait. Staff Sergeant Dunphy returned from the barn in twenty minutes. 'That's done, sir,' he said to Stelling. 'Everything is in order: detonators, timers, leads and explosives. My squad is ready to move.'

Stelling said: 'In that case everybody is. Let's get on with it.'

Giselle kissed her father and mother. Stelling said: 'I want you to stay here until we return.'

'I wish to come,' she said firmly. 'That was the general's plan for me.'

'Insubordination,' he sighed. 'All right, come.'

'It is difficult, the way is not straight. I will show you. There is only one place where you can see into the valley, the ravine.'

They were leaving the room when she saw the photograph which Dunphy had dislodged on the dresser. It was of her father and two German soldiers posing with a British fighter pilot in a field. 'Oh, my God. Toby,' she breathed. She swiftly turned to her mother. 'Mama, it is amazing. It is my Toby.'

'We have to go,' said Stelling.

* * *

From her childhood she knew another concealed way among the rocks and stunted trees, and she easily found it in the dark. The commando sergeant, Wilson, led the way with Colonel Stelling behind him and then Giselle with Cartwright who had kept his revolver in its holster.

They were silent, scarcely breathing, careful with each step along the narrow way. Giselle could hardly believe that big men could move so secretly. Dunphy and his squad were last but one in the line, bearing their wires and explosives. The final commando kept looking over his shoulder.

It was not far, about half a mile, until Giselle tapped Stelling on the arm and indicated that they should change direction. In the dungarees, her hair pulled below a beret and her face blackened, she looked like a thin man. They went the way she indicated until the path flattened out on to a ridge. She pointed again and Sergeant Wilson, like a man investigating the lair of an animal, parted the rough scrub growth in front of him and, with a sense of achievement, they looked down on the great gun.

It was in the deep, rocky depression, its outline like a dark finger, with illumination from four dim lights at ground level. They could see four sentries wandering disconsolately around its base, two of them marked by the red pinpoints of half-concealed cigarettes. The gun was projecting directly out to sea through a gap dug out of the coastal hill, and was standing on the short bridge over a deep natural declivity. Dunphy was pleased. He crawled to Stelling's side. 'We'll blow the bridge okay,' he said. 'That will do for the gun. We need to have the guards dealt with first.'

The officer nodded. 'What about the other gun?'

'We can't do that, sir.'

Stelling agreed: 'It would take an army.'

Dunphy went back to his men. He kept, almost affectionately, touching the wires and explosives they were carrying, hoping to God they had got the connections right. They did not see the commandos detach themselves from the party on the ridge and they were only faintly aware of some activity around the gun. A pinpoint of light shone fractionally. Stelling appeared alongside the engineers. Again he nodded and patted Dunphy on the arm. Still at a crouch they moved from their concealment, and laden with equipment picked their way an inch at a time down the ravine.

The commandos were still around the gun, with four dead German sentries spread almost in a pattern on the ground. 'Evening,' one of the raiders whispered and Dunphy grunted.

It took only fifteen minutes. They crawled secretly like busy spiders over the supports of the prefabricated bridge. Their days, hours, months of practice made it work.

Dunphy remained on the ground and checked every connection, every length of wire, the timer and the secondary timer, in case the first did not work, and finally the packs of explosives, fixed to the legs of the bridge. Nothing, he kept telling himself, could go wrong. Nothing. He could hear his men's breathing, which worried him. He kept looking around for the Germans. The commandos were still in position. He began to feel they might be able to get away with it.

When everything was in place he checked again. Ardley, Jenkins, Tugwell and Sproston each gave him a nod of their blackened faces in turn. When he hoped he was satisfied he jerked his head and they moved off almost casually the way they had come.

* * *

There were only two commandos and the sergeant left on the ridge above the gun. The four who had dealt so silently with the guards followed the engineers up the slope. Giselle and Cartwright had been ordered to go back towards the house. The five engineers followed and outside the farmhouse joined up with Colonel Stelling.

Now they had to wait. 'Any second now, sir,' confirmed Dunphy to Stelling, hoping to God it was. He had his watch face close to his own. Ardley also watched his watch, and the others watched him. The minute went. And then another. Dunphy dared not look towards Stelling.

Ardley said: 'The timer, staff. I'll go back.'

'*We'll* go back,' said Dunphy to Stelling.

The moment after he had said it there came a huge crack of an explosion; the ground rattled under their feet, a gust of air hit them and the sky lit up from the direction of the gun. The engineers whooped exultantly. Dunphy said: 'A bit late, that's all.'

Stelling said: 'Retire in good order, no broken legs, please.' He saw Giselle's movement towards her father's front door and said tensely to Cartwright: 'No time for goodbyes.'

Cartwright said: 'Giselle, you must come.'

'I am coming,' Giselle said quietly. She looked back just once. They could hear her dog and it abruptly shot from the house and began prancing and barking about their feet. Giselle saw the sergeant move to silence it but Stelling said: 'Leave it, Wilson. A few yaps are not going to make a difference now. Let's get going.'

With the colonel and his sergeant at the front they began to move, spaced out and swiftly but with great care, along the fringe of the road towards the path that would lead them back to the beach. The dog followed Giselle obediently now making no sound. Cartwright ushered her on. They had almost reached the entrance to the descending path to the beach when a sudden searchlight streaked towards them, fixing some of the men in its beam. They dropped out of sight. A burst of automatic fire came from the road and they saw a vehicle loaded with men coming towards them. There were more soldiers panting along the road. Sergeant Wilson dropped to one knee and in the same movement fired his tommy-gun extinguishing the light with the first burst.

'Move!' shouted Stelling. They descended the path like a rabble, half-falling, getting up, cursing. Cartwright, protecting Giselle with his arm, let some of the men go past. A moment later, from below, came their returning bursts of fire.

Giselle was gasping. 'Nearly there,' said Cartwright trying to keep her steady. 'When we get there, run fast for the boat. If there's no boat, swim.'

She fell and he tugged her upright. Soldiers were rushing by. They could hear the sergeant bellowing orders through the trees. Abruptly they felt the sand; they were out on the beach.

The dinghy was against the tide line, just discernible in the first of the dawn. Cartwright hurried Giselle forwards staggering over the sand. They were both gasping. There was a sudden hard crackle of firing from above them. He pushed her flat.

The firing paused and he shouted: 'Get to the boat!'

She ran, then realised she was running without him. Looking behind she saw that he was doubled up in the sand. She sobbed loudly and went back towards him. He waved her towards the boat but she tried to pull him to his feet.

Two of the commandos ran to them and lifted Cartwright bodily. 'We'll not leave you, sir,' said one. They stood for a moment and one pointed his tommy-gun at random towards the dark head of the cliffs. But the other pulled him back. 'They'll pick us out.'

They carried Cartwright again and with Giselle staggered towards the dinghy. There were two men and the sailor with the paddle already in the boat. They heaved Cartwright in and almost threw Giselle over the side after him. One of the commandos picked up a second paddle and they splashed towards the lurking outline of the bigger vessel.

Dunphy with his four men got to the waterline. Behind them the remaining commandos were keeping up a fire on the upper ground and the direction of the downward path. Giselle's dog was running around the beach barking.

'We missed the boat,' groaned Dunphy.

'Dump everything and swim.' He caught sight of Ardley's face. 'Just as well you learned.'

'Just swim like you did in the baths,' said Jenkins. 'I'll be with you.'

At that moment they came under fire from a new direction, from the raised ground to their left. Another searchlight flew across them.

'Come on, boys!' shouted Dunphy. He pulled off his equipment in three movements, dropping it and his rifle on to the sand. They all did the same. As they stood the Germans did not have a full field of fire but as they plunged into the cold sea the enemy could see them at once. Bullets chopped up the water.

Ardley flung his arms in sheer terror. He tried to tell himself: 'Big strokes, long strokes.' He could hear the bullets splashing into the surface. To his amazement he made it to the side of the RAF boat. 'I'm here!' he gasped. 'Help me, help me.'

Two sailors hauled him from the water and he flopped on to the metal deck, trying to breathe, being sick on his chest. Dunphy was the next over the side and then Tugwell and then Sproston. But no Jenkins.

The dinghy had turned and made for the shore again. It took aboard some of the commandoes. Others began to swim. When the boat was halfway back to the larger vessel it slowed and the men pulled something heavy from the sea.

'Welshy? Where is he? Where's Welshy, for Christ's sake?' asked Ardley wildly.

The men crowded to the side, searching the

indistinct water. The dinghy was approaching the boat.

'Welshy!' Ardley shouted. The others joined in. 'Welshy! Welshy!'

There was no response. Ardley fell back on to the deck. 'Oh Christ, Welshy.'

'Move aside, boys,' said one of the sailors. 'Let the others get off the boat.'

'Maybe they rescued our lad,' said Dunphy.

They waited until the men climbed from the boat. Something was splashing behind them. 'Welshy,' said Tugwell but it was Giselle's dog. The sailors pulled it from the water.

Colonel Stelling was on the deck. His sergeant was missing. Ardley was weeping. The dog stood soaked and wagging its tail.

'Your chap was dead in the water,' said one of the men from the dinghy to Dunphy. They brought out Jenkins's soaked body.

'Oh Christ, no,' mumbled Ardley. 'Welshy.'

Stelling said: 'My sergeant is somewhere back there. And two men.'

There was a big explosion in the water fifty yards from the bow. Instow shouted forward from the bridge: 'I'm casting off, sir.'

'I'm not leaving them,' answered Stelling. Another shell landed in the water.

'We've got to go,' insisted Instow. Another shell exploded alongside. The boat rocked violently. Instow was now in command.

'Get going then!' Stelling shouted back. 'We'll have to leave them.' He collapsed to his knees on the deck. 'The Huns will look after them. They're very sporting like that.' He closed his eyes with exhaustion. 'I'm too bloody old for this, staff,' he whispered to Dunphy.

* * *

They carried Cartwright below to a cabin as the vessel began to move. The throaty engines sounded. A naval orderly looked briefly at him and said: 'We'll get him to hospital in no time.'

'I'll stay with him,' said Giselle. She found she had a tumbler of whisky in her hand. She had never tried whisky. She choked but took another drink.

In fifteen minutes they were out in the Channel, the dawn just breaking. Colonel Stelling came to the bridge. 'Well, we blew one gun,' he said. 'But I've lost three of my men. One of the engineers is dead and the liaison officer's got a hole in himself.'

Instow said: 'The girl got back.'

'Thank God for that.' Stelling was drinking from a tumbler. 'It's madness the elementary mistakes you can make.'

'Like what?' Instow felt guilty he had remained on the boat.

'The Huns turning up like that, right after the explosion. Minutes. They *couldn't* have moved as quickly as that. They were already on the way.'

'They'd been alerted.'

'By us,' sighed Stelling. 'There was a guard post on top of the cliff, but away from the place where we went ashore — a couple of dopey sentries settled in for the night and listening to dance music on a gramophone. I sent two men to deal with them and they did. But . . . I know what happened.' He paused. 'The gramophone came to the end of the record. When it eventually sank in that no dance music was sounding the other Krauts went to have a look and found their dead mates. That's when they sounded the alarm. And they just caught us, dammit.'

He stood wearily. 'We all learn,' he said. 'Eventually.'

⋆ ⋆ ⋆

They stretched Cartwright on a bunk in the middle of the vessel. He drifted in and out of consciousness. Giselle remained with him, sitting on a stool, with her dog asleep beside her.

Cartwright stirred as they were nearing the end of the journey. 'My orders were to look after you,' he said to Giselle, regarding her distantly. 'Are you all right?'

'I am safe,' she said in a low voice. 'You will soon be in the hospital. I will visit you.'

'How long now?' he asked.

She stood and looked from the forward porthole. 'It is not far,' she said. 'We are just now going into Dover, into the harbour. I can see the beach.'

'Dover Beach,' he whispered. She was holding his hand and she felt it go still.

⋆ ⋆ ⋆

As usual, word swiftly spread about the town that something was happening at the port and a knot of people began to gather to see what they could see. Once again, Cotton wondered at their gloomy curiosity. There were two ambulances and other military vehicles on the dock. It was daylight now.

An army officer strode purposefully towards him and he abruptly realised it was the major who had come to visit him and Nancy two evenings before. 'So sorry about your house, sergeant,' he said as if he meant it. 'Damn nuisance. But they'll probably move you to a manor house or somewhere. Some of these requisitioned properties are rather grand.'

Cotton said: 'We don't want a manor house.'

'No. Well, exactly.' The officer began to sidle away. 'Or they may change their minds. They often do that.'

He went off at his important little pace. Cotton disdainfully watched him go. Then his attention was caught by an old perambulator, being pushed along the pavement across from the quay, its front wheel wobbling. Harold Barker was sitting in the pram with his two everyday companions pushing behind. Cotton crossed the road. Harold called an order: 'Vehicle patrol, halt!'

Cotton surveyed the pram. 'What's this then, lads?'

'Transport,' said Harold. 'It gets us around quicker.'

'Us pushing and 'im sitting there,' said Spots.

'Yeah,' said Boot.

'Where did you get it?'

'Found it. Up London Road way,' said Harold glancing at the others.

'It was nobody's,' said Spots.

'No baby in it,' confirmed Boot.

Cotton looked over his shoulder towards the entrance to the harbour. The low, vague shape of a boat was approaching. Harold asked: 'What's going on, sarge?'

'Don't know,' answered Cotton truthfully. 'Something is.'

Boot said abruptly: 'I been a victim of the Nazis again. When those shells landed last week they thought I was dead.'

'They nearly got us,' said Harold. 'Knocked us over.'

Cotton was not sure whether to believe them. 'There was only one slight casualty, wasn't there?'

'That was me,' said Boot determinedly. 'Blood all over. Unconscious.'

'For two minutes,' said Spots grumpily.

'But you're all right now?' asked Cotton.

'It was the second time the Nazis tried to get me,' answered Boot.

Harold announced firmly: 'My old man's coming out of prison next week.'

Boot gave up and began trying to adjust the wheel of the pram. Harold climbed out. Spots got down on his knees and inspected the underneath.

'That's good,' said Cotton. 'Your mother will be glad.'

'I don't know,' said Harold. 'He reckons he

wants to help with the war.'

'How's he going to do that?'

'Join something.' Harold brightened. 'I reckon he ought to join the police.'

* * *

Instow brought the vessel gently, almost tenderly, alongside the jetty. It was out of the view of the group of civilians waiting on the quay. A military ambulance was already there, its rear doors open.

He got his small crew on the deck and the soldiers, the commandos and the unkempt engineers made two ranks on the other side of the lowered gangway. Colonel Stelling was in front and Staff Sergeant Dunphy on the flank of his remaining three men. A stretcher was carried from below with Cartwright's body covered with a blanket. Another blanket-shrouded stretcher followed. Tears coursed down Ardley's face, but after one glance he and the others stared directly ahead. Small, white-cheeked, Giselle followed the stretchers.

The soldiers and sailors were called to attention. The naval commander and the army colonel saluted, and Stelling went down to the dockside. He indicated that Dunphy should follow him. 'Staff, come and see your soldier off,' he said. 'Did you know Captain Cartwright as well? He was Royal Engineers too.'

'A few weeks ago, sir,' said the Irishman quietly, 'we were conversing alongside an unexploded bomb.'

'That's how you get to know people,' said the colonel. He walked towards Giselle.

'I am going with him,' she said.

'He'll go to the hospital,' said Stelling. 'First.'

She regarded him with a calm face. 'He came to look after me,' she said. 'Now I must look after him.'

Three orderlies slid the stretchers into the back of the ambulance. 'I believe I must write to his wife,' Giselle added.

Stelling reached into a pocket. 'This,' he said, 'is from his personal effects. I took charge of it.' He handed an envelope with an American stamp to Giselle. 'If you read it, perhaps you will think that you ought to write to this lady in the USA. They appear to have been close.'

Glancing at the stamp, Giselle took the letter.

The ambulance driver said: 'Will you come up the front with me, miss?'

'I will go in the back.' She turned briefly to study the grey and grim vessel with its sailors and tattered soldiers, then said: 'Thank you,' to Stelling and Dunphy. They each saluted her. She climbed into the ambulance, the doors were closed and it drove quietly away.

'Get your chaps ashore, staff,' said Stelling. 'They need some rest, same as mine do.'

'Yes, sir.'

Along the quay came a sergeant and a corporal. The corporal had a hare lip. 'Staff,' said the sergeant, 'we've got transport. Get your blokes aboard and we'll get them a shit, shave and shampoo. And some grub and some kit, of course.' He glanced towards the deck. 'It looks like they need it.'

* * *

It was one of the cliffside entrances to the military caves. Ardley, Sproston and Tugwell climbed from the back of the truck. They had said nothing to each other on the journey, their heads hung with weariness and their grief for Jenkins. They tramped into the cave behind the corporal with the hare lip. 'Ave a shower, get some sleep,' he said. 'There's some char coming. Anybody hungry?' He attempted to sound cheery. They stared at him as if he spoke a foreign language and shook their heads. Each soldier stripped his soggy uniform away and crawled beneath blankets. When a NAAFI girl appeared in the doorway with a tray and mugs of tea she did not rouse them. Sproston was snoring.

At four in the afternoon Dunphy, freshly uniformed, came into the cave. Ardley eased himself on his elbow, realised where he was, and said: 'What's next, staff? Berlin?'

Sproston and Tugwell stirred and opened their eyes. Sproston groaned and Tugwell said: 'Sod almighty.'

'There's some new kit in the next dungeon,' said Dunphy. 'Very smart some of it is. There's mugs of tea on the way. You didn't drink the last lot. Then there's showers and some grub, very decent too. I've had mine. They treat fighting men very well, if they survive.'

‘We ought to write to Welshy’s mother,’ said Ardley.

‘That’s the commanding officer’s duty,’ replied Dunphy. ‘We’ll all write to her after that.’ For a moment he looked shaky. His usually robust face was pale.

‘Where now, sarge?’ asked Tugwell. ‘It’s not back to bloody Thorncliffe, is it?’

‘I hope not,’ agreed the staff sergeant. ‘Back to digging trenches and training schemes, I expect. What else is there to do?’

Tugwell said: ‘At least we know now what it’s like to blow up a real bridge.’

‘Well, you won’t need to do it for a while,’ answered Dunphy. ‘Everybody gets seven days’ leave from eighteen hundred hours.’

* * *

In the truck going to the station, each one holding his rail warrant, Sproston suddenly said: ‘Where are you going on leave, staff?’ Tugwell and Ardley looked up with interest.

‘I may travel,’ said Dunphy in his pensive way. They smiled, their first smiles for several days.

‘To Ireland?’ suggested Ardley. They were going to drop him at the bus station.

‘I’ve no reason, no people to go and see, except some daft old auntie,’ said Dunphy. ‘In any case, I’d never get across, all travel to Southern Ireland being banned, in case you tell them secrets which they then tell the Germans. That’s the reason they give, anyway. Maybe I’ll take myself to London for a few days, stay at the Union Jack Club, five bob a night with all grub, and find myself a nice jolly woman.'

Tugwell said lugubriously: 'The bombing's getting worse in London.'

'I could do with some excitement,' said Dunphy.

'I bet you're back in barracks in two days,' guessed Ardley.

Dunphy nodded. 'There's a lot to be said for taking your leave in barracks. Free board and lodging, and you can stay in bed when everybody else is playing soldiers.'

The truck dropped Ardley outside the East Kent Bus Company terminus, still a bombed shell with a corrugated-iron building set within it. They all shook hands. He said a quiet goodbye and caught the seven o'clock bus. He was going home to his wife.

It seemed only hours since he had walked through the cottage gate to say goodbye to Rose; in those few days he had been to war and back, to the sheer fright of it. Looking from the top-deck window he thought again of Welshy and covered his face for a while. None of it seemed possible.

The evening was cloudy and it moved into dimness as they reached the farm. Although the dusk was deepening he found Spatchcock wedged in his chair outside the garden door. 'Oh, oh, it's you,' the old man said. 'Still here? I must have dozed off.'

Ardley patted his shoulder.

'She's up the village hall,' said Spatchcock.

'They're practising their singing, tryin' to get into tune.'

'I'll leave my kit,' said Ardley. He put his pack inside the door.

'Still no Jerries,' said Spatchcock squinting at the evening sky. 'I'm beginning to wonder whether they're really over there.'

'Keep looking,' Ardley replied going through the gate and up the lane. He felt weary and low. He shook himself and practised a smile in the dark. From a distance he heard the singing coming from the hall.

'For the merriest fellows are we,
Tra-la, tra-la, tra-la, tra-la-la-la-la, la-la-la-la.'

He pushed the door. There were two oil lamps illuminating the interior of the building. The large woman Polly was astride the stool, thumping the piano keys with her heavy hands. About twenty singers were doing their best to keep up. He tried to see Rose.

It was Polly who turned and exclaimed: 'Here's a real pianist! Come on, young fellow, sit yourself up here!'

Ardley felt himself shuffle forward as she rose from the round stool. Barely aware of what he was doing he took her place; his hands went uncertainly to the discoloured keys and he banged them fiercely beginning to sing 'Underneath the Spreading Chestnut Tree'. He had hardly got beyond the second line before he sensed Rose behind him. He almost fell. He turned his riven face to her and held up his arms. She enfolded him and bent to put her face to his. They were both weeping. She could see in a moment what had happened to him. The other singers stood dumbly.

Rose drew him up from the stool and held him to her like a mother with a son. 'How was the Isle of Wight?' she asked through her tears.

'Bloody noisy,' he said through his.

* * *

Said the soldier to the sailor: ' 'Ow come you're in this pub so much? Don't they ever send you to sea?'

'Don't like the sea,' said the sailor. 'It makes me sick. That's why I'm in the stores.'

'Dead cushy in the stores.'

'Ammo stores. All right if you don't drop a match.'

'Action, that's what I want,' said the soldier. 'A bit of fightin'. 'And to 'and. All I do now is weed the fucking colonel's garden.'

'It's fresh air,' said the sailor philosophically.

'I 'spect I'll go back to the coal yard when the war's over. Money was good, three quid a week, but it was dusty.'

They had each finished their beers, timed to perfection. It was the sailor's turn and he ordered two more halves. He had scarcely finished doing so when a high-explosive shell landed half a mile away, shaking the pub and bringing down yet more of the ceiling. Again the clock fell from the wall behind the bar.

The landlord did not even turn from placing

the beers in front of the men. He shrugged and said: ‘I wonder ’ow long it’s all going to go on?’

‘God knows,’ answered the soldier.

The sailor said: ‘Until that bugger ’Itler surrenders.’

Afterword

Dover Beach is a work of fiction. Many of the incidents which go to make up the novel, however, are based on fact, although in some cases the chronology has been altered. Some of the more bizarre occurrences include the German spy with the sausage, the stage contortionist caught in her tangled act by an invasion alarm, and the evacuation of elderly people from Dover to a West Country lunatic asylum. At the height of the bombing and shelling there was also a murder in the town.

More than 3,000 bombs and high-explosive shells fired from occupied France fell on the town but its wartime civilian casualties, just over 200 deaths and 700 people injured, were remarkably light in the context of civilian casualties throughout Britain of 60,595 deaths and 238,000 wounded. This was due to the evacuation of two thirds of the town's population, and to the sheltering caves of the vicinity. At the beginning of hostilities the town council bought a thousand funeral shrouds at two shillings and ninepence each but half this number was later sold on to other authorities.

While emphasising again that *Dover Beach* is a novel, I would like to acknowledge help from the following sources on researching the stories on which it is based:

Christopher Dowling and the staff of the

Imperial War Museum library; the National Archives, Kew; Jon Iveson and the staff of the Dover Archives, Library and Museum; and Denis Donovan, formerly of BBC Television News. I would also like to thank Susan Sandon and Justine Taylor of William Heinemann; Mary Chamberlain, who once again was my diligent editor; my wife Diana for her editorial contributions and research; and Rebecca Dann, who typed the manuscript (so many times).

Books which I consulted include: *How We Lived Then* by Norman Longmate (Hutchinson, 1971), still the best record of civilian life in the Second World War; *Dover Front* by Reginald Foster (Secker & Warburg, 1941); *Dover at War* by Roy Humphreys (Alan Sutton, 1993); *1940 — Year of Legend, Year of History* by Laurence Thompson (Collins, 1966); *1940 — The World in Flames* by Richard Collier (Hamish Hamilton, 1979); *The People's War* by Angus Calder (Cape, 1969); and *Invasion 1940* by Peter Fleming (Rupert Hart-Davis, 1957); and *Some Were Spies* by Earl Jowitt (Hodder & Stoughton, 1954).

Other titles published by
The House of Ulverscroft:

WAITING FOR THE DAY

Leslie Thomas

Midwinter, 1943 — six months before D-Day: RAF officer Martin Paget has been on covert operations in France. His trip back to England brings him to the resurrection of a passion he thought was long over . . . In a freezing hut on Salisbury Plain, Sergeant Harris is wondering how his young and ebullient wife is coping with their separation . . . US officer Harry Miller's division has set up its headquarters in an all-but-derelict Somerset mansion. His affair with an Englishwoman is both bittersweet and potentially dangerous . . . Enjoying fishing off the coast of occupied Jersey is German cook sergeant Fred Weber. But his calm is soon to be shattered . . . Each man is heading inexorably towards the beaches of France, where the great battle will begin . . .

OTHER TIMES

Leslie Thomas

James Bevan was conceived, according to his father's account, on the very night of the wild celebrations for the new century. But at the start of the war in 1939 Bevan is a junior officer approaching middle-age, attached to a small anti-aircraft unit on the south coast. He and his wife are separated, and the soldiers he commands are now his family. Settling comfortably into the local community, it is a rude awakening when they are called upon for the real war. Interwoven with the soldiers' escapades is Bevan's own story. From the sinking of the Titanic to the Great War, his boyhood is marked by incident — when all he wants is security.

DANGEROUS DAVIES AND THE LONELY HEART

Leslie Thomas

Dangerous Davies has retired from the Metropolitan Police (although no-one told him he was going to), and he has set up as a private eye above the Welsh Curry House in Willesden. Cases are hard to come by until he is abruptly thrown into two mysteries — the murders of women answering lonely hearts advertisements, and the disappearance of a young girl student, a psychologist and a secret worth millions. Peopling Davies's world is a range of eccentric and amazing characters, including Mod the philosopher, who is Davies's sidekick. But will the new career be a success? The fates seem set against it, but Davies never gives up.

MY WORLD OF ISLANDS

Leslie Thomas

Leslie Thomas's travels have taken him to islands as distant and diverse as Saint-Pierre et Miquelon off Newfoundland and Lord Howe Island in the Tasman Sea between New Zealand and Australia, and to places more familiar, at least in name, including Nantucket, Fair Isle and Capri. His descriptive, evocative narrative — liberally sprinkled with anecdotes and accompanied by his own colour photographs — enables the reader to feel the unique mystery and character of each island as he himself has experienced it.

DANGEROUS BY MOONLIGHT

Leslie Thomas

Blundering Detective Constable Davies — nicknamed Dangerous because they say he is harmless — is never dispatched on any assignment unless it is risky or there is no one else to send. After being beaten up, he is recuperating at the coast (in January) when he is asked by Louise Dulciman to find out whether her husband, who disappeared five years before, is deceased or merely decamped. Dangerous Davies begins moonlighting. The necessity for keeping these private investigations separate from his official casework leads him into outlandish adventures — and a many-layered mystery, which unfolds before his frequently bewildered eyes.